'Light is a remarkable book – easily my favourite sf novel in the last decade, maybe longer'
Neil Gaiman

'The ride is uproarious, breathtaking, exhilarating . . . This is a novel of full-spectrum literary dominance, making the transition from the grainily commonplace now to a wild far future seem not just easy but natural, and connecting the minimal and the spectacular with grace and elegance. It is a work of – and about – the highest order.'
Iain Banks, *Guardian*

'*Light* is a literary singularity: at one and the same time a grim, gaudy space opera that respects the physics, and a contemporary novel that unflinchingly revisits the choices that warp a life. It's almost unbearably good.'
Ken MacLeod

'M. John Harrison's jubilant return to science fiction constitutes something of an event. *Light* depicts its author as a wit, an awesomely fluent and versatile prose stylist, and an sf thinker as dedicated to probing beneath the surfaces as William Gibson is to describing how the world seems when reflected in them. SF fans and sceptics alike are advised to head towards this *Light*.'
Independent

'M. John Harrison proves what only those crippled by respect-ability still doubt – that science fiction can be literature, of the very greatest kind. *Light* puts most modern fiction to shame. It's a magnificent book.'
China Miéville

'Light is dark, and heavy. Certainly quantum mechanics – both propellant and unifying force in this remarkable novel – is nobody's idea of falling off a log. But its strange conjunctions, disregard for causality and meticulous examination of the coming-into-being of things are the background to Harrison's first pure science-fiction book for 30 years. This is a serious philo-sophical book, beautifully constructed . . . it will soon be regarded as one of the most dazzling novels of its genre.' *Daily Telegraph*

'Having read (not by choice) all the shortlisted Bookers for the last seven years, *Light* knocks the shit out of the majority of them. It's profound, unique, complex, but the drawback it has on the Booker front is that it's also incredibly entertaining and gripping. Who cares about literary prizes. You'll sell warehouses full of this one.'
Muriel Gray

'The novel's style alternates between terse *pointillisme* and a lyrical intensity that is almost hallucinogenic . . . Harrison writes with fearsome, dextrous certainty about pretty much everything . . . *Light* is a novel of visionary power.'
The Times Literary Supplement

'Post-cyberpunk, post-slipstream, post-everything, *Light* is the leanest, meanest space opera since *Nova*. Visually acute, shot through with wonder and horror in equal measure, in *Light*'s dual-stranded narrative M. John Harrison pulls off the difficult trick of making the present seem every bit as baroque and strange as his neon-lit deep future. Set the controls for Radio Bay and prepare to get lost in the K-Tract. You won't regret it.'
Alastair Reynolds

'Part of the bliss of *Light* is that he is as interested in the hearts of his characters as he is in their worlds . . . it juggles storylines with exemplary balance and alternates beauty, terror and wild farce to keep us perpetually on edge'
Time Out

'Dense and complex – but also action-packed and fast-moving. An impressive novel, rare proof of what science fiction can be'
Complete Review

'I loved it. The multilayered plot worked stunningly well: in most such cases I tend to prefer one or the other, but with *Light* I was delighted to return to whichever came next. The story is somehow both bewildering and utterly clear, razor-sharp and wide enough to encompass worlds, and the language is beautiful, nailing both the bizarre and mundane with eerie skill. On every other page there's a line which makes you think 'it can't get better than this', and then it does. An amazing book: not just a triumphant return to science fiction, but an injection of style and content that will light up the genre.'   Michael Marshall Smith

'One of the most important books of science fiction to be written for a very long time. The man whom most of Britain's young guns of science fiction claim as a major inspiration is back, and he has lost none of his skills. Furthermore, he wants to travel with us into a future that is frightening but pregnant with exciting possibilities.'   *Foundation*

'At last M. John Harrison takes on quantum mechanics. The first classic of the quantum century, *Light* is a folded-down future history bound together by quantum exotica and human endurance. Taut as Hemingway, viscerally intelligent, startlingly uplifting, Harrison's ideas have a beauty that unpacks to infinity.'   Stephen Baxter

'Here we have "space opera" that brilliantly transcends its humble pulp origins while simultaneously glorying in them. The result is a gripping, thrilling, meditative novel which can be read and enjoyed on multiple levels.'   *SF Weekly*

LIGHT

Also by M. John Harrison

LIGHT

M. JOHN HARRISON

The right of M. John Harrison to be identified as the author
of this work has been asserted by him in accordance with
the Copyright, Designs and Patents Act 1988.

First paperback edition published in Great Britain in 2003 by

.Gollancz
An imprint of the Orion Publishing Group
Orion House, 5 Upper St Martin's Lane, London WC2H 9EA

A CIP catalogue record for this book is available
from the British Library

ISBN 0 575 07403 5

Printed in Great Britain by
Clays Ltd, St Ives plc

Visit M. John Harrison's web-site at:
www.mjohnharrison.com

To Cath, with love.

ONE

Disillusioned by the Actual

1999:

Towards the end of things, someone asked Michael Kearney, 'How do you see yourself spending the first minute of the new millennium?' This was their idea of an after-dinner game up in some bleak Midlands town where he had gone to give a talk. Wintry rain dashed at the windows of the private dining room and ran down them in the orange streetlight. Answers followed one another round the table with a luminous predictability, some sly, some decent, all optimistic. They would drink until they fell down, have sex, watch fireworks or the endless sunrise from a moving jet. Then someone volunteered:

'With the bloody children, I expect.'

This caused a shout of laughter, and was followed immediately by: 'With somebody young enough to be one of my children.'

More laughter. General applause.

Of the dozen people at the table, most of them had some idea like that. Kearney didn't think much of any of them, and he wanted them to know it; he was angry with the woman who had brought him there, and he wanted her to know that. So when it came to his turn, he said:

'Driving someone else's car between two cities I don't know.'

He let the silence develop, then added deliberately, 'It would have to be a good car.'

There was a scatter of laughter.

'Oh dear,' someone said. She smiled round the table. 'How dour.'

Someone else changed the subject.

Kearney let them go. He lit a cigarette and considered the idea, which had rather surprised him. In the moment of articulating it – of admitting it to himself – he had recognised how corrosive it was. Not because of the loneliness, the egocentricity, of the image, here in this enclave of mild academic and political self-satisfaction: but because of its puerility. The freedoms represented – the warmth and emptiness of the car, its smell of plastic and cigarettes, the sound of a radio playing softly in the night, the green glow of dials, the sense of it as an instrument or a series of instrumental decisions, aimed and made use of at every turn in the road – were as puerile as they were satisfying. They were a description of his life to that date.

As they were leaving, his companion said:

'Well, that wasn't very grown-up.'

Kearney gave her his most boyish smile. 'It wasn't, was it?'

Her name was Clara. She was in her late thirties, red-haired, still quite young in the body but with a face already beginning to be lined and haggard with the effort of keeping up. She had to be busy in her career. She had to be a successful single parent. She had to jog five miles every morning. She had to be good at sex, and still need it, and enjoy it, and know how to say, in a kind of whining murmur, 'Oh. That. Yes, that. Oh yes,' in the night. Was she puzzled to find herself here in a redbrick-and-terracotta Victorian hotel with a man who didn't seem to understand any of these achievements? Kearney didn't know. He looked round at the shiny off-white corridor walls, which reminded him of the junior schools of his childhood.

'This is a sad dump,' he said.

He took her by the hand and made her run down the stairs with him, then pulled her into an empty room which contained two or three billiard tables, where he killed her as quickly as he had all the others. She looked up at him, puzzlement replacing interest in her eyes before they filmed over. He had known her for perhaps four months. Early on in their relationship, she had described him as a 'serial monogamist', and he hoped perhaps she could now see the irony of this term, if not the linguistic inflation it represented.

In the street outside – shrugging, wiping one hand quickly and repeatedly across his mouth – he thought he saw a movement, a shadow on the wall, the suggestion of a movement in the orange streetlight. Rain, sleet and snow all seemed to be falling at once. In the mix, he thought he saw dozens of small motes of light. Sparks, he thought. Sparks in everything. Then he turned up the collar of his coat and quickly walked away. Looking for the place he had parked his car, he was soon lost in the maze of roads and pedestrian malls that led to the railway station. So he took a train instead, and didn't return for some days. When he did, the car was still there, a red Lancia Integrale he had rather enjoyed owning.

Kearney dropped his luggage – an old laptop computer, two volumes of *A Dance to the Music of Time* – on to the rear seat of the Integrale and drove it back to London, where he abandoned it in a South Tottenham street, making sure to leave its doors unlocked and the key in the ignition. Then he took the tube over to the research suite where he did most of his work. Funding complexities too Byzantine to unpack had caused this to be sited in a side street between Gower Street and Tottenham Court Road. There, he and a physicist called Brian Tate had three long rooms filled with Beowulf system computers bolted to equipment which, Tate hoped, would eventually isolate paired-ion interactions from ambient magnetic noise. Theoretically this would allow them to encode data in

3

quantum events. Kearney had his doubts; but Tate had come from Cambridge via MIT and, perhaps more importantly, Los Alamos, so he had his expectations too.

In the days when it housed a team of neurobiologists working on live cats, the suite had been set on fire repeatedly by extreme animal rights factions. On wet mornings it still smelled faintly of charred wood and plastic. Kearney, aware of the science community's sense of moral outrage at this, had let it be known he subscribed to the ALF and added fuel to the fire by importing a pair of oriental kittens, one black and male, the other white and female. With their long legs and savagely thin bodies, they prowled about as unassuagedly as fashion models, striking bizarre poses and getting under Tate's feet.

Kearney picked the female up. She struggled for a second, then purred and allowed herself to settle on his shoulder. The male, eyeing Kearney as if it had never seen him before, flattened its ears and retreated under a bench.

'They're nervous today,' he said.

'Gordon Meadows was here. They know he doesn't like them.'

'Gordon? What did he want?'

'He wondered if we felt up to a presentation.'

'Is that how he put it?' Kearney asked, and when Tate laughed, went on: 'Who for?'

'Some people from Sony, I think.'

It was Kearney's turn to laugh.

'Gordon is a prat,' he said.

'Gordon,' said Tate, 'is the funding. Shall I spell that for you? It starts F-U.'

'Fuck you too,' Kearney told him. 'Sony could swallow Gordon with a glass of water.' He looked round at the equipment. 'They must be desperate. Have we achieved anything this week?'

Tate shrugged.

'It's always the same problem,' he said.

He was a tallish man with mild eyes who spent his free time, to the extent he had any, devising a complexity-based architectural

4

system, full of shapes and curves he described as 'natural'. He lived in Croydon, and his wife, who was older than him by a decade, had two children from her previous marriage. Perhaps as a reminder of his Los Alamos past, Tate favoured bowling shirts, horn-rimmed glasses and a careful haircut which made him look like Buddy Holly.

'We can slow down the rate at which the q-bits pick up phase. We're actually doing better than Kielpinski there – I've had factors of four and up this week.'

He shrugged

'After that, noise wins. No q-bit. No quantum computer.'

'And that's it?'

'That's it.' Tate took off his glasses and rubbed the bridge of his nose. 'Oh. There was one thing.'

'What?'

'Come and look at this.'

Tate had installed a thirty-inch superflat display on a credenza at the back of the room. He did something to a keyboard and it lit up an icy blue colour. Somewhere off in its parallel mazes, the Beowulf system began modelling the decoherence-free subspace – the Kielpinski space – of an ion-pair. Its filmy, energetic extensions reminded Kearney of the aurora borealis. 'We've seen this before,' he said.

'Watch, though,' Tate warned him. 'Just before it decays. I've slowed it down about a million times, but it's still hard to catch – there!'

A cascade of fractals like a bird's wing, so tiny Kearney barely noticed it. But the female oriental, whose sensory-motor uptake times had been engineered by different biological considerations, was off his shoulder in an instant. She approached the screen, which was now blank, and batted it repeatedly with her front paws, stopping every so often to look into them as though she expected to have caught something. After a moment the male cat came out from wherever it had been hiding and tried to join in. She looked down at it, chattering angrily.

Tate laughed and switched the display off.

'She does that every time,' he said.

'She can see something we can't. Whatever it is goes on after the part we can see.'

'There's not really anything there at all.'

'Run it again.'

'It's just some artefact,' Tate insisted. 'It's not in the actual data. I wouldn't have shown you if I thought it was.'

Kearney laughed.

'That's encouraging,' he said. 'Will it slow down any further?'

'I could try, I suppose. But why bother? It's a bug.'

'Try,' said Kearney. 'Just for fun.' He stroked the cat. She jumped back onto his shoulder. 'You're a good girl,' he said absently. He pulled some things out of a desk-drawer. Among them was a little discoloured leather bag which contained the dice he had stolen from the Shrander twenty-three years before. He put his hand inside. The dice felt warm against his fingers. Kearney shivered over a sudden clear image of the woman in the Midlands, kneeling on a bed and whispering 'I want so much to come' to herself in the middle of the night. To Tate, he said: 'I might have to go away for a while.'

'You've only just come back,' Tate reminded him. 'We'd get on quicker if you were here more often. The cold gas people are on our heels. They can get robust states where we can't: if they make any more progress it's us who'll become the backwater. You know?'

'I know.'

Kearney, at the door, offered him the white cat. She twisted about in his hands. Her brother was still looking at the empty display.

'Have you got names for them yet?'

Tate looked embarrassed.

'Only the female,' he said. 'I thought we could call her Justine.'

'Very apt,' Kearney admitted. That evening, rather than face an empty house, he called his first wife, Anna.

TWO

Gold Diggers of 2400 AD

K-captain Seria Mau Genlicher was up in the halo with her ship, the *White Cat*, trolling for customers.

Up there, a thousand lights out of the galactic Core, the Kefahuchi Tract streams across half the sky, trailing its vast invisible plumes of dark matter. Seria Mau liked it there. She liked the halo. She liked the ragged margins of the Tract itself, which everyone called 'the Beach', where the corroded old pre-human observatories wove their chaotic orbits, tool-platforms and laboratories abandoned millions of years previously by entities who had no idea where they were – or perhaps anymore *what* they were. They had all wanted a closer look at the Tract. Some of them had steered whole planets into position, then wandered off or died out. Some of them had steered whole solar systems into position, then lost them.

Even without all that stuff, the halo would have been a hard place to navigate. That made it a good hunting ground for Seria Mau, who now lay at a kind of non-Newtonian standstill inside a classic orbital tangle of white dwarf stars, waiting to pounce. She liked this time the best. Engines were shut down. Coms were shut down. Everything was shut down so she could listen.

Some hours ago she had lured a little convoy – three dynaflow freighters, civilian ships carrying 'archeological' artefacts out of a mining belt twenty lights along the Beach, hurried along anxiously by a fast armed yawl called *La Vie Féerique* – into this benighted spot and left them there while she went and did something else. Her ship's mathematics knew exactly how to find them again: they, however, tied to standard Tate-Kearney transformations, barely knew what day it was. By the time she returned, the yawl, overburdened by its duty of care, had got the freighters into the shadow of an old gas giant while it tried to calculate a way out of the trap. She watched them curiously. She was calm, they were not. She could hear their communications. They were beginning to suspect she was there. *La Vie Féerique* had sent out drones. Tiny actinic spangles of light showed where these had begun to encounter the minefields she had sown into the gravitational subcurrents of the cluster days before the freighters arrived.

'Ah,' said Seria Mau Genlicher, as if they could hear her. 'You should be more careful, out here in empty space.'

As she spoke, the *White Cat* slipped into a cloud of non-baryonic junk, which, reacting weakly to her passage through it, stroked the hull like a ghost. A few dials woke up in the manual back-up systems in the empty human quarters of the ship, flickered, dropped back to zero. As matter, it was barely there, but the shadow operators were drawn to it. They gathered by the portholes, arranging the light that fell around them so that they could make the most tragic picture, looking at themselves in mirrors, whispering and running thin fingers across their mouths or through their hair, rustling their dry wings.

'If only you had grown like this, Cinderella,' they mourned, in the old language.

'*Such* a blessing,' they said.

Don't let me have to deal with this now, she thought.

'Go back to your posts,' she ordered them, 'or I'll have the portholes taken out.'

'We're always at our posts –'

'I'm sure we never meant to upset you, dear.'

'– always at our posts, dear.'

As if this had been a signal, *La Vie Féerique*, running fast upside the local sun, blundered into a minefield.

The mines, two micrograms of antimatter steered on to station by hydrazine engines etched into silicon wafers a centimetre square, weren't much more intelligent than a mouse; but once they knew you were there, you were dead. It was the old dilemma. You daren't move and you daren't stop moving. The crew of *La Vie Féerique* understood what was happening to them, even though it was very quick. Seria Mau could hear them screaming at one another as the yawl split lengthwise and levered itself apart. Not long after that, two of the freighters ran into one another as, dynaflow drivers clawing at the spatial fabric, they broke cover on desperate, half-calculated E&E trajectories. The third slunk quietly away into the debris around the gas giant, where it turned everything off and prepared to wait her out.

'No, no, this is not how we do it,' said Seria Mau. 'You tubby little thing.'

She appeared from nowhere on its port stern quarter and allowed herself to be detected. This produced an explosion of internal coms traffic and a satisfying little dash for safety, to which she put an end with some of her more serious – if less sophisticated – ordnance. The flare of the explosion lit up several small asteroids and, briefly, the wreckage of the yawl, which, locked into the local chaotic attractor, toppled past end over end, wrapped in a rather beautiful radioactive glow.

'What does that mean?' Seria Mau asked the shadow operators: '*La Vie Féerique*?'

No answer.

A little later she matched velocities with the wreckage and hung there while it wheeled slowly around her: buckled hull plates, monolithic items of dynaflow machinery, what looked like mile upon mile of slowly weaving cable. 'Cable?' Seria Mau laughed. 'What kind of technology is that?' You could see every strange thing out there on the Beach, ideas washed up a million years ago, modified to trick out tubby little ships like these. In the end, the bottom line was this: *everything* worked. Wherever you looked, you found. That was everyone's worst nightmare. That was the excitement of it all. Preoccupied by these thoughts, she eased the *White Cat* further in, to where the corpses turned in the vacuum. They were human. Men and women about her own age, bloated, frozen, limbs at odd, sexual angles, slowly cartwheeling through an atmosphere of their own possessions, they streamed past her bow. She nosed between them, looking for something in their expressions of dull fear and acceptance, though she was not sure what. Evidence. Evidence of herself.

'Evidence of myself,' she mused aloud.

'All around you,' whispered the shadow operators, giving her tragic glances from between their lacy fingers. 'And look!'

They had located a single survivor in a vacuum suit, a bulky white figure windmilling its arms, trying to walk on nothing, opening and closing on itself like some kind of undersea life as it doubled up in pain or perhaps only fear and disorientation and denial. I suppose, thought Seria Mau, listening to its transmissions, you would close your eyes and tell yourself, 'I can get out of this if I stay calm'; then open them and understand all over again where you were. That would be enough to make you scream like that.

She was wondering how to finish the survivor off when a fraction of a shadow passed across her. It was another vessel. It was huge. Alarms went off all over the K-ship. Shadow operators streamed about. The *White Cat* broke right and left, disappeared from local space in a froth of quantum events, non-commutative microgeometries and short-lived exotic vacuum states, then reappeared a kilometre away from her original position with all assets primed and ready. Disgusted, Seria Mau saw that she was still in the shadow of the intruder. It was so big it could only belong to her employers. She put a shot across its bows anyway. The Nastic commander edged his vessel irritably away from her. At the same time he sent a holographic fetch of himself to the *White Cat*. It squatted in front of the tank where Seria Mau lived, leaking realistically from the joints of its several yellowish legs, stridulating every so often for no reason she could see. Its bony-looking head had more palps, mosaic eyes and ropes of mucous than she preferred to look at. It wasn't something you could ignore.

'You know who we are,' it said.

'Do you think it's so clever to surprise a K-ship like that?' shouted Seria Mau.

The fetch clicked patiently.

'We were not trying to embarrass you,' it said. 'We approached in a perfectly open way. You have been ignoring our transmissions since you did . . .' It paused as if searching for a word; then, clearly at a loss, concluded uneasily: 'This.'

'That was a moment ago.'

'That was five hours ago,' the fetch said. 'We have been trying to talk to you since then.'

Seria Mau was so shaken she broke contact and – as the fetch faded away into a kind of brown smoke, a transparency of itself – hid the *White Cat* in a cloud of asteroids some distance off, to give herself time to think. She felt ashamed of herself. Why had she acted like that? What could she have been thinking of to leave herself vulnerable like that, insensible out there for five hours? While she was trying to remember, the Nastic vessel's mathematics began stalking her again, making two or three billion guesses a nanosecond at her position. After a second or two she allowed it to find her. The fetch reformed immediately.

'What would you understand,' Seria Mau asked it, 'by the idea, "Evidence of myself"?'

'Not much,' the fetch said. 'Is that why you did this? To leave evidence of yourself? Over here, we wonder why you kill your own kind so ruthlessly.' Seria Mau had been asked this before.

'They're not my kind,' she said.

'They are human.'

She greeted this argument with the silence it deserved, then after a moment said:

'Where's the money?'

'Ah, the money. Where it always is.'

'I don't want local currency.'

'We almost never use local currencies,' the fetch said, 'although we sometimes deal in them.' Its larger joints appeared to vent some kind of gas. 'Are you ready to fight again? We have several missions available forty lights down the Beach. You would be up against military vessels. It's a real part of the war, not ambushing civilians like this.'

'Oh, your war,' she said dismissively. Fifty wars, big and small, were going on out here in plain sight of the Kefahuchi Tract; but there was only one fight, and it was the fight over the spoils. She had never even asked them who their enemy was. She didn't want to know. The Nastic were strange enough. Generally, it was impossible to understand the motives of aliens. 'Motives,' she thought, staring at the collection of legs and eyes in front of her, 'are a sensorium thing. They are an *Umwelt* thing. The cat has a hard job to imagine the motives of the housefly in its mouth.' She thought about this. 'The housefly has a harder job,' she decided.

'I have what I want now,' she told the fetch. 'I won't be fighting for you again.'

'We could offer more.'

'It wouldn't help.'

'We could make you do what we want.'

Seria Mau laughed.

'I'll be gone from here faster than your vessel can think. How will you find me then? This is a K-ship.'

The fetch left a calculated silence.

'We know where you are going,' it said.

This gave Seria Mau a cold feeling, but only for a fraction of a second. She had what she wanted from the Nastic. Let them try. She broke contact and opened the ship's mathematical space.

'Look at that!' the mathematics greeted her. 'We could *go* there. Or there. Or look, *there.* We could go anywhere. Let's go somewhere!'

Things went exactly as she had predicted. Before the Nastic vessel could react, Seria Mau had engaged the mathematics; the mathematics had engaged whatever stood in for reality; and the *White Cat* had vanished from that sector of space, leaving only a deteriorating eddy of charged particles. 'You see?' said Seria Mau. After that it was the usual boring journey. The *White Cat*'s massive array – aerials an astronomical unit long, fractally folded to dimension-and-a-half so they could be laminated into a twenty-metre patch on the hull – detected nothing but a whisper of photinos. A few shadow operators, tutting and fussing, collected by the portholes and stared out into the dynaflow as if they had lost something there. Perhaps they had. 'At the moment,' the mathematics announced, 'I'm solving Schrödinger's equation for every point on a grid of ten spatial and four temporal dimensions. No one else can do that.'

THREE

New Venusport, 2400 AD

Tig Vesicle ran a tank farm on Pierpoint Street.

He was a typical New Man, tall, white-faced, with that characteristic shock of orange hair that makes them look constantly surprised by life. The tank farm was too far up Pierpoint to do much trade. It was in the high 700s, where the banking district gave out into garments, tailoring, cheap chopshop operations franchising out-of-date cultivars and sentient tattoos.

This meant Vesicle had to have other things going.

He collected rents for the Cray sisters. He acted as an occasional middleman in what were sometimes called 'off-world imports', goods and services interdicted by Earth Military Contracts. He moved a little speciality H, cut with adrenal products from the local wildlife. None of this took much of his time. He spent most of his day on the farm, masturbating every twenty minutes or so to the hologram porn shows; New Men were great masturbators. He kept an eye on his tanks. The rest of the time he slept.

Like most New Men, Tig Vesicle didn't sleep well. It was as if something was missing for him, something an Earth-type planet could never provide, which his body needed less while it was awake. (Even in the warmth and darkness of the warren, which he thought of as 'home', he twitched and mewled in his sleep, his long, emaciated legs kicking out. His wife was the same.) His dreams were bad. In the worst of them, he was trying to collect for the Cray sisters, but he had become confused by Pierpoint itself, which in the dream was a street aware of him, a street full of betrayal and malign intelligence.

It was mid morning, and already two fat cops were pulling a convulsed rickshaw girl from between the shafts of her vehicle. She was flailing about like a foundered horse, cyanosing round the lips as everything went away from her and got too small to see. Street Life was playing on her personal soundtrack, and *café électrique* had blown up another determined heart. Entering Pierpoint about halfway along its length, Vesicle found there were no numbers on the buildings, nothing he could recognise. Should he walk right to get to the high numbers, or left? He felt a fool. This feeling segued smoothly into panic, and he began changing direction repeatedly in the teeth of the traffic. In consequence he never moved more than a block or two from the side street by which he had entered. After a while he began to catch glimpses of the Cray sisters themselves, holding court outside a falafel parlour as they waited for their rents. He was certain they had seen him. He turned his face away. The job had to be finished by lunch, and he hadn't even started. Finally he went into a restaurant and asked the first person he saw where he was, to discover that this wasn't Pierpoint at all. *It was a completely different street.* It would take hours to get where he was supposed to be. It was his own fault. He had started out too late in the day.

Vesicle woke from this dream weeping. He couldn't help but identify with the dying rickshaw girl: worse, somewhere between waking and sleeping, 'rents' had become 'tears', and this, he felt, summed up the life of his whole race. He got up, wiped his mouth on the sleeve of his coat, and went out into the street. He had that oddly jointed look, that shambling look all New Men have. Two blocks down towards the Exotic Diseases Hospital, he bought a

Muranese fish curry, which he ate with a wooden throwaway fork, holding the plastic container close under his chin and shovelling the food into his mouth with awkward, ravenous movements. Then he went back to the tank farm and thought about the Crays.

The Crays, Evie and Bella, had started out in digitised art retroporn – specialising in a surface so realistic it seemed to defamiliarise the sex act into something machinelike and interesting – then diversified, after the collapse of the 2397 bull market, into tanking and associated scams. Now they were in money. Vesicle was less afraid of them than awed. He was star-struck every time they came in his shop to pick up the rents or check his take. He would tell you at length the things they did, and was always trying to imitate the way they talked.

After he had slept a little more, Vesicle went round the farm and checked the tanks. Something made him stop by one of them and put his hand against it. It felt warm, as if the activity inside it had increased. It felt like an egg.

Inside the tank, this is what was happening.

Chinese Ed woke up and nothing in his house worked. The bedside alarm didn't go off, the TV was a greyout, and his refrigerator wouldn't talk to him. Things got worse after he had his first cup of coffee, when two guys from the DA's office knocked on his door. They wore double-breasted sharkskin suits with the jackets hanging open so you could see they were heeled. Ed knew them from when he worked the DA office himself. They were morons. Their names were Hanson and Rank. Hanson was a fat guy who took things easy, but Otto Rank was like rust. He never slept. He had ambitions, they said, to be DA himself. These two sat on stools at the breakfast bar in Ed's kitchen and he made them coffee.

'Hey,' said Hanson. 'Chinese Ed.'

'Hanson,' Ed said.

'So what do you know, Ed?' Rank said. 'We hear you're interested in the Brady case.' He smiled. He leaned forward until his face was near Ed's. 'We're interested in that too.'

Hanson looked nervous. He said:

'We know you were at the scene, Ed.'

'Fuck this,' Rank said immediately. 'We don't need to *discuss* this with him.' He grinned at Ed. 'Why'd you waste him, Ed?'

'Waste who?'

Rank shook his head at Hanson, as if to say, What do you make of this shithead? Ed said:

'Kiss it, Rank. You want some more java?'

'Hey,' Rank said. 'You kiss it.' He took out a handful of brass cases and threw them across the breakfast bar. 'Colt .45,' he said. 'Military issue. Dumdum rounds. Two separate guns.' The brass cases danced and rattled. 'You want to show me your guns, Ed? Those two fucking Colts you carry like some TV detective? You want to bet we can get a match?'

Ed showed his teeth.

'You have to have the guns for that. You want to take them off me, here and now? Think you can do that, Otto?'

Hanson looked anxious. 'No need for that, Ed,' he said.

'We can go away and get the fucking warrant, Ed, and then we can come back and take the guns,' said Rank. He shrugged. 'We can take you. We can take your house. We could take your wife, you still had one, and play jump the bones with her 'til Saturday next. You want to do this the hard way, Ed, or the easy way?'

Ed said: 'We can do it either way.'

'No we can't, Ed,' said Otto Rank. 'Not this time. I'm surprised you don't know that.' He shrugged. 'Hey,' he said, 'I think you do.' He lifted his finger in Ed's face, pointed it like a gun. 'Later,' he said.

'Fuck you, Rank,' Ed said.

He knew something was wrong when Rank only laughed and left.

'Shit, Ed,' Hanson said. He shrugged. Then he left too.

After he was sure they were gone, Ed went out to his car, a four-to-the-floor '47 Dodge into which someone had shoehorned the 409 from a '52 Caddy. He fired it up and sat in it for a moment

17

listening to the four-barrel suck air. He looked at his hands.

'We can do it either way you fuckers,' he whispered. Then he dumped the clutch and drove downtown.

He had to find out what was going on. He knew a broad in the DA's office called Robinson. He persuaded her to go to Sullivan's diner with him and get lunch. She was a tall woman with a wide smile, good tits and a way of licking mayonnaise out the corner of her mouth which suggested she might be equally good at licking mayonnaise out the corner of yours. Ed knew that he could find that out if he wanted to. He could find that out, but he was more interested in the Brady case, and what Rank and Hanson knew.

'Hey,' he said. 'Rita.'

'Cut the flannel, Chinese Ed,' said Rita. She tapped her fingers and looked out the window at the crowded street. She had come here from Detroit looking for something new. But this was just another sulphur dioxide town, a town without hope full of the black mist of engines. 'Don't put that sugar on me,' she sang.

Chinese Ed shrugged. He was halfway out the door of Sullivan's when he heard her say:

'Hey, Ed. You still fuck?'

He turned back. Maybe the day was looking better now. Rita Robinson was grinning and he was walking towards her when something weird happened. The light was obscured in Sullivan's doorway. Rita, who could see why, stared past Ed in a kind of dawning fear; Ed, who couldn't, began to ask her what was wrong. Rita raised her hand and pointed.

'Jesus, Ed,' she said. 'Look.'

He turned and looked. A giant yellow duck was trying to force itself into the diner.

FOUR

Operations of the Heart

'But you never phone!' Anna Kearney said.

'I'm phoning now,' he explained, as if to a child.

'You never come and see me.'

Anna Kearney lived in Grove Park, in a tangle of streets between the railway and the river. A thin woman who fell easily into anorexia, she had a constantly puzzled expression; kept his surname because she preferred it to her own. Her flat, originally council housing, was dark and cluttered. It smelled of handmade soap, Earl Grey tea, stale milk. Early on in her tenancy she had painted fish on the bathroom walls, papered the back of every door with letters from her friends, with Polaroid photographs and memos to herself. It was an old habit, but many of the memos were new.

If you don't want to do something you don't have to, Kearney read. *Do only the things you can. Leave the rest.*

'You look well,' he told her.

'You mean I look fat. I always know I'm too fat when people say that.'

He shrugged.

'Well, it's nice to see you anyway,' he said.

'I'm having a bath. I was running it when you called.'

She kept some things for him in a room at the back of the flat: a bed, a chair, a small green-painted chest of drawers on top of which lay two or three dyed feathers, part of a triangular scented candle, and a handful of pebbles which still smelled faintly of the sea, arranged carefully in front of a framed photograph of himself at seven years old.

Though it was his own, the life these objects represented seemed unreadable and impassive. After staring at them for a moment, he rubbed his hands across his face and lit the candle. He shook the Shrander's dice out of their little leather bag: threw them repeatedly. Larger than you would expect, made from some polished brownish substance which he suspected was human bone, they skittered and rolled between the other objects, throwing up patterns he could make nothing of. Before he stole the dice, he had cast Tarot cards for the same purpose: there were two or three decks in the chest of drawers somewhere, grubby from use but still in their original cartons.

'Do you want something to eat?' Anna called from the bathroom. There was a sound of her moving in the water. 'I could make you something if you like.'

Kearney sighed.

'That would be nice,' he said.

He threw the dice again, then replaced them and looked round the room. It was small, with bare untreated floorboards and a window which looked out on the thick black foul-pipes of other flats. On the off-white wall above the chest of drawers, Kearney had years ago drawn two or three diagrams in coloured chalk. He couldn't make anything of them, either.

After they had eaten, she lit candles and persuaded him to go to bed with her. 'I'm really tired,' she said. 'Really exhausted.' She sighed and clung to him. Her skin was still damp and flushed from the bath. Kearney ran his fingers down between her buttocks. She breathed in sharply, then rolled away on to her stomach and half-knelt, raising herself so that he could reach her better. Her sex felt like very soft suede. He rubbed it until her entire body went rigid and she came, gasping, making a kind of tiny coughing groan. To his surprise this gave him an erection. He waited for it to subside, which took a few minutes, then said:

'I probably have to go away.'

She stared at him. 'But what about me?'

'Anna, I left you long ago,' he reminded her.

'But you're still here. You're happy to come and fuck me; you come for this.'

'It's you who wants this.'

She clutched his hand. 'But I see that thing,' she said. 'I see it every day now.'

'When do you see it? It doesn't want you anyway. It never did.'

'I'm so exhausted today. I really don't know what's the matter with me.'

'If you ate more—'

She turned her back on him abruptly.

'I don't know why you come here,' she whispered. Then, vehemently: 'I have seen it. I've seen it in that room. It stands in there, staring out of the window.'

'Christ,' he said. 'Why didn't you tell me before?'

'Why should I tell you anything?'

She fell asleep soon after that. Kearney moved away from her and lay staring at the ceiling, listening to the traffic cross Chiswick Bridge. It was a long time before he could sleep. When he did, he experienced, in the form of a dream, a memory of his childhood.

It was very clear. He was three years old, perhaps less, and he was collecting pebbles on a beach. All the visual values of the beach were pushed, as in some advertising image, so that things seemed a little too sharp, a little too bright, a little too distinct. Sunlight glittered on a receding tide. The sand curved gently away, the colour of linen blinds. Gulls stood in a line on the groyne nearby.

Michael Kearney sat among the pebbles. Still wet, and sorted by the undertow into drifts and bands of different sizes, they lay around him like jewels, dried fruit, nubs of bone. He ran them through his fingers, choosing, discarding, choosing and discarding. He saw cream, white, grey; he saw tiger colours. He saw ruby red. He wanted them all! He glanced up to make sure his mother was paying attention, and when he looked down again, some shift of vision had altered his perspective: he saw clearly that the gaps between the larger stones made the same sorts of shapes as the gaps between the smaller ones. The more he looked, the more the arrangement repeated itself. Suddenly he understood this as a condition of things – if you could see the patterns the waves made, or remember the shapes of a million small white clouds, there it would be, a boiling, inexplicable, vertiginous similarity in all the processes of the world, roaring silently away from you in ever-shifting repetitions, always the same, never the same thing twice.

In that moment he was lost. Out of the sand, the sky, the pebbles – out of what he would later think of as the willed fractality of things – emerged the Shrander. He had no name for it then. It had no shape for him. But it was in his dreams thereafter, as a hollow, an absence, a shadow on a door. He woke from this latest dream, forty years later, and it was a pale wet morning with fog in the trees on the other side of the road. Anna Kearney clung to him, saying his name.

'Was I awful last night? I feel much better now.'

He fucked her again, and then left. At the door of the flat she said: 'People think it's a failure to live alone, but it isn't. The failure is to live with someone because you can't face anything else.' Pinned to the back of the door was another note: *Someone loves you.* All his life Kearney had preferred women to men. It was a visceral or genetic choice, made early. Women calmed him as much as he excited them. As a result, perhaps, his dealings with men had quickly become awkward, unproductive, chafing.

What had the dice advised? He was no more certain than he had ever been. He decided he would try to find Valentine Sprake. Sprake, who had helped him on and off over the years, lived somewhere in North London. But though Kearney had a telephone number for him, he wasn't sure it was reliable. He tried it anyway, from Victoria station. There was a silence at the other end of the line then a woman's voice said:

'You have reached the BT Cellnet answering service.'

'Hello?' said Kearney. He checked the number he had dialled. 'You aren't on a cellphone,' he said. 'This isn't a cellphone number. Hello?' The silence at the other end spun itself out. In the very distance, he thought, he could hear something like breath. 'Sprake?' Nothing. He hung up and found his way down to the Victoria Line platforms. He changed trains at Green Park, and again at Baker Street, working his way obliquely to the centre of town, where he would interrogate the afternoon drinkers at the Lymph Club on Greek Street, one place he might expect to get news of Sprake.

Soho Square was full of schizophrenics. Adrift in the care of the community with their small dirty dogs and bags of clothes, they were brought together at sites like this by an attraction to movement, crowds, commerce. A middle-aged woman with an accent he couldn't quite place had annexed a bench near the mock-Tudor shack at the centre of the square and was staring around with a lively but undirected interest. Every so often her upper lip folded back and a fey, unpremeditated sound escaped her mouth, more than an exclamation, less than a word. When Kearney appeared, walking fast from the Oxford Street end, an educated look sprang from nowhere into her eyes and she began talking loudly to herself. Her topics were disconnected and various. Kearney hurried past, then on an impulse turned back.

He had heard words he didn't understand.

Kefahuchi Tract.

'What does that mean?' he said. 'What do you mean by that?'

Mistaking this for an accusation, the woman fell silent and stared at the ground near his feet. She had on a curious mixture of good-quality coats and cardigans; green wellington boots; home-made fingerless mitts. Unlike the others she had no baggage. Her face, tanned by exhaust fumes, alcohol and the wind that blows incessantly around the base of Centre Point, had a curiously healthy, rural look. When she looked up at last, her eyes were pale blue. 'I wonder if you could spare me the money for a cup of tea?' she said.

'I'll do more than that,' Kearney promised. 'Just tell me what you mean.'

She blinked.

'Wait here!' he told her, and at the nearest Pret bought three All Day Breakfasts, which he put in a bag with a classic latte. Back in Soho Square, the woman hadn't moved, but sat blinking into the weak sunlight, occasionally calling out to passers-by, but reserving most of her attention for two or three pigeons hobbling about in front of her. Kearney handed her the bag.

'Now,' he said. 'Tell me what you see.'

She gave him a cheerful smile. 'I don't see anything,' she said. 'I take my medication. I always take it.' She held the Pret bag for a moment then returned it to him. 'I don't want this.'

'Yes you do,' he said, taking things out to show her. 'Look! All Day Breakfast!'

'You eat it,' she said.

He put the bag down next to her on the bench and took her by the shoulders. He knew that if he said the right thing she would prophesy. 'Listen,' he assured her, as urgently as he knew how, 'I know what you know. Do you see?'

'What do you want? I'm frightened of you.'

Kearney laughed.

'I'm the one frightened,' he said. 'Look, have this. Have these.'

The woman glanced at the sandwiches in his hands, then looked over her left shoulder as if she had seen someone she knew.

'I don't want it. I don't want them.' She strained to keep her head turned away from him. 'I want to go now.'

'What do you see?' he insisted.

'Nothing.'

'What do you see?'

'Something coming down. Fire coming down.'

'What fire?'

'Let me go.'

'What fire is that?'

'Let me go, now. Let me go.'

Kearney let her go and walked away. Aged eighteen, he had dreamed of himself at the end of a life like hers. He was reeling and staggering down some alley, full of revelation like a disease. He was old and regretful, but for years something had been combusting its way from the centre of him towards the outer edge, where it now burst uncontrollably from his fingertips, from his eyes, his mouth, his sex, setting his clothes on fire. Later he had seen how unlikely this was. Whatever he might be, he wasn't mad, or alcoholic, or even unlucky. Looking back into Soho Square, he watched the schizophrenics passing his sandwiches from hand to hand, peeling them apart to examine the filling. He had stirred them like soup. Who knew what might come to the surface? In principle, he felt sorry for them, even amiable. The praxis of it was bleaker. They were as disappointing as children. You saw light in their eyes, but it was the ignis fatuus. In the end, they knew less than Brian Tate, and he knew nothing at all.

Valentine Sprake, who claimed to know as much as Kearney, perhaps more, wasn't at the Lymph Club; no one had seen him there for a month. Eyeing the yellowed walls, the afternoon drinkers, the TV above the bar, Kearney bought a drink and wondered where he should look next. Outside, the afternoon had turned to rain, the streets were full of people talking into mobile phones. Knowing that he would be forced, sooner or later, to face an empty apartment on his own, he sighed with impatience, turned up the collar of his jacket, and went home. There, ill at ease but worn out by what he thought of as the emotional demands of Brian Tate, Anna Kearney and the woman in Soho Square, he turned on all the lights and fell asleep in an armchair.

'Your cousins are coming,' Kearney's mother told him.

He was eight. He was so excited he ran away as soon as they arrived, off across the fields behind the house and through a strip of woodland, until he came to a pond or shallow lake surrounded by willows. It was his favourite place. No one was ever there. In winter, brown reeds emerged from the thin white cat-ice at its margins; in summer, insects buzzed among the willows. Kearney stood for a long time, listening to the diminishing cries of the other children. As soon as he was sure they wouldn't follow him, a kind of hypnotic tranquillity came over him. He pulled his shorts down and stood with his legs apart in the sun, looking down at himself. Someone at school had shown him how to rub it. It got big but he couldn't make it do anything else. Eventually he grew bored and climbed out along a cracked willow trunk. He lay there in the shade, looking down into the water, which teemed with tiny real fishes.

He could never face other children. They excited him too much. He could never face his cousins. Two or three years later, he would invent the house he called 'Gorselands', sometimes 'Heathlands', where his dreams of them, prurient yet somehow transfiguring, could be worked out in a landscape without threat.

At Gorselands it would always be full summer. From the road, people would see only trees, thick with ivy, a few yards of mossy driveway, the nameplate on the old wooden gate. Every afternoon, the pale, scarcely teenaged girls his cousins had become would squat in the warm sun-speckled gloom – their grubby feet slightly apart, their scratched knees and bundled-up skirts close to their chests – rubbing quickly and deftly at the stretched white fabric between their legs, while Michael Kearney watched them from the trees, aching inside his thick underpants and grey school shorts.

Sensing him there, they would look up suddenly, at a loss!

Whatever drove him like this to the waste ground of life, had, by the age of eight, already made Kearney vulnerable to the attentions of the Shrander. It swam with the little fishes in the shadow of the willow, just as it had sorted the stones on the beach when he was two. It informed every landscape. Its attentions had begun with dreams in which he walked on the green flat surface of canal water, or felt something horrible inhabiting a pile of Lego bricks. Dragons were expressed as the smoke from engines, while the mechanical parts of the engines themselves turned over with a kind of nauseous oily slowness, and Kearney woke to find a rubber thing soaking in the bathroom sink.

The Shrander was in all of that.

FIVE

Uncle Zip the Tailor

Much of the halo is burnt-out stuff, litter from the galaxy's early evolution. Young suns are at a premium, but you can find them. Still running on hydrogen, they welcome the human visitor with an easy warmth, like the mythic hostelries of Ancient Earth. Two days later, the *White Cat* popped out next to one of them, switched off her dynaflow drivers, and parked herself demurely above its fourth planet, which had been named, in honour of its generous facilities, Motel Splendido.

Motel Splendido was as old, in terms of human habitation, as any other rock on that quarter of the Beach. It had a tidy climate, oceans, and air no one had fucked up yet. There were spaceports on both its continents, some of them public, others less so. It had seen its share of expeditions, fitted out, kitted up and despatched under the deracinating glare of the Kefahuchi Tract, which roared across the night sky like an aurora. It had seen, and still saw, its share of heroes. Gold diggers of 2400AD, they risked everything on a throw of the dice. They thought of themselves as scientists, they thought of themselves as investigators, but they were really thieves, speculators, intellectual cowboys. Theirs was the heritage of science as it had defined itself four hundred years before. They were beachcombers. They went out one morning with their lives all washed up and returned in the evening corporate CEOs heavy with patents: that was the typical trajectory on Motel Splendido: that was the direction of things. As a result it was a good planet for money. One or two puzzling artefacts lay quarantined in its deserts, which had themselves not been deserts until the escape forty years before of a two-million-year-old gene-patching programme someone had picked up on a derelict less than two lights along the Beach. That had been the big discovery of its generation.

Big discoveries were the thing on Motel Splendido. Every day, in any bar, you could hear about the latest one. Someone had found something among all that alien junk which would turn physics, or cosmology, or the universe itself, on its head. But the real secrets, the long secrets, were in the Tract if they were anywhere, and no one had ever returned from there.

No one ever would.

Most people came to Motel Splendido to make their fortune, or their name; Seria Mau Genlicher came to find a clue. She came to make a deal with Uncle Zip the tailor. She talked to him by fetch, from the parking orbit, but not before the shadow operators had tried to persuade her to go down to the surface in person.

'The surface?' she said, laughing rather wildly. '*Moi?*'

'But you would enjoy it so. Look!'

'Leave this alone,' she warned them: but they showed her how much fun it would be, all the same, down where Carmody, a seaport long before it was a spaceport, was opening its sticky, fragrant wings against the coming night . . .

The lights had gone on in those ridiculous glass towers which spring up wherever the human male does business. The streets of the port below were filled with a warm pleasant smoky twilight, through which all intelligent life in Carmody was drifting, along Moneytown and the Corniche, towards the steam of the noodle bars on Free Key Avenue. Cultivars and high-end chimerae of every size and type – huge and tusked or dwarfed and tinted, with cocks the size of an elephant's, the wings of dragonflies or swans, bare chests patched according to fashion with live tattoos of treasure maps – swaggered the pavements, eyeing one another's smart piercings. Rickshaw girls, calves and quadriceps modified to have the long-twitch muscle fibre of a mare and the ATP transport protocols of a speeding cheetah, sprinted here and there between them, comforted by local opium, strung out on *café électrique*. Shadow boys were everywhere, of course, faster than you could see, flickering in corners, materialising in alleys, whispering their ceaseless invitation:

We can get you what you want.

The code parlours, the tattoo parlours – all run by one-eyed poets sixty years old, loaded on Carmody Rose bourbon – the storefront tailor operations and chop joints, their tiny show windows stuffed with animated designs like postage stamps or campaign badges from imaginary wars or bags of innocent-coloured candy, were already crowded with customers; while from the corporate enclaves terraced above the Corniche, men and women in designer clothes sauntered confidently towards the harbour restaurants, lifting their heads in anticipation of Earth cuisine, harbour lights on the wine-dark sea, then a late-night trip to Moneytown – wealth creators, prosperity makers, a little too good for it all by their own account, yet mysteriously energised by everything cheap and tasteless. Voices rose. Laughter rose above them. Music was everywhere, transformation dub bruising the ear, you could hear its confrontational basslines twenty miles out to sea. Above this clamour rose the sharp, urgent pheromone of human expectation – a scent compounded less of sex or greed or aggression than of substance abuse, cheap falafel and expensive perfume.

Seria Mau knew smells, just as she knew sights and sounds.

'You act as if I don't know anything about this,' she told the shadow operators. 'But I do. Rickshaw girls and tattoo boys.

Bodies! I've been there and done that. I saw it all and I didn't want it.'

'You could at least run yourself in a cultivar. You would look *so nice.*'

They brought out a cultivar for her. It was herself, seven years old. They had decorated its little pale hands with intricate henna spirals then put it in a floor-length frock of white satin, sprigged with muslin bows and draped with cream lace. It stared shyly at its own feet and whispered: 'What was relinquished returns.'

Seria Mau drove the shadow operators away.

'I don't want a body,' she screamed at them. 'I don't want to look nice. I don't want those feelings a body has.'

The cultivar fell back against a bulkhead and slid down on to the deck looking puzzled. 'Don't you want me?' it said. It kept glancing up and then down again, wiping compulsively at its face. 'I'm not sure where I am,' it said, before its eyes closed tiredly and it stopped moving. At that the shadow operators put their thin paws over their faces and retreated into the corners, making a noise like, 'Zzh zzh zzh.'

'Open me a line to Uncle Zip,' said Seria Mau.

Uncle Zip the tailor ran his operation from a parlour on Henry Street down by the Harbour Mole. He had been famous in his day, his cuts franchised in every major port. A fat, driven man with protuberant china-blue eyes, inflated white cheeks, rosebud lips, and a belly as hard as a wax pear, he claimed to have discovered the origins of life, coded in fossil proteins on a system in Radio Bay less than twenty lights from the edge of the Tract itself. Whether you believed that depended on how well you knew him. He had shipped out talented and come back focused, that was certain. Whatever codes he found, they made him only as rich as any other good tailor: Uncle Zip wanted nothing more, or so he said. He and his family lived above the business, in some ceremony. His wife wore bright red flamenco skirts. All his children were girls.

When Seria Mau fetched up in the middle of the parlour floor, Uncle Zip was entertaining.

'This is just a few friends,' he said, when he saw her at his feet. 'You can stay and learn a thing or two. Or you can come back later.'

He had got himself up in a white dress shirt and black trousers the waist of which came up to his armpits, and he was playing the piano accordion. A round, rosy patch of blusher on each chalk-white cheek made him look like a huge porcelain doll, glazed with sweat. His instrument, an elaborate antique with ivory keys and glittering chromium buttons, flashed and flickered in the Carmody neon. As he played, he stamped from side to side to keep the beat. When he sang, it was in a pure, explosive counter-tenor. If you couldn't see him you didn't know immediately whether you were listening to a woman or a boy. Only later did the barely controlled aggression of it convince you this voice belonged to a human male. His audience, three or four thin, dark-skinned men in tight pants, lurex shirts and jet-black pompadour haircuts, drank and talked without seeming to pay him much attention, although they gave thin smiles of approval when he hit his high, raging vibrato. Occasionally two or three children came to the open parlour door and egged him on, clapping and calling him Papa. Uncle Zip stamped and played and shook the sweat off his china brow.

In his own good time he dismissed his audience – who vanished with a polite sly hipster grace into the Moneytown night as if they had never been there at all – and sat down on a stool, breathing heavily. Then he shook one of his fat fingers at Seria Mau Genlicher.

'Hey,' he said. 'You come in down here in a fetch?'

'Spare me,' said Seria Mau. 'I get enough of that at home.'

Seria Mau's fetch looked like a cat. It was a low end model which came in colours you could change according to your mood. Otherwise it resembled one of the domestic cats of Ancient Earth – small, nervous, pointy-faced, and with a tendency to rub the side of its head on things.

'It's an insult to the cutter, a fetch. Come to Uncle Zip in person or not at all.' He mopped his forehead with a huge white handkerchief, laughed his high, pleasant laugh. 'You want to be a cat,' he advised, 'I make you into one no trouble.' He leaned over and put his hand several times through the hologram. 'What's this? A ghost, young lady. Without a body you're a photino, you're a weak reactor to this world. I can't even offer you a drink.'

'I already have a body, Uncle,' Seria Mau reminded him quietly.

'So why did you come back here?'

'The package doesn't work. It won't talk to me. It won't even admit what it's for.'

'I told you this is complex stuff. I said there might be problems.'

'You didn't say it wasn't yours.'

Faint disagreeable lines appeared on Uncle Zip's white forehead.

'I said I owned it,' he was ready to acknowledge. 'But I didn't say I built it. In fact, it was passed to me by Billy Anker. The guy said he thought it was modern. He thought it was K-tech. He thought it was military.' He shrugged. 'Some of those people, they don't care what they say –' he shook his head and pursed his little lips judicially '– though this guy Billy is usually very acute, very dependable.' The thought leading him nowhere, he shrugged. 'He got it in Radio Bay, but he couldn't work out what it did.'

'Could you?'

'I didn't recognise the cutter's hand.' Uncle Zip spread his own hands and examined them. 'But I saw through the cut in a day.' He was proud of his plump fingers and their clean, spatulate nails, as proud of his touch as if he cut the genes directly, like a cobbler at a last. 'Right through and out the other side. It's what you need all right: no trouble.'

'Then why won't it *work*?'

'You should bring it back. Maybe I take another look.'

'It keeps asking me for Dr Haends.'

In Dreams

At first you thought the Cray sisters were running themselves on some kind of one-shot cultivar. You soon saw they took too much care of themselves to be doing that. Nevertheless, they were big, with that sensual, more-alive-than-alive look a cultivar has because its user just doesn't care what happens. They had big, powerful behinds, over which they wore short black nylon skirts. They had big, short legs, with calves tightened and moulded by a lifetime of four-inch heels. The big shoulders of their short-sleeved white 'secretary' blouses were padded and flounced. Tattooed snakes curled and uncurled lazily around their bare, fleshy biceps.

One day they came in the shop and Evie asked Tig Vesicle did he have a twink called Ed Chianese in one of the tanks. This twink would be about yay tall (she indicated two inches taller than herself), with a partly grown out peroxide Mohican and a couple of cheap tattoos. He would have been quite a muscular guy, she said, at least before tank-life got to him.

'I never saw anyone like that,' Vesicle lied.

He was immediately full of terror. If you could help it, you did not lie to the Cray sisters. They did their faces every morning with white pan-stick, and drew in wide red liplines, voluptuous, angry and clown-like all at once. With these mouths they held the whole of Pierpoint Street to ransom. They had innumerable soldiers, shadow boys in cultivars, cheap teenage punks with guns. Also, in their antique briefcases, or big, soft leather purses, they each carried a Chambers reaction pistol. At first they seemed like a mass of contradictions, but you soon understood they weren't.

The truth was, this Chianese twink was Tig Vesicle's only regular. Who went to a tank farm in the upper 700s, Pierpoint? No one. The trade was all down at the other end, where you got any number of investment bankers, also women whose favourite dog died ten years before, they never got over it. The lunch trade was all down there, in the middle and low numbers. Without Chianese, who was twinking three weeks at a time when he could afford it, Vesicle's business would be fucked. He would be out on the street all day trying to move AbH and Earth speed to kids who were only interested in do-it-yourself gene patches which they got from some guy across the halo called Uncle Zip.

The Crays gave Tig Vesicle a look designed to say, 'You lie on this occasion, you get broken down for your rarer proteins.'

'Really,' he said.

Eventually Evie Cray shrugged.

'You see a guy like that, we're the first to know,' she said. 'The first.'

She stared round the tank farm, with its bare grey floor and shoot-up posters peeling off the walls, and gave Vesicle a contemptuous look. 'Jesus, Tig,' she said. 'Could you just make this place a little more unwelcoming? Do you think you could do that?'

Bella Cray laughed.

'Do you think you could do that for her?' she said.

After they had gone, Vesicle sat in his chair, repeating: 'Do you think you could do that?' and, 'You see a guy like that, we're the first to know,' until he thought he had the intonation right. Then he went over to look at the tanks. He got a rag out of a cupboard and wiped the dust off them. He was wiping Chianese's tank when he realised it was the warm one. 'Who is this guy,' he asked himself, 'the Cray sisters want him all of a sudden? No one ever wanted him before.' He tried to remember what Chianese looked like but he couldn't. Twinkies all looked the same to him.

He went out to a stall and got himself another fish curry. 'You see a guy like that,' he tried experimentally to the stallholder after he had paid, 'we're the first to know.'

The stallholder stared at him.

'The first,' Vesicle said.

New Men, she thought, as she watched him walk away up Pierpoint, one leg going out at an odd angle. What are they on?

Drawn by the radio and TV ads of the twentieth century, which had reached them as faltering wisps and cobwebs of communication (yet still full of a mysterious, alien vitality), the New Men had invaded Earth in the middle 2100s. They were bipedal, humanoid – if you stretched a point – and uniformly tall and white-skinned, each with a shock of flaming red hair. They were indistinguishable from some kinds of Irish junkies. It was difficult to tell the sexes apart. They had a kind of pliable, etiolated feel about their limbs. To start with, they had great optimism and energy. Everything about Earth amazed them. They took over and, in an amiable, paternalistic way, misunderstood and mismanaged everything. It appeared to be an attempt to understand the human race in terms of a 1982 Coke ad. They produced food no one could eat, outlawed politics in favour of the kind of bureaucracy you find in the subsidised arts, and buried enormous machinery in the subcrust which eventually killed millions. After that, they seemed to fade away in embarrassment, taking to drugs, pop music and the twink-tank which was then an exciting if less than reliable new entertainment technology.

Thereafter, they spread with mankind, like a kind of wrenched commentary on all that expansion and free trade. You often found them at the lower levels of organised crime. Their project was to fit in, but they were fatally retrospective. They were always saying:

'I really like this cornflakes thing you have, man. You know?'

Vesicle went back to the tank farm. The head-ends of the tanks protruded a couple of feet from their shoulder-height plyboard cubicles, like stupidly baroque brass coffins covered with cheap decorative detail. YOU CAN BE ANYTHING YOU WANT, claimed the shoot-up posters on the back wall of each cubicle. Chianese's tank was warmer than it had been. Vesicle could see why: the twink was out of credit. He had maybe half a day left, this was according to readouts in the tank fascia, and then it was the cold world for him. The tank proteome, a mucoid slime of nutrients and tailored hormones, was beginning to prepare his body for the life he left behind.

Three thirty on a grey Friday afternoon in March. The East River was the colour of puddled iron. Since midday, westbound traffic had been backing up from Honaluchi Bridge. Chinese Ed stuck his head out the side window of his ramrod Dodge, into the smell of burned diesel and lead, and tried to get a look at what was ahead. Nothing. Something was broken up there, the lights were out, someone had melted down; the people up there were on overload – office overload, 2.4 kids overload, shitcan overload – and had left their cars and were dully beating on one another to no good purpose. Who knew what had happened? It was the same old life. Ed shook his head at the futility of mankind, turned off the Capital traffic report and turned instead to Rita Robinson.

'Hey, Rita,' he said.

Two or three minutes later her peppermint and white candy-stripe skirt was up around her waist.

'Steady, Ed,' advised Rita. 'We could be here some time.'

Ed laughed. 'Steady Eddy,' he said. 'That's me.'

Rita laughed too. 'I'm ready,' she said. 'I'm ready, ready Eddy.'

It turned out Rita was right.

Two hours later they were still there.

'Doesn't this just suck?' said the woman from the pink Mustang parked a couple of cars in front of Ed's Dodge.

She looked in at Rita – who had pulled down her skirt and adjusted her garter belt and was now examining herself with a kind of morose professional intensity in the pull-down vanity mirror – and seemed to lose interest. 'Oh hi, honey,' she said. 'Just freshening up there?' Everyone had turned their engines off. People were stretching their legs up and down the pavement. A hot dog guy was working the queue, moving west ten or a dozen vehicles at a time. 'I never knew it this bad,' said the woman from the Mustang. She laughed, picked a shred of tobacco from her lower lip, examined it. 'Maybe the Russians landed.'

'You got a point there,' Ed told her. She smiled at him, stepped on the butt of her cigarette, and went back to her car. Ed turned on the radio. The Russians hadn't landed. The Martians hadn't landed. There was no news at all.

'So. This Brady thing,' he said to Rita. 'What are they saying in the DA's office?'

'Hey, Eddy,' Rita said. She looked at him for a moment or two, then shook her head and turned back to the mirror. She had her lipstick out now. 'I thought you'd never ask,' she said in a matter-of-fact voice. The lipstick didn't seem to suit her, because she put it away with an irritable gesture and looked out the window at the river running by.

'I thought you'd never ask,' she repeated bitterly.

That was when the big yellow duck started to push its head into the car through Ed's open side-window. This time, Rita didn't seem to notice it, even though it was speaking.

'Come in, Number Seven,' it was saying. 'Your time is up.'

Ed reached inside his baseball jacket, the back of which read Lungers 8-ball Superstox, and took out one of his Colts.

'Hey,' the duck said. 'I'm joking. Just a reminder. You got eleven minutes' credit to run before this facility closes down. Ed, as a valued customer of our organisation, you can put more money in or you can make the most of what's left.'

The duck cocked its head on one side and looked at Rita out of one beady eye.

'I know which I'd do,' it said.

SEVEN

The Pursuit of God

When Michael Kearney woke it was deep night outside. The lights were off. He could hear someone breathing harshly in the room.

'Who's there?' he said sharply. 'Lizzie?'

The noise stopped.

A single minimally furnished space with straw-coloured hardwood floors, galley kitchen, and a bedroom on the second floor, the apartment belonged to his second wife Elizabeth, who had moved back to the US at the end of the marriage. From its upper windows you could see across Chiswick Eyot to Castelnau. Rubbing his face, Kearney got out of the armchair and went upstairs. It was empty up there, with a drench of streetlight across the disordered bed and a faint smell of Elizabeth's clothes which had remained to haunt him after she left. He went back down again and switched on the lights. A disembodied head was balanced on the back of the Heals sofa. It was wasted and ill-looking. All the flesh had retreated to the salient points of its face, leaving the bone structure prominent and bare beneath a greyish skin. He wasn't sure what it belonged to, or even what sex it was. As soon as it saw him it began swallowing and wetting its mouth urgently, as if it hadn't enough saliva to speak.

'I can't begin to describe the grudgingness of my life!' it shouted suddenly. 'Ever feel that, Kearney? Ever feel your life is threadbare? Ever feel it's like this worn-out curtain which barely hides all the rage, the jealousy, the sense of failure, all those self-devouring ambitions and appetites that have never dared show themselves?'

'For God's sake,' Kearney said, backing away.

The head smiled contemptuously.

'It was a cheap enough curtain in the first place. Isn't that what you feel? Just like the ones at these windows, made of some nasty orange stuff with a fur of age on it the day after it was hung.'

Kearney tried to speak, but found that his own mouth had dried up.

Eventually he said: 'Elizabeth never hung curtains.'

The head licked its lips. 'Well let me tell you something, Kearney: it didn't hide you anyway! Behind it that horrible thin body of yours has been writhing and posturing for forty-odd years, laughing and making faces (oh yes, making faeces, Kearney!), shaking its huge Beardsleyesque cock about, anything to be noticed. Anything to be acknowledged. But you won't look, will you? Because pull that curtain back once and you'd be burned to a crisp by the sheer repressed energy of it.'

The head gazed exhaustedly around. After a moment or two it said in a quieter voice:

'Ever feel like that, Kearney?'

Kearney considered.

'No.'

Valentine Sprake's face seemed to fluoresce palely from within. 'No?' he said. 'Oh well.'

He got up and came out from behind the sofa where he had been crouching, an energetic-looking man perhaps fifty years old, with stooped shoulders, sandy orange hair and a goatee beard. His colourless eyes were wilful and absent-minded at the same time. He had on a brown fleece jacket too long for him, tight old Levis which made his thighs look thin and bandy, Merrell trail boots. He smelled of rolling tobacco and generic whisky. In one hand – its knuckles enlarged by years of work or illness – he held a book. He looked down at it in a startled way, then offered it to Kearney.

'Look at this.'

'I don't want it.' Kearney backed away. 'I don't want it.'

'More fool you,' said Valentine Sprake. 'I got it off the shelf there.' He tore out two or three pages of the volume – which, Kearney now saw, was Elizabeth's beloved thirty-year-old Penguin Classics edition of *Madame Bovary* – and began stuffing them in different pockets of his coat. 'I can't be bothered with people who don't know their own minds.'

'What do you want from me?'

Sprake shrugged. 'You phoned me,' he said. 'As I heard it.'

'No,' said Kearney. 'I got some sort of answer service, but I didn't leave a message.'

Sprake laughed.

'Oh yes you did. Alice remembered you. Alice quite fancies you.' He rubbed his hands busily. 'How about a cup of tea?'

'I'm not even sure you're here,' Kearney said, looking anxiously at the sofa. 'Did you understand anything you were saying over there?' Then he said: 'It's caught up with me again. In the Midlands, two days ago. I thought you might know what to do.'

Sprake shrugged.

'You already know what to do,' he suggested.

'I'm sick of doing it, Valentine.'

'You'd better get out, then. I doubt you'll finish with a whole skin whatever you do.'

'It doesn't work any more. I don't know if it ever worked.'

Sprake gave him a small colourless smile. 'Oh, it works,' he said. 'You're just a wanker.' He held up one hand in the pretence that Kearney might take offence. 'Only joking. Only joking.' He kept smiling for a moment or two, then added: 'Mind if I roll a cigarette?' On the inside of his left wrist he had a home-made tattoo, the word FUGA, in faded blue-black ink. Kearney shrugged and went into the galley. While Kearney made the tea Sprake strode about smoking nervously and picking pieces of tobacco off his bottom lip. He switched the lights off, and waited with a satisfied air for the apartment to fill with streetlight instead.

At one point he said, 'The Gnostics were wrong, you know.' Then, when Kearney didn't reply:

'There's a mist coming up over the river.'

After that there was quite a long pause. Kearney heard two or three small movements, as of someone removing a book from a shelf; then an intake of breath. 'Listen to this—' Sprake began, but fell silent immediately. When Kearney came out of the kitchen, the street door was open and the apartment was empty. Two or three books lay on the floor, surrounded by torn-out pages which looked like wings. On to the empty white wall above the sofa, in a bright parallelogram of sodium light, something outside was projecting the shadow of an enormous beaked head. It looked nothing like the head of a bird. 'Christ,' said Kearney, his heart beating so hard he could feel it rocking his upper body. 'Christ!' The shadow began to turn, as if its owner, hanging in the air two storeys above a street in Chiswick, two in the morning, was turning to look at him. Or worse, as if it wasn't a shadow at all.

'Jesus Christ, Sprake, it's here!' Kearney shouted, and ran out of the apartment. He could hear Sprake's footsteps thudding on the pavement somewhere ahead of him; but he never caught him up.

Central London, 3 a.m.

Fractals spilled across icy blue displays, developing into something that resembled the jerky frame-by-frame slow motion of a much earlier medium. Brian Tate rubbed his eyes and stared. Behind him, the suite was dark. It smelled of junk food, cold coffee. The male cat was sniffing about in a litter of discarded polystyrene cups and burger cartons around Tate's feet. The female sat quietly on his shoulder, watching with a kind of companionable complicity the mathematical monster unspooling across the screens in front of them. Every so often she dabbed out a paw, mewing impatiently, as if to draw Tate's attention to something he had missed. She knew where the action was. Tate took off his glasses and put them on the desk in front of him. Even at these speeds there was nothing to see.

Or almost nothing. At Los Alamos, bored – though he would never have admitted it to anyone – by the constant talk about physics and money, he had spent most of his free time in his room, switching restlessly from TV channel to TV channel with the sound turned down. This led him to think about choice. The moment of choice, he thought, could be located very exactly as one image flickered, broke and was replaced by the next. If you levered things apart, if you could get into the exact moment of transition, what would you find? Entertaining himself with the fantasy of an unknown station – something more watchable than reruns of *Buffy the Vampire Slayer* – transmitting into the gap, into the moment of choice, he had tried to record a series of channel changes on the VCR and play them back in stop-frame. This had proved to be impossible.

He reached back to stroke the cat's ears. She evaded him, jumped down on to the floor, where she hissed at the male until he retreated under Tate's chair.

Tate, meanwhile, picked up the telephone and tried Kearney's home number. There was no answer.

He left another message.

EIGHT

The Tailor's Cut

When Uncle Zip heard Seria Mau say the words 'Dr Haends', he sat perfectly still for a fraction of a second. Then he shrugged. 'You should bring it back,' he repeated. This was his idea of an apology. 'I'll be generous to you.'

'Uncle Zip? Do you know a Dr Haends?'

'I never heard of him,' said Uncle Zip quickly, 'and I know every tailor from here to the Core.'

'Do you think it's military?'

'No.'

'Do you think it's modern?'

'No.'

'So what can I do?'

Uncle Zip sighed. 'I already told you: bring it back to me.'

Seria Mau felt reluctant. She felt as if some other avenue should open up for her at this point. She said:

'You've lost your credibility here –'

Uncle Zip threw up his hands and laughed.

'– and I want to meet this guy, this Billy Anker.'

'I should know better than to argue with a fetch!' He stared at her, still amused but suddenly alert. 'First off, Billy Anker is not known to be a guy with a refund policy,' he said quietly. 'In addition, he is my guy, not yours. Thirdly, he is not a cutter. You understand? What do you think you'd get from him, young woman, that you won't get from me?'

'I don't know, Uncle. Something. I don't know what. But you aren't telling me what you know. And I have to start somewhere.'

He stared at her a moment longer, and she could see him think.

Then he said, in a throwaway voice: 'OK.'

'I've got money.'

'I don't want money for this,' said Uncle Zip. 'When I think about it this could work out for all of us. Even Billy.' He smiled to himself. 'I'll give you Billy as a favour. Maybe you'll do me a favour sometime down the line.' He waved one hand dismissively. 'It won't be much, no problem.'

'I'd rather pay.'

Uncle Zip got gracefully to his feet.

'Don't look a gift-horse in the mouth,' he advised her flatly. 'Take my deal, I'll let you in on Billy's whereabouts. Maybe also his present ambitions.'

'I'll think about it.'

'Hey, don't think too long.'

While he sat, he had balanced his accordion on his powerful thighs. Now he took it up, and got the straps back over his shoulders, and squeezed out a long introductory chord. 'What's money anyway?' he said. 'Money isn't everything. I go down to the Core, it's five hundred light years of money. Money all the way. They got entire planetary systems designated FTZs. They got women with two days' training, sweating out lousy little do-it-yourself splicing kits, what for? So their kids can eat. Oh, and so *Earth* kids can get a legal patch at a factor five mark-up. Break the seal on the code and give themselves metabolic collapse on a Saturday night. You know what those corporates say?'

'What do they say, Uncle Zip?'

'They say, "Money has no morality," in these voices make you want to puke. They're proud of it.'

It was 2 a.m. in Carmody, and the Kefahuchi Tract glittered across the sky as bright as Uncle Zip's accordion. He played another chord, and then a series of brash arpeggios that rippled one into the next. He puffed up his cheeks and began to stamp his feet. One by one, his audience slipped back into the parlour, giving weak apologetic grins to Seria Mau's fetch. It was as if they had been waiting somewhere down Henry Street, some bar not far down, for the music to start up again. They brought bottles in brown bags, and this time one or two shy women were with them, casting glances out of the side of their eyes at Uncle Zip then looking quickly away again. Seria Mau listened to another song, then let herself fade into brown smoke.

On the face of it, Uncle Zip was solid. He dealt with the passing trade: cultivars for pleasure, sentient tattoos, also any kind of superstitious hitch and splice, like ensuring your firstborn gets the luck gene of Elvis. Every afternoon his shop was full of nervous mothers-to-be, designing their baby to have genius. 'Everybody wants to be rich,' he would complain. 'I made a million geniuses. Also, everybody wants to be Buddy Holly, Barbra Streisand, Shakespeare. Let me tell you: no one knows what those men looked like.' It was barely illegal. It was all, as he said, a bit of fun. There was only so far he could go. It was the modern equivalent, he said, of a kiss-me-quick hat you bought on Labour Day. Or maybe that old kind of tattoo they had back then. In the lab, though, he cut for anyone. He cut for the military, he cut for the shadow boys. He cut for viral junkies, in for the latest patch to their brain disease of choice. He cut alien DNA. He didn't care what he cut, or who he cut for as long as they could pay.

As for his audience, they were cultivars: every one cloned – even the shy young women in the black tube skirts – from his own stemcells, deep-frozen insurance he took out the day he went to Radio Bay. They were his younger self, before he found his big secret, come to worship twice-nightly at the shrine he had made of his success.

Motel Splendido turned, nightside up, beneath the *White Cat*. From the parking lot, Seria Mau stared down. Carmody appeared like a sticky, abbreviated smear of light the colour or extent of which you couldn't be sure, on its island in the curve of the southern ocean. She dawdled her fetch along its magically lighted streets. Downtown was black and gold towers, designer goods in the deserted pastel malls, mute fluorescent light skidding off the precise curves of matt plastic surfaces, the foams of lace and oyster satin. Down by the ocean, transformation dub, saltwater dub, pulsed from the bars, the soundtrack of a human life, with songs like 'Dark Night, Bright Light' and others. Human beings! She could almost smell their excitement at being alive there in the warm black heart of things among the sights. She could almost smell their guilt. What was she looking for? She couldn't say. All she could be sure of was that Uncle Zip's hypocrisy had made her restless.

Suddenly it was dawn, and in a corner of the sea wall, where a water-stair went down to what was now new-washed empty sand, grey in the thin light of dawn, she came upon three shadow boys. Running on one-shot cultivars – the throwaway 24-hour kind, all tusks and rank-smelling muscles, sleeveless denim jackets, sores from bumping against things in an unconsidered manner – they were squatting in the dawn wind playing the Ship Game on a blanket, grunting as the bone dice tumbled and toppled, every so often exchanging high-speed datastreams like squeals of rage. Complex betting was in progress, less on the game than the contingencies of the world around it: the flight of a bird, the height of a wave, the colour of the sunlight. After every cast of the dice they pawed and fought pantomimically and tossed folding money at one another, laughing and snuffling.

'Hey,' they said when Seria Mau fetched up. 'Here, kitty kitty!' There was nothing they could do to her. She was safe with them.

It was like having grown-up brothers. For a moment or two they threw the dice at blinding speed. Then one of them said, without looking up: 'You don't get bored, being *not real* that way?'

They couldn't play for laughing at that.

Seria Mau watched the game until a bell rang softly on the *White Cat* and drew her away.

As soon as she was gone, two of the shadow boys turned on the third and cut his throat for cheating, then, overcome by the pure existential moment, cradled his head in the warm golden light as he smiled softly up at nothing, bubbling his life out all over them like a benediction. 'Hey you,' they comforted him, 'you can do it all again. Tonight you'll do it all again.'

Up in the parking lot, Seria Mau sighed and turned away.

'You see?' she told her empty ship. 'It always comes to this. All the fucking and the fighting, it all comes to nothing. All the pushing and the shoving. All the things they give each other. If for a moment I thought—' Could she still cry? She said, apropos of nothing: 'Those beautiful boys in the sunlight.' This made her remember what she had said to the Nastic commander, out there in the shadow of his stupidly big ship. It made her remember the package she had bought from Uncle Zip, and what she intended to do with it. It made her recall Uncle Zip's offer. She opened a line to him and said:

'OK, tell me where this Billy Anker guy is.' She laughed, and, mimicking the tailor's manner, added, 'Also his present ambitions.'

Uncle Zip laughed too. Then he let his face go expressionless.

'You waited too long for that free offer,' he informed her. 'I changed my mind about that.'

He was sitting on a stool in his front room above the shop. He had on a short-sleeve sailor suit and hat. White canvas trousers clung tight to bursting over his spread thighs. On each thigh he had a daughter sitting, plump red-faced little girls with blue eyes, shiny cheeks and blonde ringlets, caught as if in a still picture, laughing and reaching for his hat. All the flesh in this picture was lively and varnished. All the colours were pushed and rich. Uncle Zip's fat arms curved around his daughters, his hands placed in the small of each back as if they were the bellows-ends of his accordion. Behind him, the room was lacquered red and green, and there were shelves on which he had arranged his collections of polished motorcycle parts and other kitschy things from the history of Earth. Whatever you saw in Uncle Zip's house, he never let you see his wife, or gave you one thin glimpse of the tools of his trade. 'As to where the guy is,' he said, 'this is where you go . . .'

He gave her the name of a system, and a planet.

'It surveys as 3-alpha-Ferris VII. The locals – which there aren't many of them – call it Redline.'

'But that's in—'

'—Radio Bay.' He shrugged. 'Nothing comes easy in this world, kid. You got to decide how much you want what you want.'

Seria Mau cut him off.

'Goodbye, Uncle Zip,' she said, and left him there with his expensive family and his cheap rhetoric.

Two or three days later, the K-ship *White Cat*, registered as a freebooter out of Venusport, New Sol, quit the Motel Splendido parking orbit and slipped away into the long night of the halo. She had loaded fuel and ordnance. After port authority inspection she had accepted minor hull maintenance, and paid the scandalous tax upon it. She had paid her dues. At the last moment, for reasons her captain barely understood, she had taken on payload too: a team of corporate exogeologists and their equipment, headed towards Suntory IV. For the first time in a year, the lights were on in the human quarters of the ship. The shadow operators mopped and mowed. They hung in corners, whispering and clasping their hands in a kind of bony delight.

What were they? They were algorithms with a life of their own. You found them in vacuum ships like the *White Cat*, in cities, wherever people were. They did the work. Had they always been there in the galaxy, waiting for human beings to take residence? Aliens who had uploaded themselves into empty space? Ancient computer programmes dispossessed by their own hardware, to roam about, half lost, half useful, hoping for someone to look after? In just a few a hundred years they had got inside the machinery of things. Nothing worked without them. They could even run on biological tissue, as shadow boys full of crime and beauty and inexplicable motives. They could, if they wanted, they sometimes whispered to Seria Mau, run on *valves*.

NINE

This Is Your Wake-up Call

Tig Vesicle ran a tank farm, but he didn't do that stuff himself, anymore than he would have filled his arm with AbH. How he looked at it was this: his life was crap, but it was a life. So the kind of porn he liked to watch was ordinary, cheap, unimmersive, holographic stuff. It was often advertised as intrusion-porn. The fantasy of it was: some woman's room would get fitted with microcameras without her knowledge. You could watch her do anything, though things would usually end with some cultivar – all tusks, prick the size of a horse – finding her in the shower. Vesicle often turned that part off. The show he watched most was syndicated from out in the halo and featured a girl called Moaner, who was supposed to live in a corporate enclave somewhere on Motel Splendido. The story was, her husband was always away (though in fact he often arrived back unexpectedly with five of his business associates, who included another woman). Moaner wore short pink latex skirts with tube tops and little white socks. She had a little clean mat of pubic hair. She was bored, the narrative went; she was agile and spoilt. Vesicle preferred her to do ordinary things, like painting her toenails naked, or trying to look over her shoulder at herself in a mirror. One thing with Moaner was this: even though she was a clone, her body looked real. She wasn't any kind of rebuild. They advertised her as 'never been to the tailor' and he could believe that.

The other thing about her was that she was aware of you, even though she didn't know you were there.

Could you get behind that paradox? Vesicle believed you could. If he once understood it, it would tell him something about the universe or, equally important, about human beings. He felt as if she knew he was there. *She isn't a porn star!* he would tell himself.

He was dreaming this cheap, doomed, New Man dream – while Moaner herself yawned and tried on a pair of brand new yellow Mickey Mouse shorts with big buttons and matching suspenders – when the door of the tank farm banged open, letting in a gust of cold grey wind from the street, along with six or seven tiny kids. They had short black hair and tight, furious Asian faces. Snow was melting on the shoulders of their black rainslickers. The oldest was maybe eight, with lightning flashes etched into the short hair above her ears and a Nagasaki Hi-Lite Autoloader clutched in both hands. They spread out and began going through the tank cubicles as if they were looking for something, shouting and gabbling in gluey voices and pulling out the power cables so the tanks went on to emergency wake-up call.

'Hey!' said Tig Vesicle.

They stopped what they were doing and went quiet. The oldest kid shrieked and gesticulated at them. They looked warily from her to Vesicle and back again, then went on rummaging among the cubicles – where, finding a prybar, they began trying to lever the lid off Tank Seven. The girl, meanwhile, came up and stood in front of Vesicle. She was perhaps half his height. *Café électrique* had already rotted her little uneven teeth. She was wired until her eyes bulged. Her wrists trembled with the weight of the Nagasaki; but she managed to raise it until its aimspot wavered somewhere around his diaphragm, then said something like:

'Djoo-an dug fortie? Ugh?'

She sounded as if she was eating the words as fast as she spoke them. Vesicle stared down at her.

'I'm sorry,' he said. 'I'm not sure what you're saying.'

This seemed to anger her unreasonably. 'Fortie!' she shrieked.

Casting around for a reply, Vesicle remembered something the Chianese twink once told him. It was part of some anecdote from when the twink still had a life, blah, blah, blah, they all pretended to remember that. Vesicle, bored by the story but intrigued by the extremes of experience you could pack into a single statement, had memorised it gleefully. He spent a moment summoning the exact offhand gesture with which Chianese had accompanied the words, then looked down at the girl and said:

'I'm so scared I don't know whether to laugh or shit.'

Her eyes bulged further. He could see that she was hauling back on the trigger of the Hi-Lite. He opened his mouth, wondering what he could say to stem this new rage, but it was too late to say anything at all. There was a huge explosion which, oddly enough, seemed to come from somewhere near the street door. The girl's eyes bulged further, then jumped out of her head to the full length of her optic nerve. In the same instant, her head evaporated into a kind of greyish-red slurry. Vesicle stumbled backwards, rather covered with this stuff, and fell on his back, wondering what was happening.

It was this:

One-shot cultivars were queuing outside the tank farm in the Pierpoint night. Ten or a dozen of them stood about in the falling snow, stamping their feet and cocking their short reaction guns. They wore stained leather trousers, laced together over a three-inch gap all the way down the outside leg, and leather bolero vests. Their breath condensed like the breath of great dependable animals in the freezing air. Even their shadows had tusks. Their huge arms were blue with cold, but they were too fucking hard-on to care about that. 'Hey,' they told one another, 'I wish I'd put less clothes on. You know?' The entry pattern was this: they rushed the door of the twink parlour in twos, and the kiddies inside shot them down from behind the coffins.

It was bedlam in there in quite a short time after they killed the Hi-Lite girl, with the flat fizzing arcs of reaction bolts, the flicker of laser sights in the smoke, and a rich smell of human fluids. The front window was out. Big smoking holes were in the walls. Two of the tanks had fallen off their trestles; the rest, alive with shocking pink alarm graphics, were warming up fast. To Tig Vesicle it seemed that the whole issue revolved around Tank Seven. The kids had given up on getting it open: but they weren't going to leave it for anyone else. Seeing this early on, Vesicle had crawled as far away from it as possible, and got in a corner with his hands over his eyes, while cultivars rushed through the smoke, shouting, 'Hey, don't bother to cover me!' and were picked off. The kids had a tactical advantage there: but down on firepower, down on your luck, and they were being pushed back. They shrieked in their gluey argot. They pulled new guns from beneath their rainslickers. Looking over their shoulders for another way out, they got shot in the legs, or the spine, and they were soon in a condition the tailor couldn't cure. Things looked bad, then two things happened:

Somebody hit Tank Seven with a short reaction shell.

And the Cray sisters appeared in the tank farm doorway, shaking their heads and reaching for the pieces in their purses.

Chinese Ed and Rita Robinson were on the run somewhere in the weeds in back of the burning carwash. Hanson was dead, Ed guessed, and the DA too, so there would be no help from that quarter. Otto Rank had the high ground. He also had the 30.06 he had taken from Hogfat Wisconsin's kitchen after he tortured and killed Hogfat's teenage daughter. It was the way he laid her out that was the missing piece of the puzzle, Ed thought. I should have seen that, but I was too busy being the smart dick. Not seeing that was going to cost two more lives, but at least one of them was only his own.

Ed's head got too far above the weeds. The flat crack-and-whip of the 30.06 cut across the drowsy afternoon air. Some birds flew up from the river bank a quarter of a mile away.

Sixteen shots, Ed thought. Maybe he's low on ammo now.

Ed's ramrod Dodge was where he had left it parked, on the service road the other side of the lot. They weren't going to make it that far. Rita was shot. Ed was shot too, but not as bad. On the up side, he had a couple of shells left in one of the Colts. He ran harder, but this seemed to open Rita's wound.

'Hey, Ed,' she said. 'Put me down. Let's do it here.'

She laughed, but her face was grey and defeated.

'Jesus, Rita,' Ed said.

'I know. You're sorry. Well you shouldn't be, Ed. I got shot with you, which is more than most girls get.' She tried to laugh again. 'Don't you want to make it with me in the weeds?'

'Rita . . . '

'I'm tired, Ed.'

She didn't say any more, and her expression didn't change. Eventually he put her down in the weeds and began to cry. After a minute or two he shouted:

'Otto, you fucker!'

'Yo!' said Rank.

'She's dead.'

There was a silence. After a bit, Rank said:

'You want to come in?'

'She's dead, Otto. You're next.'

There was a laugh.

'If you come in—' Rank began, then seemed to be thinking. 'What is it I do?' he called. 'Hey, help me out here, Ed. Oh, wait, no, got it: *If you come in I see you get a fair trial.*' He put a shot where he estimated Ed's skull had last been. 'Guess what?' he said, when the echoes had died away. 'I'm shot too, Ed. Rita shot me in the heart, long before she met you. These women! It was point-blank, Ed. You make anything of that?'

'I make suck my dick out of it,' Ed said.

He stood up as coolly as he could. He saw Otto Rank down at

the edge of the carwash roof in the classic infantry kneel, the 30.06 up at aim, its sling tight round his elbow. Ed raised the Colt carefully in both hands. He had two shots left, and it was important he spoiled the first one. He blinked the sweat out of his eyes and squeezed off carefully. The round went ten, twelve feet wide, and Ed dropped his pistol arm to his side. Otto, who had been surprised to see him pop up out of the weeds like that, gave a wild laugh of relief.

'You got the wrong gun, Ed!' he shouted.

He stood up. 'Hey,' he said. 'Take another pop. It's free!'

He spread his arms wide. 'Nobody shoots anybody at eighty yards with a Colt .45,' he said.

Ed raised the gun again and fired.

Rank was picked up from the head end and thrown backwards with his feet in the air. He fell off the roof and into the weeds. 'Fuck you, Ed!' he screamed, but his face was half off and he was already dead. Chinese Ed looked down at his Colt. He made a gesture as if to throw it away. 'I'm sorry, Rita,' he was beginning to say, when the sky behind the carwash turned a steely colour and ripped open like a page of cheap print. This time the duck was huge. Something was wrong with it. Its yellow feathers had a greasy look, and a human tongue hung laxly out of one side of its beak.

'There will be an interruption to service,' it said. 'As a valued customer—'

At that, Chinese Ed's consciousness was pulled apart and he was received into all the bleakness and pain of the universe. All the colours went out of his world, and all the beautiful simple ironies along with them, and then the world itself was folded away until through it, try as he might, he could see nothing but the cheesy fluorescent lights of Tig Vesicle's tank farm. He erupted out of the wreckage of Tank Seven, half drowned, throwing up with disorientation and horror. He stared round at the drifting smoke, the dead kids and stunned-looking cultivars. Proteome poured sluggishly off him like the albumen of a bad egg. Poor, dead Rita was gone for good and he wasn't even Chinese Ed the detective anymore. He was Ed Chianese, twink.

'This is my *home*, you guys,' he said. 'You know? You could have knocked.'

There was a laugh from the doorway.

'You owe us money, Ed Chianese,' said Bella Cray.

She looked meditatively across the room at the two remaining gun-kiddies. 'These punks aren't from me,' she said to Tig Vesicle, who had got himself up off the floor and sidled back behind his cheap plywood counter.

Evie Cray laughed.

'They aren't mine, either,' she said.

She shot them in the face, one after the other, with her Chambers pistol, then showed her teeth. 'That's what'll happen to you if you don't pay us, Ed,' she explained.

'Hey,' said Bella. 'I wanted to do that.'

'Those punks were some of Fedora Gash's punks,' Evie told Tig Vesicle. 'So why'd you let them in?'

Vesicle shrugged. He had no choice, the shrug indicated.

The cultivars were leaving the farm now, one-handedly dragging their dead and wounded behind them. The wounded looked down at themselves, dabbling their hands and saying things like, 'I could get shot like this all day. You know?' Ed Chianese watched them file past and shivered. He stepped out of the ruined tank, plucked the rubber cables out of his spine and tried to wipe the proteome off himself with his hands. He could already feel the black voice of withdrawal, like someone talking persuasively a long way back in his head.

'I don't know you,' he said. 'I don't owe you anything.'

Evie gave him her big lipstick smile.

'We bought your paper off Fedy Gash,' she explained. She studied the wreckage of the tank farm. 'Looks as if she didn't really want to sell.' She allowed herself another smile. 'Still. A twink like you owes everyone else in the universe, Ed. That's what a twink is, a speck of protoplasm in the ocean.' She shrugged. 'What can we do, Ed? *We're* all fish.'

Ed knew she was right. He wiped helplessly at himself again, then, seeing Vesicle behind his counter, approached him and said:

'You got any tissues back there, or like that?'

'Hey, Ed,' Vesicle said. 'I got this.'

He pulled out the Hi-Lite Autoloader he had taken from the dead girl and fired it into the ceiling. 'I'm so scared I could shit!' he yelled at the Cray sisters. They looked startled. 'So, you know: *fuck you!*' He darted jerkily out from behind the counter, every nerve in his body firing off at random. He could barely control his limbs. 'Hey, fuck, Ed. How'm I doing?' he screamed. Ed, who was as surprised as the Cray sisters, stared at him. Any minute now, Bella and Evie would wake up from their trance of surprise. They would brush the plaster dust off their shoulders and something serious would start to happen.

'Jesus, Tig,' Ed said.

Naked, stinking of embalming fluid and punctured for the tank at 'neurotypical energy sites', a wasted Earthman with a partly grown-out Mohican and a couple of snake tattoos, he ran out into the street. Pierpoint was deserted. After a moment explosions and flashes of light lit up the windows of the tank farm. Then Tig Vesicle staggered out backwards, the arms of his coat on fire with blowback from the reaction pistol, shouting, 'Hey, the *fuck*,' and, 'I'm so shit!' They stared at one another with expressions of terror and relief. Chianese beat out the fire with his hands. Arms around each other's shoulders they blundered off into the night, drunk for the moment with body-chemicals and camaraderie.

TEN

Agents of Fortune

Three in the morning. Valentine Sprake was long gone. Michael Kearney stumbled along the north bank of the Thames, then hid among some trees until he thought he heard a voice. This frightened him again and he ran all the way to Twickenham in the dark and the wind before he got control of himself. There he tried to think, but all that came to him was the image of the Shrander. He decided to call Anna. Then he decided to call a cab. But his hands were trembling too hard to use the phone, so in the end he did neither but took the towpath back east instead. An hour later, Anna met him at her door, wearing a long cotton nightgown. She looked flushed and he could feel the heat of her body from two feet away.

'Tim's with me,' she said nervously.

Kearney stared at her.

'Who's Tim?' he said.

Anna looked back into the flat.

'It's all right, it's Michael,' she called. To Kearney she said, 'Couldn't you come back in the morning?'

'I just want some things,' Kearney said. 'It won't take long.'

'Michael—'

He pushed past her. The flat smelled strongly of incense and candle wax. To get to the room where he kept his stuff, he had to pass Anna's bedroom, the door of which was partly open. Tim, whoever he was, sat propped up against the wall at the head end of the bed, his face three-quarter profile in the yellow glow of two or three nightlight candles. He was in his mid thirties, with good skin and a build light but athletic, features which would help give him a boyish appearance well into his forties. He had a glass of red wine in one hand, and he was staring thoughtfully at it.

Kearney looked him up and down.

'Who the hell is this?' he said.

'Michael, this is Tim. Tim, this is Michael.'

'Hi,' said Tim. He held out his hand. 'I won't get up.'

'Jesus Christ, Anna,' Kearney said.

He went through to the back room, where a brief search turned up some clean Levis and an old black leather jacket he had once liked too much to throw away. He put them on. There was also a cycle-courier bag with the Marin logo on the flap, into which he began emptying the contents of the little green chest of drawers. Looking up blankly from this task, he discovered that Anna had washed the chalked diagrams off the wall above it. He wondered why she would do that. He could hear her talking in the bedroom. Whenever she tried to explain anything, her voice took on childish, persuasive values. After a moment she seemed to give up and said sharply, 'Of course I don't! What do you mean?' Kearney remembered her trying to explain similar things to him. There was a noise outside the door and Tim poked his head round.

'Don't do that,' Kearney said. 'I'm nervous already.'

'I wondered if I could help?'

'No, thanks.'

'It's just that it's five o'clock in the morning, you see, and you come in here covered in mud.'

Kearney shrugged.

'I see that,' he said. 'I see that.'

Anna stood angrily by the door to watch him out. 'Take care,' he said to her, as warmly as he could. He was two flights down the stone stairs when he heard her footsteps behind him. 'Michael,' she called. 'Michael.' When he didn't answer, she followed him out into the street and stood there shouting at him in her bare feet and white nightdress. 'Did you come back for another fuck?' Her voice echoed up and down the empty suburban street. 'Is that what you wanted?'

'Anna,' he said, 'it's five o'clock in the morning.'

'I don't care. Please don't come here again, Michael. Tim's nice and he really loves me.'

Kearney smiled.

'I'm glad.'

'No, you're not!' she shouted. 'No, you're not!'

Tim came out of the building behind her. He was dressed, and he had his car keys in his hand. He crossed the pavement without looking at Anna or Kearney, and got into his car. He wound the driver's window down as if he thought about saying something to one of them, but in the end shook his head and drove off instead. Anna stared after him puzzledly then burst into tears. Kearney put his arm round her shoulders. She leaned in to him.

'Or did you come back to kill me,' she said quietly. 'The way you killed all those others?'

Kearney walked off towards the Underground station at Gunnersbury. His phone chirped at him suddenly, but he ignored it.

Heathrow Terminal 3, hushed after the long night, maintained a slow dry warmth. Kearney bought underwear and toilet articles, sat in one of the concessions outside the departure lounge reading the *Guardian* and taking small sips of a double espresso.

The women behind the concession counter were arguing about something in the news. 'I'd hate to live forever,' one of them said. She raised her voice. 'There's your change, love.' Kearney, who had been expecting to see his own name on page two of the paper, raised his head. She gave him a smile. 'Don't forget your change,' she said. He had found only the name of the woman he had killed in the Midlands; no one was looking for a Lancia Integrale. He folded the paper up and stared at a trickle of Asians making their way across the departure lounge for a flight to LAX. His phone chirped again. He took it out: voicemail.

'Hi,' said Brian Tate's voice. 'I've been trying to get you at home.' He sounded irritable. 'I had an idea a couple of hours ago. Give me a ring if you get this.' There was a pause, and Kearney thought the message was over. Then Tate added, 'I'm really a bit concerned. Gordon was here again after you left. So call.' Kearney switched the phone off and stared at it. Behind Tate's voice he had heard the white cat mewing for attention.

'"Justine"!' he thought. It made him smile.

He sorted through the courier bag until he found the Shrander's dice. He held them in his hand. They always felt warm. The symbols on them appeared in no language or system of numbers he knew, historical or modern. On a pair of ordinary dice, each symbol would be duplicated; here, none was. Kearney watched them rattle across the tabletop and come to rest in the spilled coffee by his empty cup. He studied them for a moment, then scooped them up, stuffed newspaper and phone hastily into the courier bag, and left.

'Your change, love!'

The women looked after him, then at each other. One of them shrugged. By then, Kearney was in the lavatories, shivering and throwing up. When he came out, he found Anna waiting for him. Heathrow was awake now. People were hurrying to make flights, make phone calls, make headway. Anna stood fragile and listless in the middle of the concourse, staring every so often at their faces as they brushed past her. Every time she thought she saw him her face lit up. Kearney remembered her at Cambridge. Shortly after they met, a friend of hers had told him: 'We nearly lost her once. You will take care of her, won't you?' He had remained puzzled by this warning – with its image of Anna as a package that might easily slip the mind – only until he found her in the bathroom a month later, crying and staring ahead, with her wrists held out in front of her. Now she looked at him and said:

'I knew this is where you'd be.'

Kearney stared at her in disbelief. He began to laugh.

Anna laughed too. 'I knew you'd come here,' she said. 'I brought some of your things.'

'Anna—'

'You can't keep running away from it forever, you know.'

This made him laugh harder for a moment, then stop.

Kearney's adolescence had passed like a dream. When he wasn't in the fields, he was at the imaginary house he called Gorselands, with its stands of pine, sudden expanses of sandy heath, steep-sided valleys full of flowers and rocks. It was always full summer. He watched his cousins, leggy and elegant, walk naked down the beach at dawn; he heard them whisper in the attic. He was continually sore from masturbating. At Gorselands there was always more; there was always more after that. Inturned breathing, a sudden salty smell in an empty room. A murmur of surprise.

'All this dreaming gets you nowhere,' his mother said.

Everyone said that. But by now he had found numbers. He had seen how the same sequences underlay the structure of a galaxy and a spiral shell. Randomness and determination, chaos and emergent order: the new tools of physics and biology. Years before computer modelling made bad art out of the monster in the Mandelbrot Set, Kearney had seen it, churning and streaming and turbulent at the heart of things. Numbers made him concentrate more: they encouraged him to pay attention. Where he had winced away from school life, with its mixture of boredom and savagery, he now welcomed it. Without all that, the numbers made him see, he would not go to Cambridge, where he could begin to work with the real structures of the world.

He had found numbers. In his first year at Trinity someone showed him the Tarot.

Her name was Inge. He took her to Brown's and, at her request, to a film called *Black Cat White Cat* by Emir Kusturica. She had long hands, an irritating laugh. She was from another college. 'Look!' she ordered. He leaned forward. Cards spilled across the old chenille tablecloth, fluorescing in the late afternoon light, each one a window on the great, shabby life of symbols. Kearney was astonished.

'I've never seen this before,' he said.

'Pay attention,' she ordered. The Major Arcana opened like a flower, combining into meaning as she spoke.

'But it's ridiculous,' he said.

She turned her dark eyes on him and never blinked.

Mathematics and prophecy: Kearney had known instantly that the two gestures were linked, but he couldn't say how. Then, waiting for a train to King's Cross the following morning, he identified a relationship between the flutter of cards falling in a quiet room and the flutter of changing destinations on the mechanical indicator boards at the railway station. This similarity rested, he was willing to admit, on a metaphor (for while a cast of the Tarot was – or seemed – random, the sequence of destinations was – or seemed – determined): but on the basis of it he decided to set out immediately on a series of journeys suggested by the fall of the cards. A few simple rules would determine the direction of each journey, but – in honour of the metaphor, perhaps – they would always be made by train.

He tried to explain this to Inge.

'Events we describe as random often aren't,' he said, watching her hands shuffle and deal, shuffle and deal. 'They're only unpredictable.' He was anxious she should understand the distinction.

'It's just a bit of fun,' she said.

She had taken him to bed eventually, only to become puzzled when he wouldn't enter her. That, as she had said, was the end of it as far as she was concerned. For Kearney it had turned out to be the beginning of everything else. He had bought his own Tarot – a

Crowley deck, its imagery pumped up with all of that mad old visionary's available testosterone – and every journey he undertook after that, everything he did, everything he learned, had drawn him closer to the Shrander.

'What are you thinking?' Anna asked him after they landed in New York.

'I was thinking that sunlight will transform anything.'

Actually he had been thinking how fear transformed things. A glass of mineral water, the hairs on the back of a hand, faces on a downtown street. Fear had caused all these things to become so real to him that, temporarily, there was no way of describing them. Even the imperfections of the water glass, its smears and tiny scratches, had become in some way significant of themselves rather than of usage.

'Oh yes,' said Anna. 'I bet you were.'

They were sitting in a restaurant on the edge of Fulton Market. Six hours in the air had made her as difficult as a child. 'You should always tell the truth,' she said, giving him one of the haggard, brilliant smiles which had captivated him so when they were both twenty. They had had to wait four hours for a flight. She had dozed for much of the journey, then woken tired and fractious. Kearney wondered what he would do with her in New York. He wondered why he had agreed to let her come.

'What were you really thinking?'

'I was wondering how to get rid of you,' Kearney said.

She laughed and touched his arm.

'That's not enough of a joke, really, is it?'

'Of course it is,' Kearney said. 'Look!'

A steam-pipe had broken in some ancient central heating system beneath the road. Smoke rose from the pavement on the corner of Fulton Street. The tarmac was melting. It was a common sight, but Anna, delighted, clutched Kearney's arm. 'We're inside a Tom Waits song,' she exclaimed. The more brilliant her smile, the closer she always seemed to disaster. Kearney shook his head. After a moment, he took out the leather bag that contained the Shrander's dice. He undid the drawstring and let the dice fall into his hand. Anna stopped smiling and gave him a bleak look. She straightened her long legs and leaned back away from him in her chair.

'If you throw those things here,' she said, 'I'll leave you to it. I'll leave you on your own.'

This should have seemed less like a threat than it did.

Kearney considered her, then the steaming street. 'I can't feel it near me,' he admitted. 'For once. Perhaps I won't need them.' He put the dice slowly back in the bag. 'In Grove Park,' he said, 'in your flat, in the room where I kept my things, there were chalk marks on the wall above the green chest of drawers. Tell me why you washed them off.'

'How would I know?' she said indifferently. 'Perhaps I was sick of looking at them. Perhaps I thought it was high time. Michael, what are we doing here?'

Kearney laughed. 'I've got no idea,' he said.

He had run three thousand miles, and now the fear was abating he had no idea why he had come here rather than anywhere else.

Later the same afternoon they moved into the apartment of a friend of his in Morningside Heights. The first thing Kearney did there was telephone Brian Tate in London. When there was no answer from the research suite, he tried Tate's house. It was the answer service there, too. Kearney put the phone down and rubbed his face nervously.

Over the next few days, he bought new clothes at Daffy's, books at Barnes & Noble, and a laptop from a cheap outlet near Union Square. Anna shopped too. They visited Mary Boone's gallery, and the medieval Cuxa Cloister at the Metropolitan Museum of Art's branch in Fort Tryon Park. Anna was disappointed. 'I expected it to look older, somehow,' she said. 'More used.' When they ran out of other things to do they sat drinking New Amsterdam beer at the West End Gate. In the brown heat of the apartment at night, Anna sighed and walked about fractiously, dressing and undressing.

ELEVEN

Machine Dreams

Billy Anker's location, as disclosed to Seria Mau by Uncle Zip, was several days down the Beach from Motel Splendido. Little would be required in the way of navigation until they encountered the complex gravitational shoals and corrosive particle winds of Radio Bay. Seria Mau checked her supercargo into the human quarters then found herself with nothing left to do. The *White Cat's* mathematics took over the ship and sent her to sleep. She was powerless to resist. Dreams and nightmares leaked up from inside her like warm tar.

Seria Mau's commonest dream was of a childhood. She supposed it to be her own. Oddly lit but nevertheless clear, the images in this dream came and went, framed like archaic photographs on a piano. There were people and events. There was a beautiful day. A pet animal. A boat. Laughter. It all came to nothing. There was a face close to hers, lips moving urgently, determined to tell her something she didn't want to hear. Something was trying to make itself known to her, the way a narrative tries to make itself known. The final image was this: a garden, darkened with laurel and close-set silver birch; and a family, centred on an attractive black-haired woman with round, frank brown eyes. Her smile was delighted and ironic at once – the smile of a lively student, rather surprised to find herself a mother. In front of her stood two children seven and ten years old, a girl and a boy, resembling her closely about the eyes; the boy had very black hair and was holding a kitten. And there, behind the three of them, with his hand on her shoulder and his face slightly out of focus, stood a man. Was he the father? How would Seria Mau know? It seemed very important. She stared as deeply into the photograph as she would stare into a face; while it faded slowly into a drifting grey smoke which made her eyes water.

A further dream followed, like a comment on the first:

Seria Mau was looking at a blank interior wall covered with ruched oyster silk. After some time, the upper body of a man bent itself slowly into the frame of the picture. He was tall and thin; dressed in a black tailcoat and starched white shirt. In one white-gloved hand he held a top hat by its brim; in the other a short ebony cane. His jet-black hair was brilliantined close to his head. He had eyes a penetrating light blue, and a black pencil moustache. It occurred to her that he was bowing. After a long while, when he had bent as much of his body into her field of vision as he could without actually stepping into it, he smiled at her. At this, the ruched silk background was replaced by a group of three arched windows opening on to the magisterial glare of the Kefahuchi Tract. The picture, she saw, was taken in a room toppling through space. Slowly, the man in the tailcoat bowed himself back out of it.

If this dream's purpose was to elucidate the one which had preceded it, nothing was achieved. Seria Mau woke up in her tank and experienced a moment of profound emptiness.

'I'm back,' she told the ship's mathematics angrily. 'Why do you send me there? What is the point of that?'

No answer.

The mathematics had woken her, relinquished control of the ship, and slipped quietly back up into its own space, where it began to sort the quanta leaking from significant navigational events in non-local space, using a technique called stochastic resonance. Without quite knowing why, Seria Mau was left feeling angry and inadequate. The mathematics could send her to sleep when it wanted to. It could wake her up when it wanted to. It was the centre of the ship in some way she could never be. She had no idea what it was, what it had been before K-tech webbed them together forever. The mathematics was wrapped around her – kind, patient, amiable, inhuman, as old as the halo. It would always look after her. But its motives were completely unknowable.

'Sometimes I hate you,' she advised it.

Honesty made her amend this. 'Sometimes I hate myself,' she was forced to admit.

Seria Mau had been seven years old the first time she saw a K-ship. Impressed despite herself by its purposeful lines, she cried excitedly, 'I don't want to *have* one of those. I want to *be* one.' She was a quiet child, already locked in confrontation with the forces inside her. 'Look. *Look.*' Something took her and shook her like a rag; something – some feeling which would eventually marshal all of her other feelings – rippled through her. That was what she wanted then.

Now she had changed her mind, she was afraid it was too late. Uncle Zip's package taunted her with its promise, then delivered nothing. A sense of caution had led her to isolate it from the rest of the ship.

The visible part of it lay on the deckplates in a small room in the human quarters, in a shallow red cardboard box tied with shiny green ribbon. Uncle Zip had presented it to her in his typical fashion, with a signed card depicting putti, laurel wreaths and burning candles; also two dozen long-stemmed roses. The roses now lay scattered across the deck, their loose black petals stirring faintly as though in a draught of cold air.

The box, however, was the least of it. Everything inside was very old. However Uncle Zip dressed it up, neither he nor anyone else could be sure of its original purpose. Some of these artefacts had identities of their own, with expectations a million years out of date. They were mad, or broken, or had been built to do unimaginable things. They had been abandoned, they had outlived their original users. Any attempt to understand them was in the nature of a guess. Software bridges might be installed by men like Uncle Zip, but who could be sure what lay on the other side of them? There was code in the box, and that would be dangerous enough in itself: but there was a nanotech substrate of some kind too, on which the code was supposed to run. It was supposed to build something. But when you dialled it up, a polite bell rang in empty air. Something like white foam seemed to pour out and spill over the roses, and a gentle, rather remote female voice asked for Dr Haends.

'I don't know who that is,' Seria Mau told the package angrily. 'I don't know who that is.'

'Dr Haends, please,' repeated the package, as if it hadn't heard her.

'I don't know what you *want*,' said Seria Mau.

'Dr Haends to surgery, please.'

Foam continued to cover the floor, until she closed the software again. If she could smell it, she thought, it would smell strongly of almonds and vanilla. For a moment she had a recollection of these smells so clear it made her dizzy. Her entire sensorium seemed to break its twenty-year connection with the *White Cat*, toppling away into night and helpless vertigo. Seria Mau flailed about inside her tank. She was blind. She was wrong-footed. She was terrified she would lose herself, and die, and not be anything at all. The shadow operators gathered anxiously, clinging up in the corners like cobwebs, hushing and whispering, clasping their hands. 'That which is done,' one reminded another, 'and that which remains undone.'

'She is only little,' they said in unison.

Her answering cry could barely contain the force of all her grief and self-disgust and unvoiced rage. Whatever she had told them in the Motel Splendido parking orbit, she had changed her mind. Seria Mau Genlicher wanted to be human again. Although when she looked at her passengers, she often wondered why.

There were four or five of them, she thought. From the beginning they were hard to count because one of the women was a clone of the other. They had come aboard with a round tonne of field-generating equipment and a confident saunter. Their clothes looked practical until you saw how soft the fabrics were. The hair of the women was brush-cut and lightly moussed to have a semiotic of assertion. The men wore discreet brand-implants, animated logos, tributes to the great corporates of the past. The *White Cat*, with her air of stealth and clear military provenance, brought out the boy in them. None of them had ever talked to a K-captain before. 'Hi,' they said shyly, unsure where to look when Seria Mau spoke.

And then, to each other, as soon as they thought they were alone: 'Hey! Yes! Weird or what?'

'Please keep the cabins tidy,' Seria Mau interrupted them.

She monitored their affairs, especially their almost constant sexual activity, through nanocameras lodged in corners, or folds of clothing, or drifting about the human quarters like specks of dust. Dial-up, at almost any time, brought in ill-lit, undersea images of human life: they ate, they exercised, they defecated. They copulated and washed, then copulated again. Seria Mau lost count of the combinations, the raised buttocks and straddled legs. If she turned up the sound, someone would always be whispering, 'Yes.' All the men fucked one of the women; then the woman fucked her clone while the men watched. In daily life, the clone was pliable, tender, prone to fits of sudden angry weeping or to asking financial advice. She was so unsure, she said. About everything. They fucked her, slept, and later asked Seria Mau if she could turn the artificial gravity off.

'I'm afraid not,' Seria Mau lied.

She was both disgusted and fascinated by them. The poor

resolution of the nanocams gave their actions something of the quality of her dreams. Was there some connection?

She practised murmuring, 'Oh yes, that.'

At the same time she examined the equipment stowed in the *White Cat*'s hold. As far as she could see it had little to do with exogeology, but was designed to maintain small quantities of isotopes in wildly exotic states. Her passengers were prospectors. They were on the Beach, just like everyone else, looking for an earner. She became inexplicably angry, and the ship's mathematics sent her to sleep again.

It woke her almost immediately.

'Look at this,' it said.

'What?'

'Two days ago I deployed particle detectors astern,' it said (although 'astern', it felt bound to warn her, was an almost meaningless direction in terms of the geometries involved), 'and began counting significant quantum events. This is the result.'

'Two *days* ago?'

'Stochastic resonance takes time.'

Seria Mau had the data piped into her tank in the form of a signature diagram and studied them. What she saw was limited by the *White Cat*'s ability to represent ten spatial dimensions as four: an irradiated-looking grey space, near the centre of which you could see, knotted together, some worms of spectral yellow light, constantly shifting, pulsing, bifurcating and changing colour. Various grids could be laid over this model, to represent different regimes and analyses.

'What is it?' she said.

'I think it's a ship.'

Seria Mau studied the image again. She ran comparison studies. 'It isn't any kind of ship I know. Is it old? What is it doing out there?'

'I can't answer that.'

'Why?'

'I'm not yet entirely certain where "out there" is.'

'Spare me,' said Seria Mau. 'Do you know anything useful at all?'

'It's keeping pace with us.'

Seria Mau stared at the trace. 'That's impossible,' she said. 'It's nothing like a K-ship. What shall we do?'

'Keep sorting quanta,' said the mathematics.

Seria Mau opened a line to the human quarters of the ship.

There, one of the men had launched a holographic display and was clearly making some kind of presentation to the rest of them, while the female clone sat in a corner painting her fingernails, laughing with a kind of weak maliciousness at everything he said, and making inappropriate comments.

'What I don't understand,' she said, 'is why *she* never has to do that. *I* have to do it.'

The display was like a big smoky cube, showing fly-by images from the Radio Bay cluster, which contained among others Suntory IV and 3-alpha-Ferris VII. Low-temperature gas clouds roiled and swirled, failed old brown dwarf stars blinking through them like drunks crossing a highway in fog. A planet jumped into resolution, mushroom-coloured, with creamy sulphurous-looking bands. Then there were images from the surface: clouds, chaotic streaming rain, less weather than chemistry. A scatter of non-human buildings abandoned two hundred thousand years before: something that looked like a maze. They often left mazes. 'What we've got here is old,' the man concluded. 'It could be really old.' Suddenly the camera jumped to an asteroid in full view of the Tract, which blazed out of the display like costume jewellery on black velvet.

'I think we'll leave that for a later trip,' he said.

Everyone laughed except the clone, who spread her hands in front of her. 'Why do you all hate me so,' she said, looking at him over her bright red nails, 'that you make *me* do it and not her?'

He went over and drew her gently to her feet. He kissed her. 'We like you to do it because we love you,' he said. 'We all love you.' He took one of her hands and examined her fingernails. 'That's very historical,' he said. The hologram blinked, expanded until it measured four or five feet on a side, and was suddenly showing the clone's face in the throes of sexual arousal. Her mouth was open, her eyes wide with pain or pleasure, Seria Mau couldn't tell. You couldn't see what was being done to her. They all sat down and watched, giving the hologram their full consideration as if it were still showing images of Radio Bay, old alien artefacts, big secrets, the things they most wanted. Soon they were fucking again.

Seria Mau, who had begun to wonder if she knew their real motives for being aboard, watched them suspiciously for some minutes more. Then she disconnected.

Her dreams continued to distress her.

They gave her a sense of herself as a kind of bad-natured origami, a space accordion-folded to contain more than seemed possible or advisable, as full of invisible matter as the halo itself. Was this how human beings dreamed of themselves? She had no idea.

Ten days into the voyage, she dreamed of a boat-ride on a river. It was called the New Pearl River and was wider, the mother told them, than a mile. From each bank, benign but exotically-tailored vegetation hung down into the water, the surface ripples of which looked firm and nacreous and gave off smells of almonds and vanilla. The mother loved it as much as the children. She trailed her bare feet in the cool pearly water, laughing. 'Aren't we lucky!' she kept saying. 'Aren't we lucky!' The children loved her brown eyes. They loved her enthusiasm for everything in the world.

'Aren't we lucky!'

These words echoed across a change of scene, first to blackness, then to the garden again, with its dark laurels.

It was afternoon. It was raining. The old man – he was the father, and you could see how puzzled that responsibility made him, how much of an effort it was – had built a bonfire. The two children stood and watched him throw things onto it. Boxes, papers, photographs, clothes. Smoke lay about the garden in long flat layers, trapped by the inversions of early winter. They watched the hot core of the fire. Its smell, which was like any other bonfire, excited them despite themselves. They stood dressed up in coats and scarves and gloves, sad and guilty in the cold declining afternoon, watching the flames and coughing in the grey smoke.

He was too old to be a father, he seemed to be pleading. Too old.

Just as it became unbearable, someone snatched this dream away. Seria Mau found herself staring into a lighted shop window. It was a retro window, full of retro things. They were from Earth, conjuror's things, children's things made of bad plastic, feathers, cheap rubber, objects trivial in their day but now of great value to collectors. There were hanks of fake liquorice. There was a valentine heart which lit itself up by means of the loving diodes within. There were 'X-Ray Specs' and elevator shoes. There was a dark red japanned box, in which you placed a billiard ball you would never find again, though you could hear it rattling about in there forever. There was the cup with a reflected face in the bottom which turned out not to be your own. There were the trick eternity rings and handcuffs you couldn't take off. As she watched, the man in the black top hat and tails bent his upper body slowly into the window. His hat was on his head. He had removed his white kid gloves which he now held in the same hand as his beautiful ebony cane. His smile was unchanged, warm yet full of a glittering irony. He was a man who knew too much. Slowly and with a wide, generous gesture he used his free hand to take off his hat and sweep it across the contents of the window, as if to offer Seria Mau the items within. At the same time, she recognised, he was offering her himself. He was, in some way, these objects. His smile never changed. He replaced his hat slowly, unbent himself in polite silence, and disappeared.

A voice said: 'Every day, the life of the body must usurp and disinherit the dream.' Then it said: 'Though you never grew up, this is the last thing you saw as a child.'

Seria Mau woke shaking.

She shook and shook until the ship's mathematics took pity on her, flushing the tank so that specific areas of her proteome could be flooded with complex artificial proteins.

'Listen,' it said. 'We are having a problem here.'

'Show me,' said Seria Mau.

Up came the signature diagram again.

At its centre – if ten dimensions mediated as four can be said to have a centre – the lines of possibility wrote themselves so close to each other they became a solid: an inert object with the contours of a walnut, which was no longer changing much. Too many guesses had been made, was Seria Mau's first thought. The original signal, complicating itself towards infinity, had collapsed into this stochastic nugget and was now even more unreadable.

'This is useless,' she complained.

'It seems that way,' the mathematics said equably. 'But if we go to a regime that corrects for the dynaflow shift, and set N quite high, what we get is this . . .'

There was a sudden jump. Randomness resolved to order. The signal simplified itself and split in two, with the fainter component – coloured deep violet – blinking rapidly in and out of view.

'What am I looking at?' demanded Seria Mau.

'Two vessels,' the mathematics told her. 'The steady trace is a K-ship. Phase-locked to its mathematics is some kind of Nastic heavy asset: maybe a cruiser. One clear benefit is that no one can interpret their signature, but that's a sideshow. The real issue is this: they're using the K-ship as a navigational tool. I've never seen that done before. Whoever wrote the code is almost as good as me.'

Seria Mau stared at the display.

'What are they doing?' she whispered.

'Oh, they're following us,' the mathematics said.

TWELVE

The Warren

Tig Vesicle, stunned into a kind of strained passivity as his adrenalin high wore off, was lost but refused to accept it. Ed Chianese, his ears full of the faint far voices of demons, continued to follow Vesicle because he couldn't think of anything else to do. He was hungry, and faintly embarrassed by himself. After their escape from the Cray sisters, they had wandered about the streets east of Pierpoint until they found themselves on some high ground near the corner of Yulgrave and Demesne. From there they could see the whole sweep of the city, falling away, clotted with light at major intersections, to the docks. With an air of renewed confidence, Vesicle had thrown his arms wide.

'The warren!'

Plunging downhill into the maze of light and dark, they were soon nowhere again, wandering aimlessly round corners into the sudden teeth of the wind until they found themselves back on Yulgrave – the black, echoing, completely deserted perspective of which stretched away between warehouses and goods yards, apparently forever. There, they were witness to an event so strange that Chianese put it out of his mind until much later. Too much later, as it turned out. At the time all he thought was:

This isn't happening.

Then he thought, it's happening but I'm still in the tank.

'Am I still in the tank?' he said out loud.

No reply. He thought: maybe I'm someone else.

Snow was still coming down, but warm air from Clinker Bay, tainted with the smell of the inshore rigs and cracking plants, had dissolved it to sleet, falling through the mercury vapour lamps like sheaves of sparks from some invisible anvil. Walking through the sparks towards them came a small, plump, oriental-looking woman in a gold leaf cheongsam slit to the thigh. Her gait had the quick irritability lent by high heels in bad weather. One minute, Chianese was sure, she wasn't there: the next she was. He blinked. He rubbed his hand over his face. Flashbacks, hallucinations, all the bad dreams of a twink.

'Do you see her too?' he asked Vesicle.

'I don't know,' said Vesicle listlessly.

Ed Chianese looked down at the woman, and she looked up at him. There was something *so* wrong with her face. From one angle it looked beautiful in that oval, high-cheekboned oriental way. Then she turned it, or Ed altered his angle on her, and it seemed to blur and shift into a yellow and wrinkled old age. It was the same face. There was no doubt about that. But it was always moving, always blurred. Sometimes it was old and young at once. The effect was extreme.

'How are you doing that?' Ed whispered.

Without taking his eyes off her he extended a hand towards Tig Vesicle. 'Give me the gun,' he said.

'Why?' Vesicle said. 'It's mine.'

Ed said carefully: *'Give me the gun.'*

The woman got out a little gold case, which she opened, and took from it an oval cigarette.

'Do you have light?' she said. 'Ed Chianese?'

She stared up at him, her face blurring and shifting, blurring and shifting. A sudden flurry of sleet went round them both, hot orange sparks off the anvil of circumstance. Ed took the Hi-Lite Autoloader out of Tig Vesicle's hands and fired it point-blank.

'Right between the eyes,' he would say later. 'I shot her point-blank, right between the eyes.'

Nothing happened for a moment. She continued to stand there, looking up at him. Then she seemed to disassemble herself into a stream of tiny, energetic golden motes, which poured away from the point of impact to join the sparks of the rain. First her head dissolved, then her body. She burned away quite slowly, like a firework consuming itself to make light. There was no sound at all.

Then Ed heard her voice, an echoing whisper.

'Ed,' she said. 'Ed Chianese.'

The street was empty again. Ed looked down at the gun in his hand, and up from the gun at Tig Vesicle, who was staring into the sky, his face tilted so that rain fell into his open mouth.

'Jesus Christ,' Ed said.

He put the gun away and they both began to run. After a minute or two, Ed stopped and leaned against a wall. 'I'm not up to this,' he said. 'Are you?' He wiped his mouth. 'I hate the fucking dry heaves.' He looked dizzily up at the stars. They were like sparks, too, rushing and pinwheeling across the sky to coalesce, just above the warehouse roofs, into the roseate blur of the Tract. This reminded Ed of something he had been meaning to ask. 'Hey,' he said. 'What planet am I on?'

Vesicle stared at him.

'Come on,' Ed said. 'Be fair. Anyone can have a problem with that.'

New Venusport, Earth's original outpost in the halo:

The military cities sprawled across the southern hemisphere. They were less cities than EMC compounds, run as free-trade zones, pulling in migrant labour from across the halo the way a black hole rips gas out of an accretion disc. They drew the defeated races. They drew the enfeebled and stupid. They drew the New

Men, like moths to a flame. You went to New Venusport because you had nowhere else to go.

South hemisphere New Venusport was essentially a maintenance operation. K-ships filled its skies, or shot vertically into orbit at Mach 50. Night and day they crouched in the service bays with arc-light slicking down their dark grey flanks. They were restless. They flickered in and out of visibility as their navigation systems trawled through ten spatial dimensions. They never disconnected their defences or target-acquisition systems, so the air around them was constantly cooking with everything from gamma to microwaves. Work near them, you were in a lead suit. Even the paint on their hulls was deadly. The maintenance bays weren't all of it: elsewhere, EMC's resource contractors had the south hemisphere regolith up in strip-mines as wide as nation-states, using machines powered and directed by the old alien technology. They switched on, stood back, stared at one another in delighted surmise.

'Hey, this thing could *peel a planet!*'

In the cities, air and food were foul, and you had no idea what came down in the rain. The New Men, packed into their warrens, preyed upon by the usual portfolio of gangsters, high-profile political zealots and EMC police, went off to work in the grey dawn, coughing and shivering and bemused, awkwardly hunching their shoulders. But it wasn't all bad. New corporate workplace safety guidelines, self-imposed and self-policed, had brought the life expectancy of a male worker up a couple of points, to twenty-four years. Anyone could tell you that was an advance.

Meanwhile, scattered across the northern hemisphere, the corporate enclaves constructed themselves as Old Earth.

They favoured little towns – with little market squares – called Saulsignon or Brandett Hersham; little clean railway trains running through fields of chocolate-coloured ploughland. The men from EMC chose tall, beautiful women and gave them honey-coloured winter coats of real fur. The women chose men from upper management, whom they loved with a fierce mad true devotion, and gave them beautiful children with honey-coloured hair. There were grey stone churches with witch's hat steeples, chateaux and shooting boxes. Water meadows lined the tributaries of the New Pearl River – there were wild flowers all summer, long, frozen floods a mile wide to skate on every winter. You went to New Venusport if you were lucky, and a hard worker. The corporation sent you there to do a job, but you went for the blue rainwashed skies and white cumulus clouds. The horses, so beautifully groomed. The country sports. And there was such good food in Saulsignon – all those different *cheeses*!

New Venusport, the recruiting brochures said: Planet of choice.

The warren took up an entire block, bounded by the docks on two sides, the waste lot of some old industrial accident on a third, and on the fourth Straint Street, the western boundary of the garment district.

Inside, it was always lighted, but only by the hologram channels, or with lamps designed for New Men eyes: so that what actually reigned was a kind of grey-blue twilight, like the light of some antique monitor. Inside, it was crowded and hot, a chaos of plywood cubicles with no doors. These cubicles weren't joined by corridors. You never knew where you were. To get from one to the next, you went through a third. You could go through thirty small rooms to get to an outside door. Sometimes they had been partitioned further.

'Well, this is home,' said Tig Vesicle.

Ed Chianese, shaking with tank withdrawal, looked around.

'Nice,' he said. 'It's nice.'

Inside the rooms, there would always be eight or nine people doing something, you couldn't quite tell whether it was cooking or laundry. Sometimes there would be more. They had a smell about them that was hard to describe: it was like cinnamon mixed with lard. They slept on mattresses right there on the floor. The men kicked their legs out in that awkward way they had, so it was impossible not to trip over their feet as you picked your way through: they looked up for a second from masturbating, eyes as empty and reflective as the eyes of animals in the odd grey light. The women did their hair in a kind of soft short fluff over their rather beautiful oval skulls. They wore sleeveless cotton frocks in ochre colours, which fell from the shoulders with no style whatsoever. They had a body language which said that if they didn't keep busy it would be too easy to remember where they were. Kids ran about everywhere, pretending to be K-ships. Popular posters of the Kefahuchi Tract were taped up on every wall. The New Men had some kind of cult, centred round the idea that this was where they had originated. It was as sad as everything else about them. Every child knew where they came from, and it wasn't there.

Eventually Tig Vesicle stopped uncertainly, in a cubicle that looked like all the others.

'Yes. This is home,' he said.

Staring vaguely into a hologram up in one corner of the cubicle was a woman who looked just like him.

'This is Neena,' Tig Vesicle said. 'She's my wife.'

Ed looked down at her. A big grin came over his face.

'Hey,' he said. 'I'm pleased to see you, Neena. You got anything to eat?'

They had a cheap stove in every cubicle. The New Men ate a kind of noodle soup. (Sometimes there were objects in it that resembled ice cubes, only lukewarm and bluish.) Ed was in their warren four weeks. He slept on the mattress on the floor, like everyone else. In the day, when Tig Vesicle was out in the city – moving some AbH here, a little bumped-up speed there, trying to avoid the Cray sisters – Ed watched the holograms and ate the food that Neena cooked. Most of that time passed slowly. He was in withdrawal. It was painful: also, real things were very distant a lot of the time and the simple weirdness of being among New Men made that worse. He kept trying to remember who he really was. He could only remember the fictional Ed, an assembly of diamond-clear events that never happened. The afternoon of the third day he was there,

Neena Vesicle knelt down next to him where he sat on the mattress.

'Is there any way I can help?' she said.

Ed looked up at her.

'You know, I think there is.'

He reached up and put his hands either side of her ribs, and with a little sideways pressure tried to get her to kneel over him. It took her a moment to understand what he was suggesting. Then, awkward and serious, she tried to comply. 'I'm all arms and legs,' she said. She hardly smelled at all until he touched her. Then a kind of thick sweetness rolled out from her. Every time he touched her somewhere new, one of her legs would jerk, or she would catch her breath and exclaim at the same time, or shiver and half curl up. She looked down at Ed's hands, raising the cotton dress to her waist.

'Oh,' she said. 'Look at you.' She laughed. 'I mean me.'

Her ribs articulated in a way he couldn't quite understand.

Later she said, 'Is that all right? We go the wrong way for you. A bit the wrong way.' She hissed. She wiped one hand upwards, over her face, across her skull. 'Is that all right?' Tank withdrawal was in the bone. It was cellular, organic. But it was also a kind of separation anxiety. It was the sustained scream of wanting to be back in a lost world you had loved. Nothing was a cure, but sex helped. Twinks on withdrawal were desperate for sex. It was like morphine to them.

'That's good,' Ed said. 'Ah, yes. That's fine.'

The four weeks he was in the warren, everyone imitated him. Had they ever been so close to a human being before? What exactly did that mean to them? They came to the cubicle doorway and looked in at him with a kind of sombre passivity. A typical gesture of his, a manner of speaking, would go round the whole place in an hour. The kids ran from room to room imitating him. Neena Vesicle imitated him even when he was fucking her.

'Open up a little more,' she would suggest, or, 'Now me in you,' then laugh. 'I mean, you in me. Oh God. Oh fuck. *Fuck*.'

She was perfect for him because she was stranger and even

harder to understand than he was. After they finished she lay there awkwardly in his arms, said, 'Oh no, it's nice, it's quite comfortable.' She said: 'Who are you, Ed Chianese?' There was more than one way to answer that, but she had her preferences. If he said, 'I'm just some twink,' she actually looked angry. After a few days he felt himself returning from the tank. He was a long way away, and then he was closer and it was the voices of withdrawal which had retreated right to the edge. He began to remember things about the real Ed Chianese.

'I've got debts,' he explained. 'I probably owe everyone in the universe.' He stared down at her. She stared back for a moment, then looked away suddenly, as if she hadn't meant to. 'Shh, shh,' he said absently. Then: 'I guess they all want to collect off me or fuck me over. What happened in the tank farm was over who got first fuck.'

Neena put her hand over his.

'That's not who you are,' she said.

After a minute he said: 'I remember being a kid.'

'What was that like?'

'I don't know. My mother died, my sister went away. All I wanted to do was ride the rocket ships.'

Neena smiled.

'Small boys want that,' she said.

THIRTEEN

Monster Beach

Kearney and Anna stayed in New York for a week. Then Kearney saw the Shrander again. It was at Cathedral Parkway Station on 110th Street, during some kind of stalled time or hiatus, some empty part of the day. The platforms lay deserted, though you sensed that recently they had been full; the heavily riveted central girders marched off into the echoing dark in either direction. Kearney thought he heard something like the fluttering of a bird among them. When he looked up, there hung the Shrander, or anyway its head.

'Try and imagine,' he had once said to Anna, 'something like a horse's skull. Not a horse's *head*,' he had cautioned her, 'but its skull.' The skull of a horse looks nothing like the head at all, but like an enormous curved shears, or a bone beak whose two halves meet only at the tip. 'Imagine,' he had told her, 'a wicked, intelligent, purposeless-looking thing which apparently cannot speak. A few ribbons or strips of flesh dangle and flutter from it. Even the shadow of that is more than you can bear to see.' It was more than he could bear to see, alone on the platform at Cathedral

Parkway. He looked up for an instant, then broke and ran. No voice, but it had certainly told him something. Some time later he found himself stumbling about in Central Park. It was raining. Some time after that, he got back to the apartment. He was shivering, and he had thrown up over himself.

'What's the matter?' Anna asked. 'What on earth's the matter with you?'

'Pack,' he told her.

'At least change your clothes,' she said.

He changed his clothes; and she packed; and they rented a car from Avis; and Kearney drove as fast as he dared on to Henry Hudson Parkway and thence out of the city north. The traffic was aggressive, the expressways dark and dirty, knotted up into intersection after intersection like Kearney's nerves, and after less than an hour Anna had to take over because though Kearney wouldn't stop, he couldn't see any more through his headache or the glare of oncoming lights. Even the inside of the car seemed full of night and weather. The radio stations out there weren't identifying themselves, just secreting gangsta rap like a new form of life. 'Where are we?' Kearney and Anna called to one another over the music. 'Go left! Go *left*!' 'I'm stopping.' 'No, no, carry on!' They were like sailors in a fog. Kearney stared helplessly out of the windscreen, then scrambled over into the back seat and fell asleep suddenly.

Hours later he woke in a pulloff on Interstate 93. He had heard a Gothic, animal, keening noise. It was Anna, kneeling in the front passenger seat, facing away from the windscreen and tearing pages randomly out of the AAA mapbook they had got with the car. As she crumpled each one up and threw it into the footwell, she whispered to herself, 'I don't know where I am, I don't know where I am.' There was such a sense of rage and misery filling the cheap blue Pontiac – because Anna had been lost all her life and was never going to find herself now – that he fell back to sleep. The last thing he saw was an Interstate sign four hundred yards ahead, shifting and luminous in the lights of passing trucks. Then it was daylight, and they were in Massachusetts.

Anna found them a motel room at Mann Hill Beach, not far south of Boston. She seemed to have got over the night's depressions. She stood in the parking lot in the pale sunshine, blinking at the dazzle on the sea and shaking the room keys in Kearney's face until he yawned and stirred himself from the back of the car.

'Come and look!' she urged him. 'Isn't it nice?'

'It's a motel room,' Kearney acknowledged, eyeing with distrust the ruched *faux*-gingham curtains.

'It's a *Boston* motel room.'

They were in Mann Hill Beach longer than New York. There was a coast fog each morning, but it burnt off early and for the rest of the day everything was bleached out in clear winter sunshine. At night, they could see the lights of Provincetown across the bay. No one came near them. At first Kearney searched the room every couple of hours and would sleep only with the headboard lamp on. Eventually he relaxed. Anna, meanwhile, wandered up and down the beach, collecting with a kind of aimless enthusiasm the items the sea washed up; or drove the Pontiac carefully into Boston, where she ate little meals in Italian restaurants. 'You should come with me,' she said. 'It's like a holiday. It would do you good.' Then, examining herself in the mirror: 'I've got fat, haven't I? Am I too fat?'

Kearney stayed in the room with the TV on and the sound turned down – a habit he had picked up from Brian Tate – or listened to a local radio station which specialised in music from the 1980s. He quite liked this, because it made him feel convalescent, half asleep. Then one night they played the old Tom Waits song 'Downtown Train'.

He had never even liked it; but with the first chord, he was flung so completely back into an earlier version of himself that a terrible puzzlement came over him. He couldn't understand how he had aged so savagely, or how he came to be in a motel room with someone he didn't know, someone he had yet to meet, a woman older than himself who, when he touched her thin shoulder, looked sideways at him and smiled. Tears sprang into his eyes. It was only a moment of confusion, but it was carnivorous, and he sensed that by acknowledging it he had allowed it in. Thereafter it would follow him as relentlessly as the Shrander. It would always be waiting to spring out on him. Perhaps in a way it *was* the Shrander, and it would eat him moment to moment if he didn't do something. So the next morning he got up before Anna was awake and drove the Pontiac into Boston.

There, he bought a Sony handicam. He spent some time searching for the kind of soft plastic-covered wire gardeners use; but found a carbon-steel chef's knife quite easily. On an impulse he went to Beacon Hill, where he picked up two bottles of Montrachet. On his way back to the car he stood for a moment on the south side of the Charles River Basin looking across at MIT, then on an impulse tried to phone Brian Tate. No answer. Back at the motel, Anna was sitting on the bed naked with her feet tucked up, crying. Ten o'clock in the morning and she had already pinned notes to the doors and walls. *Why are you anxious?* they said, and: *Never do more than you can.* They were like beacons for a bad sailor, someone lost even in familiar straits. There was a faint smell of vomit in the bathroom, which she had tried to disguise by spraying perfume about. She looked thinner already. He put his arm round her shoulders.

'Cheer up,' he said.

'You could have told me you were going.'

Kearney held up the Sony. 'Look! Let's walk on the beach.'

'I'm not speaking to you.'

But Anna loved to be filmed. The rest of the day, while seabirds flickered over the shallows or hung like kites above the beach, she ran, sat, rolled, posed looking out to sea, against the white sand in the coastal clarity of light. 'Let me look!' she insisted. 'Let me look!' Then screams of laughter as the images poured like a stream of jewels across the little monitor. She wouldn't wait to see them on the TV. She had the impatience of a fourteen-year-old – that life had not allowed her to remain fourteen, she could sometimes imply, was her special tragedy.

'Here's something you don't know,' she said. They sat for a moment on a dune, and she told him about the Mann Hill Sea Monster—

November 1970: three thousand pounds of rotting flesh is washed on to the Massachusetts sand. Crowds gather all the next day, motoring up from Providence and down from Boston. Parents stare, startled by the blubbery flippers. Kiddies dart and dash up close enough to frighten themselves. But the thing is too decayed ever to be identified; and though its bone structure resembles that of a plesiosaur, consensus has it that the gale has brought in nothing more exotic than the remains of a basking shark. In the end, everyone goes home, but the arguments continue for thirty years—

'I bet you didn't know that!' said Anna, leaning back against Kearney's chest and encouraging him to put his arms around her. 'Though you'll say you did.' She yawned and looked out over the bay, which was darkening like the fine crust on a blob of mercury. 'I'm tired out, but in such a nice way.'

'You should go to bed early,' he said.

That evening she drank most of the wine, laughed a lot and took off her clothes, then fell asleep suddenly on the bed. Kearney pulled the covers over her, drew the *faux*-gingham curtains, and plugged the handicam into the TV. He turned off the lights and for a while ran idly through the stuff he had taken on the beach. He rubbed his eyes. Anna snored suddenly, said something indistinct. The last of the handicam images, ill-lit and grainy-looking, showed her in the corner of the room. She had got as far as unbuttoning her jeans. Her breasts were already bare, and she was turning her head as if Kearney had just spoken to her, her eyes wide, her mouth sweet but tired with acceptance, as if she already knew what was going to happen to her.

He froze that image on the screen, found a pair of scissors and cut two or three lengths of the wire he had bought that morning. These, he placed close to hand on the bedside table. Then he took off his clothes, stripped the chef's knife out of its plastic wrap, pulled back the bedclothes and looked down at her. She lay curled up, with one arm placed loosely round her knees. Her back and shoulders were as thin and unmuscled as a child's, the spine prominent and vulnerable. Her face, in profile, had a sharp, hollowed-out look, as if sleep was no rest from the central puzzle of being Anna. Kearney stood above her, hissing through his teeth, mainly in anger at the things that had led her here, led him here. He was about to start when he thought he would throw the Shrander's dice, just to be sure.

She must have heard them tumbling on the bedside table, because when he turned back she was awake and looking up at him, dull and fractious with sleep, her breath sour from the wine. Her eyes took in the knife, the wire, Kearney's unaccustomed erection. Unable to understand what was happening, she reached up with one hand and tried to pull him down towards her.

'Are you going to fuck me now?' she whispered.

Kearney shook his head, sighed.

'Anna, Anna,' he said, trying to pull away.

'I knew,' she said, in a different voice. 'I always knew you'd do it in the end.'

Kearney detached himself gently. He put the knife back on the bedside table. 'Kneel up,' he whispered. 'Kneel up.'

She knelt up awkwardly. She seemed confused.

'I've still got my knickers on.'

'Shh.'

Kearney held her with his hand. She moved against him, made a small noise and began to come immediately.

'I want you to come!' she said. 'I want you to come too!'

Kearney shook his head. He held her there quietly in the night until she buried her face in the pillow and stopped trying to control herself. He fetched the bottle of wine and gave her half a glassful and they lay on the bed and watched the television. First Anna on the beach, then Anna undressing, while the camera moved slowly down one side of her body and up the other; then, as she grew bored, a CNN news segment. Kearney turned the sound up just in time to hear the words '... Kefahuchi Tract, named after its discoverer.' Flaring across the screen in colours that couldn't be natural appeared some cosmic object no one could understand. It looked like nothing much. A film of rosy gas with a pinch of brighter light at its centre.

'It's beautiful,' Anna said, in a shocked voice.

Kearney, sweating suddenly, turned the sound down.

'Sometimes I think this is all such bollocks,' he said.

'It is beautiful, though,' she objected.

'It doesn't look like that,' Kearney told her. 'It doesn't look like anything. It's just data from some X-ray telescope. Just some numbers, massaged to make an image. Look around,' he told her more quietly. 'That's all anything is. Nothing but statistics.' He tried to explain quantum theory to her, but she just looked bemused. 'Never mind,' he said. 'It's just that there isn't really anything there. Something called decoherence holds the world into place the way we see it: but people like Brian Tate are going to find maths that will go round the end of that. Any day now we'll just go round decoherence on the back of the maths, and all this –' he gestured at the TV, the shadows in the room '– will mean as much to us as it does to a photon.'

'How much is that?'

'Not much.'

'It sounds awful. It sounds undependable. It sounds as if everything will just –' she made a vague gesture '– boil around. Spray about.'

Kearney looked at her.

'It already does,' he said. He raised himself on one elbow and drank some wine. 'Down there it's just disorder,' he was forced to admit. 'Space doesn't seem to mean anything, and that means that time doesn't mean anything.' He laughed. 'In a way that's the beauty of it.'

She said in a small voice, 'Will you fuck me again?'

The next day he managed to get Brian Tate on the phone and ask him, 'Have you seen that crap on TV?'

'Sorry?'

'This X-ray object, whatever it is. I heard someone from Cambridge talking about Penrose and the idea of a singularity without an event horizon, some bollocks like that—'

Tate seemed distracted. 'I haven't heard about any object,' he said. 'Look Michael, I need to talk to you—'

The connection went down. Kearney stared angrily at his phone, thinking of Penrose's definition of the event horizon not as a limitation of human knowledge but as *protection* against the breakdown of physical laws which might otherwise leak out into the universe. He switched the television on. It was still tuned to CNN. Nothing.

'What's the matter?' asked Anna.

'I don't know,' he said. 'Look, would you mind if we went home?'

He drove the Pontiac into Logan International. Three hours later they were on a standby flight, climbing above the Newfoundland coast, which at that point looked like a skin of mould on the sea. Up they went through a layer of cloud, then broke into glaring sunlight. Anna seemed to have put aside the events of the night. She spent much of the journey staring down at the surface of the clouds, a faint, almost ironical smile on her face; although once she took Kearney's hand briefly and whispered:

'I like it up here.'

But Kearney's mind was on other journeys.

In his second year at Cambridge, he had worked in the mornings, cast cards in his room in the afternoon.

To represent himself, he always chose The Fool.

'We move forward,' Inge had told him before she found someone who would fuck her properly, 'by the deeply undercutting action of desire. As The Fool steps continually off his cliff and into space, so we are presences trying to fill the absence that has brought us forth.' At the time, he had had no idea what she meant by this. He supposed it was some bit of patter she had learned to make things more interesting. But he began with this image of himself in mind: so that each journey would be, in every sense, a trip.

He had to remove The Fool from the deck before the cards could be dealt. Late afternoon, as the light went out of the room, he laid it on the arm of his chair, from which it fluoresced up at him, more an event than a picture.

Through simple rules, a cast of the cards determined the journey that would be based upon it. For instance: if the card turned up was a Wand, Kearney would go north only if the trip was to take place in the second half of the year; or if the next card turned up was a Knight. Further rules, whose clauses and counter-clauses he intuited with each cast and recast of the cards, covered the choice of south, west and east; of destination; even of the clothes he would wear.

He never cast the cards once the journey had started. There was too much to occupy him. Whenever he looked up there was something new in the landscape. Gorse spilled down the side of a steep little hill with a farm on top. Factory chimneys dissolved in a blaze of sun he couldn't look into. A newspaper opened suddenly just down the carriage, sounding like the spatter of rain on a window. Between each event his reverie poured itself, as seamless as golden syrup. He wondered what the weather would be like in Leeds or Newcastle, turned to the *Independent* to find out, read: 'Global economy likely to remain subdued.' Suddenly, he noticed the wristwatch of the woman sitting across the aisle. It was made of plastic, with a dial transparent to its own works, so that, in the complexity of the greenish, flickering cogs, your eye lost the position of the hands!

What was he looking for? All he knew was that the clean yellow front of an Intercity train filled him with excitement.

Kearney worked in the morning. In the afternoon he cast the Tarot. At weekends he made journeys. Sometimes he saw Inge around the town. He told her about the cards; she touched his arm with a kind of rueful affection. She was always pleasant, though a little puzzled. 'It's just a bit of fun,' she would repeat. Kearney was nineteen years old. Mathematical physics was opening to him like a flower, revealing his future inside. But the future wasn't quite enough. By following the journeys as they fell out, he believed then, he would open for himself what he thought of as a 'fifth direction'. It would lead to the real Gorselands, perhaps; it would enact those dreams of childhood, when everything had been filled with promise, and predestination, and light.

'Michael!'

Kearney stared around him, uncertain for a moment where he was. Light will transform anything: a plastic drinking glass full of mineral water, the hairs on the back of your hand, the wing of an airliner thirty thousand feet above the Atlantic. All these things can be redeemed and become for a time essentially themselves. The cabin crew had begun to run up and down the aisles, emptying the seatback trays. Shortly afterwards the engines throttled up and then down again, as the aircraft banked and slipped down into the cloud. Vapour roiled in the wingtip turbulence, then the runway was visible, and the illuminated day transformed itself suddenly into the wet, windswept spaces of London Heathrow.

'We're landing!' said Anna excitedly.

She clutched his upper arm and stared out of the window. 'We're landing!'

In the end all the journeys had led to, of course, was the Shrander. The Shrander had been waiting for him, all along, to catch up.

FOURTEEN

The Ghost Train

Seria Mau opened a line to the human quarters and found them clustered round the hologram display again. This time it was showing some of the complex machinery in the *White Cat*'s hold, being operated onsite in the middle of a desert of olivine sand and low melted-looking heaps of rock which when you studied them hard turned out to be ruins.

'The guys knew how to party all right,' one of the men said. 'This stuff went down at twelve thousand Kelvin, maybe more, from some kind of large-scale gamma emitter. Looks as though they piped the output of a small star in here,' he said. 'A million years ago, and they were fighting over assets a million years older than that. Jesus! Will you just look at this?'

'Jesus,' repeated the female clone listlessly. 'What a fucking bore.'

They all laughed and gathered round the display. The two women, who were wearing identical shocking-pink tube skirts with a satin look, held hands behind their backs.

Seria Mau stared at them. They made her angry. It was just more fucking and fighting and shoving. All they ever talked about was profit-sharing deals, art events they had seen, holidays at the Core. All they ever talked about was the rubbish they had bought or would like to buy. What use were they to anyone, even themselves? What had they brought aboard her ship? 'What have you brought aboard my ship?' she demanded in a loud voice. They started, glanced at each other, she thought guiltily. They looked around for the source of the voice. 'Why have you brought this stuff on board?'

Before they could answer she cut away from them to her signature display. There was the K-ship, and tethered to it like a blind camel on a bit of rope was the Nastic battle cruiser. She had identified it now. She had matched its signature to the fakebooks stored in the *White Cat*'s databanks. A front-line cruiser called *Touching the Void*, it was the vessel whose commander had paid her for the *Vie Féerique* ambush. He had told her, 'I know where you are going.' She shivered in her tank at this memory.

'What are they doing?' she asked the mathematics.

'Staying where they are,' it reported.

'They're going to follow me wherever I go!' Seria Mau shrieked. 'I hate this! I hate it! No one can follow us, no one is good enough.'

The mathematics thought.

'Their navigation system is nearly as clever as me,' it concluded. 'Their pilot is military. He's better than you.'

'Get rid of them,' she ordered.

'*You* brought this about,' she accused the human beings. The men were beginning to look anxious. They were still casting little glances here and there, as if she had a real presence in the cabin with them. The two women clasped hands and whispered to one another. For now, you couldn't tell which one was the cultivar. 'Turn that thing off,' Seria Mau said. They turned the hologram off. 'Now tell me what use you are to anyone.' While they were trying to think of an answer to this, a small shudder went through the fabric of the *White Cat*. A moment later a bell chimed.

'What?' said Seria Mau impatiently.

'They're coming up on us,' the mathematics reported. 'Half a light in the last thirty nanoseconds. At the moment it's a soft alarm, but it could harden.'

'Half a *light*? I don't believe this.'

'What would you like me to do?'

'Arm the ordnance.'

'At the moment I think they're just trying—'

'Put something between us and them. Something big. And make sure it outputs in all particle regimes. I want them blind. Hit them if you can, but just make sure they can't see us.'

'A quarter of a light,' said the mathematics. 'Hard alarm.'

'Well,' said Seria Mau. 'He *is* good.'

'He's here. It's down to kilometres.'

She said: 'We're ninety-five nanoseconds into a disaster. Where's that ordnance?'

There was a vague ringing in the hull. Out in the flat grey void beyond, a huge flare erupted. In an attempt to protect its client hardware the *White Cat*'s massive array shut down for a nanosecond and a half. By this time, the ordnance had already cooked off at the higher wavelengths. X-rays briefly raised the temperature in local space to 25,000 degrees Kelvin, while the other particles blinded every kind of sensor, and temporary sub-spaces boiled away from the weapons-grade singularity as fractal dimensions. Shockwaves sang through the dynaflow medium like the voices of angels, the way the first music resonated through the viscous substrate of the early universe before proton and electron recombined. Under cover of this moment – less of grace than of raw insanity and literal metaphysics – Seria Mau cut the drivers and dropped her ship out into ordinary space. The *White Cat* flickered back into existence ten light years from anywhere. She was alone.

'There, you see,' Seria Mau said. 'He wasn't that good.'

'I have to say he pulled the plug before we did,' the mathematics told her. 'But I can't tell if he got the Nastic vessel out with him.'

'Can we see him?'

'No.'

'Just take us somewhere and hide, then,' Seria Mau said.

'Do you care where?'

Seria Mau turned over exhaustedly in her tank.

'Not at the moment,' she said.

Astern – if the word 'astern' can have any meaning in ten spatial and four temporal dimensions – the explosion was still dying away as a kind of hard after-image in the eye of the vacuum itself. The entire engagement had played itself out in four hundred and fifty nanoseconds. No one in the human quarters had noticed anything, although they seemed surprised that she had stopped talking to them so suddenly.

In a second, or completing, lobe of her dream, Seria Mau was in the garden again:

Weeks after the bonfire, the house was still full of it. The smoke seeped everywhere. Everything was tainted. All those old things the father had burned just came back as their own smoke, and descended on the shelves, the furniture and the window sills. They came back as a smell. The two children stood in their coats and scarves by the circle of ashes, which was like a black pool in the garden. They crept their toes up to its exact edge, and looked down at them there. They looked at each other in a kind of solemn surprise, while the father paced about in the house behind them. How could he have done that? How could he have made a mistake that big? They wondered what would happen next.

The girl wouldn't eat. She refused to eat or drink. The father looked down at her seriously. He held her hands so that she had to look into his eyes. His eyes were a brown so light it verged on orange. People would call those eyes appealing. They were full of an appeal.

'You will have to be the mother now,' he said. 'Can you help us? Can you be the mother?'

The girl ran to the end of the garden and cried. She didn't want to be anyone's mother. She wanted someone to be hers. If this event was part of a life, she didn't like it. She didn't trust a life like that. It would all come to nothing. She ran up and down the

99

garden with her arms out to the sides making loud noises until her brother laughed and joined in, and the father came out and made her look into his sad brown eyes and asked her again if she would be the mother. She looked away from him as hard as she could. She knew how big a mistake he had made: if it's hard to get away from a photograph, it's harder still to get away from a smell.

'We could have her back,' she suggested. 'We could have her back as a cultivar. It's easy. It would be easy.'

The father shook his head. He explained why he wouldn't want that. 'Then I won't be her,' the little girl said. 'I'll be something better.'

The mathematics hid them nicely. It even found a sun, small, G-type, a bit tired, but with a row of planets that gleamed in the distance like portholes in the night.

What was memorable about the system, which was called Perkins' Rent, was the train of alien vehicles that hung nose to tail in a long cometary orbit which at aphelion was halfway to the next star. They were between a kilometre and thirty kilometres long, with hulls as tough and thick as rinds, coloured a kind of lustreless grey, shaped as randomly as asteroids – potato shapes, dumb-bell shapes, off-centre shapes with holes in them – and every one under two feet of the sifted-down dust blown out of some predictable and not very recent stellar catastrophe. The dust of life, though there was no life here. Whoever they belonged to abandoned them before proteins appeared on Earth. Their vast nautiloid internal spaces were as clean and empty as if nothing had ever lived there. Every so often part of the train fell into the sun, or ploughed ship by ship into the methane seas of the system's gas giant: but once it had been perfect.

The ghost train was the economic mainstay of Perkins' Rent. They mined those ships like any other kind of resource. Nobody knew what they did, or how they got here, or how to work them; so they cut them up and melted them down, and sold them via a sub-contractor to some corporate in the Core. It made a local economy.

It was the simple, straight-line thing to do. The used-up ones were surrounded by unpredictably shifting clouds of scrap: cinders, meaningless internal structures made of metals no one wanted or even understood, waste product from the automatic smelters. The *White Cat* found a snug place in one of these clouds, where the smallest individual unit was two or three times her size. She gave herself up to the chaotic attractor, shut down her engines and was instantly lost: a statistic. Seria Mau Genlicher woke up in a fury from her latest dream, opened a line to the supercargo.

'This is where you get off,' she told them.

She dumped their equipment from the hold and then opened the human quarters to the vacuum. The air made a thick whistling noise as it blew out. Soon the K-ship had a little cloud of its own, comprised of frozen gases, luggage, and bits of clothing. Among this floated five bodies, blue, decompressed. Two of them had been fucking and were still joined together. The clone was the hardest to get rid of. She clung on to the furniture, screaming, then clamped her mouth shut. The air roared past her, but she wouldn't give up and be evacuated. After a minute, Seria Mau felt sorry for her. She closed the hatches. She brought the human quarters back up to pressure.

'There are *five* bodies out there,' she told the mathematics. 'One of the men must have been a clone, too.'

No answer.

The shadow operators hung in corners with their hands over their mouths. They turned their heads away.

'Don't look at me like that,' Seria Mau told them. 'Those people brought some kind of transponder on board here. How else could we have been followed?'

'There was no transponder,' said the mathematics.

The shadow operators shifted and streamed like weed under water, whispering, 'What has she done, what has she done?' in soft, fey, papery voices. 'She has killed them all,' they said. 'Killed them all.'

Seria Mau ignored them.

'There must have been something,' she said.

'Nothing,' the mathematics promised her. 'Those people were just people.'

'But—'

'They were just people,' the mathematics said.

'Come on,' said Seria Mau after a moment. 'No one's innocent.'

The clone was crouched in a corner. The drop in air pressure had ripped most of her clothes off, and she was squatting with her arms wrapped round her upper body. Her skin had a hectic, wealed look where the evacuating air had scraped it. Here and there along her thin, ribby sides, blackish bruises showed where things had bounced off her on their way out into space. Her eyes were glazed and puzzled, full of a hysteria she was holding in place out of shock, puzzlement, failure to quite appreciate how much had happened. The cabin smelled of lemons and vomit. Its walls were scarred where fixtures and fittings had ripped loose. When Seria Mau spoke, the clone stared round in a panicky way and tried to force herself further into the corner.

'Leave me alone,' she said.

'Well they're dead now,' Seria Mau said.

'What?'

'Why did you let them treat you like that? I watched. I watched the things they did to you.'

'Fuck you,' said the clone. 'I can't believe this. I can't believe some fucked-up machine is giving me a lecture, that just killed everyone I know.'

'You let them use you.'

The clone hugged herself tighter. Tears rolled down either side of her nose. 'How can you say that? You're just some fucking machine.'

She said: 'I loved them.'

'I'm not a machine,' Seria Mau said.

The clone laughed.

'What are you then?' she said.

'I'm a K-captain.'

The clone got a disgusted, tired expression on her face. 'I'd do anything not to end up like you,' she said.

'So would I,' said Seria Mau.

'Are you going to kill me now?'

'Would you like me to?'

'No!'

The clone touched her bruised lip. She looked bleakly around the cabin. 'I don't suppose any of my clothes survived,' she said. Suddenly, she began to shiver and weep silently. 'They're all out there, aren't they? With my friends? All my good clothes!'

Seria Mau turned the cabin temperature up.

'The shadow operators can fix that,' she said offhandedly. 'Is there anything else I can do for you?'

The clone considered this.

'You can take me somewhere where there are real people,' she said.

The occupied planet of the system was called Perkins IV, though its inhabitants referred to it as New Midland. It had been terraformed, after a fashion. It had an agriculture based on traditional principles, some FTZ-style assembly plants in closed compounds, and two or three towns of fifty or sixty thousand people, all on one peneplained continent in the Northern Hemisphere. The agriculture ran to beet and potatoes, plus a local variety of squash which had been marketed successfully further up the Beach until some cutter worked out how to do it cheaper; which had been the fate of traditionally based agricultures for three and a half centuries. The biggest town ran to cinemas, municipal buildings, churches. They thought of themselves as ordinary people. They didn't do much tailoring, out of a vague sense of its unnaturalness. They had a religion less bleak than matter-of-fact. At the school they taught about the ghost train and how to mine it.

The first Monday of an early, squally spring, some of the younger children were playing a game of 'I went to the particle market and I bought … '

They had got as far as ' … a Higgs boson, some neutral K mesons, and a long-lived neutral kaon which decayed into two pions by CP-violating processes,' when a single flat concussion rattled the windows and a matt-grey wedge-shaped object, covered all over in intakes, dive brakes and power bulges, shot across the town a hundred feet up and stopped inside its own length. It was the *White Cat*. The children rushed to the schoolhouse windows, shouting and cheering.

Seria Mau put the clone out of a cargo port.

'Goodbye,' she said.

The clone ignored her. 'I loved them,' she said to herself. 'And I know they loved me.'

She had been saying that to herself for five hours. She looked round at the municipal buildings, the tractor park and the schoolyard, where waste paper blew about in the dust.

What a dump, she thought. Perkins' Rent! She laughed. She walked a little way away from the K-ship, lit a cigarette, and stood in the street waiting for someone to give her a ride. 'It looks like that,' she told herself. 'It looks like somewhere that would be called Perkins' Rent.'

She started crying again, but you couldn't see that from across the schoolyard, where the children were still glued to the windows, the girls eyeing enviously her pink satin tube skirt, patent leather high heels and crimson nail polish, while the boys regarded her shyly from the corners of their eyes. When they grew up, the boys thought, they would rescue her from some bad situation she found herself in, down in the Core among the gene doctors and rogue cultivars. She would be grateful and reward them by showing them her tits. Let them touch, even. How good and warm those tits would feel, resting in your hands.

Perhaps sensing some of this, the clone turned round and banged on the hull of the *White Cat*.

'Let me back in,' she called.

The cargo port opened.

'You should make up your mind,' said Seria Mau.

Local interceptor squadrons, scrambled as the K-ship hit the outer atmosphere, showed up a minute or two later. They got good locks and began to make an attack run. 'Look at these idiots,' said Seria Mau. Then, on an open channel: 'I *told* you I wasn't staying.' She torched up and quit the gravity well vertically at a little under Mach 40, on a faint but visible plume of ionised gas. The kids cheered again. Thunder rolled round Perkins IV and met itself coming the other way.

From out beyond the atmosphere, Perkins' Rent looked like a cataracted eye. The clone sat in her cabin staring listlessly down at it, while the shadow operators clustered around her, reaching out as if to touch her, whispering regretfully in their languages of guilt. 'You can stop that,' Seria Mau Genlicher warned them, 'before you start.' She saw off a couple of orbital interceptors with one of her low-end assets; then consulted the mathematics, fired up the dynaflow drivers and committed her ship to the endless dark.

A few tens of nanoseconds later, a familiar object detached itself stealthily from the ghost train and slipped after her. Its hull showed some pitting from a recent high-temperature event.

FIFTEEN

'Kill Him, Bella.'

Ed always made sure he talked to Tig as well as Neena.

It was hard on the street. The police were everywhere. The Cray sisters were everywhere. (Ed sensed them out there, nursing their grievance in the New Venusport night, cruel as fish. He knew he shouldn't feel safe in the warren, where only plankton like himself collected, just beneath the surface in the dim blue light.) Tig came in later and later at night. He was always hungry but he had no time to eat. His gait was more disconnected when he was tired.

'It's me. It's Tig,' he would say from the doorway, as if he was reluctant to enter the cubicle without Ed's permission.

Some nights, Ed went back out on the street with him. They stayed uptown, and played for small points. It was corner trade, a little here, a little there. If Tig suspected Ed was fucking his wife, he never let it show. By an unspoken agreement, they didn't mention the Cray sisters either. They didn't have much else in common, so most of the time they talked about Ed. That suited Ed. Talking helped. By his third week, thanks to Neena's generosity, he had begun to reclaim large tracts of the past. The problem was, none of them joined up. It was sudden analepsis – images, people, places, events, caught by an unsteady camera, lit with bad light. Connective tissue was missing. There was no real narrative of Ed.

'I knew some amazing guys,' he began suddenly one night, in the hope that talking about it would make it clearer. 'You know, really mad guys. Guys with charmed lives.'

'What sort of guys?'

'You know, all over the galaxy there are these guys who just *do* it,' Ed tried to explain. 'They're widely distributed. They're having fun.'

'Do what?' Tig asked him.

Ed was puzzled that Tig didn't already know. 'Well, everything,' he said. They were standing at the corner of Dioxin and Photino at the time. It was maybe half two, half three in the morning. The street was slow. In fact, it was empty. The night sky was over it all with a field of stars. Off in one corner the Kefahuchi Tract glared down on them like a bad eye. Not really meaning to, Ed made a gesture which took it all in. 'Just everything,' he said.

What it turned out was this:

From an early age, Ed Chianese had been some kind of drifter and sensationist. He couldn't remember what planet he came from. 'Maybe it was even this one!' He laughed. He left home as soon as he could. There was nothing for him there. He was a big raw black-haired kid who loved cats, excited all the time for no reason, and he felt less trapped than too well looked after. He rode the dynaflow ships. He hopped from planet to planet for three years until he fell off the edge of things on to the Beach. There, he got in with people to whom life was nothing unless it looked as if you were about to lose it. This meant doing the Kefahuchi Boogie. It meant prospecting, and the entrada. It meant surfing stellar envelopes in the one-man rockets they called dipships, which were made of nothing much more than mathematics, magnetic fields and some kind of smart carbon. Not many people did that any more.

It meant running the old alien mazes scattered across the artificial systems of the halo. Ed was good at that. He did

Cassiotone 9 in the best time since Al Hartmeyer off of the old *Heavyside Layer*, who was, as everyone agreed, a fucking madman in his own day. No one ever matched Ed's distance into the maze on Askesis, because no one else ever made it out. Maybe you did these things for money, on contract to some shit EMC subsidiary. Maybe you did them because they were a sport. One way or the other, Ed hung out with extreme people for some years, entradistas, sky pilots, particle jockeys, full-tilt people looking to score amid big, difficult alien machinery. Some of these guys were women. Ed was at the Venice Hotel on France Chance IV the day Liv Hula brought her hyperdip *Saucy Sal* out of the photosphere of the local sun. No one ever went that deep before. The instant she was safe you could hear the cheers a light year off. She was the first to go that deep: she was the fucking *first one*. He lived four weeks in a freighter in the Tumblehome parking orbit while Dany LeFebre was waiting for the unknown disease she caught on-planet to run its course. He pulled her out of there in the end. Half mad. Half dead. He didn't even know her that well.

Everywhere there was excitement to be had and determined people gathered to have it, Ed was there. Go deep was what they said to one another: Hey, go deep. Then something happened he didn't remember, and he drifted away from all that. Maybe it was someone he knew, maybe it was something he did; maybe it was Dany after all, looking up at him unable to speak ever again. One tear ran down her face. Afterwards, Ed's life seemed to go downhill a little, but it was still full of stuff. He dropped proasavin-D-2 on Badmarsh, and in the orbital cities of the Kauffman Cluster shot up Earth-heroin cut with the ribosomes of a tailored marmoset. When he ran short of money he was, in a minor way, thief, dealer, pimp. Well, maybe more than minor. But if his hands weren't clean, his heart was crazy for life, and where you got most life was on the edge of death. This is what he believed since his sister left, when he was just a kid. He wound up on the Beach at Sigma End, where he hung out with guys like the legendary Billy Anker, at that time obsessed with Radio RX1.

'Man,' Ed said to Tig, 'I can't tell you the achievements that guy did.' He grinned. 'I was on board for a few of them,' he said. 'But not the best.' He shook his head remembering that.

Vesicle was puzzled. He had kids. He had Neena. He had a life. He couldn't see the point of any of it. But that wasn't the real issue. How come Ed ended up a twink, he wanted to know, when a twink was surely the opposite of all that? What was the point of having cheap fantasies in some tank, after you had surfed the Schwarzchild radius of a black hole?

Ed grinned his slow grin.

'The way I think of it,' he explained, 'is this: when you've done all the things worth doing, you're forced to start on the things that aren't.'

The fact was, he didn't know. Maybe he was always a twink. Twinking lay in wait for him all his life. It bided its time. Then one day he went round a corner – he couldn't even remember which planet he was on – and there it was: BE ANYTHING YOU WANT TO BE. He had done everything else, so why not? Since then, being anything he wanted had cost him, if not quite everything, then most of it. Worse: if there wasn't much to him back in those old wild days of his, there was even less to him now.

He thought privately he would twink out again as soon as he made some money.

It couldn't go on. Ed knew that. He had guilt dreams. He had feelings of disaster when he woke in the night. In the end it all happened at once, one early evening when he was fucking Neena.

Each day the warren went through a cycle in which bustle segued imperceptibly into quiet and back again. This happened perhaps three or four times. To Ed, the quiet periods had a ghostly feel. Cold draughts made their way from cubicle to cubicle. Images of the Kefahuchi Tract glimmered from the cheap posters like religious icons. The kids were asleep, or out on the waste lot over towards the dockyards. Occasionally you would hear a sneeze or a sigh: that made it worse. You felt deserted by everything. Early evening was always like that: this evening it felt as if human life had stopped everywhere, not just in here.

All Ed could hear was Neena's uneven breathing. She had got into an awkward position, on her front with one knee bent under her and her cheek pressed against the wall. 'Push harder,' she kept saying indistinctly. This caused Ed, full of memory and melancholy, to shift his own position a little, allowing him to see across her long white back to the doorway where a shadowy figure was observing them. For a minute, Ed thought he was hallucinating his own father. A kind of raw gloom poured over him, a memory he couldn't identify. Then he shuddered ('Yes,' said Neena: 'Oh, yes.') and blinked.

'Jesus. Is that you, Tig?'

'Yes. It's me.'

'You're never home this early.'

Vesicle, peering uncertainly into the room, seemed more puzzled than hurt. 'Is that you, Neena?' he said.

'Of course it is.' She sounded angry and impatient. She pushed Ed away and jumped up, straightening her dress, running her fingers through her hair. 'Who else did you expect?'

Tig seemed to think for a moment.

'I don't know.' After a moment he gave Ed a direct look and said, 'I didn't expect it would be anybody. I thought—'

'Maybe I'll leave,' Ed offered, anxious to make a gesture.

Neena stared at him.

'What? No,' she said. 'I don't want you to.' Suddenly she turned away from them both and went over to the stove. 'Turn the lights up,' she said. 'It's cold in here.'

'We can't breed with them, you know,' Tig said.

Her left shoulder seemed to shrug of its own accord. 'Do you want noodles?' she demanded. 'Because it's all we've got.'

By this time, Ed's heart rate had gone down, his concentration had returned, and he was hearing noise again in the warren. At first it sounded normal – squeals of kids, hologram soundtracks, a general domestic clatter. Then he heard louder voices. Shouts coming closer. Then two or three loud, flat explosions.

'What's this?' he said. 'People are running. Listen!'

Neena looked at Tig. Tig looked at Ed. They looked at one another, the three of them.

'It's the Cray sisters,' Ed said. 'They've come for me.'

Neena turned back to the stove as if she could ignore this.

'Do you want *noodles*?' she said impatiently.

Ed said, 'Get the gun, Tig.'

Vesicle got the gun, which he kept in a thing that looked like a meat safe. It was wrapped in a piece of rag. He unwrapped it, looked at it for a moment, then offered it to Ed.

'What are we going to do?' he whispered.

'We're going to leave here,' Ed said.

'What about the children?' shouted Neena suddenly. 'I'm not leaving my children!'

'You can come back later,' Ed told her. 'It's me they want.'

'We haven't *eaten anything*!' Neena said.

She held on to the stove. Eventually they pulled her away from it and made off through the warren in the direction of the Straint Street entrance. It took forever. They blundered over outstretched limbs in the bluish light. They couldn't get up any speed. Neena hung back as hard as she could, or made off in inappropriate directions. Every time they went through a door they upset something or someone. Every cubicle seemed connected to every other. If the warren was like a maze in a cheap nightmare, so was the pursuit: it would seem to diminish, then, just as Ed relaxed, start up from another direction, more energetic than before. A firefight developed, ran away with itself, guttered into silence. There were screams and explosions. Who was shooting who, amid the echoes in a cubicle full of smoke? Miniature gun-punks in rainslickers. One-shot cultivars with tusks a foot long. Silhouettes of men, women and children scattering with disconnected motions against the sudden flash of guns. Neena Vesicle looked back. A shudder went through her. She laughed suddenly.

'You know, I haven't run like this for ages!' she said.

She hugged Ed's arm. Her eyes, lively and slightly unfocused with excitement, glittered into his. Ed had seen it before. He laughed back.

'Steady down, kid,' he said.

Shortly after that, the light got greyer and less blue. The air got colder. One minute they were scattering someone's evening meal across the floor – Ed had time to see an arc of liquid, a ceramic bowl spinning on its edge like a coin, an image of the Kefahuchi Tract glittering out of some hologram display to the sound of cathedral music – the next they were out on Straint Street, panting and banging one another on the back.

It was snowing again. Straint, a perspective made of walls and streetlights, stretched off into the distance like a canyon full of confetti. Old political posters flapped off the walls. Ed shivered. Sparks, he thought suddenly: Sparks in everything. He thought: Shit.

After a minute he began to laugh.

'We made it,' he said.

Tig Vesicle began to laugh too. 'What are we like?' he said.

'We made it,' Neena said experimentally. She said it once or twice more. 'We *made* it,' she said.

'You certainly did, dear,' Bella Cray agreed.

Her sister said: 'We thought you'd come out this side.'

'In fact we banked on it, dear.'

The two of them stood there in the middle of the street in the blowing snow, where they had been waiting all along. They were fully made up, and clutching their big purses to their chests like women out for fun on the edge of the garment district seven o'clock at night, ready to drink and do drugs and meet what the world had to offer. To keep the chill off they had each added a little waist-length fake-fur jacket to their black skirts and secretary blouses. In addition, Bella was wearing a pillbox hat of the same material. Their bare legs were reddened and chapped above black calf-length winter boots. Evie Cray began to unzip her purse. She looked up from the operation halfway through.

'Oh, you can go, dear,' she said to Neena, as if she was surprised to find her still there. 'We won't need you.'

Neena Vesicle looked from Ed to her husband. She made an awkward gesture.

'No,' she said.

'Go on,' Ed said gently. 'It's me they want.'

Neena shook her head stubbornly.

'You can go,' Ed told her.

'It's him we want,' agreed Evie Cray. 'You go on, dear.'

Tig Vesicle took Neena's hand. She let him draw her away a pace or two but she kept her body and her eyes turned to Ed. He gave her his best smile. *Go on*, he mouthed silently. Then out loud he said:

'Thanks for everything.'

Neena smiled uncertainly back.

'By the way,' Evie Cray said, 'we want your fucking husband too.'

She reached into her purse, but Ed already had the HiLite Autoloader out, which he held close enough to her face so that the muzzle just touched her under the left eye, indenting the flesh there. 'Keep your hand in the bag, Evie,' he advised. 'And don't do anything.' He looked her up and down. 'Unless this is a cultivar you're running.'

'You'll never know, dipshit,' she said.

She said: 'Kill him, Bella.'

Ed found himself looking across the top of her head into the muzzle of Bella Cray's big Chambers pistol. He shrugged.

'Kill me, Bella,' he said.

Tig Vesicle observed this standoff for a moment, backing away quietly. He still had hold of Neena's hand. 'Goodbye, Ed,' he said. He turned away and ran off down the street. At first he had to pull Neena along, but soon she seemed to wake up, and began to run in earnest. They were like some kind of tall, awkward bird. The snow whirled round them, half-obscuring their poorly articulated limbs and curious running style. Ed Chianese felt a kind of relief, because he owed them both so much. He hoped they would work it out between themselves, and come back for their kids, and be happy.

'Hey,' he said absent-mindedly. 'Go deep, you guys.'

'Dipshit,' said Evie Cray.

There was a loud bang as the gun in her purse went off. The purse exploded and a Chambers bolt hummed off down the street. Ed jumped in surprise and shot Evie in the side of the face. She went rigid and backed into her sister's hand, so that Bella shot her too, in the back of the head. Ed let Evie fall, stepped away and got the HiLite under Bella's chin.

'I hope it was a cultivar, Bella,' he said. Then he warned her: 'Drop the pistol unless you're running one too.'

Bella looked down at her sister's body, then at Ed.

'You fucking cunt,' she said. She let the pistol fall. 'You won't be safe anywhere now. You won't be safe anywhere ever again.'

'Not a cultivar, then,' said Ed. He shrugged. 'Sorry.'

He waited until he was sure that Tig and Neena Vesicle had escaped. Then he collected up all the weapons and ran off down Straint in the opposite direction to the one they had taken. He had no idea where he was going, and the snow was already turning to rain. Behind him he could hear Bella Cray screaming for the gun-punks. When he looked back she was trying to get her sister to sit up. The remains of Evie's head flopped backwards like a bit of wet rag in the streetlight. Point-blank, he thought. Shot right in the eyes.

SIXTEEN

The Venture Capital

The day he got back to London, Michael Kearney closed the Chiswick house and moved into Anna's flat.

There wasn't much to move, which was lucky because Anna accumulated things as a way of insulating herself against her own thoughts. The place was a warren to start with: linear in plan, but each room sized differently or acting as a passage between two others. You never knew where you were. There wasn't much natural light. She had reduced it further by doing the walls a kind of Tuscan yellow then rag-rolling on top of that in pale terracotta. The kitchen and lavatory were tiny, and the latter had been painted with blue-gold fishes. There were masks everywhere, streamers, Chinese lampshades, bits of dusty curtain, chipped glass candelabra, and large dried fruits from countries to which she had never been. Her books spilled off their bowed softwood shelves to drift across the molasses-coloured floor.

Kearney had planned to use the futon in the back room, but as soon as he lay on it his heart raced and he was racked with inexplicable anxieties. After a night or two he began sleeping in Anna's bed. This was perhaps a mistake.

'It's as if we're married again,' Anna said, waking up one morning and giving him a painfully bright smile.

When Kearney got out of the bathroom, she had made poached eggs and stale toast, also stale croissants. It was 9 a.m. and the table was carefully set with place mats and lighted candles. Generally, though, she seemed better. She signed up for yoga classes at Waterman's Arts Centre. She stopped writing notes to herself, though she left the old ones pinned up on the back of the bedroom door where they confronted Kearney with forgotten emotional responsibilities. *Someone loves you.* He spent much of each night staring at the wash of streetlight on the ceiling of the room, listening to the traffic murmur to and fro across Chiswick Bridge. As soon as he felt settled, he went to Fitzrovia to see Tate.

It was a raw Monday afternoon. Rain had emptied the streets east of Tottenham Court Road.

The research suite – an annexe of Imperial College orphaned recently into the care of free market economics – was entered through a bleak, clean basement area with a satin-finish nameplate and newly blacked iron railings. A few streets further east it would have housed a literary agency. The ventilators were open and noisy, and through the frosted glass windows Kearney could see someone moving about. The faint sound of a radio filtered out. Kearney went down the steps and punched his access code into the keypad by the door. When it didn't work, he pressed the intercom button and waited for Tate to buzz him in. The intercom crackled, but no one spoke at the other end, and no one buzzed.

After a moment he called, 'Brian?'

He pressed the buzzer again, then held it down with his thumb. No answer. He went back to street level and peered through the railings. This time he couldn't see anyone moving, and all he could hear was the sound of the ventilators.

'Brian?'

After a moment, he assumed he had been mistaken. The lab was empty. Kearney turned up the collar of his leather jacket and walked off in the direction of Centre Point. He hadn't got to the end of the street when he thought of phoning Tate at home. Tate's wife picked up. 'Absolutely not here,' she said. 'I'm glad to say. He was out before we woke up.' She thought for a moment, then added dryly: 'If he came home at all last night. When you see him tell him I'm taking the kids back to Baltimore. I mean that.' Kearney stared at the phone, trying to remember what she was called or what she looked like. 'Well,' she said, 'in fact I don't mean it. But I will soon.' When he didn't answer she said sharply, 'Michael?'

Kearney thought her name was Elizabeth, but people called her Beth. 'Sorry,' he said. 'Beth.'

'You see?' said Tate's wife. 'You're all the same. Why don't you just bang on the fucking door until he wakes up?' Then she said: 'Do you think he's got a woman in there? I'd be relieved. It would be such human behaviour.'

Kearney said, 'Look, hang on, I—'

He had turned round just in time to see Tate come up the steps from the suite, pause for a moment to look both ways, then cross the street and walk off at a rapid pace towards Gower Street. 'Brian!' called Kearney. The phone picked up the tone of his voice and began squawking urgently at him. He broke the connection and ran after Tate, shouting, 'Brian! It's me!' and, 'Brian, what the fuck's going on?'

Tate showed no sign of hearing. He stuck his hands in his pockets and hunched his shoulders. By now it was raining heavily. 'Tate!' shouted Kearney. Tate looked over his shoulder, startled, then began to run. By the time they reached Bloomsbury Square, which was where Kearney caught up with him, they were both breathing heavily. Kearney grasped Tate by the shoulders of his grey snowboarder jacket and swung him round. Tate made a kind of sobbing gasp.

'Leave me alone,' he said, and stood there suddenly defeated with water pouring down his face.

Kearney let him go.

'I don't understand,' he said. 'What's the matter?'

Tate panted for a bit, then managed to say: 'I'm sick of you.'

'What?'

'I'm sick of you. We were supposed to be in this together. But you're never here, you never answer your phone, and now bloody Gordon wants to sell forty-nine per cent of us to a merchant bank. I can't deal with the financial side. I'm not supposed to have to. Where have you been for the last two weeks?'

Kearney gripped him by the forearms.

'Look at me,' he said. 'It's *all right*.' He made himself laugh. 'Jesus, Brian,' he said. 'You can be hard work.' Tate watched him angrily for a moment, then he laughed too.

'Look,' said Kearney, 'let's go to the Lymph Club and have a drink.'

But Tate wouldn't let himself be won over that easily. He hated the Lymph Club, he said. Anyway he had work to do. 'I suppose you could come back with me,' he suggested.

Kearney, permitting himself a smile, agreed that this would be the best thing.

The suite smelled of cats, stale food, Giraffe beer. 'Most nights I'm sleeping on the floor,' Tate apologised. 'I don't get time to go home.' The cats were burrowing about in a litter of burger cartons at the base of his desk. Their heads went up when Kearney walked in. The male hurried up to him and fawned about at his feet, but the female only sat where she was, the light making a transparent corona out of her white fur, and waited for him to come to her. Kearney passed his hand over her sharp little head and laughed.

'What a house of prima donnas,' he told her.

Tate looked puzzled. 'They've missed you,' he said. 'But look here.'

He had prolonged the typical useful life of a q-bit by factors of eight and ten. They cleared the rubbish from around the credenza at the back of the room and sat down in front of one of the big flatscreen displays. The female cat prowled about with her tail in the air, or sat on Kearney's shoulder purring into his ear. Test results evolved one after the other like puffs of synaptic activity in decoherence-free space. 'It's not a quantum computer,' Tate said, after Kearney had congratulated him, 'but I think we're ahead of Kielpinski's team, as of now. Do you see why I need you here? I don't want Gordon selling us down the river just when we can ask anybody for anything.' He reached out to tap the keyboard. Kearney stopped him.

'What about the other thing?'

'What other thing?'

'The glitch in the model, whatever it was.'

'Ah,' said Tate, 'that. Well, I did what I could with it.' He tapped a couple of keys. A new programme launched. There was a flash of arctic-blue light; the female oriental stiffened on Kearney's shoulder; then the earlier test result bloomed in front of them as the Beowulf system began faking space. This time the illusion was much slower and clearer. Something gathered itself up behind the code somewhere and shot out across the screen. A million coloured lights, boiling and sweeping about like a shoal of startled fish. The white cat was off Kearney's shoulder in a second, hurling herself at the display so hard it rocked. For fully half a minute the fractals poured and jerked across the screen. Then everything stopped. The cat, her coat reflecting ice-blue in the wash of the display, danced about for half a minute more, then lost interest and began to wash herself affectedly.

'What do you make of it?' said Tate. 'Kearney?'

Kearney sat full of a kind of remote horror, stroking the cat. Just before the burst of fractals, just as the model collapsed, he had seen something else. How was he going to save himself? How was he going to put all this together? Eventually he managed to say:

'It's probably an artefact, then.'

'That's what I thought,' said Tate. 'There's no point going any further with it.' He laughed. 'Except maybe to amuse the cat.'

When Kearney didn't rise to this, he went off and started setting up another test. After about five minutes he said, as if continuing an earlier conversation:

'Oh, and some maniac was here to see you. He came more than once. His name was Strake.'

'Sprake,' said Kearney.

'That's what I said.'

Kearney felt as if he had woken in the night, out of luck. He put the white cat down carefully and stared around the suite, wondering how Sprake had found his way here.

'Did he take anything?' He indicated the monitor. 'He didn't see this?'

Tate laughed.

'You're joking. I wouldn't let him in. He walked up and down in the area, swinging his arms and haranguing me in a language I didn't recognise.'

'His bark's worse than his bite,' Kearney said.

'After the second time, I changed the door code.'

'So I noticed.'

'It was just in case,' said Tate defensively.

Kearney had met Sprake perhaps five years after he stole the dice. The meeting occurred on a crowded commuter train passing through Kilburn on its way to Euston. The walls of the Kilburn cutting were covered with graffiti, explosions of red and purple and green done with deliberation and exuberance, shapes like fireworks going off, shapes bulging like damp tropical fruit, effects of glistening surfaces. *Eddie, Daggo, Mince* – less names than pictures of names. After you had seen them everything else became oppressive and dull.

The platform at Kilburn was empty but the train stopped there for a long time, as if it was waiting for someone, and eventually a man pushed his way on. He had red hair, pale hard eyes, and an old yellow bruise across the whole of his left cheek. He wore a belted military surplus coat with no jacket or shirt underneath it.

Though the doors closed, the train remained still. As soon as he got in, he rolled a cigarette and began smoking it with relish, smiling and nodding around at the other passengers. The men stared at their polished shoes. The women studied the mass of sandy hairs between his pectoral muscles; they exchanged angry glances. Though the doors had closed, the train remained where it was. After a minute or two, he pulled back his cuff to consult his watch, a gesture which revealed the word FUGA tattooed inside his grimy wrist. He grinned, and indicated the graffiti outside.

'They call it "bombing",' he said to one of the women. 'We ought to live our lives like that.' Instantly she became involved with her *Daily Telegraph*.

Sprake nodded, as if she had said something. He took his cigarette out of his mouth and examined the flattened, porous, spittle-stained end of it. 'You lot, now,' he said. 'Well, you look like a lot of self-satisfied bullies.' They were corporate IT workers and estate agents in their mid twenties, passing themselves off with a designer tie or a padded shoulder as dangerous accountants from the City. 'Is that what you want?' He laughed. 'We should bomb our names on to the prison walls,' he shouted. They edged away from him, until only Kearney was left.

'As for you,' he said, staring interestedly up at Kearney with his head at an odd, bird-like angle on his neck, and dropping his voice to a barely audible murmur:

'You just have to keep killing, don't you? Because that's the way to keep it at arm's length. Am I right?'

The encounter already had the same edge of unease – the aura, the heightened epileptic foreboding – many events had taken on in the wake of the Shrander, as if that entity cast some special kind of illumination of its own. But at the time Kearney still considered himself as a kind of apprentice or seeker. He still hoped to gain something positive. He was still trying to see his retreat from the Shrander as accompanied by a counter-trajectory – a movement *towards* it – from which something like a transformational encounter might yet proceed. But the truth was that, by the time he met Sprake, he had been throwing the dice, and making random journeys, and getting nowhere, for what seemed like a lifetime. He felt a flicker of vertigo (or perhaps it was only the train starting up again, to drift, slowly at first then faster and faster, towards Hampstead South) and, thinking he was going to fall, reached a hand out to Sprake's shoulder to steady himself.

'How do you know?' he said. His own voice sounded hoarse and threatening to him. It sounded disused.

Sprake eyed him for a second, then chuckled round at the occupants of the carriage.

'A nudge,' he said, 'is as good as a wink. To a blind horse.'

He had slyly removed himself as Kearney reached for him. Kearney half fell into the woman hiding behind the *Daily Telegraph*, righted himself with an apology, and in that instant saw how good the body is at making metaphors. Vertigo. He was in flight. Nothing good would ever come of this now. He had been falling from the moment the dice came into his hands. He got off the train with Sprake, and they walked off across the noisy, polished concourse and out into Euston Road together.

In the years that followed they developed their theory of the Shrander, though it contained no elements of explanation, and was rarely articulated except by their actions. One Saturday afternoon on a train to Leeds, they murdered an old woman in the draughty space between the carriages, and, before stuffing her into the toilet cubicle, wrote in her armpit with a red gel pen the lines, 'Send me an eon heart/Seek it inside.' It was their first joint effort. Later, in an ironic reversal of the usual trajectory, they flirted with arson and the killing of animals. At first Kearney gained some relief, if only through the comradeship – the complicity – of this. His face, which had taken on a look so hollow he might have been dead, relaxed. He gave more time to his work.

But in the end, complicity was all it turned out to be. Despite these acts of propitiation, his circumstances remained unchanged, and the Shrander pursued him everywhere he went. Meanwhile,

Sprake took up more and more of his time. His career languished. His marriage to Anna ended. By the time he was thirty, he was sclerotic with anxiety.

If he relaxed, Sprake kept him up to the mark.

'You still don't think it's real,' he would say suddenly, in his soft, insinuating way: 'Do you?'

Then: 'Go on, Mick. Mickey. Michael. You can admit it to me.'

Valentine Sprake was already in his forties and still lived at home. His family ran a second-hand clothes shop in North London. There was an old woman with a vaguely middle-European accent, who spent her time staring up in a kind of exhausted trance at the curiously wrenched space of the religious art on the walls. Sprake's brother, a boy of about fourteen, sat day in and day out behind the counter of the shop, chewing something which smelled of aniseed. Alice Sprake, the sister, with her heavy limbs, vacant heavy smile, her olive skin and faint moustache, regarded Kearney speculatively from large brown eyes. If they were ever left alone together, she sat next to him and put her damp hand softly on his cock. He became erect immediately, and she smiled at him in a possessive way, revealing that her teeth weren't good. No one ever saw this, but whatever their other limitations that whole family had a withering emotional intelligence.

'You'd like to give her one, wouldn't you?' said Sprake. 'Give her a bit of a slippery hot one, Mikey old chap. Well I don't care, mind –' here he gave a shout of laughter '– but the other two wouldn't let you.'

It was Sprake who took them into Europe.

They killed Turkish prostitutes in Frankfurt, a Milanese dress-designer in Antwerp. Towards the end of what became a six-month spree, they found themselves in The Hague one evening, eating at a good-quality Italian restaurant opposite the Kurrhaus Hotel. The evening wind came up off the sea, blew sand into the square outside before it died away. The lamp swung above the table and the shadows of the wineglasses shifted uncomfortably on the tablecloth, like the complex umbrae and penumbrae of planets. Sprake's hand moved between them, then lay flat as if exhausted.

'We're like bears in a pit here,' he said.

'Do you wish we hadn't come?'

' "Crespelle and ricotta",' said Sprake. He threw the menu on to the table. 'What the fuck's that about?'

After an hour or two, a boy sauntered past outside in the twilight. He was perhaps five feet ten inches tall and twenty-six years old. His hair had been dragged back and plaited tightly, and he was wearing yellow high-waisted shorts with their own yellow crossover braces. He carried a matching yellow soft toy. Though he was slightly built, his shoulders, hips and thighs had a rounded, fleshy look, and on his face was the self-satisfied and yet somehow wincing expression of someone acting out a fantasy in public.

Sprake grinned at Kearney.

'Look at that,' he whispered. 'He wants you to put him in a death camp for his sexuality. You want to choke him because he's a prat.' He wiped his mouth and stood up. 'Maybe the two of you can get together.' Later, in their hotel room, they looked down at what they had done to the boy. 'See that?' Sprake said. 'If that doesn't tell you something, nothing will.' When Kearney only stared at him, he quoted with the intense disgust of the master to the apprentice:

' "It was a mystery to them that they were in the Father all along without knowing it." '

'Excuse me?' the boy said. 'Please?'

In the end these promises of understanding amounted to little. While their association never quite came to seem like anything as positive as a mistake, Sprake revealed himself over the years to be an undependable accomplice, his motives as hidden – even from himself – as the metaphysics by which he claimed to understand what was happening. That afternoon on the Euston train he had been looking for a cause to attach himself to, the *folie à deux* which would advance his own emotional ambitions. For all his talk, he knew nothing.

It was late. Candlelight flickered on the walls of Anna Kearney's apartment, where she turned in her sleep, throwing out her arms and murmuring to herself. Sparse traffic came out of Hammersmith on the A316, crossed the bridge and hummed away west and south. Kearney threw the dice. They rattled and scattered. For twenty years they had been his secret conundrum, part of the centralising puzzle of his life. He picked them up, weighed them for a moment in the palm of his hand, threw them again, just to watch them tumble and bounce across the carpet like insects in a heatwave.

This is how they looked:

Despite their colour they were neither ivory nor bone. But each face had an even craquelure of faint fine lines, and in the past this had led Kearney to think they might be made of porcelain. They might have been porcelain. They might have been ancient. In the end they seemed neither. Their weight, their solidity in the hand, had reminded him from time to time of poker dice, and of the counters used in the Chinese game of mah-jong. Each face featured a deeply incised symbol. These symbols were coloured. (Some of the colours, particularly the blues and reds, always seemed too bright given the ambient illumination. Others seemed too dim.) They were unreadable. He thought they came from a pictographic alphabet. He thought they were the symbols of a numerical system. He thought that from time to time they had *changed* between one cast and another, as if the results of a throw affected the system itself. In the end, he did not know what to think. Instead he had given them names: the Voortman Move; the High Dragon; the Stag's Great Horns. What part of his unconscious these names emerged from, he had no clue. All of them made him feel uneasy, but the words 'the Stag's Great Horns' made his skin crawl. There was a thing that looked like a food processor. There was another thing that looked like a ship, an old ship. You looked at it one way and it was an old ship. You looked at it another way and it was nothing at all. Looking was no solution: how could you know which way was up? Over the years Kearney had seen pi in the symbols. He had seen Planck's constants. He had seen a model of the Fibonacci sequence. He had seen what he thought was a code for the arrangement of hydrogen bonds in the primitive protein molecules of the autocatalytic set.

Every time he picked them up, he knew as little as he had the first time. Every day he started new.

He sat in Anna Kearney's bedroom and threw the dice again. How could you know which way to look at them?

With a shiver he saw that he had thrown the Stag's Horns. He turned it over quickly, shovelled the dice back into their leather bag. Without them, without the rules he had made up to govern their combinations, without *something*, he could no longer make decisions. He lay down next to Anna, supporting himself on one elbow, watched her sleep. She looked hollowed-out and yet at peace, like someone very old. He whispered her name. She didn't wake, but murmured, and moved her legs slightly apart. A palpable heat came up from her.

Two nights previously, he had found her diary, and in it read this passage:

I look at the images Michael made of me in America, and I hate this woman already. Here she stares out across the bay from Monster Beach with one hand shading her eyes. Here she undresses, drunk; or picks up driftwood, her mouth full of smiles. She dances on the sand. Now she is seen lying back on her elbows in front of an empty fireplace, wearing light-coloured trousers and a soft wool jumper. The camera moves across her. She is laughing out at the lover behind the handicam. Her legs are raised at the knees and slightly parted. Her body looks relaxed but not in the least sensual. Her lover will be disappointed because of this: but even more because she looks so well. Is it something about the room? That fireplace betrays her instantly, it makes too bare a frame, it throws her into high relief. Her energy is projected beyond the picture space. She is making eye contact. It is a disaster. He is used to a thinner

*face, gaunt cheekbones, body language pivoting between the
grammars of pain and sex. Neither folded in on herself nor
quivering with need, she is no longer the woman he knows. He
is used to more urgency.*

He will not be so attracted to someone this happy.

Kearney turned away from the sleeping woman and pondered
the justice of this. He thought about what he had seen on Tate's
flatscreen monitor that afternoon. He would have to talk to Sprake
again soon; he fell asleep thinking about that.

When he woke up, Anna was kneeling over him.

'Do you remember my Russian hat?' she said.

'What?'

Kearney stared up at her, feeling stupid with sleep. He looked at
his watch: 10 a.m. and the curtains were open wide. She had
opened the window too. The room was lively with light, the sound
of people, traffic. Anna had one arm behind her back, and was
leaning forward with her weight on the other one. The neck of her
white cotton nightgown had fallen forward so that he could see her
breasts, which for some complicated reason of her own she had
never encouraged him to touch. She smelled of soap and
toothpaste.

'We went to the pictures in Fulham, to see a Tarkovsky film, I
think it was *Mirror*. But I went to the wrong cinema, and it was
bitterly cold, and I was sitting on the steps outside waiting for you
for an hour. When you got there, all you could look at was my
Russian hat.'

'I remember that hat,' Kearney told her. 'You said it made your
face look fat.'

'Broad,' said Anna. 'I said it made my face too broad. And you
said, without a moment's hesitation, "It makes your face your face.
That's all, Anna: your face." Do you know what else you said?'

Kearney shook his head. All he really remembered was angrily
searching the cinemas of Fulham for her.

'You said: "Why spend any more of your life apologising?"'

She looked down at him, and after a pause said, 'I can't tell you how much I loved you for that.'

'I'm glad.'

'Michael?'

'What?'

'I want you to fuck me in my Russian hat.'

She brought her arm from behind her back and there it was in her hand, a silky grey fur thing the size of a cat. Kearney began to laugh. Anna laughed too. She put the hat on her head and instantly looked ten years younger. Her smile was wide and pretty, as vulnerable as her wrists. 'I never could understand someone who wore a Russian hat to watch Tarkovsky,' he said. He gathered her nightgown up into the small of her back and reached down. She groaned. He was still able to think, as he often thought, Perhaps this will be enough, release me at last, push me through the wall between me and me.

He thought: Perhaps this will save her from me.

Later he made a phone call, and that afternoon, as a result, found Valentine Sprake wandering up and down the taxi rank at Victoria station with two or three blackened pigeons running in and out between his feet. They were all lame. Sprake looked irritated.

'Never phone me on that number again,' he said.

'Why?' asked Kearney.

'Because I fucking don't want you to.'

He showed no signs of remembering what had happened when they last met. His engagement with the Shrander – his flight, if it could be described like that – was as private as Kearney's, as private as madness: a dialogue so internalised it could only be inferred, partially and undependably, from the sum of his actions. Kearney got him in a cab and they went through the coagulated traffic of Central London then out to the Lea Valley, where the shopping parks and industrial estates were still embedded with a vestigial tissue of residential streets, neither clean nor dirty, new or old, inhabited by mid-day joggers and half-dead feral cats. Sprake stared sullenly out the windows at the alloy siding and empty buildings. He seemed to be whispering to himself.

'Have you seen this Kefahuchi thing?' Kearney asked him tentatively. 'On the news?'

'What news?' said Sprake.

Suddenly he pointed out a display of flowers on the pavement in front of a florist's. 'I thought those were wreaths,' he said, with a bleak laugh. 'Sombre though colourful,' he added. After that, his mood improved, but he kept saying, 'News!' under his breath in a contemptuous fashion until they reached the offices of MVC-Kaplan, which were hushed, warm and empty at the end of the working day.

Gordon Meadows had begun his career in gene-patenting then, after a series of high-profile drug launches for a Swiss-based pharmaceuticals house, moved laterally and with ease into money. He specialised in ideas, kickstarts, original research. His style was to a blow a pure, weightless bubble: boost capitalisation, float, talk the stock up, and profit-take a stage or two before the product was due onstream. If you didn't get that far, he dumped you for what he could get. As a result, Meadows Venture Capital had the whole of a curious bolted-glass structure which glittered uneasily between the tailored alloy façades of a Walthamstow 'excellence' park; and no one remembered Kaplan, a puzzled highbrow who, unable to meet the challenge of free market thinking, had returned only briefly to molecular biology before becoming a teacher in a Lancashire comprehensive.

Meadows was tall and thin, with a kind of willowy fitness. When Kearney first knew him, fresh from his pharmaceutical triumphs, he had favoured the merciless saffron haircut and goatee of the internet entrepreneur. Now he wore suits from Piombo, and his workspace – which had a grim view of trees along the towpath of the old Lea Valley Navigation – seemed to have been furnished from an issue of *Wallpaper*. B&B Italia seating faced a desk made from a single slab of re-melted glass, on which stood, as if they had something to do with one another, a Mac Cube and Sottsass coffee pot. This he sat behind, eyeing Valentine Sprake with a cautious amusement.

'You must introduce us,' he told Kearney.

Sprake, who had worked himself up into a fever in the lift, now stood with his face pressed up against the glass wall of the building, staring down at two or three lumps of packing material the size of refrigerators, floating along the canal in the gathering twilight.

'Let's talk about him later,' recommended Kearney. 'He's got a great idea for a new drug.' He sat on the end of Meadows's desk. 'Brian Tate is worried about you, Gordon.'

'Is he?' said Gordon. 'I'm sorry if that's so.'

'He says you're progress-chasing. He's worried that you're going to sell us to Sony. We don't want that.'

'I think Brian is—'

'Shall I tell you why we don't want that, Gordon? We don't want that because Brian's a prima donna. You've got to show confidence in a prima donna. Try this thought-experiment.' Kearney held up his hands, palms uppermost. He looked at the left one. 'No confidence,' he said, and then, looking at the right one, 'no quantum computer.' He repeated this pantomime. 'No confidence, no quantum computer. Are you intelligent enough to see the connection here, Gordon?'

Meadows laughed.

'I think you're less naïve than you suggest,' he said. 'And Brian is certainly less nervous than he pretends. Now let's see . . .' He tapped a couple of keys. Spreadsheets blossomed on his monitor like ripening fruit. 'Your burn-rate's quite high,' he concluded after a moment. He raised his hands, palms upward, and mimicked the way Kearney had looked from one to the other. 'No money,' he said, 'no research. We need fresh capital. And a move like this – as long as we thought it was good for the science – would expand our opportunities, not limit them.'

'Who's "we"?' said Kearney.

'You aren't listening. Brian would have his own department.

That would be part of the package. He wonders if you work hard enough, Michael. He's worried about his idea.'

'I think you're getting ready to dump us. Here's some advice. Don't try it.'

Meadows examined his hands.

'You're being paranoid, Michael.'

'Imagine that,' Kearney said.

Valentine Sprake turned away from the darkening view and walked in a jerky, hurried fashion across the room, as if he had seen, out there in the marshes, something which surprised him. He leaned over Meadows's desk, picked up the coffee pot and drank its contents directly from the spout. 'Last week,' he said to Meadows, 'I learned that Urizen was back among us, and His name is Old England. We are all adrift on the sea of time and space here. Think about that too.' He stalked out of the office with his hands folded on his chest.

Meadows looked amused.

'Who *is* that, Kearney?'

'Don't ask,' said Kearney absently. On the way out he said: 'And keep off Brian's back.'

'I can't protect the two of you forever,' Meadows called after him. That was when Kearney knew Meadows had already sold them to Sony.

Lightweight separators in pastel colours were used to create privacy inside MVC-Kaplan's otherwise featureless tent of bolted glass. The first thing Kearney saw outside Meadows's workspace was the shadow of the Shrander, projected somehow from *inside* the building on to one of these. It was life-size, a little blurred and diffuse at first, then hardening and sharpening and turning slowly on its own axis like a chrysalis hanging in a hedge. As it turned, there was a kind of rustling noise he hadn't heard for twenty years; a smell he still recognised. He felt his whole body go cold and rigid with fear. He backed away from it a few steps, then ran back into the office, where he hauled Meadows over the glass desk by the front of his suit and hit him hard, three or four times in succession, on the right cheekbone.

'Christ,' said Meadows in a thick voice. 'Ah.'

Kearney pulled him all the way over the desk, across the floor and out of the door. At the same time the lift arrived and Sprake got out.

'I saw it, I saw it,' Kearney said.

Sprake showed his teeth. 'It's not here now.'

'Get a fucking move on. It's closer than ever. It wants me to do something.'

Together they bundled Meadows into the lift and down three floors. He seemed to wake up as they dragged him across the lobby and out to the canal bank. 'Kearney?' he said repeatedly. 'Is that you? Is there something wrong with me?' Kearney let go of him and began kicking his head. Sprake pushed his way between them and held Kearney off until he had calmed down. They got Meadows to the edge of the water, into which they dropped him, face down, while they held his legs. He tried to keep his head above the surface by arching his back, then gave up with a groan. Bubbles came up. His bowels let go.

'Christ,' said Kearney reeling away. 'Is he dead?'

Sprake grinned. 'I'd say he was.' He tilted his head back until he was looking straight up at the faint stars above Walthamstow, raised his arms level with his shoulders, and danced slowly away north along the towpath towards Edmonton.

'Urizen!' he called.

'Fuck this,' said Kearney. He ran in the opposite direction, all the way to Lea Bridge, then got a minicab to Grove Park.

Every murder reminded him of the Shrander's house, which in a sense he had never left. His fall had begun there, his deeply fallen knowledge imprisoned him there. In another sense, the Shrander's pursuit of him in succeeding years *was* that knowledge: it was the constant fall into the awareness of falling. When he killed, especially when he killed women, he felt released from what he knew. He felt for an instant as if he had escaped again.

Bare grey dusty floorboards, net curtains, cold grey light. A dull house on a dull street. The Shrander, intact, irrefragable, enduring, stood in its upper room gazing magisterially out of the window like the captain of a ship. Kearney ran away from it because, as much as anything, he was frightened of the *coat* it wore. He was frightened of the smell of wet wool. That smell would be his last unfallen sensation.

The beak opened. Words were spoken. Panic – it was his own – filled the room like a clear liquid, an albumen or isinglass so thick he was forced to turn and swim his way through the open door. His arms worked in a sort of breaststroke while his legs ran beneath him in useless slow motion. He stumbled across the landing outside and straight down the stairs – full of terror and ecstasy, the dice in his hand – into the rainy streets, looking for someone to kill. He knew he wouldn't be saved unless he did. A kind of lateral gravity was in his favour: he fell all the way from the Shrander's house towards the railway station. To travel, he hoped, would be to *fall away* from falling, at some more acceptable, some more merciful angle.

It was late on a wet winter afternoon. The trains were reluctant, overheated, empty. Everything was slow, slow, slow. He caught a local, grinding its way out of London into Buckinghamshire. Every time he looked down at the dice in his hand, the world lurched and he had to look away. He sat there sweating until, two or three stops beyond Harrow-on-the-Hill, a tanned but tired-looking woman joined him in the carriage. She was dressed in a black business suit. In one hand she carried a briefcase, in the other a plastic Marks & Spencer carrier bag. She fussed with her mobile phone, leafed through a self-help book which seemed to be called *Why Shouldn't I Have the Things I Want?* Two stations further north, the train slowed and stopped. She got to her feet and waited for the door to open, staring at the darkening platform, the lighted ticket office beyond. She tapped her foot. She looked at her watch. Her husband would be waiting in the car park with the Saab, and they would go straight on to the gym. Up and down the train, other doors opened and closed, people hurried away. She looked nervously right and left. She looked at Kearney. In the overheated emptiness, her journey pulled out like chewing gum, then snapped.

'Excuse me,' she said. 'They don't seem to be letting me out.' She laughed.

Kearney laughed too.

'Let's see what we can do,' he said.

Five or six thin gold chains, each bearing either her initial or her Christian name as a pendant, clung to the prominent tendons of her neck. 'Let's see what we can do, Sophie.' As he reached down to touch with his fingertip the make-up caked in the faint blonde down at the corner of her mouth, the train pulled slowly away. Her shopping had spilled when she fell. Something – he thought it was a shrink-wrapped lettuce – rolled out of the carrier bag and along the empty carriage. The platform slid backwards and was replaced by black night. The doors had never opened.

Kearney, expecting discovery at any moment, lived from newscast to newscast: but there was no mention of Meadows. The upper half of a body recovered from the Thames near Hungerford Bridge proved to be decomposed, and a woman's. A second Nigerian boy was found dead in Peckham. Apart from these incidents, nothing. Kearney regarded the screen with growing disbelief. He couldn't understand how he had got away with it. No one likes a venture capitalist, he found himself thinking one night, but this is ridiculous.

'And now,' said the anchorwoman brightly, 'sport.'

He was less afraid of discovery, he found, than of the Shrander itself. Would Meadows be enough to keep it at bay? One minute he was confident; the next he had no hope. A noise in the street outside was enough to send his heart rate up. He ignored the phone, which was often ringing two or three times in a morning. Messages were backing up at his answer service, but he didn't dare call in and get them. Instead, he cast the dice obsessively, watching them bounce across the floor away from him like bits of human bone. He couldn't eat, and the slightest rise in temperature made him sweat. He couldn't sleep, and when he did, dreamed it was himself he had killed. When he woke from this dream – filled with a mixture of depression and anxiety that felt for all the world like grief – it was to find Anna lying on top of him, weeping and whispering fiercely:

'It's all right. Oh please. It's all right.'

Awkward and unpractised, she had wrapped her arms and legs tightly round him, as if to stifle his cries. It was so unlike Anna to attempt to comfort someone else that Kearney pushed her off in a sort of terror and willingly fell back over the edge into the dream.

'I don't understand you,' she complained the next morning. 'You were so nice until a few days ago.'

Kearney peered cautiously at himself in the bathroom mirror, in case he saw some other thing. His face, he noted, looked pouchy and lined. Behind him through the steam he could see Anna lying in a bath which smelled of rose oil and honey, her colour heightened by heat, her expression made petulant by a genuine puzzlement. He put down his razor, bent over the bath, and kissed her on the mouth. He put his hand between her legs. Anna writhed about, trying to turn over and present herself, panting and slopping water over the side of the bath. Kearney's cellphone rang.

'Ignore it,' Anna said. 'Don't answer it. Oh.'

Later, Kearney made himself listen to his messages.

Most of them were from Brian Tate. Tate had been calling two or three times a day, sometimes leaving only the number of the research suite, as if he thought Kearney might have forgotten it, sometimes talking until the answer service cut him off. To begin with his tone was hurt, patient, accusatory; soon it became more urgent. 'Michael, for God's sake,' he said: 'Where have you been? I'm going mad here.' The call was timed at eight in the evening, and bursts of laughter in the background suggested he was phoning from a pub. He put the phone down suddenly, but the next message came in less than five minutes later, from a mobile:

'This is such a *shitty* signal,' it began, followed by something indistinguishable, then: 'The data's useless. And the cats—'

After two or three days things seemed to come to a head for him. 'If you won't come over,' he threatened, 'I'm giving up. I'm sick of dealing with it all.' There was a pause, then: 'Michael? I'm sorry. I know you wanted this to be—'

There were no further calls after that, until the most recent one. And all that said was:

'Kearney?'

There was a background noise like rain falling. Kearney tried to return the call, but Tate's phone seemed to be switched off. When he replayed the original message, he heard behind the rain another noise, like a signal feeding back then swallowing itself abruptly.

'Kearney?' Tate said. Rain and feedback. 'Kearney?' It was hard to describe how tentative he sounded.

Kearney shook his head and put on his coat.

'I knew you'd go out again,' said Anna.

As soon as Kearney let himself in, the black cat, the male, ran up to him, fawning and mewling for attention. But he extended his hand too suddenly, and, lowering its haunches as if he had hit it, it ran off.

'Shh,' said Kearney absently. 'Shh.'

He listened. The temperature and humidity of the suite were supposed to be tightly controlled, but he couldn't hear the fans or the dehumidifiers. He touched a switch and the fluorescents came on, buzzing in the silence. He blinked. Everything but the furniture had been crated up carefully and moved somewhere else. There was plastic packing material scattered over the carpet, along with discarded strips of heat-seal tape. Two damaged cardboard boxes, bearing the logo of a firm called Blaney Research Logistics, lay discarded in a corner. The benches and desks were empty but for the dust which had built up over the months of their occupation, to make circuit-like patterns between the installations.

'Puss?' said Kearney. He drew with his finger in the dust.

On Tate's credenza he found a single yellow Post-it note. There was a phone number, an email address.

'Sorry, Michael,' Tate had scribbled underneath.

Kearney stared around. Everything Gordon Meadows had said about Tate came back to him. It made him shake his head. 'Brian,' he murmured, 'you conniving bastard.' He was almost amused.

Tate had taken his ideas to Sony, with or without the help of MVC-Kaplan. He had clearly been planning it for weeks. But something else had happened here, something less easy to understand. Why had he left the cats? Why had he disconnected the flatscreen displays, then swept them on to the floor and kicked them apart in a rage? You didn't associate Tate with rage. Kearney stirred the pieces with his foot. They had fetched up among the usual litter of junk food wrappers and other refuse, some of which was more than a week old. The cats had been using it as a lavatory. The male was cowering in the wreckage now, staring up at him like a little live gargoyle.

'Shh,' he said.

He reached down more carefully, and this time it rubbed against his hand. Its sides were trembling and emaciated, its head as sharp as an axe, its eyes bulging with opposites – distrust and relief, fear and gratitude. Kearney picked it up and held it close to his chest.

He fondled its ears, called the female cat's name, looked around hopefully. There was no response.

'I know you're here,' he said.

Kearney turned the lights out and sat down on Tate's credenza. He thought that if the female got used to him being there she would eventually come out from wherever she was hiding. Meanwhile, her brother ceased to tremble and began instead to purr, a clattering rumble, disjointed, hoarse as machinery. 'That's a bizarre noise,' Kearney told him, 'for an animal your size.' Then he said: 'I'd imagine he called you Shrödinger in the end. Is that what

137

he called you? Is he that dull?' The cat purred a moment more then stopped and stiffened suddenly. It peered down into the pile of wrecked equipment and burger cartons.

Kearney looked down too.

'Hello?' he whispered.

He was expecting to see the female, and indeed, there was a whitish flicker down near his feet; but it wasn't a cat. It was a quiet spill of light, emerging like fluid from one of the ruptured displays and licking out across the floor towards Kearney's feet. 'Jesus!' he shouted. He jumped up. The male cat made a panicky hissing noise and squirmed out of his arms. He heard it hit the floor and run off into the dark. Light continued to pour out of the broken screen, a million points of light which shoaled round his feet in a cold fractal dance, scaling into the shape he most feared. Each point, he knew – and every point which comprised it, and every point which comprised the point before that – would also make the same shape. 'There is always more,' Kearney whispered. 'There is always more after that.' He threw up suddenly: staggered away, bumping into things in the dark, until he found the outside door.

It hadn't been rage that made Tate destroy the equipment; it had been fear. Kearney ran into the street without looking back.

SEVENTEEN

The Lost Entradas

Human beings, hooked by the mystery of the Kefahuchi Tract, arrived on its doorstep two hundred years after they got into space.

They were arrant newcomers, driven by the *nouveau* enthusiasms of a cowboy economy. They had no idea what they had come for, or how to get it: they only knew they would. They had no idea how to comport themselves. They sensed there was money to be made. They dived right in. They started wars. They stunned into passivity five of the alien races they found in possession of the galaxy and fought the sixth – which they called 'the Nastic' out of a mistranslation of the Nastic's word for 'space' – to a wary truce. After that they fought one another.

Behind all this bad behaviour was an insecurity magnificent in scope, metaphysical in nature. Space was big, and the boys from Earth were awed despite themselves by the things they found there: but worse, their science was in a mess. Every race they met on their way through the Core had a star drive based on a different theory. All those theories worked, even when they ruled out one another's basic assumptions. You could travel between the stars, it began to seem, by assuming anything. If your theory gave you a foamy space to work with – if you had to catch a wave – that didn't preclude some other engine, running on a perfectly smooth Einsteinian surface, from surfing the same tranche of empty space. It was even possible to build drives on the basis of superstring-style theories, which, despite their promise four hundred years ago had never really worked at all.

It was affronting to discover that. So when they fetched up on the edge of the Tract, looked it in the eye, and began to despatch their doomed entradas, the Earthlings were hoping to find, among other things, some answers. They wondered why the universe, which seemed so harsh on top, was underneath so pliable. Anything worked. Wherever you looked, you found. They were hoping to find out why. And while the entradistas were dying in ways no one could imagine, crushed, fried, expanded or reduced to mists of particles by the Tract itself, lesser hearts took with enthusiasm to the Beach, where they found Radio Bay. They found new technologies. They found the remains of ancient races, which they ragged about like bull terrier pups with an old bone.

They found artificial suns.

There had been, some time in the deep past, such a premium on the space closest to the Tract that there were more artificial suns in the Radio Bay cluster than natural ones. Some had been towed in from other locations; others had been built from scratch, *in situ*. Planets had been steered into place around them, and inserted into unnatural orbits designed to keep the Tract in maximum view. Ferociously goosed magnetic fields and ramped-up atmospheres protected them from radiation. Between the planets, under the sleets of raging light, rogue moons wove their way, in fantastically complex orbits.

These were less star systems than beacons, less beacons than laboratories, and less laboratories than experiments in themselves: enormous detectors designed to react to the unimaginable forces pouring out of the uncontained singularity hypothetically present at the centre of the Tract.

This object was massively energetic. It was surrounded by gas clouds heated to 50,000 degrees Kelvin. It was pumping out jets and spumes of stuff both baryonic and non-baryonic. Its gravitational effects could be detected, if faintly, at the Core. It was, as one commentator put it: 'A place that had already been old by the time the first great quasars began to burn across the early universe in the unimaginable dark.' Whatever it was, it had turned the Tract around it into a region of black holes, huge natural accelerators and junk matter – a broth of space, time, and heaving event horizons; an unpredictable ocean of radiant energy, of deep light. Anything could happen there, where natural law, if there had ever been such a thing, was held in suspension.

None of the ancient races managed to penetrate the Tract and bring back the news; but they all had their try. They had their try at finding out. By the time human beings arrived, there were objects and artefacts up to sixty-five million years old hanging off the edge, some clearly left by cultures many orders stranger or more intelligent than anything you saw around today. They all came prepared with a theory. They brought a new geometry, a new ship, a new method. Every day they launched themselves into the fire, and turned to cinders.

They launched themselves from places like Redline.

Whoever built Redline, whoever built its actinic, enraged-looking sun, wasn't even broadly human. Added to which a peculiar orbital motion, designed to keep the artefact at its south pole presented to a location deep inside the central area of the Kefahuchi Tract, gave it nauseous, undependable rhythms. On Redline, spring arrived twice in five years, then for a whole year in the next twenty; then every other day. When it came it was the colour and quality of cheap neon. Steaming radio-jungles and blue-lit, UV-scoured deserts precluded much in the way of direct dealing by human beings. (Though, in a broad metaphor of the exploration of the Bay itself, the brave, the unlucky and the morally dyslexic still despatched themselves on hasty half-planned entradas. In search of what? Who knew. They were quickly lost in the mists among the foetid ruins. Those that returned, having cracked their faceplates better to examine what they found, would brag around the Motel Splendido spaceport bars for a week or two on their return, then die in the tradition of the entrada, from indescribable diseases.)

Seria Mau consulted her fakebooks. 'The South Polar Artefact,' they informed her, 'resists analysis, though it appears to be a receiver rather than a transmitter.' And later: 'While "day" and "night" can be said to occur on Redline, their occurrence does not seem to be determined simply.' This was the place that lay below her, so pure and unambiguous it was a joy to behold. Also, her fate, at least in a sense. She opened a line.

'Billy Anker,' she said. 'I'm here to see you.'

After some time a voice replied, patched and faint, bracketed by static. 'You want to come down?' it said. Immediately she was nervous.

'I'll send a fetch,' she temporised.

Billy Anker had a thin stubbly face, from which the dark hair swept back into a brutal little ponytail freighted with grey. His age was uncertain, his skin darkened by the light of a thousand suns. His eyes were greeny-grey, set in deep sockets: if he liked you they considered you for some time, often becoming warmly amused; if he didn't, they slid away. They delivered nothing. Billy Anker had an enthusiasm to be out there in the Bay (some said he was born there, but what did they know? They were junkie entradistas and particle-jockeys whose soft voices, wrecked by Carmody bourbon laced with the ribosomes of local bats, told only their own romantic inner legend) always searching for something. He had no patience with anyone who didn't feel the same. Or who at least didn't feel *something*.

'We're here to look,' he'd say, 'and be amazed. We're not here long. Look at this. See that? Look!'

He was a thin, active, seeking little man, skin and tendons, who at all times wore the bottom half of an ancient air-pilot's G-suit, two leather coats, a red and green do-rag tied in a fanciful knot. He lost two fingers of one hand in a bad landing on Sigma End, on the edge of the accretion disc of the notorious black hole they called Radio RX-1 (nearby was the entrance to an artificial wormhole which, he believed at the time, had its eye on the same target as the Redline South Polar Artefact). These he never had replaced.

When Seria Mau fetched up at his feet, he studied her a moment.

'What do you look like, the real you?' he asked.

'Nothing much,' said Seria Mau. 'I'm a K-ship.'

'So you are,' said Billy Anker, consulting his systems. 'I see that now. How has that worked out for you?'

'None of your business, Billy Anker.'

'You shouldn't be so defensive,' was how he replied. And then, after a moment or two: 'So what's new in the universe? What have you seen that I haven't?'

Seria Mau was amused. 'You ask me that when you stay in this piece-of-shit old heap,' she said, looking round the inside of Billy Anker's quarters, 'wearing a glove on one hand?' She laughed. 'Plenty of things, though I was never down in the Core.' She told him some of the things she had seen.

'I'm impressed,' he admitted

He rocked back in his chair. Then he said:

'That K-ship of yours. It'll go deep. You know what I mean, "go deep"? I heard one of those will go almost anywhere. You ever think of the Tract? You ever think of taking it there?'

'The day I get tired of this life.'

They both laughed, then Billy Anker said:

'We've got to leave the Beach some day. All of us. Grow up. Leave the Beach, dive in the sea –'

'– because why else be alive, right?' said Seria Mau. 'Isn't that what you're going to say? I heard a thousand men like you say that. And you know what, Billy Anker?'

'What?'

'They all had better coats than you.'

He stared at her.

'You aren't just a K-ship, you're the *White Cat*,' he said. 'You're the girl who stole the *White Cat*.' She was surprised he worked that out so fast. He smiled at her surprise. 'So what can I do for you?'

Seria Mau looked away from him. She didn't like to be worked out so quickly, on some junk planet in Radio Bay in the back passage of nowhere. Also, even in a fetch she couldn't manage those eyes of his. She knew bodies, whatever the shadow operators said. That was part of the problem. And when she saw Billy Anker's eyes she was glad she didn't have one now, which would find them irresistible.

'The tailor sent me here,' she said.

Billy Anker got a dawning expression on his thin face.

'You bought the Dr Haends package,' he said. 'I see that now. You're the one bought it, from Uncle Zip. Shit.'

Seria Mau cut the connection.

'Well, he's cute,' the clone said.

'That was a private transmission,' Seria Mau told her. 'Do you want to get put out into empty space again?'

'Did you see his hand? Wow.'

'Because I can do that if you want,' said Seria Mau. 'He's too quick, this Billy Anker guy,' she told herself, and then out loud added: 'Did you really like that hand? I thought it was overdone.'

The clone laughed sarcastically.

'What does someone who lives in a tank know?'

Since her change of mind on Perkins' Rent, the clone – whose name was Mona or Moehne or something similar – had fallen into a kind of short-swing bipolar disorder. When she was up, she felt her whole life was going to change. Her skirts got pinker and shorter. She sang to herself all day, saltwater dub like 'Ion Die' and 'Touch-out Hustle'; or the fantastic old outcaste beats which were chic in the Core. When she was down she hung about the human quarters biting her nails or watching hologram pornography and masturbating. The shadow operators, who adored her, took care of her in the exaggerated way Seria Mau had never allowed. She let

144

them dress her in the kind of outfits Uncle Zip's daughters might wear to a wedding; or fit her quarters out with mirrors to optical-astronomy standard. Also, it was important to them to see she ate properly. She was sharp enough to understand their needs and play to them. When the mood compass pointed north, that was when she had them wrapped round her little finger. She had them make her Elvis food and lurex halter tops that showed off her nipples. She got them to change the width of her pelvis by quick fix cosmetic surgery. 'If that's what you want, dear,' they said. 'If you think it will help.' They would do anything to cheer her up. They would do anything to keep her out of the housecoat with the food stains on the front, including encourage her to smoke tobacco, which was even illegal in the FTZs since twenty-seven years ago.

'I wasn't listening deliberately,' she said.

'Keep off this band from now on,' Seria Mau warned her. 'And do something with that hair.' Ten minutes later she sent her fetch back down to Billy Anker.

'We get a lot of interference here,' he said wisely. 'Maybe that was why I lost you.'

'Maybe it was.'

Whatever Billy Anker had done, whatever he was famous for, he wasn't doing much of it now. He lived in his ship, the *Karaoke Sword*, which Seria Mau suspected would never leave Redline again. The neon vegetation, bluish, pale and strong, grew over its half-mile length like radioactive ivy over a fluted stone column. The *Karaoke Sword* was made of alien metals, pocked from twenty thousand years of use and ten of Redline rain. You could only guess at its history before Billy found it. Inside, ordinary Earth stuff was hot-wired into its original controls. Bundles of conduit, nests of wires, things like TV screens four hundred years old and full of dust. This was not K-tech. It was as old-fashioned as nuts and bolts, though nothing like as kitschy and desirable. Also, there were no shadow operators on board the *Karaoke Sword*. If you wanted something doing, it was do it yourself. Billy Anker mistrusted the shadow operators though he never would say why. Instead he sat in what looked like an ancient fighter-pilot's chair, with tubes of coloured fluid and wires going into him, and a helmet he could put on if he felt like it.

He watched Seria Mau's fetch sniffing around in the rubbish at his feet and said:

'In its day this shit took me some weird places.'

'I can imagine that,' said Seria Mau.

'Hey, if it's good enough it's good enough.'

'Billy Anker, I'm here to tell you the Dr Haends package doesn't work.'

Billy looked surprised; then unsurprised.

A sly expression came to his face. 'You want your money back,' he guessed. 'Well, I'm not known –'

'– as a refund guy. I know. But look, that's not—'

'It's policy, babe,' said Billy Anker. He shrugged sadly, but his look above that was comfortable. 'What can I say?'

'You can say nothing and listen for once. Is that why you're alone here with all this historical stuff, because you never listen to anyone? I didn't come here for a refund. If I wanted that I could have it from Uncle Zip. Only I don't trust him.'

'Fair point,' admitted Billy Anker. 'So what do you want?'

'I want you to tell me where you got it from. The package.'

Billy Anker pondered this.

'That isn't usual,' was his reply.

'All the same it's what I want.'

They regarded one another evenly. Billy Anker tapped the fingers of his good hand on the arm of his acceleration chair. In response the screens in front of him cleared, then began showing planets. They were big. They came in fast towards the viewer, swelling and blooming like something live then diving left and right in the moment they disappeared. They were layered with swirling bands of cloud, magenta, green, dirty brown and yellow.

'This is footage I took,' said Billy Anker, 'on a sweep through here just after they discovered it. See how complex this shit is? And the people who built it didn't even have a sun to work with. They towed a brown dwarf into place and torched it up. They knew how to do that so it became a kind of star doesn't fit on any sequence we're aware of. Then they brought in these *eight* gas giants, along with sixty smaller planetary objects, and injected Redline into the most complex artificial gravitation alley anyone ever saw. Some kind of resonance libration did the rest.' He considered this. 'These guys weren't hobbyists. That operation alone must have taken them a million years. Why do you start a project like that, never finish it?'

'Billy Anker, I don't care.'

'Maybe you just get bored and drift away. There's another thing, though, and it's this: if you can do all that, if you can muster the psychic energy to do all that just to build some kind of scientific instrument, how fucking serious is what you're looking for? You ever think of that? *Why* these people bothered to spend their time like this?'

'Billy—'

'Anyway: as a result of that and other important aspects of its history, this system is a particle-jockey's nightmare. Interference, as the fakebooks say, is common. So that's probably why our previous connection broke down. Do you think? Which I regretted because I was enjoying it so much.'

He killed the screens and looked down at Seria Mau's fetch.

'Tell me how you stole the *White Cat*,' he invited her.

The control room of the *Karaoke Sword* smelled of hot dust. The monitors ticked and cooled, or switched themselves on suddenly in random patterns. (They showed the Redline surface, an eroded mesa here, a ruined structure there, nothing much to tell between the two; they always came back to the South Polar Artefact, dimly observable in its wastes of radio-snow.) A flickering light went across the control room walls, which had original hieroglyphs on them similar to ancient Earth civilisations. Billy Anker absently rubbed his right hand as if to alleviate the pain of his missing fingers. Seria Mau knew that she had to give something to get something, so she let the silence draw out, then said:

'I didn't. The mathematics stole it.'

Billy Anker laughed in disbelief.

'The *mathematics* stole it? How does that come about?'

'I don't know,' she said. 'How do I know? It put me to sleep. It can do that. When I woke up we were a thousand lights from anywhere, looking down at the halo.' She had woken from the usual disturbing dreams – though in those days they did not yet feature the man in the top hat and tails – to find herself nowhere. In her tank, she shivered at the recollection. 'It was empty space,' she said. 'I had never been in empty space before. You have no idea. You just have no idea.' She remembered only dislocation, feelings of panic that really had nothing to do with her situation. 'You know,' she said, 'I think it was trying to show me something.'

Billy Anker smiled.

'So the ship stole you,' he said, more to himself than her.

'I suppose it did,' she admitted.

'Oh,' she said, 'I was happy enough to be stolen. I was sick of EMC anyway. All those "police" actions in the Free Trade Zones! I was sick of Earth politics. Mostly I was sick of myself...' This made him look interestedly at her, so she stopped. 'I was sick of a lot of things which aren't your business.' She struggled to formulate something. 'And yet if the ship stole me, you know, it had no agenda. It hung there. It just hung there in empty space for hours. After I had calmed down, I took it back into the halo. We were running flat out for months. That was when I really deserted. That was when I made my own plans.'

'You went rogue,' said Billy Anker.

'Is that what they say?'

'You play for anyone who pays.'

'Oh, and that makes me *so different* from all of you people! Everyone has to earn a living, Billy Anker.'

'EMC want you back. You're just an asset to them.'

It was Seria Mau Genlicher's turn to laugh.

'They'll have to catch me first.'

'How close are they to that?' Billy Anker asked her. He waggled the fingers of his good hand. 'This close. When you came in here, my systems had a look at your hull. You were in an exchange of top-end ordnance not long ago. You have particle scouring from some kind of high volume X-ray device.'

'It was no "exchange",' said Seria Mau. 'I was the only one who fired.' She laughed grimly. 'They were gas in eighty nanoseconds,' she claimed, hoping it was true.

He shrugged to show that though he was impressed he would not be deflected from the issue.

'But who were they? They're on to you, kid.'

'What do you know?'

'It's not what I know. It's what *you* know, which you're trying to deny. It's all over you. It's in the way you speak.'

'*What do you know, Billy Anker?*'

He shrugged.

'No one can catch the *White Cat*!' she screamed at him.

At that moment Mona the clone walked out from among the hieroglyphs on the wall of Billy Anker's control room. Her fetch, a smaller and cheaper version of herself, flickered like bad neon. It was wearing red fuck-me pumps with five-inch heels, a calf-length latex tube – lime green – and a bolero top in pink angora wool. Its hair was done up in bunches with matching ribbon.

'Oh, hi, sorry,' she said. 'I must have pressed the wrong thing.'

Billy Anker looked irritated.

'You want to be more careful, kid,' he advised her. She gave him a casual up-and-down, then ignored him.

'I was trying to find some music,' she said to Seria Mau.

'Get out of here,' said Seria Mau.

'I just can't work this stuff,' the clone complained.

'If you don't remember what happened to your friends,' Seria Mau reminded her, 'I can show you the footage.'

The clone stood biting her lips for a moment, outrage struggling in her expression with despair, then tears ran down her face and she shrugged and faded slowly away into brown smoke. Though he must have wondered what was behind it all, Billy Anker watched this performance with a studied lack of interest. After a minute he said to Seria Mau:

'You changed the name of the ship. I'm interested why.'

She laughed. 'I don't know,' she said. 'Why do you do anything like that? We hung there in the dark, the ship, the mathematics and me. There was nothing to orient ourselves by except the Tract – faint, distant, winking like a bad eye. Suddenly I remembered the legend the original space-captains had, when they first used the Tate-Kearney transformations all those hundreds of years ago to find their way from star to star. How in the long watches of the night they would sometimes see, inside their navigational holograms, *a ghostly vision of Brian Tate himself*, toppling through the vacuum with his white cat on his shoulder. That's when I chose the name.'

Billy Anker stared at her.

'Jesus,' he said.

Seria Mau fetched up on the arm of his chair.

'Are you going to tell me where you got the Dr Haends package?' she said, staring into his eyes.

Before he could answer, she was pulled away from the *Karaoke Sword* and back to the *White Cat*. Soft, persistent alarms filled the ship. Up in the corners, the shadow operators were wringing their hands.

'Something is happening here,' the mathematics said.

Seria Mau turned restively in the narrow volumes of her tank. What limbs she had left made vague, nervous motions.

'Why tell me?' she said.

The mathematics brought up the signature diagram of an event five or six hundred nanoseconds old. It presented as faint grey fingers knotting and unknotting against spectral light: 'Why does this always look like *sex*?' complained Seria Mau. The mathematics, unsure how to answer, remained silent. 'Choose a new regime,' she ordered irritably. The mathematics chose a new regime. Then another. Then a third. It was like trying on coloured spectacles until you saw what you wanted. The image flickered and changed like ancient holiday snaps in a slide projector. Eventually it began to toggle regularly between two states. If you knew exactly how to look into the gap between them you could detect, like weakly reacting matter, the ghost of an event. Two AUs distant, deep in a band of hot gas and asteroidal rubbish, something had moved and then become still again. The nanoseconds spooled away, and nothing further happened.

'You see?' said the mathematics. 'Something is there.'

'This is a difficult system to see in. The fakebooks are clear on that. And Billy Anker says—'

'I appreciate that. But you do agree that something is there?'

'Something's there,' admitted Seria Mau. 'It can't be them. That ordnance would have melted a planet.'

She thought for a moment.

'We'll ignore it,' she said.

'I'm afraid we can't do that,' the mathematics told her. 'Something is happening here and we don't know what it is. They slipped away, like us, just as the ordnance went off. We have to assume this is them.'

Seria Mau thrashed in her tank.

'How could you let this happen!' she shrieked. 'They were gas in eighty nanoseconds!'

The mathematics sedated her while she was still speaking. She heard herself dopplering away into silence like an illustration of some point in General Relativity. Then she dreamed she was back in the garden, one month before the first anniversary of her mother's death. Damp spring now reigned, with Earth-daffodils in the beds beneath the laurel bushes, Earth-sky pale blue between towering white clouds. The house, opening its doors and shutters reluctantly after the long winter, had breathed the three of them forth like an old man's breath. The brother found a slug. He bent down and poked it with a stick. Then he picked it up and ran about with it, going, 'Yoiy yoiy yoiy.' Seria Mau, nine years old, dressed carefully in her red woollen coat, wouldn't look at him, or laugh.

All winter she had dreamed of a horse, a white horse which would step so delicately! It would come from nowhere and after that follow her everywhere she went, touching her with its soft nose.

Smiling sadly, the father watched them play.

'What do you want?' he asked them.

'I want this slug!' cried the brother. He fell down and kicked his legs. 'Yoiy yoiy.'

The father laughed.

'What about you, Seria Mau?' he said. 'You can have anything you want!'

He had lived by himself all winter, playing chess in his cold room upstairs, with his hands in fingerless mitts. He cried every lunchtime when he saw Seria Mau bringing the food. He wouldn't let her leave the room. He put his hands on her shoulders and made her look into his hurt eyes. She didn't want that every day of her life. She didn't want his tears; she didn't want his garden, either, with its patch of ashes and its smell of loss among the birch trees. The moment she thought that, she did want him, after all! She loved him. She loved her brother. All the same, she wanted to run far away from them both and sail the New Pearl River.

She wanted to go right up into some space of her own, clutching the mane of a great white horse whose gentle breath would smell of almonds and vanilla.

'I want not to have to be the mother,' Seria Mau said.

Her father's face fell. He turned away. She found herself standing in front of a retro-shop window in the rain.

Hundreds of small items were on display behind the steamy glass. Every one of them was false. False teeth, false noses, fake ruby lips, false hair, X-ray spectacles that never worked. Old, corrupt stuff made of tin or plastic, whose only purpose was to become something else the moment you picked it up. A kaleidoscope that blacked your eye. Puzzles which, taken apart, would never go back together. False-bottom boxes that laughed when they were touched. Musical instruments which farted when you blew in them. It was all false. It was a paradigm of undependability. In the middle of all the other objects, in pride of place, lay Uncle Zip's gift-box with its green satin ribbon and its dozen long-stemmed roses. The rain stopped. The lid of the box lifted a little of its own accord. A nanotech substrate like white foam poured out and began to fill the shop window, while the soft bell chimed and the woman's voice whispered:

'Dr Haends? Dr Haends please. Dr Haends to surgery!'

At this there came a light but peremptory tap on the inside of the glass. The foam cleared, revealing the display to be empty but for a single item. Against a background of ruched oyster satin stood a piece of stiff white card, on which was reproduced the crude and lively drawing of a man in black top hat and tails, caught preparing to light an oval Turkish cigarette. He had shot his cuffs with a flourish. He had tamped the tobacco on the back of his long white hand. Frozen in that moment, he was full of elegant potential. His black eyebrows made ironic arcs. 'Who knows what will happen next?' he seemed to be saying. The cigarette would vanish. Or the magician would vanish. He would tip back his hat with the end of his ebony cane and fade slowly into nothing while the Kefahuchi Tract slithered across the ruched satin void behind him like a cheap Victorian necklace and the streetlight flashed – ting! – off one of his white, even, incisor teeth. Everything would vanish.

Beneath this image, in bold art deco letters, someone had printed the words:

DR HAENDS, PSYCHIC SURGEON.
Appears twice nightly.

Seria Mau woke puzzled, to find her tank flooded with benign hormones. The mathematics had changed its mind. 'I believe after all that we're alone,' it said, and left for its own space before she could comment. This compelled her to call up the relevant displays and give them her attention.

'Now I'm not so sure,' she said.

No reply.

Next, a line opened from the planet below.

'So what happened here?' Billy Anker wanted to know. 'One minute you're talking, the next you aren't?'

'This interference!' said Seria Mau gaily.

'Hey, well, don't do me any favours,' he grumbled. Then he said: 'You want to know the history of that package, maybe I'll help. But first you got to do something for me.'

Seria Mau laughed.

'No one can help you with your dress-sense, Billy Anker; I want to say that from the start.'

This time it was Billy Anker who broke the connection.

She sent down her fetch. 'Hey, come on,' she said, 'it was a joke. What do you want me to do?'

You could see him swallow his pride. You could see he had his own reasons to keep her attention. 'I wanted you to come with me,' he said. 'See some things on Redline, that's all.' She was touched, until his voice got that note she already recognised. 'Nothing special. Or only as special as everything else we know out here on the edge—'

'Let's go,' she interrupted. 'If we're going.'

In the end, though, there wasn't time to do that. Alarms chimed. The shadow operators flew about. The *White Cat* went up to full readiness. Her battle clocks, reset to zero, began to count off in femtoseconds, the last stop before the unknowable realtime of the universe. Meanwhile, she diverted fusion product into engines and ordnance and began, as a precautionary spoiling measure, to flicker in and out of the dynaflow at random. From this behaviour, Seria Mau judged they were in an emergency.

'What?' she demanded of the mathematics.

'Look,' it recommended, and began increasing the connections between her and the *White Cat* until, in important ways, Seria Mau *became* the ship. She was on ship-time. She had ship consciousness. Processing rates ramped up by several orders of magnitude from the paltry human forty bits a second. Her sensorium, analogued to represent fourteen dimensions, echoed with replicas of itself like a cathedral built in 'brane-space. Seria Mau was now alive in a way, in a place – and at a speed – which would burn her out if it lasted for more than a minute and half. As a precautionary measure the mathematics was already sluicing the tank proteome with endorphins, adrenalin inhibitors and warm-down hormones which, operating at biological speeds, would take effect only after any encounter was finished.

'I was wrong,' it said. 'Do you see? There?'

'I see,' said Seria Mau. 'I see the fuckers!'

It was EMC. There was no need for signature diagrams or fakebooks. She knew them. She knew their shapes. She even knew their names. A pod of K-ships – coms shrieking with fake traffic, decoys flaring off in several dimensions – flipped themselves down the Redline gravitational alley along a trajectory designed for maximum unpredictability. Second-guessed from instant to instant, this appeared in the *White Cat's* sensorium as neon, scripted recursively against the halo night. The *Krishna Moire* pod, on long-distance ops out of New Venusport, comprised: the *Norma Shirike*, the *Kris Rhamion*, the *Sharmon Kier* and the *Marino Shrike*, and was led by the *Krishna Moire* itself. In they came, their crosslinked mathematics causing them to constantly exchange positions in a kind of randomised braid or plait. It was a classic K-ship ploy. But the centre thread of the plait (though 'centre' was a meaningless term in these circumstances) presented as an object Seria Mau recognised: an object with a weird linked signature, half-Nastic, half-human.

As they roared down upon her, the *White Cat* flickered and fluttered, miming uncertainty and perhaps a broken wing. She vanished from her orbit. The pod took note. You could hear their sarcastic laughter. They assigned a fraction of their intelligence to finding her; bored on in. Seria Mau – her signature dissembled to mimic that of an abandoned satellite at the Redline L2 – needed no further evidence. Her intuition was operating in fourteen dimensions too.

'I know where they're going.'

'Who cares?' said the mathematics. 'We're out of here in twenty-eight nanoseconds.'

'No. It's not us. It's not us they want!'

There was a prickle of white light in the upper atmosphere of Redline as mid-range ordnance, despatched into the dynaflow before the raid began, popped out to engage Billy Anker's nominal complement of minefields and satellites. Down on the surface in the streaming rain, the *Karaoke Sword* began to wake up to its situation, coms reluctant, engines slow to warm, countermeasures half-blind to the day: a rocket with a ten-year hangover, entering Seria Mau's sensorium as a pained, lazy worm of light.

Too slow! she thought. Too old.

She opened a line, 'Too slow, Billy Anker!' she called. No answer. The entradista, tapping in a panic at the arms of his acceleration couch, had dislocated his left index finger. 'I'm coming down!'

'Is this wise?' the mathematics wanted to know.

'Disconnect me,' said Seria Mau.

The mathematics thought.

'No,' it said.

'Disconnect me. We're a side-issue here. This isn't a battle, it's a police raid. They've come for Billy Anker, and he doesn't have a clue how to help himself.'

The *White Cat* reappeared 200 kilometres above Redline. Ordnance burst around her. Someone had predicted she would come out *there* and *then*. 'Oh yes,' said Seria Mau, 'very clever. Fuck you too.' Tit for tat, she cooked off a high-end mine she had slipped into the path of the incoming pod. 'Here's one I prepared earlier,' she said. The pod broke up, temporarily blinded, and toppled away in several directions. 'They won't forgive us for that,' she told her mathematics. 'They're arrogant bastards, that team.' The mathematics, which was using the respite to normalise her relationship with the *White Cat*, had no comment to make. The ship's sensorium collapsed around her. Everything slowed down. 'In and out now,' she ordered. 'Quick as we can.' The *White Cat* pitched over into entry attitude. Retrofire pulsed and flared.

Outside, the colours of space gave way to weird smeary reds and greens. Seria Mau airbraked relentlessly in the thickening atmosphere, letting speed scrub off as heat and noise until her ship was a roaring yellow fireball across the night sky. It was a rough ride. The shadow operators streamed about, their lacy wings rippling out behind them, their long hands covering their faces. Mona the clone, who had looked out of a porthole as the ship stood on its nose, was throwing up energetically in the human quarters.

They breached the cloudbase at fifteen hundred feet, to find the *Karaoke Sword* immediately below them. 'I don't believe this,' said Seria Mau. The old ship had lifted itself a foot or two out of the mud and was turning hesitantly this way and that, shaking like a cheap compass needle. A fusion torch fired up at the rear, setting nearby vegetation alight and generating gouts of radioactive steam. After twenty seconds, its bows dropped suddenly and the whole thing slumped back to earth with a groan, breaking in two about a hundred yards forward of the engine. 'Jesus Christ,' Seria Mau whispered. 'Put us down.'

The mathematics said it was unwilling to commit.

'Put us down. I'm not leaving him here.'

'You aren't leaving him here, are you?' Mona the clone called up anxiously from the human quarters.

'Are you deaf?' said Seria Mau.

'I wouldn't put it past you, that's all.'

'Shut up.'

The *Krishna Moire* pod, realising what had happened, swept in, fanned out into the parking orbit with a kind of idle bravado, the way shadow boys in one-shot cultivars occupy a doorway so they can spit, gamble and clean their nails with replicas of priceless antique flick-knives. They could afford to wait. Meanwhile, to move things along, Krishna Moire himself opened a line to the *White Cat*. He had signed on younger than Seria Mau, and his fetch, though it was six feet tall and presented itself in full Earth Military Contracts chic, including black boots, high-waist riding breeches and a dove-grey double-breasted tuxedo with epaulettes, had the demanding mouth of a boy.

'We want Billy Anker,' he said.

'Go through me,' Seria Mau invited.

Moire looked less certain. 'This is a wrong thing you are doing, resisting us,' he informed her. 'To add to all those other wrongdoings you done. But, hey, we didn't come for you, not this time.'

'I done?' said Seria Mau. 'Wrongdoings I *done*?'

Outside, explosions marched steadily across the mud, flinging up rocks and vegetation. Elements of the pod, becoming impatient with the half-minute wait, had entered the atmosphere and begun to shell the surface at random. Seria Mau sighed.

'Fuck off, Moire, and take speaking lessons,' she said.

'You're only alive because EMC don't care about you one way or another,' he warned her as he faded to brown smoke. 'They could change their minds. This operation is double red.' His fetch flickered, vanished, reformed suddenly in a kind of postscript. 'Hey, Seria, I got my own pod now!' it said.

'I knew that. So?'

'So next time I see you,' the fetch promised, 'I'll let the machine speak.'

'Jerk,' said Seria Mau.

By this time she had the cargo bay open. Billy Anker, dressed in a vintage EV suit, was shuffling head down towards it with all the grim patience of the physically unfit. He fell. He picked himself up. He fell again. He wiped his faceplate. Up in the stratosphere, the *Krishna Moire* pod shifted and turned in hungry disarray; while high above it in the parking lot, the hybrid ship awaited what would happen, its ambivalent signature flickering like a description of the events unfolding below. Who was up there, Seria Mau wondered, along with the commander of *Touching the Void*? Who was presiding over this fumbled op? Down in the cargo bay, Mona the clone called Billy's name. She leaned out, caught his hand, pulled him inside. The cargo ramp slammed shut. As if this was a signal, long vapour trails emerged from the cloudbase at steep angles. Billy Anker's ship burst open. Its engines went up in a sigh of gamma and visible light.

'Go,' Seria Mau told the mathematics. The *White Cat* torched out in a low fast arc over the South Pole, transmitting ghost signatures, firing off decoys and particle-dogs.

'Look!' cried Billy Anker. 'Look down!'

The South Polar Artefact flashed beneath them. Seria Mau caught a fleeting glimpse of it – a featureless gunmetal ziggurat a million years old and five miles on a side at the base – before it vanished astern. 'It's opening!' cried Billy Anker. Then, in an awed whisper: 'I can see. I can see inside—' The sky lit up white behind them, and his voice turned to a despairing wail. The pod, growing frustrated, had hit the ziggurat with something from the bottom shelf of its arsenal, something big. Something EMC.

'What did you see?' Seria Mau asked three minutes later, as they skulked at Redline L2 while the *White Cat*'s mathematics tried to guess them a way out under the noses of their pursuers.

Billy Anker wouldn't say.

'How could they do that?' he railed. 'That was a unique historical item, and a working one. It was still receiving data from somewhere in the Tract. We could have *learned* something from that thing.' He sat white-faced in the human quarters, panting and wiping the adrenalin sweat off his face with his do-rag, the top half of the muddy EV suit peeled back. The shadow operators were cooing and fluttering round him, trying to fix his dislocated finger, but he kept batting them away with his other hand. 'This old stuff,' he said, 'it's all we have. It's our only resource!'

'Where you look, you find,' she told him. 'There will always be more, Billy Anker. There will always be more after that.'

'Nevertheless, everything I learned, I learned from that thing.'

'And what did you learn, Billy Anker?'

He tapped the side of his nose.

'You'd like to know,' he said, laughing as if this assertion showed how sharp and clean his intuition was. 'But I won't tell.' He was a beachcomber, with all the tidal scouring of the personality that implies. His big discovery shored him up. He had to believe she would be interested in whatever tacky insight into the nature of things he thought it gave him. 'I can tell you what EMC want, though,' he offered instead.

'I know that already. They want you. They followed me all the way from Motel Splendido to find you. And here's another thing to think about: the *Moire* pod wanted to try me out. They think they're good enough. But whoever's in that other ship wouldn't let them, in case you were caught in the crossfire. That's why Krishna Moire bumped your artefact, Billy. He's pissed at his superiors.'

Billy Anker grinned his sly grin.

'And are they good enough?' he said. 'To try you out?'

'What do you think?'

Billy Anker contemplated this answer with approval. Then he said, 'EMC don't want me. They want what I found.'

Seria Mau felt cold in her tank.

'Is it on board my ship?' she said.

'In a manner of speaking,' he acknowledged. He made a gesture meant to take in all of Radio Bay, maybe even the vast sweep of the Beach itself. 'It's out there too.'

EIGHTEEN

The Circus of Pathet Lao

Some hours after he shot Evie Cray, Ed Chianese found himself on the waste ground behind the New Men warren.

It was pitch black out there, lit with oddly angled flashes of white light from the docks. Occasionally a K-ship left its slip on a vertical line of fusion product, and for perhaps two or three seconds Ed could see low hummocks, pits, ponds, piles of broken engineering objects. The whole place had a smell of metal and chemicals. Vapour drifted out the yards like a ground mist. Ed was throwing up again, and the tank voices were back in his head. He dumped the guns in the first pool he came to. A life like his, and finally he had killed someone. He remembered boasting to Tig Vesicle:

'Once you've done all the things worth doing, you begin on the things that aren't.'

A little smoke came up from the pool, as if there was more in it than water. Shortly after he got rid of the guns, he came across an abandoned rickshaw. It loomed up in front of him suddenly – out of context, one wheel in a flooded hole – tilted at an odd angle against the sky. Detecting his approach, advertisements crawled across the sides of its hood, coalesced as soft lights in the air above it. Music started up. A voice echoed across the waste ground:

'Sandra Shen's Observatorium and Native Karma Plant, Incorporating the Circus of Pathet Lao.'

'No thanks,' Ed said. 'I'll walk.'

In the light of the next flare from the rocket yards, he discovered the rickshaw girl. She was on her knees, bowed down between the shafts, breathing in with a kind of hoarse whistle, letting it out as a grunt. Every so often her whole body tensed up as tight as a fist and began to tremble. Then she seemed to relax again. Once or twice she laughed to herself and said, 'Hey, man.' She was occupied with dying the way she had been occupied with life, to the exclusion of everything else. Ed knelt down beside her. It was like kneeling next to a foundered horse.

'Hold on,' he said. 'Don't die. You can make it.'

There was a painful laugh.

'The fuck you know about it,' the girl said thickly.

He could feel the heat pouring off her. He had the feeling it would rush away like that, full tilt, and then stop and never be replaced. He tried to put his arms round her to hold it in. But she was too big, so he just held one of her hands.

'What's your name?' he said.

'What's it to you?'

'You tell me your name, you can't die,' Ed explained. 'It's like somehow, you know, we made contact. So you owe me something, and all that.' He thought. 'I need you not to die,' he said.

'Shit,' she said. 'Other people go out in peace. I get a twink.'

Ed was surprised she could guess that.

'How do you know?' he said. 'You can't know that.'

She drew her breath in raggedly.

'Look at yourself,' she advised. 'You're as dead as me, only it's on the inside.' She narrowed her eyes. 'You got blood all on you, man,' she told him. 'You're all over blood. At least I haven't got blood on me.' This seemed to cheer her up in some way. She nodded to herself, settled back.

'I'm Annie Glyph,' she said. 'Or I was.'

'Visit today!' boomed the rickshaw's advertising chip suddenly. 'Sandra Shen's Observatorium and Native Karma Plant, Incorporating the Circus of Pathet Lao. Also: the future descried. Prophecy. Fortune Telling. Atheromancy.'

'I worked this city five years, on *café électrique* and sheer fucking guts,' Annie Glyph said. 'That's two years more than most.'

'What's atheromancy?' Ed asked her.

'I got no idea.'

He stared at the rickshaw. Cheap spoked wheels and orange plastic, totally Pierpoint Street. The rickshaw girls ran eighteen hours a day for speed money, and opium money to take the edge off the speed; then they blew up. *Café électrique* and guts: that was their boast. All they had in the end was a myth of themselves. They were indestructible: this destroyed them. Ed shook his head.

'How can you live with it?' he said.

But Annie Glyph wasn't living with it any more. Her eyes were empty, and she had slumped to one side, tipping the rickshaw over with her. He couldn't quite believe something as alive as her could die. Her huge body still had the sheen of sweat on it. Her rawboned face, dwarfed by the muscles of her neck and shoulders, masculised by the inboard testosterone patch the tailor had specified as part of the cheap conversion kit, had a kind of etched beauty. Ed studied it a moment or two then leaned forward to close her eyes. 'Hey, Annie,' he said. 'Sleep at last.' At this, something weird happened. Her cheekbones rippled and shifted uneasily. He put it down to the unsteady illumination of the rickshaw ads. But then her whole head blurred, and seemed to break up into lights.

'Shit!' Ed said. He jumped to his feet and fell over backwards.

It lasted a minute, maybe two. The lights seemed to flutter up into the softly glowing region where the rickshaw ads blossomed out of the air. Then lights and ads together poured back down into her face, which received them like a dry sponge soaking up tears. Her left leg contracted, then kicked out galvanically. 'The fuck,' she said. She cleared her throat and spat. Pushing into the mud with her feet and hands, she got herself and the rickshaw upright. She shook herself and stared down at Ed. Steam was already coming up off the small of her back into the cold night. 'Nothing like that ever happened to me before,' she complained.

'You were dead,' Ed whispered.

She shrugged. 'Too much speed. I can fix that with more speed. You wanna go somewhere?'

Ed got up and backed away.

'No thanks.'

'Hey, climb in, man. It's free. You got a ride.' She looked up at the stars, then slowly around at the waste ground, as if she wasn't sure how she came to be there. 'I owe you, I can't remember why.'

It was the weirdest ride Ed ever had.

2.30 a.m.: the streets were deserted, silent but for the steady soft slap of Annie Glyph's feet. The shafts moved up and down as she ran, but the cab had a chip to damp the effect of that. To Ed it was like gliding and being motionless, both at once. All he could see of the rickshaw girl was her massive lats and buttocks, painted with electric-blue Lycra. Her gait was an energy-saving shuffle. She was designed to run forever. Every so often she shook her head, and an aerosol of sweat sprayed up into the cab's soft corona of advertising light. The heat of her streamed around him, so that he was insulated against the night. He felt insulated from everything else too, as if being Annie's passenger allowed him to withdraw from the world: take a rest from its mysteries.

When he admitted this, she laughed.

'Twinks!' she said. 'Rest is all you fuckers ever do.'

'I had a life once.'

'They all say that,' Annie advised him. 'Hey,' she said. 'Don't you know not to talk to the rickshaw girl? She's got work to do if you ain't.'

The night ran past, the garment district flowing into Union Square and then East Garden. EMC adprop was everywhere. 'War!' announced the hologram hoardings: 'Are you ready?' Annie turned briefly on to downtown Pierpoint, which was as deserted as if the war had already happened. The tank parlours and chopshops were all closed. Here and there some loser drank Roses whiskey in an empty bar while a cultivar in an apron wiped the bartop with his dirty rag and pondered the difference between life and the semblance of it. They would be like that 'til dawn then go home, still wondering.

'So what did you do, this other life you had?' Annie asked Ed suddenly. 'This, "I wasn't always a twink" life of yours?'

Ed shrugged.

'One thing I did,' he began, 'I flew dipships—'

'They all say that.'

'Hey,' Ed said. 'We don't have to talk.'

Annie laughed to herself. She hung a left off Pierpoint on to Impreza, then another at the corner of Impreza and Skyline. There, she had to pull hard into a half-mile grade, but her breathing barely altered. Hills, her body language implied, were the small change of life to a rickshaw girl. After a while, Ed said:

'One thing I remember, I had a cat. That was when I was a kid.'

'Yeah? What colour was that?'

'It was black,' Ed said. 'It was a black cat.'

He could make a clear mental picture of the cat, juggling with a coloured feather in the hall. For twenty minutes it would put its whole heart into whatever you offered – paper, a feather, a painted cork – then lose interest and fall asleep. It was black and thin, with nervous, fluid movements, a pointed little face and yellow eyes. It was always hungry. Ed could make a clear mental picture of the cat, but he couldn't remember anything about the family house. Instead he had a lot of tank memories, which he knew weren't real because of their shiny completeness, their perfection of structure. 'Maybe there was another cat too,' he said: 'A sister.' But on reflection he knew that wasn't true.

'We're here,' Annie said suddenly.

The rickshaw stopped with a jerk. Ed, thrown back out into the world, stared cluelessly around. Fences and gates, dripping with condensation, rattled in the onshore wind. Behind that, a chilly strip of concrete stretched away into saltmarsh and sand dunes, where an encrustation of cheap, sea-soured wooden hotels and bars could be seen.

'Where's this?' he said. 'Shit.'

'The customer doesn't give a destination, I bring them here,' Annie Glyph explained. 'Don't you like it? I'm on a percentage from the circus. See? Over there.' She drew his attention to a distant cluster of lights, then, when he seemed unimpressed, gave him an anxious look. 'It's not so bad,' she said. 'They got hotels and stuff here too. It's the noncorporate spaceport.'

Ed stared over the fence.

'Shit,' he said again.

'I get a percentage to bring in trade,' Annie said. 'I can take you in if you like.' She shrugged. 'Or I could take you on somewhere. But you have to pay for that.'

'I'll walk,' Ed said. 'No money.'

'No money?'

He shrugged.

'Not much of anything,' he said.

She stared at him with an expression he couldn't interpret.

'I was dying out there,' she said. 'But you took time over me. So I'll run you back to the city.'

'The fact is,' Ed admitted, 'I got nowhere to be, either. No money. Nowhere to be. No reason to be there.' He could see her trying to process this. Her lips moved a little as she looked at him. He understood suddenly that she had a good heart, and that made him feel anxious on her behalf. It made him feel depressed. 'Hey,' he said. 'So what? You don't owe me anything, I enjoyed the ride.' He looked her immense body up and down. 'Your action is good.'

She stared at him puzzledly; then down at herself; and then, across the chain-link fence and the rattling gate in the wind, at the circus by the shore. 'I keep a room over there,' she said. 'See those lights? I bring in custom, they let me have a room. That's the deal I have with them. You want to stay there?'

The gate rattled, the sea air got a little colder. Ed thought about Tig and Neena, what happened to them.

'OK,' he said.

'In the morning you could ask for a job.'

'I always wanted to work in a circus.'

Opening the gate, she looked at him sidelong.

'Kids do,' she said.

The room was hardly bigger than she was, with cheap fibreboard walls that creaked and gave in the sea wind. The walls were off-white, with a couple of loose shelves. There was a toilet and shower in a translucent plastic cubicle in one corner; an induction-oven and a couple of pots and pans in another. She had a futon rolled up against the wall. It was as bleak and transitional a space as you liked, smelling of oil-fried rice and sweat. *Café électrique* sweat. Rickshaw-girl sweat. But she had some things of her own on the shelves, which was more than most of them could say. She had two spare Lycra outfits, three old books, and some tissue-paper flowers.

'It's nice,' Ed said.

'Why lie?' she said. 'It's shite.' She indicated the futon. 'I could make us something to eat,' she said, 'or maybe you'd just like to lie down?'

Ed must have looked reluctant.

'Hey,' she said. 'I'm gentle. I never hurt anyone yet.'

She was right. She enfolded him with care. Her olive skin, with its faint down of hair, had a strange strong smell, like cloves and ice. She touched him softly, protected him from her convulsions by coming somewhere deep down inside herself, and gently encouraged him to batter against her as hard as he wanted. When he woke in the night, he found she had curved round him with awkward consideration, as if she was not used to someone being there. The tide was in. Ed lay and listened to the sea roll the stones about in the undertow. The wind hissed. It was soon bluish dawn. He felt the circus begin to wake up around him, though he didn't yet know what that might mean for him. Annie Glyph's tranquil downer

167

breath, the rise and fall of her huge ribcage, soon sent him to sleep again.

In a time like that, who needed a circus? The halo was a circus in itself. Circus was in the streets. It was inside people's heads. Eat fire? Everyone was a fire-eater. Everyone had geek genes and a story to tell. Sentient tattoos made everyone the Illustrated Man. Everyone was high on some flying trapeze issue of their own. It was the flight into the grotesque. The tusked cultivar on Electric Avenue, the twink curled foetally in the twink-tank: whether they knew it or not, they had asked and answered all the questions the universe could support for now. They were their own audience, too.

The only thing you couldn't be was an alien, so Sandra Shen kept a few of those. And prophecy was still popular, because no one could quite do it yet. But in the face of the uniform grotesque, the Circus of Pathet Lao had been forced to look elsewhere for the cheap thrill at the heart of performance, and – through a series of breathtaking acts of the imagination devised and sometimes acted in by Sandra Shen herself – present the vanished normal.

As a result, Ed Chianese's age was able to define itself as the cultural opposite of 'Having Breakfast, 1950'. It could thrill to 'Buying an Underwired Bra at Dorothy Perkins, 1972', or 'Novel Reading, early 1980s', and snigger over the perverse 'A New Baby', and 'Toyota Previa with West London School Children', both 2002. Most extraordinary of all – perched as it was so exactly on the historical cusp – was the astonishing 'Brian Tate and Michael Kearney Looking Into a Computer Monitor, 1999'. These gemlike tableaux – acted out behind glass under powerful lights by the clones of fat men about to have heart attacks on a Zurich metro platform, anorexic women dressed in the Angelino sport-fuck wear of 1982 – brought to life the whole bizarre comfortingness of Old Earth. Such desperate fantasies were the real earners. Like fairy godmothers they had blessed the Circus at its inception, funded its early whirlwind travels across the halo, and now supported its declining years in the twilight zone of New Venusport.

Success is often its own downfall. People weren't coming to watch any more. They were coming to get their own ideas. They weren't content to spectate the vanished past; they wanted to be it. The retro lifestyles emerging from the corporate enclaves had less historical accuracy than a Shen tableau but a softer, more buyable feel. The look was 'Dress Down Friday'. It was the Erickson phone and an Italian wool sweater worn across the shoulders with its arms knotted loosely in front. Meanwhile, at the radical edge, a gene tailor and ex-entradista from Motel Splendido was reputed to have made himself over as the exact replica of a Victorian music hall star, using actual DNA.

In the face of competition like that, Madame Shen was thinking of moving on. But there were other reasons for that, too.

You go too deep, you expect to get burned. There isn't any way around that. Ed dreamed of a dipship breaking up in slow motion in the photosphere of a G-type star. The dipship was Ed. Then he dreamed he was back in the twink-tank but the tank world had come apart and he could already hear voices from every cupboard, every corner, every pretty girl's petticoat. Then he woke with a start and it was full day, and he could hear the sea one side of the dunes and the circus on the other. He found two vegetable samosas wrapped in a slip of greaseproof paper, also some money, together with a note which read: Go see the receptionist about work. Annie Glyph's handwriting was as careful and literate as her way of having sex. Ed ate the samosas, looking comfortably around the little room, with the marine light falling into it and the sea air filling it. Then he crumpled the paper, took a shower to get the blood off him, and went out.

Sandra Shen's Observatorium and Native Karma Plant, Incorporating the Circus of Pathet Lao, occupied a two-acre concrete site on the boundary of the noncorporate spaceport.

The Observatorium, housed in a series of bizarre pressure tanks and magnetic vessels, took up less than a quarter of this; while the Circus itself was contained in a single building the curves and volutes of whose composite construction had been designed to resemble a carnival tent. The rest of the compound was living quarters. All exactly what you would expect – weeds, salt-streaked alloy siding, blistered paint, old carnie holograms with no memory of themselves as human, which, faded but energetic, woke into life as you passed, pursuing, hectoring, cajoling. Everyone who worked here would be like that – lively but disconnected. Ed felt like that too. He had to walk across the whole site to find the front office, which was in another clapped-out wooden building, greyish white under a faulty neon sign.

The receptionist wore a blonde wig.

It was big hair, platinum hair, piled high and sold cheap. In front of her she had a holographic terminal of a type with which Ed was unfamiliar. This resembled an old-fashioned fishtank, in which he thought he discerned now and then a stream of bubbles, a fake clamshell open on a miniature mermaid. The receptionist was like a mermaid herself. Older than she looked, she sat demurely beneath her hair, a small woman with a personal sense of humour and an accent he could not place.

When Ed explained his purpose the whole thing took on a curiously formal air. She asked him for his details, which except for his name he made up. She asked him what he could do. That was easier.

'Fly any kind of ship,' he boasted.

The receptionist pretended to look out the window.

'We don't need a pilot momentarily,' she said. 'As you can see, we're on the ground.'

'Sunjammers, deep freighters, star ships, dipships. I've been there,' Ed went on, 'and flown it.' He was surprised how close to the truth this was. 'Fusion engines to dynaflow drivers. Some stuff I never knew what it was, Earth controls bolted onto alien equipment.'

'I'm sympathetic,' the receptionist said. 'But is there anything else you can do?'

Ed thought.

'I rode navigator on Alcubiere ships,' he said. 'You know, the big ones that bunch reality up in front of them as they go? It's like a ruckle in cloth.' He shook his head, trying to visualise the Alcubiere warp. 'Or maybe not like that at all. Anyway, space gets wrenched, matter gets wrenched, time goes out the window with everything else. Close into the ship you can just about survive it. The navigators surf that part of the wave. They go out in EVA pods and park in the warp, trying to see what's next. One thing they can see from there, it's their lives flushing away in front of them.'

He felt bleak now when he talked about it. 'They call it the bow wave,' he explained.

'The kind of jobs we have—' the receptionist began.

'You see some weird shit as a navigator. It looks like all these silvery eels, under the sea. Migrating. It's some kind of radiation, that was how it was explained to me, but you don't see it as that. Your life kind of leaks away as eels under the sea, and you watch it go. Afterwards,' Ed said, 'you can't work out why you'd do a job like that.' He looked at his hands. 'I surfed that wave and a few others too. Anyway, I can fly any kind of rocket. Except K-ships of course.'

The receptionist shook her head.

'I meant,' she said, 'can you do anything like stack crates, clean up after animals. That kind of work.' She consulted the terminal again and added: 'Or prophecy.'

Ed laughed. 'Pardon?'

She regarded him evenly.

'Telling the future,' she explained, as if to someone who didn't know the word but was bright enough to learn it.

Ed leaned forward and looked into the terminal.

'What is going on in there?' he said.

Her eyes were a confusing colour. Sometimes it was jade, sometimes the green of a salt wave; sometimes, somehow, both at once. There were dots of silver in her pupils which seemed ready to break up, drift away. Suddenly, she switched off the terminal and stood up as if she had to be somewhere else and had no more time to talk to Ed. Standing up, she seemed taller and younger, though some of it was shoes and she still had to look up to make eye contact. She wore a pale denim jacket with cowboy pockets and patterns of rhinestones, and a black patent-leather tube skirt. She smoothed the skirt across the front of her thighs and said: 'We're always on the lookout for a prophet.'

Ed shrugged. 'I was never interested in that,' he said. 'With me it was more a question of *not* knowing the future. You know?'

She gave him a sudden warm smile.

'I imagine it was,' she said. 'Well, talk to her. You never know.'

'Talk to who?'

The receptionist finished smoothing her skirt then went to the door. Her back swayed, balancing the big hair. This gave her an interesting gait, Ed thought, for an older person. Curiously enough, he seemed to remember that walk. He followed her out and stood at the top of the steps, shading his eyes. It was full morning now. Maritime light was spraying up off the naked concrete, maritime light and heat to daze and irritate the unwary.

'Talk to who?' he repeated.

'Madam Sandra,' she said, not turning round.

For some reason this name made him shiver. He watched the receptionist walk away across the site towards the Circus of Pathet Lao in its blinding white carnival tent.

'Hey! So where do I find her?' he called.

The receptionist kept walking.

'Madam Sandra finds you, Ed. She finds you.'

Later that morning he stood on the dunes looking out to sea. The light was harsh and violet. Little red-throat lizards scuttled through the marram at his feet. He could hear saltwater dub basslines, bumping away in some cocktail lounge further down the access road. In front of him a faded sign on a tilted wooden post in the sand announced 'Monster Beach'. You couldn't tell which direction it was pointing, but Ed thought it was straight up. He grinned. Beats me, he told himself; but he was thinking less of the beach sign than of the elusive Sandra Shen. He was hungry again. On his way back to Annie Glyph's room, he heard some sounds he recognised issuing from the bar of the deserted Dunes Motel, a clapboard box in a weedy oyster-shell lot a little apart from the motel itself.

Ed stuck his head round the open door, out of the frying light and into the cool gloom inside, where he found three skinny old men in white caps and bronze polyester pleat-front trousers too big for them, throwing dice onto a blanket on the floor.

'Hey,' said Ed. 'The Ship Game.'

They looked up at him without interest, down again immediately. Their eyes were like dark brown studs, the whites curded with age. Neat stained moustaches. Skin coffeed by sunlight. Thin big-veined hands which looked fragile but weren't. Lives lived out slower and slower, steeped in the preservative of Black Heart Rum. Eventually one of them said in a soft, distant voice:

'You to pay to play.'

'It's the narrative of capital,' Ed agreed, and reached in his pocket.

The Ship Game –

Also known as Entreflex or Gobetween, this full-on collision of jacks and craps – with its hair-trigger jargon, its bone pieces like dead men's knuckles, its twelve coloured characters nobody really knew the meaning of any more – was endemic. It was galaxy-wide. Some said it arrived with the New Men, aboard their flagship the *Remove All Packaging*. Some said it originated on the ancient trundling sublight ships of the Icenia Credit. It was a pastime which had seen many forms. In the present one, an ironic subtext to everything that happened in empty space, the characters, and the names the players gave them, were supposed to represent the notorious $N = 1000$ Engagement, an early human/Nastic encounter during which, faced by the sheer number of events and conditions

173

in fight-space – so many ships, so many dimensions to misappropriate, so much different physics to hide behind, so many nanosecond strategies in operation at once – the EMC admiral Stuart Kauffman abandoned the Tate-Kearney transformations and simply threw dice to decide his moves. Ed, who saw it less as a subtext than a source of income, had played the game all his adult life, the first ship he stowed away on to the last ship he jumped. The soft voices of the old men filled the bar.

'Give me an overend.'

'You don't want no overend. You fucked.'

'So tell me now, what you think to that?'

'I think you double-fucked.'

Ed laid down his money. He smiled across the blanket and bid Vegan Snake Eyes.

'That get you in the water,' acknowledged the old men.

He blew on the dice – they were heavy and cool to the touch, some smart alien bone that would leach the heat of your hand, the energy of motion, to change the characters as they fell. They scattered and tumbled. They jumped like grasshoppers. Symbols fluoresced briefly – interference patterns, ancient holographies blue, green and red – as they passed through a slanting bar of light. Ed thought he saw the Horse, the Tract, a clipper ship in a tower of cloud like smoke. Then the Twins, which gave him a sudden shiver. One of the old men coughed and reached for his rum. A few minutes later, when money began to change hands, there was a brusque but reverent air to each transaction.

Ed was at the circus for several days before anything happened. Annie Glyph came and went in her shy, calm way. She seemed pleased to see him at the end of her shift. She always had something for him. Always seemed a little surprised to find him still there. He grew used to her huge body moving behind the plastic shower curtain. She was so careful! Only at night, when she sweated out the *café électrique*, did he have to move away in case he got hurt.

'Do you like someone as big as me?' she would ask him. 'Everyone you've fucked, they were small and nice.'

This made him angry, but he didn't know how to tell her.

'You're OK,' he said. 'You're beautiful.'

She laughed and looked away.

'I have to keep the room empty,' she said, 'in case I break things.'

She was always gone in the morning. Ed woke late, ate breakfast at the Café Surf on the maritime strip, where he also got the news. War came closer every day. The Nastic were killing women and children off civilian ships. Who knew why? Space wrecks filled the holograms. Somewhere out near Eridani IV, children's clothes and domestic artefacts drifted slowly around in the vacuum as if they had been stirred. Some meaningless ambush, three freighters and an armed yawl, *La Vie Féerique*, destroyed. Crews and passengers, gas in eighty nanoseconds. You couldn't make anything of it. After he'd eaten, Ed combed the circus for work. He talked to a lot of people. They were well disposed, but none of them could help.

'It's important you meet Madam Shen first,' they said.

Looking for her became a game with him. Every day he picked someone new to represent her, some figure seen at a distance, sexually ambiguous, half-visible in the violent uplight from the concrete. In the evening he would pressure Annie Glyph with, 'Is she here today?' and Annie Glyph would only laugh.

'Ed, she's always busy.'

'But is she here today?'

'She has things to do. She's working on behalf of others. You'll meet her soon.'

'So, OK, look: is that her, over there?'

Annie was delighted.

'That's a man!'

'Well, is that her?'

'Ed, that's a *dog*!'

Ed enjoyed the bustle of the circus, but he couldn't understand the exhibits. He stood in front of 'Brian Tate and Michael Kearney' and felt only confused by the manic gleam in Kearney's eye as he stared at the monitor over his friend's shoulder, the oddness of Tate's gesture as he looked up and back, the beginnings of understanding dawning on his harassed features. Their clothes were interesting.

He did little better with the aliens. The huge bronze pressure tanks or mortsafes floating three or four feet off the ground with a kind of oily resilience – so that if you touched one of them, however lightly, you could feel it respond in a simple, massively Newtonian fashion – filled him with a kind of anxiety. He was afraid of their circuitry inlays, and the baroque ribs that might as easily have been decoration as machinery. He was afraid of the way they followed their keepers across the site in the distance in the deceptive sea-light at noon. In the end, he could rarely bring himself to look in the tiny armoured-glass window that enabled you to see the MicroHotep or Azul or Hysperon they were supposed to contain. They hummed silently, or gave off barely visible flashes of ionising radiation. He imagined that looking into them was like looking into some kind of telescope. They reminded him of the twink-tank. He was afraid of seeing himself.

When he admitted this to Annie Glyph, she laughed.

'You twinks are always afraid of seeing yourselves,' she said.

'Hey, I looked once,' he said. 'Once was enough. It was like there was a kitten in there, some kind of black kitten.'

Annie smiled ahead of herself at something invisible.

'You looked at yourself and saw a kitten?' she said.

He stared at her. 'What I mean,' he explained patiently, 'I looked into one of those brass things.'

'Still: a kitten, Ed. That's real cute.'

He shrugged.

'You could barely see anything at all,' he said. 'It could have been anything.'

Madam Shen was a daily no-show. Nevertheless Ed believed he could sense her out there: she would come in her own good time, and he would have employment. In the meantime he rose late, drank Black Heart from the bottle, and crouched with the old men on the floor of the bar at the Dunes Motel, listening to them talk their desultory talk as the dice tumbled and fell. Ed won more than he lost. Since he left home he was lucky that way. But he kept throwing the Twins and the Horse and in consequence his dreams became as unsettled as Annie's. The two of them sweated, thrashed, woke, took the only route they could out of there. 'Fuck me, Ed. Fuck me as hard as you like.' Ed was hooked on Annie by then. She was his bulwark against the world.

'Hey, concentrate. Or you playing catch-up now,' the old men told him gleefully.

If Annie worked late, he played that shift too. The old men never switched on the light in their empty bar. The neon glow of the Tract, seeping in through the open door, was light enough for them. Ed thought they were beyond most things younger people needed. He was shaking the dice one night about ten when a shadow fell across the game. He looked up. It was the receptionist. Tonight she wore a fringed, soft-washed denim skirt. Her hair was up, and she had that fishtank-looking terminal of hers clutched under one arm like some white goods item she just that moment bought. She looked down at the money on the blanket.

'Call yourselves gamblers?' she challenged the old men.

'Yes, we do!' was their unison reply.

'Well I don't,' she said. 'Give me those dice, I'll show you how to gamble.'

She took the bone in one small hand, flexed her wrist and threw it. Double Horses.

'You think that's something?'

She threw again. And again. Two Horses, six in a row.

'Well now,' she admitted. 'That's on the way to being something.'

This trick, clearly familiar, made the old men more animated than Ed had ever seen them. They laughed and blew on their fingers to indicate scorching. They nudged each other, they grinned at Ed.

'You'll see something now,' they promised.

But the receptionist shook her head. 'I haven't come to play,' she said. They were upset, she could see. 'It's just,' she explained, looking meaningfully at Ed, 'I've got other things to do tonight.' They nodded their heads as if they understood, then looked at their feet to hide their disappointment. 'But, hey,' she said, 'it's Black Heart rum at the Long Bar too, and you know how you like the girls down there. What do you say?'

The old men winked and grinned. They could be interested by that, they allowed, and filed out.

'Why you old goats!' the receptionist chided them.

'I'll come too,' Ed said. He didn't feel like being alone with her.

'You'll stay,' she advised him quietly. 'If you know what's good for you.'

After the old men had gone the room seemed to get darker. Ed stared at the receptionist and she stared back at him. Faint glimmers in the fishtank under her arm. She patted her hair. 'What sort of music do you like?' she said. Ed didn't answer. 'I listen to a lot of Oort Country,' she said, 'as you can probably tell. I like its grown-up themes.' They stood in silence again. Ed looked away, pretended to study the broken old bar furniture, the slatted shutters. A breeze came up off the dunes outside, fingered the objects in the room as if trying to decide what to do with them. After a minute or two, the receptionist said softly:

'If you want to meet her, she's here now.'

Ed felt the hairs rise on the back of his neck. He kept himself firmly facing away.

'I just need a job,' he said.

'And we have one for you,' said a different voice.

Tiny lights began to pour into the room from somewhere behind Ed. He knew where they must be coming from. Nothing would be gained by admitting it, though: an admission like that could fuck up everything. I've seen a lot, Ed told himself, but I don't want the shadow operators in my life. The receptionist had put the fishtank down on the floor. White motes were pouring from her nostrils, from her mouth and eyes. Something pulled Ed's head round so that like it or not he had to witness this event: give it form by recognising it. The lights were like foam and diamonds. They had some kind of music with them, like the sound of the algorithm itself. Soon enough there was no receptionist, only the operator that had been running her, now busily reassembling itself as the little oriental woman he had already shot on Yulgrave Street. The exchange was denim for slit cheongsam, Oort Country drawl for fiercely plucked eyebrows and the faintest delicate swallowing of consonants. After the transition was complete, her face shifted in and out of its own shadows, old then young, young then old. Strange then perfect. She had the charisma of some unreal alien thing, more powerful than sex though you felt it like that.

'Things here are truly fucked up,' Ed whispered. 'Lucky I can just run away.'

Sandra Shen smiled up at him.

'I'm afraid not, Ed,' she said. 'This isn't a tank parlour. There are consequences out here. Do you want the job or don't you?' Before he could answer this, she went on: 'If not, Bella Cray would like a word.'

'Hey, that's a threat.'

She shook her head fractionally. Ed looked down at her, trying to see what colour her eyes were. She smiled at his anxiety.

'Let me tell you something about yourself,' she suggested.

'Oh ho. Now we get to it. How you know all about me though you never saw me before?' He grinned. 'What's in the fishtank?' he said, trying to see past her to where it lay on the floor. 'I've wondered about that.'

'First things first. Ed, I'll tell you a secret about yourself. You're easily bored.'

Ed blew on his fingers to indicate scorching.

'Wow,' he said. 'That's something I never once thought of.'

'No,' she said. 'Not that boredom. Not the boredom you manage from a dipship or a twink-tank. You've been hiding the real boredom behind that your whole life.' Ed shrugged a little, tried to look away, but now her eyes held his somehow, and he couldn't. 'You have a bored soul, Ed; they handed it to you before you were born. Enjoy sex, Ed? It's to fill that hole. Enjoy the tank? It fills the hole. Prefer things edgy? You aren't whole, Ed: it's to fill you up, that's the story of it. Another thing anyone can see about you, even Annie Glyph: you have a piece missing.'

Ed had heard this more often than she thought, though usually in different circumstances he had to admit.

'So?' he said.

She stepped to one side.

'So now you can look in the fishtank.'

Ed opened his mouth. He closed it again. Suckered in some way he didn't follow. He knew he would do it, out of that very boredom she mentioned. He looked sideways in the light leaking through the open door. Kefahuchi light, which made Sandra Shen harder, not easier, to see. He opened his mouth to say something, but she got there first. 'The show needs a prophet, Ed.' She started to turn away. 'That's the opening. That's the deal. And you know, Annie could do with a little more cash. There's not much left after she scores the *café électrique.*'

Ed swallowed.

Sea shushing behind the dunes. An empty bar full of dust and Tract-light. A man kneels with his head inside some kind of fishtank, unable to pull himself free, as if whatever smoky yet gelid substance that fills it has clutched him and is already trying to digest him. His hands tug at the tank, his arm muscles bulge. Sweat pours off him in the shitty light, his feet kick and rattle against the floorboards, and – under the impression that he is screaming – he produces a faint, very high-pitched whining noise.

After some minutes this activity declines. The oriental woman lights an unfiltered cigarette, watching him intently. She smokes for a while, removes a shred of tobacco from her lip, then prompts him:

'What do you see?'

'Eels. Like eels swimming away from me.'

A pause. His feet drum the floor again. Then he says thickly: 'Too many things can happen. You know?'

The woman blows out smoke, shakes her head.

'It won't do for an audience, Ed. Try again.' She makes a complex gesture with her cigarette. 'All the things it might be,' she reminds him, as if she has reminded him before: 'the one thing it is.'

'But the *pain*.'

She doesn't seem to care about the pain. 'Go ahead.'

'Too many things can happen,' he repeats. 'You know.'

'I do know,' she says, in a more sympathetic voice. She bends down to touch his knotted shoulders briefly and absent-mindedly, like someone calming an animal. It's a kind of animal she knows very well, one with which she has considerable experience. Her voice is full of the sexual charisma of old, alien, made-up things. 'I do know, Ed, honestly. But try to see in more dimensions. Because this is circus, baby. Do you understand? It's entertainment. We've got to give them something.'

When Ed Chianese came to, it was three in the morning. Sprawled face down on the oceanside at the back of the Dunes Motel, he gently felt his face. It wasn't as sticky as he had expected: though the skin seemed smoother than usual and slightly sore, as if he had used cheap exfoliant before a night out. He was tired, but everything – the dunes, the tidewrack, the surf – looked and smelled and sounded very sharp. At first he thought he was alone. But there was Madam Shen, standing over him, her little black shoes sinking into the soft sand, the Tract burning up the night sky behind her.

Ed groaned. He closed his eyes. Vertigo was on him instantly, an after-image of the Tract pinwheeling against the nothing blackness.

'Why are you doing this to me?' he whispered.

Sandra Shen seemed to shrug. 'It's the job,' she said.

Ed tried to laugh. 'No wonder you can't fill it.'

He rubbed his face again, felt in his hair. Nothing. At the same time knew he would never get rid of the sensation of that stuff, sucking at him. And this was the thing about it: it wasn't actually *in* the tank. Or if it was it was somewhere else as well . . .

'What did I say? Did I say I'd seen anything?'

'You did well for your first lesson.'

'What *is* that stuff? Is it still on me? What's it done to me?'

She knelt briefly beside him, stroking his hair back from his forehead. 'Poor Ed,' she said. He felt her breath on his face. 'Prophecy!' she said. 'It's a black art yet, and you're at the forefront of it. But try and see it like this: everyone's lost. Ordinary people, they walk down the street, they've all had bad directions: everyone has to find their way. It's not so hard. They do it on a daily basis.'

For a moment it looked as if she might say something more. Then she patted him on the back, picked up the fishtank and trudged off with it under her arm, up over the dunes and back to the circus. Ed crawled away through the marram grass to where he could throw up quietly. He had bitten his tongue, he discovered, while he was trying to lever the fishtank off his head.

He had already made up his mind to try and forget the stuff he saw in there. That stuff made tank withdrawal seem like fun.

NINETEEN

Chimes of Freedom

After he left the laboratory, Michael Kearney was afraid to stop moving.

It began to rain. It got dark. Everything seemed to be surrounded by the pre-epileptic corona, a flicker like bad neon. A metallic taste filled his mouth. At first he ran around the streets, reeling with nausea, clutching park railings as he passed.

Then he blundered into Russell Square station, and thereafter took tube trains at random. The evening rush had just begun. Commuters turned to watch him squat in the crook of a dirty tiled passage or the corner of a platform, his shoulders hunched over protectively as he shook the Shrander's dice in the basket of his clasped hands; turned away quickly again when they saw his face or smelled the vomit on his clothes. After two hours in the Underground system his panic diminished: he found it hard to stop moving, but at least his heart rate had decreased and he could begin to think. On a swing back through the centre, he had a drink at the Lymph Club, kept it down, ordered a meal he couldn't eat. After that he walked a little more, then caught a Jubilee Line train to Kilburn, where Valentine Sprake lived at the end of a long street of inexpressive three-storey Victorian stock-brick houses, the rubbish-choked basement areas and boarded-up windows of which attracted a floating population of drug dealers, art students, economic refugees from the former Yugoslavia.

Political posters clung to the lamp-posts. None of the stained and rusty cars half up on the pavement among the wastepaper and dogshit were less than ten years old. Kearney knocked at Sprake's door, once, twice, then a third time. He stepped back and with the rain falling into his eyes called up at the front of the building. 'Sprake? Valentine?' His voice echoed off down the street. After a minute something drew his attention to one of the top floor windows. He craned his neck to look, but all he could see was a piece of grey net curtain and the reflection of the streetlight on the dirty glass.

Kearney put his hand out to the door. It swung inward, as if in response. Kearney stepped back suddenly.

'Jesus!' he said. 'Jesus!'

For a moment he had thought he saw a face peering round the door at him. It was smeared with streetlight, lower than you would expect to see a face, as if quite a young child had been sent to answer his knock.

Inside, nothing had changed. Nothing had changed since the 1970s, and nothing ever would. The walls were papered a yellowish colour like the soles of feet. Low wattage bulbs on timers allowed you twenty seconds of light before they plunged the stairs back into darkness. There was a smell of gas outside the bathroom, stale boiled food from the second floor rooms. Then aniseed everywhere, coating the membranes of the nose. Near the top of the stairwell a skylight let in the angry orange glare of the London night.

Valentine Sprake lay under a wash of fluorescent light, inside a chalk circle drawn on the bare floorboards of one of the upper rooms. He was sprawled up against an armchair, his head thrown back and to one side, as if he was at that moment being shot. He was naked, and he seemed to have covered himself with some sort of oil. It glistened in the sparse ginger hair between his legs. His mouth had fallen open, and the expression on his face was at once pained and restful. He was dead. His sister Alice sat on a broken sofa outside the circle, her legs out in front of her. Kearney remembered her in adolescence, slow-moving and vague. She had grown into a tall woman of thirty or so, with black hair, very white skin, and a faint downy moustache. Her skirt was drawn up to reveal white, fleshy thighs, and she was staring across Sprake's head at a picture on the opposite wall. From this strange cheap piece of religious art, a Gethsemane rendered stereoscopically in greens and bluish greys, the face and upper body of Christ yearned out into the room in a wrenched but determined gesture of embrace.

'Alice?' said Kearney.

Alice Sprake made a noise like, 'Yoiy. Yoiy yoiy.'

Kearney held his hand over his mouth and went a little further into the room.

'Alice, what happened here?'

She stared at him blankly; then down at herself; then back up at the picture on the wall. She began to masturbate absent-mindedly, working her fingers into her groin.

'Christ,' said Kearney.

He took another look at Sprake. Sprake was clutching an old electric kettle in one hand and a pamphlet edition of Yeats's *Hodos Chameleontos* in the other. A moment before, perhaps, he had been holding them up with his arms outspread in the hieratic gesture of a figure on a Tarot card. The floor in front of him was littered with objects that seemed to have fallen out of his lap as he died. Seashells, the skull of a small mammal: Serbian gypsy ornaments which had belonged to his mother. There was a feeling that something else was going to happen in the room. Despite the finality of what had already taken place, something else could easily happen.

Alice Sprake said: 'He was good boy.'

She groaned loudly. The broken springs of the sofa creaked and were silent. After a moment she got to her feet and smoothed her skirt down over her thighs. She was six feet tall, Kearney thought, perhaps more. Her great size had a calming effect on him, and she seemed aware of that. She smelled powerfully of sex.

'I will see to this, Mikey,' she said. 'But you must go.'

'I came because I needed his help.'

The idea seemed to give her no satisfaction.

'It is your fault that he is like this. Ever since he met you he has been mad. He was going to do wonderful things with his life.'

Kearney stared at her.

'Sprake?' he said in disbelief. 'Are you talking about Sprake?' He started to laugh. 'The day we met he was a fuck-up in a railway carriage. *He did tattoos on himself with a Bic pen.*'

Alice Sprake drew herself up.

'He was one of the five most powerful magicians in London,' she said simply. Then she added: 'I know what you are afraid of. If you don't go now I will send it after you.'

'No!' said Kearney.

He had no idea what she might be able to do. He stared panickily from her to the dead man, then ran out of the room, down the stairs and into the street.

Anna was asleep when he let himself back into the flat. She had wound herself in the duvet so that only the top of her head showed, and there were new notes everywhere. *Other people's problems are their own*, she had tried to remind herself: *You aren't responsible for other people's problems.*

Kearney went quietly into the back room and began to empty the chest of drawers, stuffing clothes, books, packs of cards and personal items into his Marin courier bag in the dark. The room looked out on to the central well of the block. Kearney hadn't been in there long when he began to hear voices echoing up from one of the lower floors. It sounded like a man and a woman arguing, but he couldn't make out any words, only a feeling of loss and threat. He got up off his knees and drew the curtains. The voices seeped in anyway. When he had what he wanted, he tried to zip up the bag.

The zip caught. He looked down. The bag and everything in it was covered in a thick soft even layer of dust. This image gave him such a sense of his life draining away that he was filled with terror again. Anna woke up in the other room.

'Michael?' she said. 'Is that you? That's you isn't it?'

'Go to sleep,' Kearney advised her. 'I just came for some things.'

There was a pause while she assimilated this. Then she said:

'I'll make you a cup of tea. I was just going to make tea but I fell asleep. I was so exhausted I just fell asleep.'

'There's no need to do that,' he said.

He heard the bed creak as she got up. She came and leaned in the doorway in her long cotton nightdress, yawning and rubbing her face. 'What are you doing?' she said. She must have smelt the vomit on the front of his jacket, because she said: 'Have you been ill?' She switched the light on suddenly. Kearney made a futile gesture with the bag in his hand. They stood there blinking at each other.

'You're leaving.'

'Anna,' Kearney said, 'it's for the best.'

'How can you bloody say that!' she shouted. 'How can you bloody say it's for the best?'

Kearney began to speak, then shrugged.

'I thought you were going to stay! Yesterday you said this was good, you said it was good.'

'We were fucking, Anna. I said that was good.'

'I know. I know. It *was* good.'

'I said it was good fucking you, that's all,' he said. 'That was all I meant.'

She slid down in the doorway and sat with her knees drawn up.

'You let me feel as if you were going to stay.'

'You did that yourself,' Kearney tried to persuade her.

She stared up at him angrily. 'You wanted it too,' she insisted. 'You practically said as much to me.' She sniffed, wiped her eyes with the back of her hand. 'Oh well,' she said. 'Men are always so stupid and frightened.' She shivered suddenly. 'Is it cold in here?

I'm awake now anyway. At least have some tea. It won't take a minute.'

It took longer. Anna fussed about. She wondered if there was enough milk. She began the washing up, then abandoned it. She left Kearney to finish the tea while she went into the bathroom and ran the taps. After that he heard her rooting about somewhere else in the flat. Drawers opened and closed. 'I saw Tim the other day,' she called. This was so transparent Kearney didn't bother to answer. 'He remembered you.' Kearney stood in the kitchen, staring at the things on the shelves and drinking the weak Earl Grey he had made. He kept hold of the courier bag, feeling that if he put it down he would weaken his position. Every so often a wave of anxiety licked over him, starting somewhere deep in the brainstem, as if some very old part of him could detect the Shrander long before Kearney himself heard or saw it.

'I've got to go,' he said. 'Anna?'

He emptied his cup into the sink. When he got to the door she was already there, standing so he couldn't open it. She had dressed for going out, in a big cable-knit cardigan and fake Versace skirt, and there was a bag at her feet. She saw him looking down at it. 'If you can go I can go too,' she said. Kearney shrugged and reached over her shoulder for the knob of the Yale lock.

'*Why* don't you trust me?' she said, as if it was already established that he didn't.

'It isn't anything like that.'

'Oh yes it is. I try to help you –'

He made an impatient gesture.

'– only you won't let me.'

'Anna,' he said quickly, 'I help *you*. You're a drunk. You're anorexic. You're ill most days, and on a good day you can barely walk down the pavement. You're always in a panic. You barely live in the world we know.'

'You bastard.'

'So how can you help?'

'I'm not letting you go without me,' she said. 'I'm not letting you open this door.'

She struggled against him.

'Jesus, Anna.'

He got the door open and pushed past her. She caught up with him on the stairs and held on to the collar of his jacket and wouldn't let go even when he started to drag her down the stairs.

'I hate you,' she said.

He stopped and stared at her. They were both panting.

'Why are you doing this, then?'

She hit him in the face.

'Because you have no idea!' she shouted. 'Because no one else will help you. Because you're the useless one, the damaged one. Are you so stupid you can't see that? Are you so stupid?'

She let go of his coat and sat down suddenly. She glanced up at him, then away again. Tears poured down her face. Her skirt had ridden up as she fell, and he found himself staring at her long, thin thighs as if he had never seen her before. When she saw that, she blinked her tears away and pulled the skirt up further. 'Christ,' Kearney whispered. He turned her over and pushed her into the cold stone stairs, while she pushed back hard against his hand, sniffing and crying throughout.

When, ten minutes later, he dragged himself away and walked off towards the tube station, she simply followed.

He had met her in Cambridge, perhaps two years after he stole the dice. He was looking for someone to murder, but Anna took him to her room instead. There he sat on the bed while she opened a bottle of wine, showed him photographs of her most recent brush with anorexia, walked nervously about in a long cardigan and nothing else. She told him: 'I like you but I don't want to have sex. Is that all right?' It was all right with Kearney, who – constrained by the Gorselands fantasies and worn out by the evasions he normally had to practise on these occasions – often found himself saying much the same thing. Every time the cardigan fell open thereafter, he gave her a vague smile and looked politely away. This only seemed to make her more nervous. 'Will you just sleep next to me?' she begged him when it was time to go. 'I really like you but I'm not ready for sex.' Kearney spent an hour stretched out next to her, then, at perhaps three in the morning, left the bed and masturbated violently into the bathroom sink. 'Are you all right?' she called in a muffled, sleepy voice.

'You're so nice,' she said, when he came back. 'Hug me.'

He stared at her in the dark. 'Were you even asleep?' he said. 'Please.'

She rolled against him. As soon as he touched her, she groaned and pulled away, raising her behind in the air and burying her face in the pillow while he manipulated her with one hand and himself with the other. At first she tried to join in, but he wouldn't let her touch him. He kept her at the edge of coming, breathing in great sobbing gasps, whimpering into the pillow between each breath. He watched her like this until watching her had made him so hard again his cock hurt. Finally he brought her off with two or three quick little circular rubs and let himself come on to the small of her back. Gorselands had never seemed so close. He had never felt so in control. Engineering that, he supposed, was her way of feeling in control. With her face still in the pillow she said:

'I really didn't mean to do that right up until I did it.'

'Didn't you?' said Kearney.

'You've made me very sticky.'

'Stay there, stay there,' he ordered her, 'don't move,' and fetched tissue to wipe her dry.

He went everywhere with her after that. He was attracted by her cleverly chosen clothes, sudden bursts of laughter, dissembled narcissism. At nineteen, her fragility was already obvious. She had a confusing relationship with her father – some kind of academic in the north – who had wanted her to attend a university closer to home. 'He's sort of disowned me,' she said, looking up at Kearney with a soft, dawning surprise, as if it had just happened. 'Can you understand why anyone would do that?' She had tried to kill herself twice. Her friends, in the way students are, were almost proud of this; they took care of her. Kearney, they intimated fiercely, had responsibilities too. Anna herself seemed only embarrassed: forgotten for a minute, though, she began to waste away. 'I don't think I'm eating much,' she would say helplessly on the telephone. She had the air of someone the simplest levels of whose personality must be held together, hands on, daily.

Kearney was drawn to her by all that (not to say by a species of deep gallantry he detected in her, the presence at some level beneath all these gestures of panic and self-defeat, of a woman determined to have what life her demons would allow). But it was her way of having sex that kept him there. If Kearney wasn't precisely a voyeur, Anna wasn't quite an exhibitionist. Neither of them ever knew quite what they were. They were a mystery to one another.

Eventually that in itself would enrage them: but those early encounters were like water in a desert. They married in a register office two days after he got his doctorate – he bought for the occasion a Paul Smith suit. They were together ten years after that. They never had children, though she said she wanted them. He saw her through two stretches of therapy, three more bouts of anorexia, a last, almost nostalgic attempt to do away with herself. She watched him follow the funding from university to university, doing what he called 'MacScience' for the corporates, keeping track of the new discipline of complexity and emergent properties, all the time staying ahead of the game, the Shrander, the body count. If she suspected anything, she never spoke. If she wondered why they moved so often, she never said. In the end he told her everything one night, sitting on the edge of her bed at the Chelsea and Westminster hospital, staring down at her bandaged wrists and wondering how they had come to this.

She laughed and took his hands in hers. 'We're stuck with each other now,' she said, and within the year they were divorced.

TWENTY

Three Body Problem

Two days out from Redline, and the *White Cat* was changing course every twelve nanoseconds. Dyne-space enfolded the ship in a figured, incalculable blackness, out of which reached the caressing fingers of weakly reacting matter. The shadow operators hung motionless at the portholes whispering to one another in the old languages. They had taken on their usual form, of women biting their knuckles in regret. Billy Anker wouldn't have them near him. 'Hey,' he said, '*we* don't know what they want!' He tried to exclude them from the human quarters, but they crept in like smoke while he was asleep and hung up in the corners watching him dream his exhausted dreams.

Seria Mau watched him too. She knew that she would soon have to have his account of himself, and of the object she had bought from Uncle Zip. Meanwhile she spent her time with the ship's mathematics, trying to understand what was going on behind them, where, several lights adrift, the *Krishna Moire* pod wove itself chaotically round the curious hybrid signature of the Nastic ship, to make a single, watery, undependable trace in the display.

'It's hard to feel threatened, when they stay back so far.'

'Perhaps they don't want us to panic,' the mathematics suggested. 'Or –' with its equivalent of a shrug '– perhaps they do.'

'Can we lose them?'

'Their computational success is high, but not as high as mine. With luck, I can keep them at arm's length.'

'But can we lose them?'

'No.'

She couldn't bear that idea. It was a limitation. It was like being a child again. '*Well then, do something!*' she screamed. After some thought the mathematics put her to sleep, which for once she welcomed.

She dreamed again of the time they were all still happy. 'Let's go away!' the mother said. 'Would you like to go away?' Seria Mau clapped her hands, while her brother ran up and down the family room, shouting, 'Let's go away! Let's go away!' though when the time came he threw a tantrum because he couldn't take his little black cat. They caught the Rocket Train north, to Saulsignon. It was a long journey in a lost season – not quite winter, not quite spring – slow and exciting by turns. 'If it's a Rocket Train it should go faster!' the little boy shouted, running up and down the aisle. The sky was a stretched blue over long hypnotic lines of plough. They got down at Saulsignon the afternoon of the next day. It was the tiniest of stations, with wrought iron posts and tubs of Earth flowers, washed bright as a new pin by the little showers of rain falling through the sunlight. The platform cat licked its tortoiseshell fur in a corner, the Rocket Train departed, and a white cloud obscured the sun. Outside the station a man walked by. When he stopped to look back, the mother shivered and wrapped her honey-coloured fur coat about her, drawing its collar tight with one long white hand.

Then she laughed and the sun came out again. 'Come along, you two!' And there, moments later it seemed, was the sea!

Here the dream ended. Seria Mau waited attentively for the reprise, or second act, in which the conjuror would appear, dressed in his beautiful top hat and tails. When nothing happened she was disappointed. As soon as she woke up she switched on all the lights in the human quarters. The shadow operators, caught bending solicitously over Billy Anker's bed in the dark, fled right and left.

'Billy Anker,' Seria Mau called. 'Wake up!'

A few minutes later he stood blinking and rubbing his eyes in front of the Dr Haends package in its red gift box.

'This?' he said.

He looked puzzled. He poked about behind the box. He picked up one of Uncle Zip's roses and sniffed it. He raised the lid of the box cautiously (a bell chimed, a soft spotlight seemed to shine down from above) and eyed the upwelling and slow purposive spill of white foam. The bell chimed again. A female voice whispered, 'Dr Haends. Dr Haends, please.' Billy Anker scratched his head. He put the lid back on the box. He took it off again. He reached out to touch the white stuff with his finger.

'Don't do that!' warned Seria Mau.

'Shh,' said Billy Anker absently, but he had thought better of it. 'I look inside,' he said, 'and I don't see anything. Do you?'

'There's nothing to see.'

'Dr Haends to surgery, please,' insisted the quiet voice.

Billy Anker cocked his head to listen, then closed the box. 'I never saw anything like this before,' he said. 'Of course, we don't know what Uncle Zip did to it.' He straightened up. Cracked the knuckles of his undamaged hand. 'It didn't look like this when I found it,' he said. 'It looked the way K-tech always looks. Small. Slippery but compact.' He shrugged. 'Packaged in those slinky metals they had back then, beautiful like a shell. It didn't have these theatrical values.' He smiled in a way she didn't understand, looking off into the distance. 'That's Uncle Zip's signature, if you like,' he said, in a bitter voice. Seria Mau's fetch wove nervously around his ankles.

'Where did you find it?' she said.

Instead of answering Billy Anker sat down on the deck to get more on a level with her. He looked perfectly comfortable there, in his two leather jackets and three-day stubble. He stared into the fetch's eyes for a while, as if he was trying to see through to the real Seria Mau, then surprised her by saying:

'You can't outrun EMC forever.'

'It's not me they're after,' she reminded him.

'All the same,' he said, 'they'll catch you in the end.'

'Look around at these million stars. See anything you like? It's easy to lose yourself out here.'

'You're already lost,' Billy Anker said. 'I admire that you stole a K-ship,' he went on quickly: 'Who wouldn't? But you're lost, and you aren't finding yourself. Anyone can see that. You're doing the wrong thing. You know?'

'How come you say these things?' she shouted. 'How come you make me feel bad like this?'

He couldn't answer that.

'What's the right thing to do, Billy Anker? Beach my ship on some shithole and wear two coats that creak? Oh, and be big about how I'm not a refund kind of guy?' She regretted saying this immediately. He looked hurt. From the start he had reminded her of someone. It wasn't his clothes, or all the rigmarole with the antique consoles and obsolete technology. It was his hair, she thought. Something about his hair. She kept looking at him from different angles, trying to remember who it brought to mind. 'I'm sorry,' she said, 'I don't know you well enough to say that.'

'No,' he said.

'I was wrong,' she said, after she had left him a pause which he didn't fill. 'It was wrong of me.'

She had to be content with a shrug.

'So. What then? What should I do? You tell me, you with your emotional intelligence you're clearly so proud of.'

'Take this ship deep,' he said. 'Take it to the Tract.'

'I don't know why I'm talking to you, Billy Anker.'

He laughed.

'I had to try,' he said. He said, 'OK, so this is how I found the package. First, you got to know a little about K-tech.'

She laughed.

'Billy Anker, what can *you* tell *me* about that?' He went on anyway.

Two hundred years before, humanity stumbled over the remains of the oldest halo culture of all. It was thinly represented compared to some, scattered across fifty cubic lights and half a dozen planets, with outstations huddled so close to the Tract it soon became known as the Kefahuchi Culture or K-culture. There was no clue what these people looked like, though from their architecture you could tell they were short. The ruins were alive with code, which turned out to be some kind of intelligent machine interface.

Working technological remains, sixty-five million years old.

No one knew what to do with it. The research arm of Earth Military Contracts arrived. They threw a cordon round what they called the 'affected area' and, working out of hastily thrown-up colonies of pressurised sheds, modified tools from various strains of shadow operator, which they ran on nano- and biotech substrates. With these they tried to manipulate the code direct. It was a disaster. Conditions in the sheds were brutal. Researchers and experimental subjects alike lived on top of the containment facilities. 'Containment' was another meaningless EMC word. There were no firewalls, no masks, nothing above a Class IV cabinet. Evolution ran at virus speeds. There were escapes, unplanned hybrids. Men, women and children, shipped in down the Carling Line from the branded prison hulks orbiting Cor Caroli, accidentally ingested the substrates, then screamed all night and in the morning spoke in tongues. It was like having a wave of luminous insects spill out of the machine, run up your arm and into your mouth before you could stop them. There were outbreaks of behaviour so incomprehensible it had to be an imitation of the religious rituals of the K-culture itself. Dancing. Sex and drugs cults. Anthemic chanting.

After the Tampling-Praine Outbreak of 2293, which escaped the halo and infected parts of the galaxy itself, attempts to deal directly with the code, or the machinery it controlled, were abandoned. The big idea after that was to contain it and connect the human operator via a system of buffers and compressors, cybernetic and biological, which mimicked the way human consciousness dealt with its own raw eleven-million-bit-a-second sensory input. The dream of a one-to-one realtime link with the mathematics faded, and, a generation after the original discoveries, EMC installed what they had into hybridised ships, drives, weapons and – especially – navigational systems which had last run sixty-five million years before.

The pressure-sheds were demolished, and the lives of the people in them quietly forgotten.

K-tech was born.

'So?' said Seria Mau. 'This is not news.'

She knew all this, but was embarrassed to hear it spoken out loud. She felt some guilt for all those dead people. She laughed. 'None of this is news to my life,' she said. 'You know?'

'I know,' said Billy Anker. He went on:

'EMC was born in those pressure-sheds, too. Before that you had a loose cartel of security corporations, designed so the neo-liberal democracies could blame subcontractors for any police action that got out of hand. So all those boyish decent-looking presidents could make eye contact with you out of the hologram display and claim in those holy voices of theirs, "We don't make the wars," and then have "terrorists" killed in numbers. After K-tech, well, EMC *became* the democracies: look at that little shit we just talked to.' He grinned. 'But here's the good news. K-tech has run out. For a while, it was a gold rush. There was always something new. The early prospectors were picking stuff up with their bare hands. But by the time Uncle Zip's generation came along, there was nothing left. Now they're adding refinements to refinements, but only at the human interface. They can't build new code, or back-engineer those original machines.

'Do you understand? We don't have a technology here. We have alien artefacts: a resource mined until it ran out.' He looked around him, gestured to indicate the *White Cat.* 'This may have been one of the last of them,' he said. 'And we don't even know what it was for.'

'Hey, Billy Anker,' she said. '*I* know what it's for.'

He looked her fetch in the eye and she felt less sure.

'K-tech has run out,' he repeated.

'If that's a good thing, why are you so pissed off?'

Billy Anker got up and walked about to stretch his legs. He had another look at the Dr Haends package. Then he came back to her and knelt down again.

'Because I found a whole planet of it,' he said.

Silence strung itself out like packets in a wire in the human quarters of the ship. Under the dim fluorescent lights the shadow operators whispered to one another, turning their faces to the wall. Billy Anker sat on the floor scratching the calf of one leg. His shoulders were hunched, his stubbled face set in creases as habitual as the creases in his leather coats. Seria Mau watched him intently. Every tiny camera drifting in the room gave her a different view.

'Ten years ago,' he said, 'I was obsessed with the Sigma End wormhole. I wanted to know who put it there, how they did it. More than that, I wanted whatever was at the other end of it. I wasn't alone. For a year or two, every hot guy with a theory was hanging off the edge of the accretion disc, doing what he called "science" from some piece of junk he'd salvaged further down the Beach. A lot of them ended up as plasma.' He laughed softly. 'A thousand sky-pilots, entradistas, madmen. Amazing guys like Liv Hula and Ed Chianese. At that time we all thought Sigma End was the gateway to the Tract. I was the one found out it wasn't.'

'How?'

Billy Anker chuckled. His whole face changed.

'I went down it,' he said.

She stared at him. 'But . . .' she said. She thought of everyone who had died trying that.

She said: 'Didn't you care?'

He shrugged. 'I wanted to know,' he said.

'Billy Anker—'

'Oh, it's no way to travel,' he said. 'It broke me. It broke the ship. That weird twist of light just hangs like a crack in nowhere. You can barely see it against the stars: but shoot through and it's like—' He examined his damaged hand. 'Who knows what it's like? Everything changes. Things happened in there I can't describe. It was like being a kid again, some bad dream of running down an endless hallway in the dark. I heard things I still can't give a meaning to, filtering through the hull. But, hey, I was out there! You know?' The memory of it made him rock to and fro with excitement where he sat. He looked twenty years younger than when she woke him up. The lines had vanished from round his mouth. His greeny-grey eyes, harder to bear than usual, were lighted from inside by his joke, his hidden narrative, his fierce construction of himself; at the same time they made him seem vulnerable and human. 'I was somewhere no entradista had ever been before. I was in front, for the first time. Can you imagine that?'

She couldn't.

She thought: If you can't stop yourself trying to attract people this way, Billy Anker, it's because you have no self-esteem. We want a human being, all you dare show us is the Jack of Hearts. Then suddenly she realised who he reminded her of. The ponytail, if it had still been black; the thin dark-skinned face, if it hadn't been so tired, so burned out by the rays of distant suns: neither would have looked out of place at the tailorshop party on Henry Street in downtown Carmody, in the soft humid night of Motel Splendido –

'You're one of Uncle Zip's clones,' she said.

At first she thought this would shock him into saying something new. But he only grinned and shrugged it off. 'The personality didn't take,' he said. A complex expression crossed his face.

'*He made you for this.*'

'He wanted a replacement. His entradista days were over. He thought the child would follow the father. But I'm my own man,' Billy Anker said. He blinked. 'I say that to everyone, but it's true.'

'Billy—'

'Don't you want to know what I found?'

'Of course I do,' she said. She didn't care one way or another at that moment, she was so chilled by his fate. 'Of course I do.'

He was silent for a time. Once or twice he started to speak, but language seemed to fail him. Finally he began:

'That place: it butts up against the Tract so tight you can practically *hear* the rush and roar of it. You fall out the wormhole, toppling end over end, all your control systems redlined, and there it is. Light. Deep light. Fountains, cascades, falling curtains of light. All the colours you can imagine and some you can't. Shapes they used to see through optical telescopes, in the old days back on Earth. You know? Like gas clouds, and clouds of stars, but evolving there in human time in front of you. Building and falling like surf.' He was silent again, looking inside himself as if he'd forgotten she was there. Eventually he said: 'And you know, it's small, that place. Some used-up old moon they sent down the wormhole for their own purposes. No atmosphere. You can make out the curve of the horizon. And bare. Just white dust on a surface like a cement floor . . .

'A cement floor,' he whispered. 'You hear the K-code resonating in it like the sound of a choir.' He raised his voice. 'Oh, I didn't stay,' he said. 'I wasn't up to it. I saw that at once. I was too scared to stay. I could feel the code, humming in the fabric, I could hear the light pour over me. I could feel the Tract at my back, like something watching. I couldn't believe they would drive a wormhole through to somewhere so insane. I grabbed a few things – just like the old prospectors, the first few things I saw – and I got out of there as fast as I could.'

He jerked his thumb over his shoulder at the Haends package. 'That was one of them,' he said. After a moment he shivered. 'I got the *Karaoke Sword* off the moon, but it was a long time before I could go anywhere. We just hung there in the wash of light. Even the ship felt a kind of terror. I couldn't make myself enter the wormhole again. A wormhole is a lottery. It's a one-shot thing, even for a man like me. In the end I took absolute navigational fixes – fixes from the standing gravity wave, also fixes I was less certain of, from the anisotropy of the whole universe – to find out where I was. Then I came back the long way round, by dynaflow. I was broke, so I got together a few of the things I'd found, and sold them on. It was a mistake. After that I knew everyone in the galaxy would want to know what I knew. I hid up.'

'But you could find the place again,' said Seria Mau. She held her breath.

'Yes,' he said.

'Then take me there, Billy Anker. Take me to that planet!'

He looked down at his hands, and after a time shook his head. 'It's important we don't lead them there,' he said. 'You can see that.' He held up his hand to forestall her arguments. 'But that's not the reason. Oh, I'd take you there despite them, because I can tell how much that package means to you. Between you and me and the *White Cat*, we might lose them on the way—'

'Then why not take me? Why?'

'Because it's no place for you or me.'

Seria Mau walked her fetch away from him and through a bulkhead. Billy Anker looked surprised. The next time he heard her voice, it was the ship's voice. It came from all around him. 'I see right through you, Billy Anker,' she said. She tut-tutted mildly. 'All this talk about leaving the Beach, and you're too scared to swim.'

He looked angry then stubborn. 'That's no place for human beings,' he insisted.

'I'm not a human being!'

He smiled. His face lit up softly and shed the years, and she saw he was his own man after all.

'Oh yes you are,' he said.

TWENTY-ONE

War

Ed Chianese continued his training as a visionary.

Madam Shen liked to work in the Observatorium, preferably among the tableaux themselves. She had a personal fondness for 'Brian Tate and Michael Kearney Looking Into a Monitor in 1999'. Ed, made nervous by the fixed gazes and untrustworthy expressions of the two ancient scientists, felt more comfortable in the front office, or the bar at the Dunes Motel.

His tutor remained unpredictable. Sometimes she came as herself; sometimes as the receptionist with her Dolly Parton tits and Oort Country chat; sometimes as an ill-tempered hermaphrodite carnie called Harryette who wore black singlets to show off the points of her little breasts, often teaming them with colored spandex tights which bulged alarmingly at the crotch. Sometimes she didn't come at all, and Ed could go back to throwing dice on the blanket. (Though now he had begun to lose regularly. You forfeit your luck when you start trying to see the future in this life, the old men told him, cackling dutifully as they sheafed up his money.) Whoever she came as, Sandra Shen was short. She wore short skirts. She smoked the short local cigarettes of tobacco and bat guano, oval in cross-section, acrid in use. He tried to think of her as a human being: never got to know her well. She wasn't young any more, he was certain of that. 'I'm tired, Ed,' she would complain. 'I've been doing this too long.' She didn't say what, though he took her to mean the Circus of Pathet Lao.

Her moods were as unpredictable as her appearance. One day, pleased with his progress, she would promise him a show of his own – 'A main tent show, Ed. A real show'. The next she would shake her head, throw away her cigarette and say in a voice of professional disgust:

'A kiddie sees better futures than you. I can't sell them this.'

One afternoon at the Dunes she told him, 'You're a true visionary, Ed. That's your tragedy.'

They had been working for perhaps an hour, and Ed, slumped in one corner so tired he thought he could feel himself slipping down through the floor, had prised the fishtank off his head for a breather. Outside, the seabirds croaked and wheeled over the beach. Harsh violet light fell between the slatted louvres and sliced Sandra Shen's emerald green cheongsam into the uneasy colouration of some jungle predator. She lifted a shred of tobacco from her lower lip. Shook her head.

'It's my tragedy too,' she admitted. 'Mine too.'

If Ed had hoped to learn something from her about the process itself, he was wrong. She seemed as confused by it as he was.

'What I want to know,' he said, 'is what my head's in.'

'Forget the *tank*, Ed,' she said. 'There's nothing in there. That's what I want you to understand: nothing there at all.' When she saw how this failed to reassure him, she seemed at a loss. Once she said, 'Never forget: with prophecy you find your own heart at the heart of it.' Finally she recommended: 'You've got to duck and dive in there. It's a full-on Darwinian environment. You've got to be quick to bring back the goods.'

Ed shrugged.

'That *so* doesn't describe the experience,' he told her.

He really didn't know what happened to him when his head was in the fishtank, but he knew it wasn't anything as twitchy or aggressive as that. He thought that was her temperament showing. As a description it revealed more about her than it did about prophecy. 'Anyway,' he told her, 'direction was always the difficulty with me. Speed was never a problem.'

He added, for no reason he could see: 'My dreams have been bad lately.'

'Things are tough all over, Ed.'

'Thanks a lot.'

Sandra Shen grinned at him. 'Talk to Annie,' she advised. A few white motes seemed to drift out of her eyes. Unsure whether this was menace or a joke, he put his head back in the tank so he didn't have to watch. After a moment he heard her say:

'I'm sick of selling the past, Ed. I want to start on the future.'

'Do I say anything when I'm in here?'

The more he worked with the fishtank, the worse Ed's dreams became.

Space, but not empty. A kind of inchoate darkness wrapped over itself like the bow wave of the Alcubiere warp but worse than any of that. The cold water of a meaningless unsalted sea, the information supersubstance, substrate of some universal algorithm. Lights which shivered and writhed away from him in shoals. This was the work Sandra Shen had given him, prophecy, or the failure of prophecy, nothing revealed, a journey that went on forever, then stopped quite suddenly to leave him looking down on things from above.

Bits and pieces of landscape, but notably a house. There would be some damp countryside, a pretty old railway station, hedges, a field tipped up at an angle, then this house, dour, four-faced, made of stone. There was a sense that these items had assembled themselves only a moment before. But that they were – or had been – in some sense real, he had no doubt. He always approached the house from above like that, and from an angle, as if arriving by plane: a tall house with a roof of purple grey slate, Flemish gables, extensive gloomy gardens in which the laurels and lawns were always wintered. White birch trees grew a little way away. It was often raining, or misty. It was dawn. It was late afternoon. After a moment or two, Ed found himself entering the house, and at that point he was woken up by the tail end of his own despairing cry.

'Hush,' said Annie Glyph. 'Hush, Ed.'

'I remember things I haven't seen,' Ed cried out.

He clung to her, listening to her heart, which beat thirty times a minute or less. It was always there to reclaim him, that huge dependable heart, to fetch him out of the standing wave of his own terror. On the down side, it soothed him almost instantly back into unconsciousness, where one night the dream moved on and he was the one place he didn't want to be. Inside the house. He saw stairs. *'Waraaa!'* he shouted, ambushing his sister in the hall. She dropped the lunch tray and the two of them stared down silently at the mess. A boiled egg rolled away and into a corner. It was too late to help. He looked into his sister's face, full of some rage he couldn't name. He ran away, shouting.

'After she left, our father stood on the kitten,' he told Annie next morning. 'It died. He didn't mean that to happen. But that was when I made up my mind I'd leave too.'

She smiled. 'Travel the galaxy,' she said.

'Fly the ships,' he said.

'Have all the pussy you could find.'

'That and more,' Ed said with a grin.

He sat for a minute after Annie had gone to work, thinking:

That was the black kitten I remembered, then: but there was more to it than that. Before the sister went away. He thought he saw a river, a woman's face. Fingers trailed in water. A voice saying delightedly but far off:

'Aren't we lucky? Aren't we lucky to have this?'

We were all together then, Ed thought.

Ed did his first show in a tuxedo.

Thereafter, for obvious reasons, he would favour a cheap blue boiler suit made of easily washable fabrics: but the first time he was resplendent. They built a cramped little stage for him, between 'Brian Tate and Michael Kearney Looking Into a Monitor in 1999' and 'Toyota Previa with Clapham Schoolchildren, 2002', lighting it with racks of antique coloured spots and some careful holographic effects designed to maintain the theme. In the centre of the stage Ed had the bare wooden chair on which he would sit while he used the fishtank; also a microphone as old as the lights.

'It won't actually be connected to anything,' Harryette said. 'We'll handle the sound in the usual way.'

The hermaphrodite seemed nervous. She had fussed around all afternoon. She specialised in stage management, and was always describing how she had worked her way up to it from being an ordinary stagehand. It was Harryette who had insisted on the tuxedo. 'We want you to seem commanding,' she said. She was proud of her ideas. Privately, Ed thought they bordered on the fatuous. With her shaved head, live tattoos and thatch of reddish armpit hair, he thought she was the least appealing of Sandra Shen's manifestations. He kept wanting to say, 'Look, you're a shadow operator, you could run on anything. So why this?' but he couldn't find the right moment. Also he wasn't sure how an algorithm would take that sort of criticism. Meanwhile he had to listen to her explain, as she indicated the tableaux on each side of the tiny stage:

'We site ourselves on the cusp like this to exploit suggestions of impermanence and perpetual change.'

'I can see we'd want to do that.' Ed said.

He didn't see why they had to have the hologram backdrop of the Kefahuchi Tract, shimmering away behind the stage as if projected on a satin curtain. But when he asked Harryette about it, she changed the subject immediately, morphing into Sandra Shen and advising him: 'What you've got to recognise, Ed, is that they want you dead. All prophecy is a sending-on-before. The audience need you to be dead for them.'

Ed stared at her.

On the night, he wasn't sure what the audience wanted from him. They filed into the performance space in a kind of rustling hush, a broad sample of New Venusport life. There were corporates from the enclaves, dressed in careful imitation of the tableaux in the offstage shadows; geeks and cultivars from Pierpoint Street; little perfect port prostitutes smelling of vanilla and honey; rickshaw girls, tank addicts, eight-year-old gun punks and their accountants. There were quite a few New Men with their pliable-looking, etiolated limbs and inappropriate facial expressions. They were quieter than a circus audience ought to be, they had bought less food and drink than Ed had expected. They were ominously attentive. They didn't look as if they wanted him dead. He sat on the wooden chair in his tuxedo in the coloured spotlight and stared out at them. He felt hot and a bit sick. His clothes felt too tight.

'Ah,' he said.

He coughed.

'Ladies and gentlemen,' he said. Rows of white faces stared at him. 'The future. What is it?'

He couldn't think of anything to add to that, so he bent forward, picked up the fishtank, which had been placed on the floor between his feet, and set it on his lap. Ed's duty was to see. It was to speak. He had no idea if prophecy was entertainment or a service industry. Madam Shen had not been clear on that.

'Why don't I get my face in this?' he suggested.

Silver eels streamed out of him, something leaking out of his life, and Ed leaking after it like a current of warmer water in a cold sea. That night was no different to any other experience in the fishtank, except perhaps for an added, gluey distance to everything he saw. Everything in there was an effort that night. He woke up on the spaceport concrete perhaps an hour later. A salt night wind was blowing. He felt sick and cold. Annie Glyph was kneeling by him. He had the feeling that she had been there for some time. That she was prepared to wait however long it took. He coughed and heaved. She wiped his mouth.

'There,' she said.

'Jesus,' said Ed. 'Hey,' he said. 'How was I?'

'It was a short show. As soon as you put the fishtank on your head, you had some sort of spasm. That was what it looked like.' Annie smiled. 'They weren't convinced,' she went on, 'until you got out of the chair.' He had got out of the chair, she told him, to stand facing the audience for maybe a minute in the shifting light, during which time he trembled and slowly pissed himself. 'It was a real twink moment, Ed. I was proud of you.' After that some muffled sounds came out of the smoky-looking substance in the tank. He shrieked suddenly and began trying to wrestle it off his head. Then he passed out and fell his length into the front row of the audience. 'They weren't happy, and we had some problems with them after that. You know, they were corporates who had paid for special seats and you were sick on their good clothes. Madam Shen talked to them, but they seemed disappointed. We had to drag you out the back way.'

'I don't remember that.'

'It didn't look much. You spoilt your tuxedo, rolling about in your own piss.'

'But did I say anything?'

'Oh, you told the future. You did that all right.'

'What'd I say?'

'You talked about war. You said things no one wanted to hear. Blue babies floating out of wrecked ships in empty space. Frozen babies in space, Ed.' She shivered. 'No one wants to hear that kind of thing.'

'There isn't any war,' Ed pointed out. 'Not yet.'

'But there will be, Ed. That's what you said: "War!"'

This meant nothing to Ed. After he had passed the part with the eels, instead of seeing his childhood in the house with the grey roof, he had watched himself step off his first rocket ship – a tubby little dynaflow freighter called the *Kino Chicken* – on to the parched soil of his first alien planet, with a broad sixteen-year-old leer on his face. The monkey was on his back. He was grooving on concepts of infinite travel and empty space. Always more. Always more after that. He stood at the top of the cargo ramp and shouted, 'Alien planet!' Never regret anything, he promised himself there and then. Never go back. Never see them again, mothers, fathers, sisters who abandon you. It was no distance at all from that position to the death of Dany LeFebre which had hurt him so bad. It all led so inevitably from the *Kino Chicken*, through hyperdip, to the twink-tank.

He told Annie Glyph this, as they walked back across the concrete to her room.

'I had another name then,' he said.

Suddenly he thought he was going to be sick again. He crouched down and put his head between his knees. He cleared his throat. Annie touched his shoulder. After a bit he felt better, and was able to look up at her. 'I let those people down tonight,' he said. She made him see, the way she always did, that massive calm patience of hers. He threw himself against it because it was what he had.

'If I'm predicting the future,' he said desperately, 'why do I always see the past?'

TWENTY-TWO

Persistent Entities

It was late. People hurried in and out of the restaurants and cinemas, heads down into the wet and windy night. The trains were still running. Michael Kearney zipped his jacket up. While he walked, he got on his cellphone and made an effort to raise Brian Tate, first at Tate's home, then at the Sony offices in Noho. No one was answering – although at Sony a recording tried to lure him into the maze of automated corporate response – and he soon put the phone away again. Anna caught up with him twice. The first time was at Hammersmith, where he had to stop and buy a ticket.

'You can follow me all you like,' Kearney told her. 'It won't help.'

She gave him a flushed, obstinate look, then pushed her way through the ticket barrier and down to the eastbound platform where – the light of a malfunctioning fluorescent flickering harshly across the upper half of her face – she challenged him: 'What good's your life been? Honestly, Michael: what good has it been?'

Kearney took her by the shoulders as if to shake her; looked at her instead. Began to say something ugly; changed his mind.

'You're being ridiculous. Go home.'

She set her mouth.

'You see? You can't answer. You haven't got an answer.'

'Go home now. I'll be all right.'

'That's what you always said. Isn't it? And look at you. Look how frightened and upset you are.'

Kearney shrugged suddenly.

'I'm not afraid,' he said, and walked off again.

Her disbelieving laugh followed him down the platform. When the train came she stood as far away from him as she could in the crowded carriage. He lost her briefly in the late-night mêlée at Victoria, but she picked him up again and struggled grimly after him through a crowd of laughing Japanese teenagers. He set his teeth, got off the train two stops early and walked as fast as he could for a mile or so, into the light and activity of West Croydon and out into the suburban streets the other side. Whenever he looked back she had fallen further behind: but she always kept him in sight somehow, and by the time he knocked at Brian Tate's door she had caught him up again. Her hair was slicked down to her scalp, her face was flushed and exasperated; but she blinked the rain out of her eyes and gave him one of those brilliant, strained smiles, as if to say:

'You see?'

Kearney knocked at the door again, and they stood there in an angry truce with their luggage in their hands, waiting for something to happen. Kearney felt a fool.

Brian Tate's house was situated in a quiet, hilly, tree-lined street with a church at one end and a retirement home at the other. It boasted four floors, a short gravelled driveway between laurels, mock-Tudor timbering over pebbledash. On summer evenings you would be able to watch foxes sniffing about among the licheny apple trees in the garden at the rear. It had the air of a house that had been used mildly and well all its existence. Children had been brought up there, and sent on to the kinds of schools suited to children from houses like these, after which they had made careers in brokerage and then had children of their own. It was a modest, successful house, but there was something gloomy about it now, as if Brian Tate's occupancy had disconcerted it.

When no one answered the door, Anna Kearney put down her bag and went to stand on tiptoe in the flower bed beneath one of the windows.

'Someone's in,' she said. 'Listen.'

Kearney listened, but he couldn't hear anything. He went round to the back of the house and listened there, but all the windows were dark and there was nothing to hear. The rain came down quietly on the garden.

'He's not here.'

Anna shivered. 'Someone's in,' she repeated. 'I saw him looking out at us.'

Kearney rapped on the window.

'See?' Anna called excitedly. 'He moved!'

Kearney got his cellphone out and dialled Tate's number. 'Knock on the door again,' he said, putting the phone to his ear. He got an old-fashioned answer machine and said, 'Brian, if you're there, pick up. I'm outside your house and I need to talk to you.' The tape ran for half a minute then stopped. 'For God's sake Brian, I can see you in there.' Kearney was dialling again when Tate opened the front door and looked out uncertainly. 'It's no good doing that,' he said. 'I keep the phone somewhere else.' He was wearing some kind of heavily insulated silver parka over cargo pants and a T-shirt. A wave of heat came out of the door behind him. The hood of the parka obscured his face, but Kearney could see that it was hollow and tired-looking, in need of a shave. He looked from Kearney to Anna, then back again.

'Do you want to come in?' he said vaguely.

'Brian—' Kearney began.

'Don't go in,' Anna said suddenly. She was still standing in the flower bed under the window.

'You don't have to come with me,' Kearney told her.

She stared at him angrily. 'Oh yes I do.'

Inside, the house was thick with heat and humidity. Tate led them into a small room at the back.

'Could you shut the door after you?' he said. 'Keep the warmth in.'

Kearney looked around.

'Brian, what the fuck are you doing?'

Tate had made the room into a Faraday cage by tacking copper chicken wire to the walls and ceiling. As an extra precaution he had covered the windows with Bacofoil. Nothing electromagnetic could get into him from outside that room; nothing could get out. No one could know what he was doing, if he was doing anything. Boxes of tacks, rolls of chicken wire and Bacofoil cartons lay everywhere. The central heating was turned up full. Two stand-alone heaters running off bottled gas roared away in the middle of the room next to a Formica kitchen table and chair. On the table Tate had racked six G4 servers connected in parallel, a keyboard, a hooded monitor, some peripherals. He also had an electric kettle, instant coffee, plastic cups. Takeaway food cartons littered the floor. The room stank. It was immeasurably bleak and obsessive in there.

'Beth left,' Tate explained. He shivered and put his hands out to one of the heaters. His face was hard to see inside the hood of the parka. 'She went back to Davis. She took the kids.'

'I'm sorry to hear that,' Kearney said.

'I bet you are,' Tate said. 'I bet you are.' He raised his voice suddenly. 'Look,' he said, 'what do you want? I keep the phone in another room, you know? I've got work to do here.'

Meanwhile, Anna Kearney was staring around as if she couldn't believe any of it. Every so often her eyes went across Tate with the calm contempt of one neurotic for another, and she shook her head. 'What's that?' she said suddenly. The white cat had emerged cautiously from under the desk. It looked up at Michael Kearney and ran off a little way. Then it stretched itself with a kind of careful self-regard and walked up and down purring, its tail stuck in the air. It seemed to be enjoying the heat. Anna knelt down and offered her hand. 'Hello, baby,' she said. 'Hello, little baby.' The cat ignored her, leapt lightly up on to the hardware, and from there on to Tate's shoulder. It looked thinner than ever, its head more than ever like the blade of an axe, ears transparent, fur a corona of light.

'I'm living in just the one room,' Tate said.

'What's happened, Brian?' Kearney said gently. 'I thought you said it was a glitch.'

Tate held his hands out from his sides.

'I was wrong.'

Rooting about in the tangle of USB cable, stacked peripherals and old coffee cups that covered the desk, he came up with a 100Gb pocket drive in a polished titanium shell. This he offered to Kearney, who weighed it cautiously in his hand.

'What's this?'

'The results of the last run. It was decoherence-free for a whole minute. We had q-bits that survived a whole fucking minute before interference set in. That's like a million years down there. That's like the indeterminacy principle is *suspended.*' He gave a strained laugh. 'Is a million years long enough for us, do you think? Will that do? But then ... I don't know what happened then. The fractals ...'

Kearney felt this wasn't going anywhere. He thought results like these were probably wrong, and that anyway they couldn't explain what he had seen in the laboratory.

'Why did you smash the monitors up, Brian?'

'Because it wasn't physics any more. Physics was *off.* The fractals started to –' he couldn't think of a word, nothing had prepared him for whatever he was seeing in his head '– leak. Then the cat went inside after them. She just walked through the screen and into the data.' He laughed, looking from Kearney to Anna. 'I don't expect you to believe that,' he said.

Underneath it all – underneath the inexplicable fear, the weirdness, the simple guilt of selling the project out first to Meadows then to Sony – Tate was just a teenager good at physics.

He hadn't developed past a hip haircut and the idea that his talent gave him some sort of edge in the world, if only he would always be forgiven by adults. Now his wife had disabused him of that. Worse, perhaps, physics itself had come looking for him in some unfathomable way he couldn't live with. Kearney felt sorry for him, but he only said carefully:

'The cat's here, Brian. She's on your shoulder now.'

Tate glanced at Kearney, then at his own shoulder. He didn't seem to see the white cat perched there, purring and kneading the material of his coat. He shook his head.

'No,' he said abjectly. 'She's gone now.'

Anna stared at Tate, then the cat, then Tate again.

'I'm leaving,' she said. 'I'll call a taxi, if no one minds.'

'You can't call from in here,' Tate told her, as if he was talking to a child. 'It's a *cage*.' Then he whispered, 'I had no idea Beth felt so badly about things.'

Kearney touched his arm.

'Why do you need the cage, Brian? What really happened?'

Tate began to cry. 'I don't know,' he said.

'Why do you need the cage?' Kearney persisted. He made Tate face him. 'Are you afraid something will get in?'

Tate wiped at his eyes. 'No, I'm frightened it will get out,' he said. He shivered and made a curious half-turn away from Kearney, raising his hand to zip the neck of the parka; this brought him face to face with Anna. He jerked in a startled way, as if he had forgotten she was there. 'I'm cold,' he whispered. He felt around behind him with one hand, pulled the chair out from behind the table and sat down heavily. All the time the white cat rode on his shoulder, shifting its balance fluently, purring. Tate looked up at Kearney from the chair and said:

'I'm always cold.'

He was silent for a moment, then he said: 'I'm not really here. None of us are.'

Tears rolled down the dark grooves around his mouth.

'Michael, we're none of us here at all.'

Kearney stepped forward quickly and, before Tate could react, pulled back the hood of the parka. Fluorescent light fell mercilessly across Tate's face, stubbled, exhausted, old-looking, and with an abraded appearance about the eyes, as if he had been working without spectacles, or crying all night. Probably, Kearney thought, he had been doing both. The eyes themselves were watery, a little bloodshot, with pale blue irises. Nothing was odd about them in the end except the tears pouring in a silvery stream from their inner corners. There were too many of them for Tate's grief. Every tear was made up of exactly similar tears, and those tears too were made from tears. In every tear there was a tiny image. However far back you went, Kearney knew, it would always be there. At first he supposed it was his own reflection. When he saw what it really was he grabbed Anna by the upper arm and started dragging her out of the room. She struggled and fought all the way, hitting out at him with her luggage, staring back in horror at what was happening to Brian Tate.

'No,' she said reasonably. 'No. Look. We have to help him.'

'Christ, Anna! Come *on*!'

The white cat was crying too. As Kearney watched, it turned its thin, savage little head towards him, and its tears poured out into the room like points of light. They flowed and flowed until the cat itself began to dissolve and spill off Brian Tate's shoulder like a slow glittering liquid on to the floor, while Tate rocked himself to and fro and made a noise like:

'Er er er.'

He was melting too.

An hour later they were sitting in the brightest place they could find open in the centre of London, a pick-up bar at the Cambridge Circus end of Old Compton Street. It wasn't much of a place, but it was as far away as they could get from the cold endless suburbs and those streets of decent, bulky stockbroker homes with one lighted room visible between laurels and rhododendrons. The bar did food – mainly odds and ends of tapas – and Kearney had tried to get Anna to eat something, but she had only looked at the menu and shuddered. Neither of them was speaking, just staring out into the street outside, enjoying the warmth and the music and the feeling of being with people. Soho was still awake. Couples, mostly gay, were hurrying past the window arm in arm, laughing and talking animatedly. There was some human warmth to be had by holding your glass steady in both hands and watching that.

Eventually Anna finished her drink and said:

'I don't want to know what happened back there.'

Kearney shrugged. 'I'm not sure it was actually happening like that anyway,' he lied. 'I think it was some sort of illusion.'

'What are we going to do?'

Kearney had been waiting for her to ask this. He found the pocket drive he had taken from Tate, weighed it in his hand for a moment then put it on the table between them, where it lay gleaming softly in the coloured light, a nicely designed object not much bigger than a pack of cigarettes. Titanium has a look to it, he thought. Today's popular metal. He said:

'Take this. If I don't come back, get it to Sony. Tell them it's from Tate and they'll know what to do with it.'

'But that stuff,' she said. 'That *stuff* is in there.'

'I don't think it has anything to do with the data,' Kearney said. 'I think Tate is wrong about that. I think it's me this thing wants, and I think it's the same thing that's wanted me all along. It's just found a new way of talking to me.'

She shook her head and pushed the drive back towards him.

'I'm not letting you go anyway,' she said. 'Where can you go? What can you do?'

Kearney kissed her and smiled at her.

'There are some things I can still try,' he said. 'I've saved them until last.'

'But—'

He slid back his stool and got up.

'Anna, I can get out of this. Will you help me?' She opened her mouth to speak, but he touched her lips with his fingers. 'Will you just go home and keep this thing safe and wait for me? Please? I'll be back in the morning, I promise.'

She glanced up at him, her eyes hard and bright, then away again. She reached out and touched the pocket drive, then put it quickly inside her coat. She shook her head, as if she had tried everything and was now consigning him to the world. 'All right,' she said. 'If that's what you want.'

Kearney felt an enormous relief.

He left the bar and took a cab to Heathrow, where he booked himself on the first available flight to New York.

The airport was stunned into calmness by the late hour. Kearney sat in an empty row of seats in the departure lounge, yawning, peering out through the plate glass at the huge fins of the manoeuvring aircraft and throwing the Shrander's dice compulsively as he waited for night to turn into dawn. He had his bag on the seat beside him. He was going to America not because he wanted to, but because that was what the dice had suggested. He had no idea what he would do when he arrived. He saw himself driving through the heartlands trying to read a Triple A map in the dark; or staring out of a train window like someone in a Richard Ford story, someone whose life has long ago pivoted on to its bad side and is being held down by its own weight. All his strategies were bankrupt. They had been hollowed out years ago by a kind of persistent internal panic. Whatever was happening to him now, though, was new. It had a culminatory feeling. He was going to run again, and probably be caught this time, and perhaps find out what his life had been about. Anything else he had told Anna was a lie. She must have expected that, because just before 5 a.m. he felt her lean over him from behind and kiss him and close her thin hands over his so that he couldn't throw the dice again.

'I knew you'd come here,' she whispered.

TWENTY-THREE

Star-crossed

The commander of *Touching the Void* tried to contact Seria Mau by fetch.

Something was wrong with his signal. It had lost part of itself, or got mixed up with something else, some of the baroque matter of the universe, before it reached her. The fetch squatted in front of her tank for a full minute, fading in and out of view, then vanished. It was much smaller than she remembered from their previous dealings – a bundle of yellowish limbs barely bigger than a human head, crouching in what looked like a puddle of sticky liquid. Its skin had the shine of roasted poultry. She wondered if that meant there was something wrong, not just with the signal but with the commander himself. She asked mathematics what it thought.

'Contact broken,' the mathematics said.

'For Christ's sake,' Seria Mau told it, 'I could work that out on my own.'

Over the next two days the apparition reappeared at intervals of a minute or two in different parts of the ship, caught by the drifting cameras as a brief subliminal flicker. The shadow operators drove it into corners, where it became panicked. Eventually it flickered to life in front of Seria Mau's tank, from which position, stabilising quickly but still too small, it regarded Seria Mau patiently from its cluster of eyes and made several attempts to speak.

Seria Mau eyed it with distaste.

'What?' she said.

Eventually it managed to say her name:

'Seria Mau Genlicher, I –' Interference. Static. Echoes of nothing, with nothing to echo in. '– important to warn you about your position,' it said, as if completing some argument she had missed the beginning of. The signal faded, then blurted back loudly. '– modified the Dr Haends package,' it said, and was silent again. It faded into brown smoke, moving its palps agitatedly: but if it was trying to communicate further, she couldn't hear. When it had gone, Seria Mau asked the mathematics:

'What are they doing back there?'

'Nothing new. The Moire pod has lost way a little. *Touching the Void* is still phaselocked to an unknown K-ship.'

'Can you make any sense of this?'

'I don't think so,' the mathematics admitted.

What does an alien think anyway? What use does it make of the world? As soon as they arrived on a planet the Nastic turned its indigenous population over to excavation projects. They wanted silos, a mile across and perhaps five miles deep. After the lithosphere was laced with these structures, the Nastic would hover by the million in the air above them, on wings which looked as cheap and brand new as a plastic hairslide. No one knew why, although the best guess was that it had religious significance. If you tried to hold more than a practical conversation with a Nastic, it began saying things like, 'The work fails only when the worker has turned from the wheel,' and, 'In the morning, they face inward like the Moon.' The Nastic colonies, substantial in number, spread from the rim of the galaxy towards its centre, in the shape of a slice from a pie chart. The inference was obvious: they had originated from outside. That being so, no one could suggest how they had travelled the distances involved. Their own myths, in which the Ur-swarm travelled without ships at all, beating its wings down some lighted fracture in the continuum, alternately warmed and fried by radiation, could be discounted.

There were no more attempts at communication. The *White Cat* fled through empty space, while her pursuers hung back like cunning hounds. It was no easier to work out what to do.

Meanwhile, Billy Anker filled the ship. He did the most ordinary things in too large a way. Seria Mau, drawn and repelled at the same time, watched him carefully from the hidden cameras as he washed, ate, scratched his armpits sitting on the lavatory with his pressure-suit down round his knees. Billy Anker smelled of leather, sweat, something else she couldn't identify, though it might have been machine oil. He never took off his fingerless glove.

Sleep was no consolation to him. Dreams lifted his top lip off his teeth in a frightened snarl; in the mornings he looked at himself askance in the mirror. What was there to see? What kind of inner resources could he have, with such an indifferent start in life? Invented and set in motion as an extension of his own father, he had flung himself into the void as a way of validating himself. He had done that mad thing among many other mad things, and got so worn out by them he crept away and spent ten years putting himself back together, while war came closer, and the big secrets got more remote instead of less, and the galaxy fell apart a little more, and everything strayed that bit farther from being fixable –

Give it all up, Billy Anker, she wanted to urge him. Live for the big discovery and you only feed the fat man inside. Also he profits from everything you find. She wanted to beg him:

'Give it all up, Billy Anker, and come away with me.'

What did she mean by that? What *could* she mean? She was a rocket ship and he was a man. She thought about that. She watched over him while he slept, and had her own dreams.

In Seria Mau's dreams, which played themselves out as inaccurately as memories in the extended sensorium of the *White*

Cat, Billy Anker knelt over her, smiling down endlessly while she smiled up at him. She was in love, but didn't quite know what to want. Puzzled by herself, she simply exhibited herself to him in a daze. She wanted to feel the weight of his gaze, she realised, in a room full of light, on a summer afternoon. But a kind of shadow version of this event dogged her imagination and sometimes made things seem absurd – it was cold in the house, there was food cooling on a tray, the boards were bare, she was so much smaller than him; all she felt was embarrassment and a kind of uninspired chafing. In an attempt to discover how she should act, she ran footage of Mona the clone's companions in the days before she blew them out the airlock. From this she learned to say, with a kind of angry urgency, 'I want to do it. I want to fuck.' But in the end Seria Mau had no interest in being penetrated; indeed, she was rather upset by the absurdity of the idea.

Mona the clone also examined herself, frankly or anxiously according to her mood, in the mirrors. She was interested in her body and her face, but she was obsessed with her hair, which at the time they rescued Billy Anker from Redline was a long pinkish-blonde floss that smelled permanently of peppermint shampoo. She would pile it up this way and that on her head, looking at it from different angles until she let it fall with an expression of disgust and said, 'I'm committing suicide.'

'Come away now dear and eat,' the shadow operators said listlessly.

'I mean it,' Mona threatened.

She and Billy Anker inhabited the human quarters like two species of animal in the same field. They had nothing to say to one another when it came to it. This became plain the first day he was aboard. Mona had the operators turn her out in a white leather battledress jacket with matching calf-length kick-pleat skirt, which they accessorised by adding a little gold belt, also block-heeled sandals in transparent urethane. She looked good and she knew it. She poached a sea bass with wild lemon grass, cuisine she had learned in the middle-management enclaves of Motel Splendido, and – over a dessert of fresh summer berries steeped in grappa – told him about herself. Her story was a simple one, she said. It was a story of success. At school she had excelled in synchronised swimming. Her place in the corporate order was affirmed by a real knack for working with others. She had never felt encumbered by her origins, never felt jealous of her sister-mother. Her life was on track, she confided, with the added ingredient that it had only just begun.

She asked him if he could fly the *White Cat*.

Billy Anker didn't seem to catch that. He scratched the stubble under his jaw.

'What life's that, kid?' he said vaguely.

Four feet away from one another, they looked as if they had been filmed in different rooms. 'This is where I live,' Mona informed him the next day: 'And this is where you live.'

She had the shadow operators make over her half of the human quarters to look like a breakfast bar or diner from Earth's deep past, with a clean chequerboard floor and antique milkshake machines that didn't need to work. Billy Anker left his half the way it was, and sat naked in the middle of the floor in the mornings, his unbuffed body running to a kind of scrawny middle age, doing the exercises of some complicated satori routine. Mona watched holograms in her room. Billy spent most of the day staring into space and farting. If he farted too loud, Mona came and stood in the communicating doorway and said, 'Jesus!' in a disgusted voice, as if she was recommending him to the attention of a third party.

Seria Mau followed these domestic encounters with a kind of amused tolerance. It was like having pets. Their antics could often bring her out of her recurrent cafards, ill-humours and tantrums where the *White Cat*'s hormonal pharmacopoeia could not. She was reassured by Mona and Billy. She expected nothing new of them.

All the more surprising then, four or five days out of Redline, to catch them together in Mona's bedroom.

*

The lighting mimicked afternoon leaking through half-closed blinds somewhere in the temperate zones of Earth. An atmosphere of *cinq à sept* prevailed. There was a dish of rosewater by the bed for Billy Anker to dip his fingers in if he started to come too soon. Mona wore a short grey silk slip, which was up round her waist, and lots of lip colour to make it look as if she had already bitten them. She had hold of the chrome bedhead in both hands. Her mouth was open and through the bars her eyes had a faraway look. One breast had come free of the slip.

'Oh yes, fuck me, Billy Anker,' she said suddenly.

Billy Anker, who was curved over her in a manner both protective and predatory, looked younger than he had. His forearms were long and brown, corded in the yellow light. His unbound hair hung down round his face; he still had on his fingerless mitt. 'Oh, fuck me through the wall,' Mona said. This gave him pause; then he shrugged, lost his inturned look and carried on with what he had been doing. Mona went pink and gave a fluttering, delicate little cry. That was the last straw for Billy, who after a series of spasms groaned loudly and slumped over her. They slipped apart immediately and began to laugh. Mona lit a cigarette and let him take it from her without asking. He sat up against the bedhead with one arm round her. They smoked for a while then Billy Anker, casting around for something to slake his thirst, drank the rosewater from the bedside dish.

Seria Mau watched them in silence for a moment or two, thinking, Is this how he would have been with me?

Then she took control of the human quarters. She reduced the temperature by tens of degrees. She brought up the lights until they had the glare of hospital fluorescents. She introduced disinfectants into the air-conditioning. Mona the clone threw her arm across her eyes then, realising what must have happened, shoved Billy Anker away from her. 'Get off me before it's too late,' she said. 'Oh God, get off me.' She scrambled out of bed and into the corner of the room, where she clung with both hands to the nearest fixed object, shaking with fear and whispering, 'It wasn't me. It wasn't me.'

Billy Anker stared at her puzzledly. He wiped away the aerosol of disinfectant which stood on his face like sweat. Looked down at the palm of his hand. Laughed.

'What's going on?' he said.

Seria Mau examined him carefully. He looked like a plucked chicken in that light. His flesh looked as grey as his hair. She wasn't quite sure what she had seen in him.

She said in her ship's voice: 'This is your stop, Billy Anker.'

The clone whimpered, clung on harder, shut her eyes as tight as she could. 'You might well do that,' Seria Mau advised her: 'It's your stop too.' She dialled up the mathematics.

'Open the airlock,' she ordered.

She thought for a moment.

'No, wait,' she said.

Two minutes later, something levered its way out of nowhere on a remote curve of the Beach, at the edge of a system no one had ever bothered to name. Empty space convulsed. A splatter of particles organised itself in a millisecond or two from a fireworks display into the ugly lines of a K-ship – the *White Cat*, her torch already alight, heading in-system at a shallow angle to the ecliptic on a brutally straight line of fusion product.

Surveys of the system, carried out fifty years after humanity arrived on the Beach, had found a single solid object in a braiding orbital dance with gas giants. Though a little large, it was strictly a moon. Tidal heating in its core had raised the surface to temperatures resembling Earth's, generating also a loose and wispy atmosphere which featured the gases that support life. Against a curious greenish arc of sky ballooned the salmon-pink bulk of the nearest gas giant. A single fractal structure occupied the entire planet. Though from a distance this resembled vegetation, it was neither alive nor dead. It was just some mad old algorithm which, vented from a passing navigational system, had run wild then run out of raw materials. The effect was of endless peacock feathers a million different sizes: a clever drawing ramped into three dimensions. Mathematics trying to save itself from death.

Plush and velvety, surrounded by a vanishingly thin mist of itself, this structure defeated the eye at all scales. It did something strange and absorbent to the light. It lay brittle and exfoliated, fragmenting into a viral dust of itself, a useless old calculation which had accidentally become an environment. There was a biome: among its quaint bracts and stalks, local life forms moved with a kind of puzzled stealth. The logic of the ecology was unclear, its terminal fauna provisional. At dawn or dusk, something between a bird and a marmoset might be seen, making its way painfully to the tip of some huge feather to stare anxiously at the face of the gas giant, before it closed its eyes and began a fluting territorial aubade. No one had stayed long enough to find out any more.

The *White Cat* burned a clearing among the feathers, hovered above them momentarily, and lowered herself down. For a minute or two nothing more happened. Then a cargo port opened and two figures debouched. After a pause in which they turned back and seemed to be arguing with the ship itself, they hurried down the already-closing cargo ramp and stood in silence. They were naked, although they had between them what seemed to be some party clothes and the bottom half of an old G-suit. As they watched, the *White Cat* stood on its tail, shot into the sky, and vanished, all in the same easy, practised gesture.

Mona the clone stared helplessly about.

'She might at least have dropped us near a town,' she said. 'The bitch.'

Thrown into a fugue to which – for once – the mathematics of the *White Cat* had made no contribution, Seria Mau Genlicher, pilot of the spaceways, dreamed she was ten years old again. One moment her mother was smiling and excited; the next she was dead and in a photograph, which not long later went up into the wet afternoon air in grey smoke.

The father couldn't bear anything that reminded him of his wife. That photograph was too hard to bear, he said. Just too hard to bear. All winter, he locked himself in his study, and when Seria Mau brought him the tray at lunchtime, touched her cheek and cried. Stay for a moment, he urged her. Be the mother for just a moment. She couldn't begin to articulate the embarrassment she felt at this. She looked at the floor, which only made it worse. He kissed her gently on the top of the head, then with one finger under her chin, gently compelled her to face him again. You look like her, he said. You look so like her. A gasp came from him. Sit here, no here, like this. Like this. He put his fingers down between Seria Mau's legs then gasped and burst into tears. Seria Mau took the tray and went out. Why would he do that? She felt as stiff and awkward as someone learning how to walk.

'*Waraaa!*' said her brother, ambushing her on the landing. She dropped the lunch tray and the two of them stared down silently at the mess. A boiled egg rolled away and into a corner.

All that winter, K-ships roared low over the New Pearl River. They made sudden dirty white arcs across the sky. The father took Seria Mau and her brother to the base, to watch those ships come in. It was war. It was peace. Who knew what it would be, out there on the edge of the galaxy, with the Nastic only three systems away, and unknown assets at large in the Kuiper Belt, presenting as lumps of dirty ice? The children loved it. There followed the best and worst of times, marked by parades and marches, economic crashes, political speeches, the overturning of scientific paradigms: fresh news every day. That was when Seria Mau made up her mind. That was when she made her own plans. She collected holograms – little black cubes full of stars, roseate nebulae, wisps of floating gas – the way other girls collected cosmetics. 'This is Eridon Omega,' she explained to her brother, 'south of the White Cawl. The *Vittor Neumann* pod rules there. Just let the Nastic try anything against them!' Her eyes glowed. 'They have ordnance that evolves itself, generation by generation, in a medium *outside* the ship. Whole worlds are at stake here!' She watched herself say this in the mirror, with no idea why she looked so wild-eyed and excited. The morning of her thirteenth birthday, she signed up. EMC were always looking for recruits, and for the K-pods they only wanted the youngest, fastest people they could find.

'You should be proud of me,' she told the father.

'I'm proud,' her brother said. He burst into tears. '*I* want to be a space ship too.'

Saulsignon was a training camp by then. There were wire fences everywhere. The little railway station had lost its look of Ancient Earth, its flower tubs and the tabby cat which made the brother angry because it reminded him of his little black kitten. They stood there, the three of them, on her last day, awkward in the wind and rain.

'Will you get leave?' the father said.

Seria Mau laughed triumphantly.

'Never!' she said.

As soon as this word was out, the dream faded to nothing, like lights going down. When they came up again, they came up in the magic shop window. Ruby-coloured plastic lips. Feathers dyed bright orange and green. Bundles of coloured scarves that would go into the magician's shiny hat and then hop out as live white pigeons. All that stuff which, though sometimes pretty, was always fake: always made to mislead and dissemble. Seria Mau stood in front of the glass for some time, but the conjuror never came. Just as she was turning to leave, she heard a faint bell ring, and a voice whispered, 'When will you come for me, Dr Haends?' She looked around in surprise at the empty street. There was no doubt about it. The voice had been her own. When she woke, she thought for a moment that someone was bending over her: in the same instant, she saw herself marooning Billy Anker and Mona the clone in the shadow of the gas giant. The memory of an act that bad could only make you feel absurd.

'Why did you let me do it?' she said.

The mathematics gave its equivalent of a shrug. 'You weren't ready to listen.'

'Take us back there.'

'I wouldn't recommend that.'

'Take us back.'

The *White Cat* shut her torch down and fell as silently as a derelict between the gas giants. Course changes were made in increments, using tiny, ferocious pSi engines which worked by blowing oxygen on to porous silicon compounds. Meanwhile, the particle-detectors and massive arrays, extending like veinous systems in a leaf, sifted vacuum for the track of the *Krishna Moire* pod. 'Power up,' the mathematics instructed quietly. 'Power down.' What was left of Seria Mau's body moved impatiently in its tank. She had a need to see Billy Anker that anyone else would have described as physical. If she had remembered how, she would have bitten her lip. 'Why did I do this?' she asked herself. The shadow operators shook their heads: sooner or later something like it had been bound to happen, they inferred. In the end the *White Cat* got close enough to examine the planet itself. Something moved among the feathers. It might have been whatever lived down there; it might have been ancient calculations crumbling into dust.

'What's that?' said the mathematics.

'Nothing,' said Seria Mau. 'Go in,' she ordered. 'I've had enough of this.'

She found Billy Anker and Mona the clone lying half out of the long cobalt shadows. Mona was already dead, her pretty blonde head resting on the upper part of Billy's chest. He had one arm round her shoulders. With his other hand he was still stroking her hair. As she died she had been looking intently into his face, and had placed one leg between both his, trying to get some final comfort out of life. Under the instructions of the old algorithm – which, provided so suddenly with raw material for its endless repetition, had sifted stealthily down on to them from the structures above – their cells were turning to feathers. Billy Anker's legs looked like a peacock satyr's. Mona was gone all the way to diaphragm, blue-black dusty feathers which seemed to shift and grow and do something odd to the light.

Seria Mau's fetch – in these conditions little more than a shadow itself – wove nervously about in front of the lovers. How could I have done this? she thought, while she said aloud:

'Billy Anker, is there any way I can help?'

Billy Anker never stopped stroking the dead woman's hair, or looking away from her.

'No,' he said.

'Does it hurt?'

Billy Anker smiled to himself. 'Kid,' he said, 'it's more comfortable than you'd think. Like a good downer.' He laughed suddenly. 'Hey, the wormhole was the spectacle. You know? That's what I keep remembering. That was how I expected to go.' Silent a moment, he contemplated that. 'I could never even describe what it was like in there,' he said. Then he said, 'I can hear this thing counting. Or is that some sort of illusion?'

Seria Mau came as close to him as she could.

'I can't hear anything. Billy Anker, I'm sorry to have done this.'

At that, he bit his lip and finally looked away from Mona the clone.

'Hey,' he said. 'Forget it.'

He convulsed. Dust billowed up from the stealthily shifting surface of his body. The algorithm was reorganising him at all scales. For a moment his eyes filled with horror. He hadn't expected this. 'It's eating me!' he shouted. He flailed with his arms, clutched at the dead woman as if she might help him. Forgetting she was only a fetch, he tried to clutch at Seria Mau too. Then he got control of himself again. 'The more you deny the forces inside, kid, the more they control you,' he said. His hand went through her like a hand through smoke. He stared at it in surprise. 'Is this happening?' he asked.

'Billy Anker, what am I to do?'

'That ship of yours. Take it deep. Take it to the Tract.'

'Billy, I—'

Above them, streaks of violet ionisation went across the face of the gas giant. There was a great whistling thud of displaced air; then another; then a vast emerald fireball somewhere in orbit, as the

231

White Cat began to defend herself against what must be the attentions of the *Krishna Moire* pod. Suddenly, Seria Mau was half up there with her ship, half down here with Billy Anker. Alarms were going off everywhere along the continuum between these two states, and the mathematics was trying to disconnect her fetch.

'Leave me!' she cried. 'I want to stay with him! Someone must stay with him!'

Billy Anker smiled and shook his head.

'Get out of here, kid. That's Uncle Zip up there. Get out while you can.'

'Billy Anker, I brought them down on you!'

He looked tired. He closed his eyes.

'I brought them down on myself, kid. Get out of here. Take it deep.'

'Goodbye, Billy Anker.'

'Hey, kid—'

But when she turned to answer, he was dead.

I fell for it, she told herself in despair. All the fucking and the fighting. Despite everything I promised myself, I fell for it too.

Then she thought: Uncle Zip! Terror dissolved her, because she had so underestimated that fat man, how intelligent he was, how galaxywide. She had been in his hands from the moment she began to deal with him.

What would she do now?

TWENTY-FOUR

Tumbling Dice

'If I'm predicting the future, how come I always see the past?'

When Ed asked Sandra Shen that question, she was no more help than Annie Glyph. All she did was shrug lightly.

'I think we need practice, Ed,' she said. She lit a cigarette and gave her attention amusedly to something in the corner of the room. 'I think we need to work harder.'

Ed never could decode that distant look of hers. If anything, she seemed pleased by the débâcle in the main tent. It filled her full of energy: her other projects languished, and she was around on a daily basis. She kicked the old men out of the bar of the Dunes Motel. He came in and found her fitting it out with equipment of her own, which she was bringing in at night in unmarked crates. This stuff was uniformly old. It featured cloth-covered electric cable, Bakelite casings, dials across which tiny needles rose and fell. There was some kind of amplifier that worked by valves.

'Jesus,' he said. 'This is *real*.'

'Fun, isn't it?' Sandra Shen said. 'Four hundred and fifty years old, give or take. Ed, it's time we began to work together on this.

Put our heads together. What I need to do is fasten these straps round your wrists . . .'

The idea was that Ed sat with his arms and legs strapped to the arms and legs of a big raw-looking wooden chair that came with the rest of the equipment, while Sandra Shen connected herself to the valve amplifier. She then settled the fishtank on Ed's head and asked him questions until she got an answer that suited her. Her voice came to him close and intimate, as if she was in there with him and the eels on their weird, tiring journey beneath the Alcubiere sea, forward towards some unwelcome revelation of his youth. The questions were meaningless to Ed.

'Is life a bitch or isn't it, Ed?' she would say. Or: 'Can you count to twelve?'

He never heard his own answers anyway. The part of him inside the fishtank wasn't hooked up to the part outside: not in any way as simple as that. The bar at the Dunes Motel lay in its baking afternoon darkness, split by a single ray of white sunlight. The oriental woman leaned against the bar, smoked, nodded to herself. When she got an answer that suited her, she cranked a handle on her apparatus. Curious bluish jolts of light were emitted undependably from its cathodes. The man in the chair convulsed and screamed.

In the evenings, Ed still had to give his performance. He was exhausted. Audiences dwindled. Eventually, only Madam Shen, dressed in a frankly décolleté emerald cocktail dress, was there to watch. Ed began to suspect the audiences weren't the point of it. He had no idea what Sandra Shen wanted from him. When he tried to talk to her about it before the show, she only told him not to worry. 'More practice, Ed. That's all you need.' She sat in the best seats, smoking, applauding with soft claps of her little strong hands. 'Well done, Ed. Well *done*.' Afterwards two or three carnies would drag him away. Or if Annie happened to be around, she would pick him up with a kind of tender amusement and carry him back to her room.

'Why are you doing this to yourself, Ed?' Annie asked him one night.

Ed coughed. He spat into the sink.

'It's a living,' he said.

'Oh, very entradista,' she said sarcastically. 'Tell me about it, Ed. Tell me about the dipships again, and what hard-ons you all were. Tell me how you fucked the famous lady-pilot.'

Ed shrugged.

'I don't know what you mean.'

'Yes you do.'

Annie looked as near exasperated as she could, and went outside so she could stalk about without breaking anything.

'What do you know about her, Ed?' she called back in. 'Nothing. Why is she making you do this? What does she expect you to *see*?' When he didn't answer, she said, 'It's just another version of the tank. You twinks will accept any amount of shit not to face the world.'

'Hey, it was you who introduced me to her in the first place.'

Annie was silent at that. After a while she changed her tack.

'It's a beautiful night out here. Let's walk on the sand. At least you should have a rest from it sometimes. Let me take you to town, Ed! I'll come home early one evening, run you over there. We could see a show!'

'I am a show,' Ed said.

Nevertheless, he saw the point. He started going into town. He went at night, and avoided both Pierpoint Street and Straint. He didn't want to meet Tig or Neena again. He didn't want Bella Cray back in his life. He spent his time in the quarter they called East Dub, where the narrow streets were choked with rickshaws and the tank farms called out to him from their animated shoot-up posters. Ed walked on by. He got into the Ship Game instead, squatting in the street in the smell of falafel and sweat with cultivars twice his size. These guys were always on the edge of violence when life brought them next to someone who had something real to lose.

The dice fell and tumbled. Ed walked away whole but cleaned out, and thanked them for it. They viewed his receding back with monstrous tusky grins. 'Any time, man.'

When she found out, Madam Shen regarded him curiously.

'Is this wise?' was all she said.

'Everyone,' he said, 'deserves a break.'

'And yet, Ed, there's Bella Cray.'

'What do you know about Bella?' he demanded.

When she shrugged, he shrugged too.

'If you're not scared of her, I'm not either.'

'Be careful, Ed.'

'I'm careful,' he said. But Bella Cray had already found him.

He was followed one night by two corporate-looking guys with loosely knotted apricot sweaters. He led them the mystery dance for half an hour, round the crooked alleys and arcades, then dodged into a falafel joint on Foreman Drive and out the back.

Had he lost them? He couldn't be sure. He thought he saw the same two guys the next day, on the concrete at the noncorporate spaceport. It was wide noon, with white heat blazing up from the concrete, and they were pretending to look in one of the alien exhibits, goofing about round the viewing port, turning away and pretending to barf at what they saw inside. The giveaway was that one of them always kept the whole site in view while the other was bent to the glass. Ed still had twenty yards on them when he turned quietly off into the crowd. But they must have seen him, because the next night in East Dub a gun-kiddie mob calling themselves The Skeleton Keys of the Rain tried to kill him with a nova grenade.

He didn't get much time to think. There was a characteristic wet-sounding thump. At the same time, everything seemed to brighten and fade simultaneously. Half the street went out right in front of his eyes, and it still missed him.

'Jesus,' whispered Ed, backing away into a crowd of prostitutes tailored to look and act like sixteen-year-old Japanese girls from late twentieth-century internet fuck sites. 'There was no need for that.' He touched his face. It felt hot. The prostitutes staggered about giggling nervously, their clothes in tatters, their skin sunburned to bright red. As soon as he could think again, Ed went off at a run. He ran until he didn't know where he was, except that it was waste lot midnight. The Kefahuchi Tract almost filled the sky, always growing as you watched, like the genie raging up out of the bottle, yet somehow never larger. It was a singularity without an event horizon, they said, the wrong physics loose in the universe. Anything could come out of there, but nothing ever did. Unless of course, Ed thought, what we have out here is already a result of what happens in there . . . He stared up and thought long and hard about Annie Glyph. It was like this the night he met her, bad light flickering across waste lots. Somehow he had brought her back to life just by asking her name. Now he was responsible for her.

He went back to the circus and found her sleeping. The room was full of her slow, calm heat. Ed lay down beside her and buried his face where her neck and shoulder met. After a moment or two she half woke and made room for him inside the curve of her body. He put his hand on her and she gave a big guttural grunt of pleasure. He would have to leave New Venusport before something happened to her because of him. He would have to leave her here. How would he tell her? He didn't know.

She must have read his thoughts, because she came home a few nights later and said:

'What's the matter, Ed?'

'I don't know,' Ed lied.

'If you don't know, Ed, you should find out,' she said.

They stared puzzledly at one another.

Ed liked to walk around in the cold bright morning through the circus itself, moving from the salt smell of the dunes to the smell of warm dusty concrete that filled the air around the tents and pavilions.

He wondered why Sandra Shen had chosen this site. If you

landed here, it was because you had no corporate credentials. If you left from here, no one wished you good luck. It was a transit camp, where EMC processed refugee labour before moving it on to the mines. Paperwork could maroon you at the noncorporate port for a year, during which your own bad choices would take the opportunity to stretch it to ten. Your ship rusted, your life rusted. But you could always go to the circus. This in itself worried Ed. What did it mean for Madam Shen? Was she trapped here too?

'This outfit ever move on?' he asked her. 'I mean, that's what a circus does, right? Every week another town?'

Sandra Shen gave him a speculative look, her face shifting from old to young then back again around its own eyes, as if they were the only fixed point in her personality (if personality is a word with any meaning when you are talking about an algorithm). They were like eyes looking out from cobwebs. She had a fresh drink beside her. Her little body was leaning back, elbows on the bar, one red high-heel hooked in the brass bar rail. Smoke from her cigarette rose in an exact thin stream, broke up suddenly into eddies and whorls. She laughed and shook her head.

'Bored already, Ed?' she said.

The next night Bella Cray was in the audience for his show.

'Christ!' whispered Ed. He looked around for Sandra Shen: she was off on other business. Ed was stuck there in the glare of the old theatre lights, the cold white glare of Bella Cray's smile. There she was, sitting in the front row not two yards away, knees together, handbag in her lap. Her white secretary blouse had a little saddle of perspiration under each armpit, but her lipstick was bright and fresh and she was mouthing something he couldn't quite make out. He remembered her saying, just before he shot her sister, 'What can we do, Ed? *We're* all fish.' To get away from her, he plunged his head into the tank. As the world went out he heard her call:

'Hey, Ed! Break a leg!'

When he woke up she was gone. His head was full of a high, pure ringing sound. Annie Glyph lugged him into the dunes, where she laid him down in the cool air and distant sound of the surf. He rested his head in her lap and held her hand. She told him he had prophesied war again, and worse; he didn't tell her about seeing Bella Cray in the audience. He didn't want to worry her. Also, he had spent a tiring hour inside the tank. He had watched his dead mother's things thrown on the bonfire, seen his sister leave for other worlds, resented his father for being ordinary and weak, left for other worlds himself: then he had been led past his own past, into some completely unknowable state. He was worn out with it.

'It's good you're here,' he said.

'You should stop doing this, Ed. It isn't worth it.'

'Do you think they'll let me stop? Do you think *she'll* let me stop? Everyone but you wants to kill me or use me. Maybe both.'

Annie smiled and shook her head slowly.

'That's ridiculous,' she said.

She gazed out to sea. After a minute or two she said in a different voice, 'Ed, don't you sometimes want someone smaller? Really? Someone nice and small to fuck, and not just that: to be with?'

He squeezed her huge hand.

'You're a rock,' he told her. 'Everything breaks on you.'

She pushed him away and went down to the water.

'Jesus, Ed,' she shouted into the sea wind. 'You fucking twink.'

Ed watched her striding up and down at the tideline, picking up large stones and pieces of driftwood and hurling them far out into the ocean. He got himself carefully to his feet and left her there to her demons.

The spaceport was empty. Everyone had gone home long ago. The night was just chain-link rattling in the wind, smell of the tide, a voice calling out from some motel cabin. Mercury vapour light made everything look half real. Empty sheds, intermittent traffic. It was like that most nights. Nothing for hours, then four ships in twenty minutes – two tubby freighters in from the Core; the tender of a vast Alcubiere ship hanging somewhere up in the parking lot like an asteroid; some semi-corporate short-hauler, skulking down on business no one could afford to acknowledge. There would be bursts of flame the orange colour of New Men hair, then darkness and cold wind until morning. Ed didn't feel like going back to the room until Annie was asleep. Instead he wandered over and stood between the rocket sheds, looking up at the huge ships, enjoying their smells of stressed metal and burnt pSi fuel.

After a while he noticed a figure pushing a wheeled waste bin slowly across the concrete in his direction. It was Bella Cray. Since her sister's death her skirts were tighter. Bella was making-up for two, with several colours of eye shadow and lips that resembled a pumped-up rosebud. Those lips were the first thing you saw coming towards you. Going away, she presented as buttocks. Somewhere in between was her handbag full of guns.

'Hey, Ed,' she said, 'look at this!'

The waste bin was almost as big as her. Folded awkwardly into it, their long legs hanging over the side, were Tig and Neena Vesicle. Their expressions were puzzled. They were dead. Up from the bin came a smell of alien fluids, bitter and hopeless. Neena's eyes were still open, and she was looking up at the Kefahuchi Tract the way she had looked at Ed while he was fucking her in the warren, so that he expected her to laugh breathlessly and say, 'Oh I'm so far in you!' Tig Vesicle didn't even look like Tig any more.

Bella Cray chuckled.

'Like it, Ed?' she said. 'This is what's going to happen to you. But first it's going to happen to everyone you know.'

Neena Vesicle's long legs hung out of the waste bin. Bella Cray, as if she needed something to busy herself with, began to try and stuff them back in. 'If I could fold the bugger up a bit more,' she said. She leaned in over the bin until her feet came off the ground, then gave up. 'They're just as fucking awkward as they were alive, your friends,' she said. She wrenched at her skirt and blouse until she got them back into place. She patted her hair.

'Well, Ed,' she said.

Ed looked on at this performance. He felt cold; he didn't know what he felt. Annie would be next, that was obvious enough. Annie was the only other person he knew.

'I could pay you something now,' he said.

Bella pulled a lace-edged handkerchief out of her bag to wipe her hands. While she was at it she checked her look in a little gold compact mirror. 'Whoa!' she said. 'Is that me?' Out came the lipstick. 'Tell you what, Ed,' she said, applying it freely. 'Money isn't going to help with this.'

Ed swallowed.

He had another look in the bin. 'You didn't have to do this,' he said. Bella Cray chuckled.

At that moment Annie Glyph, who had worn off her irritation throwing stones into the tide, walked up out of the darkness, calling, 'Ed? Ed, where are you?' She saw him standing there. 'Ed, you shouldn't be out here in the cold like this,' she said. Then she seemed to notice the contents of the waste bin. She stared at it puzzledly, and then at Bella Cray, and then Ed, with a sort of slow, patiently dawning anger. Finally, she said to Bella: 'These people got no one to speak for them, they live in a warren, they get the shit end of every stick: you got no call to stuff them in a waste bin too.'

Bella Cray looked amused.

'"You got no call",' she mimicked. She stared interestedly up at Annie, who was perhaps twice her height, then went back to working with the lipstick. 'Who's this horse?' she asked Ed. 'Hey, let me guess. I bet you're fucking her, Ed. I bet you're fucking this horse!'

'Look,' Ed said. 'It's me you want.'

'That's clever of you, to work that out.'

Bella replaced the compact in her purse and started to zip the purse up. Then she seemed to remember something.

'Wait,' she said. 'You've got to see this—'

She had the Chambers gun half out when Annie Glyph's hands – big-knuckled and clumsy, calloused from five years in the rickshaw shafts, trembling a little from all that *café électrique* – closed over it. Ed loved those hands but he never got the wrong side of them. There was a barely noticeable struggle then Annie had passed the pistol to him. He checked the load, which resembled a black oily fluid but was really a kind of particle-jockey's nightmare held in place by magnetic fields. He swept the shadows for tell-tale signs of gun-punks, which were generally raincoats, shoes with big soles, anyone with a nova grenade or a bad haircut. Meanwhile, Annie had one hand still clamped over both of Bella's: this simple grip she used to hoist Bella slowly off the floor.

'Now we can talk face to face,' she said.

'What's this?' Bella said. 'Is this your dubious shot at fame? You think you won't get hurt for this?' She raised her voice. 'Hey, Ed, you think I don't have guys out there?'

'That's a valid point,' Ed told Annie.

'There's no one out there,' Annie said. 'It's the night.'

Her free hand went up, curled all the way round Bella's neck and met itself coming the other way. Bella made a noise. Her face got red, she milled her arms about like a baby. One of her shoes fell off.

'Jesus, Annie,' Ed said. 'Put her down and let's get out of here.'

The fact was, it filled him with anxiety to see one of the Cray sisters treated like this. He owed his recent personality to being her victim. Bella was everywhere. In this city at least she was broadband, nationwide. She earned from everyone she saw. She had her finger in every pie from Earth-heroin to giftwrap. Bella bought gun-punks and love-kiddies. For relaxation she had a patch which made her come all day then, like a female mantis, eat Mr Lucky with her favourite sauce. This was the woman who had sworn to revenge herself after Ed killed her sister. If she proved so easy to show up on her own turf, where did that leave Ed? Besides, no one, as he knew from the personal evidence in the waste bin, turned the tables on Bella Cray for long. He shivered.

'There's a fog coming up, Annie,' he said.

Annie was explaining to Bella, 'You don't see the consequences of your acts, you might as well be in a twink-tank.' She forced Bella to look in the waste bin. 'I want you to understand what you did when you did this,' she said. 'What you *really* did.'

Bella tried to laugh. What came out was, 'Guck guck guck.'

Annie's grip tightened. Bella's colour deepened. She squeezed out one more guck and went limp. At that Annie seemed to lose interest. She dropped Bella on the floor and picked up Bella's purse instead. 'Hey Ed, look! It's full of money!' She sheafed the money into her hands and held it up and laughed like a kid. Annie's delight never knew any bounds. She was a rickshaw girl. Everything she did, she was full-on inside it. They would have called her simple in another age; but that was the last thing she was. 'Ed, I never *saw* so much money!' While she was counting it, Bella Cray scraped herself off the concrete and limped quickly away into the fog. She seemed a little one-sided.

Ed raised the Chambers gun, but it was too late to get a shot. Bella was gone. He sighed.

'No good will come of this,' he said.

'Oh yes it will,' said Annie. She rolled up the money. 'Better I have it than that little cow. You'll see.'

'She won't rest until you're dead too.'

Towards dawn the two of them trundled the waste bin across the concrete and into the dunes, where Ed buried Tig and Neena and stuck the Monster Beach sign in the sand over them. Annie stood in the fog for a moment, then said, 'I'm sorry about your friends, Ed,' and went to bed; but Ed stayed until the fog cleared, the seabirds began to call and the onshore wind ruffled the marram grass, thinking of Neena Vesicle and how when he was inside her she would tremble and say, 'Push harder. Oh. Me.' Something changed for Ed that night. The next show he did, he dreamed right through his childhood and into another place.

TWENTY-FIVE

Swallowed by the God

Michael and Anna Kearney, with their English accents, careful clothes and slightly puzzled air, drove north from New York City again. This time they were in no hurry. Kearney rented a little grey BMW from an uptown dealer, and they dawdled north into Long Island, then, back on the mainland, followed the coastline up into Massachusetts.

They stopped to look at anything that caught their eye, anything the highway signs suggested might be of interest. There wasn't much, unless you counted the sea. Kearney, with the air of a man suddenly able to accept his own past, browsed the flea markets and thrift stores of every town they passed through, unearthing used books, ancient videotapes and CD remasterings of albums he had once liked but had never been able to acknowledge in public. These had titles like *The Unforgettable Fire* and *The Hounds of Love*. Anna looked at him sidelong, amused: puzzled. They ate three times a day, often in waterfront fish restaurants, and though Anna put on weight, she no longer complained. They stayed a night here, a night there, avoiding motels, seeking instead the picturesque bed-and-breakfast offered by retired lipstick lesbians or middle-aged brokers fleeing the consequences of the Great Bull Market. Genuine English marmalade. Views of gulls, tidewrack, upturned dories. Clean and seaside places.

In this roundabout way they came again to Monster Beach, where Kearney got them a clapboard cottage facing the ocean across a narrow road and some dunes. It was as bare inside as the beach, with uncurtained windows, scrubbed wooden floors, and bunches of dried thyme hanging in corners. Outside, a few shreds of pale blue paint clung to the grey boards in the onshore winds.

'But we've got TV,' Anna said. 'And mice.' Later she said: 'Why are we here?'

Kearney wasn't sure how to answer that.

'We're hiding, I suppose.'

At night he still dreamed of Brian Tate and the white cat, melting like tallow in the foetid heat of the Faraday cage: but now he saw them increasingly in situations that made no sense. Taking up bizarre formal seated postures, they toppled away from him against a fundamental blackness. The cat, though it looked exactly like an ornament on a shelf, was as big as the man. (This curious detail of scale, the dream's comment upon itself, caused Kearney a rush of misery – strengthless, stark, unbelievably depressing.) Still toppling, they became smaller and smaller, to vanish from sight, gesticulating hieratically, against a background of slowly exploding stars and nebulae.

Compared to this, the death of Valentine Sprake, though it lost in memory nothing of its grotesqueness, had begun to seem like a side-issue.

'We're hiding,' Kearney repeated.

During his third year at Cambridge, before he met Anna, or murdered anyone, he had glanced into a stationer's window one day on his way into Trinity College. Inside was a display of engraved wedding cards which, as he walked past it, seemed for a moment to merge indistinguishably with the discarded bus tickets and ATM receipts which littered the pavement at his feet. The inside and the outside, he saw, the window display and the street, were only extensions of one another.

He was still making journeys under the auspices of the Tarot cards. Two or three days later, somewhere between Portsmouth and Charing Cross, his train was delayed first by repair works along the line then by a fault in one of its power cars. Kearney dozed, then woke abruptly. The train wasn't moving and he had no idea where he was, though it must be a station: passengers prowled outside the windows in the bitter cold, among them two clergymen with that uniform whiteness of hair which has been lost to the laity. He fell asleep again, to dream briefly of the lost pleasures of Gorselands, then woke suddenly in the horrified certainty that he had called out in his sleep. The whole carriage had heard him. He was twenty years old, but his future was clear. If he continued to travel like this he would become someone who made noises in his sleep on the London express: a middle-aged man with bad teeth and a cloth briefcase, head resting uncomfortably in the corner of the seat back as his mind unravelled like a pullover and everything became illegible to him.

That was the last of his epiphanies. By its light the Tarot, generator of epiphanies, looked like a trap. It looked like the drabbest of careers. Journeys – perhaps infinite numbers of them – remained nested within it like fractal dimensions: but the medium had become as transparent to him as the stationer's window, and they were too easy to unpack. He was twenty years old, and the clean yellow front of an Intercity train, rushing towards the platform in the sunlight, no longer filled him with excitement. He had slept in too many overheated rooms, eaten in too many station cafés. He had waited for too many connections.

He was ready, without knowing it, for the next great transition of his life.

'*Are* we hiding?' Anna said.

'Yes.'

She came and put herself in front of him, close to, so that he could feel the heat from her skin.

'Are you sure?'

Perhaps he wasn't. Perhaps he was waiting. He sat out there on Monster Beach each night after she had gone to sleep. If he expected his nemesis, he was disappointed: for once it was nowhere near. Something in that relationship had changed forever. For the first time since their original encounter, Kearney – though he shook with fear upon confronting the idea – was encouraging the Shrander to catch up. Did he feel it stop? Turn its head, as intelligently as a bird, to listen for him now? Did it wonder why he was trailing his coat?

Out there at night he hadn't much else to do but wait, and watch the ocean waves go in and out beneath the hard stars. Cold offshore winds picked up the sand and trickled it, hissing, between the marram grass on the dunes. There was a shivering luminescence. Kearney had a sense of things as endless: in this scheme the beach became a metaphor for some other transitional site or boundary, a beach at the edge of which lapped the whole universe. What kinds of monsters might wash up on a beach like that? More than the rotten, devolved carcass of a basking shark; more than the plesiosaur for which it had been so briefly and headily mistaken in 1970. Most nights he would go back into the cottage and take out the pocket drive containing Brian Tate's last data. Most nights he turned it over for a minute or two in his hands in the cold blue light of the TV screen, then put it away again. Once, he got out his laptop and connected the drive to it, though he switched neither of them on, going instead into the bedroom where he got fully clothed into bed beside Anna and placed the palm of his hand against her sex until she half-woke and groaned.

By day he played those old records, or sifted through the TV channels looking for anything that passed for science news. Everything seemed to amuse him. Anna didn't know what to make of it. One morning at breakfast she asked him:

247

'Will you kill me, do you suppose?'

'I don't think so,' he answered. 'Not now.' Then he said, 'I don't know.'

She put her hand over his.

'You will, you know,' she said. 'You won't be able to stop yourself in the end.'

Kearney stared out of the window at the ocean.

'I don't know.'

She took away her hand and kept herself to herself all morning. Equivocation always made her puzzled and, he thought, angry. It had to do with her childhood. Her problem with life was really the same as his: not giving it much credit, she had sought something which seemed more demanding. But there was more to what was happening than that. They'd driven themselves past the norms of their relationship, they had no idea what to make of each other. He didn't want her to be healthy. She didn't want him to be reliable or good-natured. They paced around one another by night, looking for openings, looking for less ordinary attitudes to force on one another. Anna was good at it. She surprised him by inviting him, off the back of one those brilliant, vulnerable smiles of hers:

'Would you like to put your cock inside me?'

They had taken the patchwork quilt off the bed and arranged it in front of the hearth, where driftwood was burning down to pure white ash. Anna, almost as white, lay half on her side in the firelight. He looked down thoughtfully at the hollows and shadows of her body.

'No,' he told her. 'I don't think I would.'

She bit her lip and turned her back.

'What's the matter with me?'

'You never wanted it,' he said cautiously.

'I did want it,' she said. 'I wanted it from the beginning, but it was easy to see you didn't. Half the girls at Cambridge knew. All you'd do was wank them off, and you never even came yourself. Inge Neumann – the girl with the Tarot cards? – was quite puzzled about it.' At this he looked so mortified she laughed. 'At least I *got* you to come,' she said.

The only reprisal he had was to tell her about Gorselands.

'You would never see the house from the road,' he said. He leaned forward, anxious with the effort of imagining it all. 'It was so well hidden. Only trees thick with ivy, a few yards of mossy driveway, the nameplate.' In the grounds, everything was cool and shadowy except where the sun struck through on to a lawn like a broad pool. 'It looked so real.' The same light struck through into a third floor room, where, in the heat under the roof, it was always late afternoon and there was always a deep, inturned breathing sound, like the breath of someone who has lost all consciousness of themselves. 'Then my cousins would arrive and begin taking their clothes off.' He laughed. 'That's what I imagined, anyway,' he said. When Anna looked puzzled, he said: 'I would watch them and masturbate.'

'But this wasn't real?'

'Oh no. It was just a fantasy.'

'Then I don't—'

'I had nothing to do with them in life.' He had never once approached them in life. They had seemed too energetic, too brutal. 'The Gorselands fantasy spoilt everything for me. When I got to Cambridge I couldn't do anything.'

He shrugged.

'I don't know why,' he admitted. 'I just couldn't forget it. The promise of it.'

She stared at him.

'But that's so exploitative,' she said, 'using other people for something that only ever goes on inside you.'

'I ran away from the things I wanted—' he tried to explain.

'No,' she said. 'That's awful.'

She took the quilt by one corner and dragged it back into the bedroom. He heard the bed creak as she flung herself down on it. He felt abashed, caved-in. He said miserably, at least half-believing himself:

'I always thought the Shrander was my punishment for that.'

'Go away.'

'*You* used *me*,' he said.

'I didn't. I never did.'

TWENTY-SIX

50,000 degrees K

'We had some luck of course,' admitted Uncle Zip.

Seria Mau had returned to orbit to find the *Moire* pod all over everything like a cheap suit. She had given them some grief on her way out of there, and was now holed up among the gravitational rocks and shoals of the inner system, talking to Uncle Zip via a network of randomly switching proxy transmitters. The *Moire* pod – accepting this precaution as a challenge, and rather glad to be out of a fight Uncle Zip wouldn't allow them to win – had licked their wounds, pooled their mathematics and were rolling up the network at a rate of ten million guesses a nanosecond. Meanwhile, Seria Mau's fetch looked up at Uncle Zip, and Uncle Zip looked down at her. She could barely see his pipe-clayed face and fancy waistcoat for the creaking under-curve of his belly, clad in captain's ducks and restrained by a black leather belt fully eight inches wide. He had in one hand something that resembled a brass telescope, and in the other an ancient paper fakebook, 'The Galaxy and its Stars'. His sailor hat was on his head, with Kiss Me Quick in cursive script around the crown.

'There's no substitute for luck,' he said.

What had happened was this: in their haste to beat one another to the *White Cat*, Uncle Zip and the commander of the Nastic heavy cruiser *Touching the Void* had collided in the Motel Splendido parking lot. At the time of the collision, Uncle Zip's vehicle of choice – the K-ship *El Rayo X*, on loan, along with the *Krishna Moire* pod, from undisclosed contacts in the bureaucracy of EMC – had already torched up to around twenty-five per cent the speed of light. Thirty or forty seconds later, it was buried deep below the Nastic vessel's greenish rind-like hull, having penetrated the whorled internal structures as far as the command and control centre before losing momentum. *Touching the Void* absorbed this incoming energy in a simple Newtonian fashion, retransmitting it as heat, noise, and – finally – a sluggish acceleration in the direction of the Lesser Magellanic Cloud. Its ruptured hull was promptly surrounded by clouds of shadow operators trying to make damage estimates. A caul of tiny repair machines – low-end swarming programmes mediating via a substrate of smart ceramic glue – began to seal the hole.

'Meanwhile,' said Uncle Zip, 'I find that by his own lights the guy is in fact already dead, though his ship-math maintains him as some sort of fetch. I say, "Hey, we can still work together. Being dead this way is no impediment to that," and he agrees. It made sense we worked together. Working together can sometimes be the right thing.'

So that was how it was. Uncle Zip's shadow operators, correctly assuming that neither ship was going anywhere on its own, began to build software bridges between the K-ship's mathematics and the propulsion systems of its new host. No one had ever done this before: but within hours they were back up and running and in pursuit of the *White Cat*, their origin, position and motives cloaked beneath the curious double signature which had so puzzled Seria Mau. 'Some luck was involved,' Uncle Zip repeated. He seemed to like the idea. He spread his hands comfortably. 'Things came unstuck a couple of times along the way. But here we are.'

He looked down at her. 'You and me, Seria Mau,' he said, 'we got to work together too.'

'Don't hold your breath, Uncle Zip.'

'Why is that?'

'Because of everything. But mainly because you killed your son.'

'Hey,' he said. '*You* did that. Don't look at me!' He shook his head. 'It must be convenient to forget events so soon.'

Seria Mau had to acknowledge the truth of that.

'But it was you involved me with him,' she said. 'You wound me up and set me going. And why bother, anyway, when you already knew where Billy was? You knew it all along, or else you couldn't have told me. You could have found him any time. Why the charade?'

Uncle Zip considered how to answer.

'That's true,' he admitted in the end: 'I didn't need to find him. But I knew he would never share that secret source of his. He was down there on that shithole rainy planet for ten years, just hoping I would ask, so he could say no. So instead I sent him what he needed: I sent him a sad story. I showed him he could still do something good in the world. I sent him someone worse off than he was, someone he could help. I sent him you. I knew he'd offer to take you there.'

He shrugged.

'I figured I could follow you,' he said.

'Uncle Zip, you bastard.'

'Some people have said that,' admitted Uncle Zip.

'Well, Billy told me nothing in the end. You didn't guess him right. He only came aboard my ship to have sex with the Mona clone.'

'Ah,' said Uncle Zip. 'Everyone wants sex with Mona.'

He smiled reminiscently.

'She was one of mine, too,' he said. Then he shook his head sadly. 'Things weren't good between me and Billy Anker since his first day out the incubator. It sometimes happens with a father and a son. Maybe I was too tough on him. But he never found himself, you know? Which was a pity, because he so much resembled me when I was young, before I did one entrada too many and as a consequence got this fat disease.'

Seria Mau cut the connection.

The sound of alarms. Under its shifting blue and grey internal light, the *White Cat* felt empty and haunted at the same time. Shadow operators hung beneath the ceilings of the human quarters, pointing at Seria Mau and whispering among themselves like bereaved sisters. 'For God's sake what's the matter now?' she asked them. They covered one another's bruised-looking mouths with their fingers. The *Moire* pod had chased down most of the RF proxies and were running about after the rest like a lot of dogs on the Carmody waterfront at night. 'We have a buffer a few nanoseconds thick,' her mathematics warned her. 'We should either fight or leave.' It thought for a moment. 'If we fight, they'll probably win.'

'Well then, go.'

'Where?'

'Anywhere. Just lose them.'

'We might lose the K-pod, but not the Nastic ship. Their navigational systems aren't as good as me, but their pilot is better than you.'

'*Don't keep saying that!*' shrieked Seria Mau. Then she laughed. 'What does it matter, after all? They won't hurt us – not until they find out where we're going, anyway. And maybe not even then.'

'Where are we going?'

'Wouldn't you like to know!'

'We can't go there unless I do,' the mathematics reminded her.

'Ramp me up,' said Seria Mau. Instantly, the fourteen dimensions of the *White Cat's* sensorium folded out around her, and she was on ship-time. One nanosecond, she could smell vacuum. Two, she could feel the minute caress of dark matter against the hull. Three, she could tune into the hideous fusion life of the local sun, with its sounds no one has ever described. Four nanoseconds, and she had the shifting constantly redesigned command languages of the *Moire* pod drifting up to her through something like layers of clear liquid, which was the encryption they were suspended in. In five nanoseconds she knew everything about them: propulsion status, rate of burn, ordnance on call. What damage they were carrying from the day's encounter – the hulls thinned at crucial points from particle ablation, the arsenals depleted. She could feel the nanomachines working overtime to shore up their internal architecture. They were too young and stupid to realise how damaged they were. She thought she could beat them, whatever the mathematics said. She hung there a further nanosecond, warming herself in the fourteen-dimensional night. Blinks and fibres of illumination came and went. Distant things like noises. She heard Krishna Moire say, 'Got it!' but knew he hadn't.

This was the place for her.

It was the place for people who didn't know what they were any more. Who had never known. Uncle Zip had called her 'a sad story'. Her mother was long dead. She had not seen her brother or father for fifteen years. Mona the clone had felt only contempt for her, and Billy Anker had pitied her even as she killed him: in addition his hard death still hung before her, like the menu for her own. Then she conned herself that all the complex stuff of being human was transparent at this level of things, and she could see straight through it to the other side – right to the simple code beneath. She could stay or go: in this place as in life. She was the ship.

'Arm me,' she commanded.

'Is this what you want?'

'Arm me.'

At that exact juncture, the K-pod found the last of her proxies and began unspooling the thread that led to her. But she was connected, and they were still thinking in milliseconds. Each time they found her, she was somewhere else. Then, in the instant it took them to realise what had happened, she had got into their personal space.

The engagement had to take place within one and a half

minutes, or Seria Mau would burn out. During that time she would flicker unpredictably in and out of normal space fifty or sixty thousand times. She would remember little of it afterwards, an image here, an image there. In ship-space, a high-end gamma burst, generating 50,000K for an endless fourteen nanoseconds, looked like a flower. Targets turned under the gaze of her acquisition systems like diagrams, to be flipped this or that number of degrees in seven dimensions until they bloomed like flowers too. To the targets themselves the *White Cat* seemed to come out of nowhere on three or four different arcs which though sequential appeared simultaneous, in a mist of decoys, false signals and invented battle languages, a froth of code and violence which could have only the one conclusion. 'The fact is, boys,' she commiserated, '*I'm* not sure which of these is me.' The *Norma Shirike*, struggling to connect, broke up into a cloud of pixels, like jigsaw pieces blown off a table in a high wind. The *Kris Rhamion* and the *Sharmon Kier*, trying not to run into one another in their haste to get away, ran into a small asteroid instead. Suddenly, it was all unmatched bits and pieces, floating in nowhere. They had ragged edges. None of them looked human, at any scale she chose. Local space was cooling down, but it was still like a cooker, resonating with light and heat, glittering with exotic particles and phase states. It was beautiful.

'I love it in here,' she said.

'You have three milliseconds left,' the mathematics warned her. 'And we didn't get them all. I think one of them left the system. But Moire himself is loose and I'm still looking for him.'

'Leave me in here.'

'I can't do that.'

'Leave me in, or we're stuffed anyway. He used his team as decoys, went on ship-time late. The bet was he would have a millisecond or two left to bounce me as I slowed down.' It was a textbook tactic and she had fallen for it. '*Moire, you fucker, I know what you're up to!*' Too late. She was back on normal time. The tank proteome, flushed with nutrients and hormonal tranquillisers, was beginning to try and repair her. She could barely stay awake. 'Fuck,' she told the mathematics. 'Fuck, fuck, fuck.' There was laughter on the RF frequencies. Krishna Moire flickered briefly into existence in front of her, dressed in his powder-blue stormtroop uniform.

'Hey, Seria,' he said. 'What's this, you ask? Well it's goodnight from me. And a *fucking* goodnight to you.'

'He's on us,' said the mathematics.

Moire's ship flickered towards her through the wreckage. It looked like a ghost. It looked like a shark. Nothing she could do would be fast enough. The *White Cat* turned and turned in panic like one of her own victims, looking for a way out. Then everything lit up like a Christmas tree, and the *Krishna Moire* was batted away in the blast, a black needle toppling end over end against the dying flare of the explosion. In the same instant, Seria Mau became aware that something huge had materialised beside the *White Cat*. It was the Nastic cruiser, its vast, mouldy-looking hull, like a rotting windfall in some old orchard, still crawling with autorepair media.

'Jesus,' she said. 'They bumped him. Uncle Zip bumped his own guy.'

'I don't think it was Uncle Zip,' the mathematics said. 'The command came from somewhere else in the ship.' A dry laugh. 'It's like the bicameral mind in there.'

Seria Mau felt weepy when she heard this.

'It was the *commander*,' she said. 'He always liked me. And I always liked him.'

'You don't like anyone,' the mathematics pointed out.

'Usually I don't,' said Seria Mau. 'But I'm very up and down today. I can't work out what's the matter with me.' Then she said: 'Where's that bastard Moire?'

'He's down in the outer layers of the gas giant. He got out by surfing the expansion wave of the bump. He's taken damage, but his engines still work. Do you want to go in after him?'

'No. Cook it up.'

'Pardon?'

'Cook the fucker up.'

'?'

'If you want something done,' sighed Seria Mau, 'do it yourself. There.' Ordnance disengaged from one of the complex outer structures of the *White Cat*, hung for the blink of an eye while its engine fired, then streaked down into the gas giant's atmosphere. Gravity tried to crush it out of existence, but between here and there it had turned itself into the voice of God. Something like lightning flared across the face of the gas giant, as it began to torch itself up. Uncle Zip opened a line to the *White Cat*. He was puffing out his cheeks angrily. 'Hey,' he said, 'all that was unnecessary. You know? I paid good money for those guys. In the end I wouldn't of let them hurt you.'

Seria Mau ignored him.

'Better light out,' she advised her mathematics. She yawned. 'This is where we're going,' she said. And finally: 'I really didn't want to be bothered with that fucker again. I was just too tired.'

As they left the system, a new star had begun to burn behind them.

Seria Mau slept for a long time, dreamlessly at first. Then she began to see images. She saw the New Pearl River. She saw the garden, gloomy under rain. She saw herself from a great distance, very small but clear. She was thirteen. She had gone to sign up for the K-ships. She was saying goodbye to her brother and her father. The scene was this: the station at Saulsignon, still pretty under its wartime skies, which were just like the wartime skies of Antique European Earth, blue, turbulent, vapour-trailed but full of hope. She saw herself wave, and she saw the father raise his hand. The brother refused to wave. He didn't want her to go, so he refused even to look at her. This scene faded slowly. After that, she glimpsed herself when she was last human, sitting on the edge of a bed shivering, vomiting into a plastic bowl while she tried to hold around her a cotton robe that fell open constantly at the back.

You sign up for the K-ships in sterile white rooms at even

temperatures: nevertheless, whatever you do you can't get warm. You mustn't have eaten. They give you the emetics anyway. They give you the injection. They give you the tests, but to be honest that is only to pass the two or three days it takes the injection to work. By then your bloodstream is teaming with selected pathogens, artificial parasites and tailored enzymes. You present with the symptoms of MS, lupus and schizophrenia. They strap you down and give you a rubber gag to bite on. The way is cleared for the shadow operators, running on a nanomech substrate at the submicrometre level, which soon begin to take your sympathetic nervous system to pieces. They flush the rubbish out continually through the colon. They pump you with a white paste of ten-micrometre-range factories which will farm exotic proteins and monitor your internal indicators. They core you at four points down the spine. You are conscious all the way through this process, except for the brief moment when they introduce you to the K-code itself. Many recruits, even now, don't make it past that point. If you do, they seal you in the tank. By then they have broken most of your bones, and taken some of your organs out: you are blind and deaf, and all you are aware of is a kind of nauseous surf rolling through you forever. They have cut into your neocortex so that it will accept the software bridge known ironically as 'the Einstein Cross' from the shape you see the first time you use it. You are no longer alone. You will soon be able to consciously process billions of billions of bits per second; but you will never walk again. You will never laugh or touch someone or be touched, fuck or be fucked. You will never do anything for yourself again. You will never even shit for yourself again. You have signed up. It comes to you for an instant that you were able to choose this but that you will never, ever, ever be able to unchoose it.

In the dream, Seria Mau saw herself from above. All these years on, she wept at what she had done to herself back then. Her skin was like a fish's skin. She was trembling in the tank like a damaged experimental animal. But her brother would not even wave her goodbye that day. That in itself was reason enough. Who wanted a

259

world like that, where you had to be the mother all the time, and your brother wouldn't even wave goodbye?

Abruptly Seria Mau was looking at a picture of a blank interior wall covered with ruched grey silk. After some time, the upper body of a man – he was tall, thin, dressed in a black tailcoat and starched white shirt; he held in one white-gloved hand a top hat, in the other an ebony cane – bent itself slowly into the frame of the picture. Seria Mau trusted him immediately. He had laughter in his eyes – they were a penetrating light blue – and a black pencil moustache, and his jet-black hair was brilliantined close to his head. It occurred to her that he was bowing. After a long while, when he had bent as much of his body into her field of vision as he could without actually stepping into it, he smiled at her, and in a quiet, friendly voice said:

'You must forgive yourself all this.'

'But—' Seria Mau heard herself reply.

At this, the ruched silk background was replaced by a group of three arched windows opening on to the blunt glare of the Kefahuchi Tract. This made the room itself appear to be toppling through space at a measured, subrelativistic pace.

'You must forgive yourself for everything,' the conjuror said.

Slowly, he tipped his hat to her, and bowed himself back out of the picture. Before he had quite gone, he beckoned her to follow him. She woke up suddenly.

'Send the shadow operators to me,' she told her ship.

TWENTY-SEVEN

The Alcubiere Break

Ed's fishtank movie showed him his sister leaving again.

'But will you come back?' the father begged her. There was no answer to that. 'But will you?'

Ed wrenched his head around on his neck as far as it would go, stared at anything – the flower tubs, the white cumulus clouds, the tabby cat – so as not to look at either of them. He wouldn't have a kiss from her. He wouldn't wave goodbye. She bit her bottom lip and turned away. Ed knew this was a memory. He wished he could piece it together with the other stuff he remembered, make sense of the shitty retrospective project of his life. But her face wavered as if behind water, decoherent and strange, and suddenly he was right through it and out the other side.

Everything lurched as he went through, and there was nothing but blackness and a sense of enormous speed. A few dim points of light. A chaotic attractor churning and boiling in the cheap iridescent colours of 400-year-old computer art. Like a wound in the firmament.

'You believe this shit?' Ed said.

His voice echoed. Then he was out the other side of that too, and toppling in empty space forever, where he could hear the precise roaring surf of the songs of the universe, nested inside each other like fractal dimensions –

– and then woke and found he was still on stage. It was unusual for that to happen, and maybe what had wakened him was this unlooked-for noise he had heard, swelling up to penetrate his prophetic coma like the sound of the waves as they fall on Monster Beach. He opened his eyes. The audience, still on its feet, was applauding him for the third solid minute. Of them all, Sandra Shen was the only one still seated. Eyeing him from the front row with an ironic smile, she tapped her little oriental paws slowly together. Ed leaned forward to try and hear the sound they made. Fainted.

Next he woke with the smell of salt in his nostrils. The great bulk of the dunes was black over him. Above that, the neck of the night with its cheap ornaments strung round it. Both of those were more comforting than the silhouette of the circus owner, the red ember of her bat-shit cigarette. She seemed pleased.

'Ed, you did so well!'

'What did I *say*? What happened?'

'What happened, they loved you Ed,' she answered. 'You shot right through. I'd say you were their boy.' She laughed. 'I'd say you were my boy too.'

Ed tried to sit up.

'Where's Annie?'

'Annie had to be somewhere else, Ed. But I'm here.'

Ed stared up at her. She was kneeling behind his head, bent over so she could look in his face. Her face was upside down to him, faint, sallow with clues. A few lively motes spilled from her eyes, blew away on the sea wind. She smiled and stroked his forehead.

'Still bored, Ed? No need to be. The circus is yours. You can name your price. We can start selling futures. Oh, and Ed?'

'What?'

'We leave in a fortnight.'

*

He felt relieved. He felt doomed. He didn't know how to tell Annie. He drank all day in the bars of the coastal strip; or – which was not like him – practised voluntarily with the fishtank in the afternoons. He would have played the Ship Game, but the old men were long gone from the Dunes Motel. He would have twinked out but he was afraid to go downtown. Annie, meanwhile, absented herself from his life. She worked all night, and came in quietly after she thought Ed had gone to sleep. When they did meet, she was preoccupied, quiet, withdrawn. Had she guessed? She looked away from him when he smiled. This made him wretched enough to say:

'We have to talk.'

'Do we, Ed?'

'While we still remember each other.'

A week after he hit the jackpot, she didn't come home at all.

She was away three days. During that time, Madame Shen prepared to leave New Venusport. The exhibits were folded. The attractions were packed. The big tent was struck. Her ship, *The Perfect Low*, came down from the parking lot one bright blue morning. It turned out to be a tubby brass-coloured little dynaflow HS-SE freighter, forty or fifty years old, built cheap and cheerful with a pointed nose and long curved fins at the back. 'Well, Ed, what do you think of the rocket?' Sandra Shen asked. Ed stared up at the ripe-avocado geometry of its hull, blackened by tail-down landings from Motel Splendido to the Core.

'It's a dog,' he told her. 'You want my opinion.'

'You'd prefer a hyperdip,' she said. 'You'd prefer to be back on France Chance IV, going dive for dive with Liv Hula in a smart carbon hull. She couldn't have done it without you, Ed. She went on record later, "I only pushed so hard because I was afraid Ed Chianese would get there first".'

Ed shrugged.

'I did all that,' he said. 'I'd prefer to be with Annie now.'

'Oh ho. Now he can go, he can't bring himself to leave. Annie's got things to do at the moment, Ed.'

'Things for you?'

It was Sandra Shen's turn to shrug. She continued to gaze wryly up at her ship. After a moment she said: 'Don't you want to know why they love your show? Don't you want to know why they changed their minds about you?'

Ed shivered. He wasn't sure he did.

'Because you stopped the war-talk, Ed, and all the stuff about eels. You gave them a future instead. You gave them the Tract, glittering in front of them like an affordable asset. You took them in there, you showed them what they might find, what it might make them. Everything's worn out down here, and they know it. You didn't offer them retro, Ed. You said it *hadn't* all been done. You said, "Go deep!" That's what they wanted to hear: one day soon they were going to get off the beach at last, and into the sea!'

She laughed. 'You were very persuasive. Then you were sick.'

'But I've never been there,' Ed said. 'No one has.'

Sandra Shen licked a flake of local tobacco from the corner of her lower lip.

'That's right,' she said. 'They haven't, have they?'

Ed waited for Annie, she didn't come. One day, then two. He cleaned the room. He washed out her spare Lycra. He stared at the wall. Suddenly, when he didn't want to go anywhere, or be reminded there was anywhere to go, the port was full of activity. Rocket flare lit the dunes all night. Rickshaws bustled in and out. The circus was shipped, except for the aliens in their decorated mortsafes which you saw in the distance just after dawn, following their handlers across the concrete on some unknown errand. The third day, Ed got out an aluminium folding chair and sat in the sun with a bottle of Black Heart. Half past ten in the morning, a Pierpoint Street rickshaw entered the port from the city side and came on at a good clip.

Ed jumped to his feet. 'Hey, Annie! Annie!' he called. The chair went over, but he saved the rum. 'Annie!'

'Ed!'

She was laughing. He heard her call his name all the way across the concrete. But when the rickshaw pulled up in front of him in a cloud of advertisements like coloured smoke and tissue paper, it wasn't Annie between the shafts, only some other girl with big legs who looked him up and down ironically.

'Hey,' he said. 'Who are you?'

'You ain't ready to know,' said the rickshaw girl. She jerked her thumb over her shoulder. 'Your squeeze is in there.'

At that moment, Annie Glyph stepped down on to the concrete. Those missing three days she had put to use, and had herself made over – an investment unknowingly underpinned by the humiliated Bella Cray. The cut was radical. New clean flesh had flourished like magic in the tailor's soup. The old Annie was gone. What Ed saw was this: a girl not more than fifteen years old. She wore a calf-length pink satin skirt with a kick pleat at the back, and a bolero top in lime green angora wool that showed off her nipples. This she had accessorised with a little gold chain belt, also block-heeled sandals in transparent urethane. Her hair, a blonde floss, was done up in bunches with matching ribbon. Even with the shoes she was less than five foot two and a half inches tall.

'Hi Ed,' she said. 'Like it? It's called Mona.'

She looked down at herself. Looked back up at him and laughed. 'You like it!' she said.

She said anxiously: 'You do like it, don't you?' She said, 'Oh Ed. I'm so happy.'

Ed didn't know what to say. 'Do I know you?'

'Ed!'

'It was a joke,' he said. 'I see the resemblance now. It's nice, but I don't know why you did this.'

He said: 'I liked you the way you were.'

Annie stopped smiling.

'Jesus, Ed,' she said. 'It wasn't for you. It was for me.'

'I don't get this.'

'Ed, *I* wanted to be smaller.'

'This isn't smaller,' Ed said. 'It's Pierpoint Street.'

'Oh, great,' she said. 'Fuck off. It's what I am, Ed. Pierpoint Street.'

She got back in the rickshaw. To the rickshaw girl she said, 'Take me away from this fucker.' She got down out of the rickshaw again and stamped her foot. 'I love you Ed, but it has to be said you're a twink. What if I wanted to be fucked by someone bigger than me? What if that was what *I* needed to get off? You don't see that, that's why you're a twink.'

Ed stared at her. 'I'm having an argument with someone I don't even recognise,' he complained.

'*Look at me then.* You helped me when I was down, only I found out too late that being your mother was the price. Twinks always need a mother. What if I didn't want to be that any more?'

She sighed. She could see he didn't get it.

'Look,' she said. 'What's my life to you? You saved me, and I don't forget that. But I got my ideas about things. I got my ambitions, I always did. You're shipping out with Madam Shen anyway. Oh yes! You think I didn't know that? Ed, I was there before you. Only a twink would think I wasn't.

'We already saved each other, now it's time to save ourselves. You know I'm right.'

A long curved wave of bleakness raced towards Ed Chianese's shore: the Alcubiere break, which is the black surf gravity; which is the coiled swell of empty space that sucks into itself one significant event of your life after another and if you don't move on you're left there gazing out across nothing at nothing much again.

'I guess,' he said.

'Hey,' she said. 'Look at me.' She came close and made him look in her eyes. 'Ed, you'll be OK.'

Her tailored pheromones caused his head to spin. Her very voice gave him an erection. He kissed her. 'Mmmm,' she said. 'That's nice. You'll soon be out there again, flying those famous lady-pilots. Which I have to say I'm jealous of them.' Her eyes were the colour of speedwell in the water meadows of a New Venusport corporate village. Her hair smelled of peppermint shampoo.

Despite all this, she had completely natural lines. It was art not artifice. You would never know she had been to the tailor. She was sex on a stick, Mona the clone, the porn in your pocket.

'I got what I wanted, Ed –'

'I'm glad,' Ed made himself say. 'I really am.'

'– and I hope you will too.'

He kissed the top of her head. 'You take care, Annie.'

She let him see her smile.

'I will,' she said.

'Bella Cray . . .'

Annie shrugged.

'You didn't know me, Ed. How will she?'

She detached herself from him gently and got back in the rickshaw. 'You certain about this?' the rickshaw girl was prompted to enquire. 'Because you been in and out of there before.'

'I'm certain,' Annie said. 'I'm sorry.'

'Hey,' said the rickshaw girl, 'don't apologise. You work the port you're on a diet of raw sentiment.'

Annie laughed. She sniffed and wiped her eyes.

'You take care too,' she told Ed.

With that she was gone. Ed watched the rickshaw grow smaller and smaller as it crossed the bare concrete to the spaceport gate, its advertisements streaming after it like a cloud of coloured scarves and butterflies in the sun. Annie's little hand appeared for a moment, to be waved back at Ed, forlorn and cheerful at the same time. He heard her call something which he worked out later was, 'Don't spend too much time in the future!' Then she turned the corner to the city, and he never saw her again in that life.

Ed went and got drunk the rest of the day at the Café Surf and was dragged home in the dark by his former gambling partners from the Dunes Motel. There, he found Sandra Shen waiting for him with the fishtank under her arm. The old men laughed and blew on their hands to indicate scorching. 'You in trouble now, my man!' they predicted. All that night, pale white motes flickered in the dark in Annie Glyph's old room; then, later, on the dunes outside. Next day he woke exhausted aboard *The Perfect Low*. He was alone, and the ship was warming for take-off. He felt the hum of engines through her frame. He felt the tremble in the tips of her fins. The oily preflight roll of the dynaflow drivers came up to him from somewhere below and the hair rose on the back of his neck for the millionth time because he was alive in *this* place and *this* time, and leaving it all only to find something else out there.

Always more. Always more after that.

The little freighter shook with the excitement of it too. She balanced herself carefully on a column of flame and in her own tubby fashion hurled herself skyward.

'Hey Ed,' came Sandra Shen's dry voice a minute or two later. 'Look at this!'

The New Venusport parking orbit was full of K-ships. Pods and superpods stretched away as far as Ed could see, hundreds of them, in restlessly layered and shifting formations. They dipped in and out of local space, extruding weapons, as suspicious of one another as animals, hulls simmering gently in a bouillabaisse of particles. They shimmered with navigational fields, defensive fields, fields for target acquisition and ordnance control, fields which shed everything from soft X-rays to hard light. Local space miraged and twisted around them. They were hunting without moving. He could almost hear the poisonous throb of their engines.

War! he thought.

The Perfect Low, receiving clearance, edged between them and out of the lot.

TWENTY-EIGHT

Sparks in Everything

After the argument with Anna, Michael Kearney dressed and took the rental car into Boston, where he drank beer and caught Burger King before it closed, after which he sped deliberately up and down the coast road, driving in and out of thick white pockets of fog while he ate a bacon double cheeseburger with fries. The ocean, when you could see it, was a silver strip far out, the dunes at the south end of the bay heaped up black against it. Seabirds cackled on the beach even in the dark. Kearney parked the car, cut the engine, listened to the wind in the grass. He made his way down through the dunes and stood on the damp sand, stirring with the toe of one shoe the bands of tide-sorted shingle. After a moment, he had the impression of something huge sweeping in across the bay towards him. The monster was returning to its beach. Or perhaps not the monster itself, but whatever lay behind it, some condition of the world, the universe, the state of things, which is black, revelatory and, in the end, a relief – something you don't want to know but are perversely glad to have confirmed. It swept in directly from the east, directly from the horizon. It passed over him, or perhaps into him. He shivered and turned away from the beach, and trudged back up the dunes to the car, thinking about the woman he had killed in the English Midlands, where their idea of a dinner-table game was to ask:

'How do you see yourself spending the first minute of the new millennium?'

Even as he spoke he had wished he could answer differently. He had wished he could say the decent, optimistic kinds of things they were saying. Remembering this, he saw clearly how he had marginalised his own life. He had brought his life upon himself. Driving back to the cottage, he lowered the side window and threw the Burger King packaging out into the night.

When he got back, the cottage was silent.

'Anna?' he called.

He found her in the front room. The TV was on, with the sound turned down. Anna had dragged the quilt off the bed again and now sat cross-legged on it by the fire, her hands resting, palms upwards, on her knees. The pound or two she had put on over the last month made her thighs, belly and buttocks seem smooth and young; above, she was still as ribby as a horse. He had a feeling there was some insight in all this he wasn't quite close enough to see. Her wrists were so white that the veins in them looked like bruises. Next to her she had placed the carbon-steel chef's knife he had bought on their first visit to the beach. Its blade flickered in the TV light, uncertain and grey, which filled the room.

'I'm trying to scrape up all the courage I have, here,' she said, without looking away from the fire. Her voice was friendly. 'I knew you wouldn't want me if I got well.'

Kearney picked up the knife and put it out of her reach and his. He bent over her and kissed her spine where it snaked up between the thin scapulae.

'I do want you,' he said. He touched her wrists. They were hot but bloodless. 'Why are you doing this?'

She shrugged. She laughed a little fake laugh. 'It's a measure of last resort,' she said. 'It's a vote of no confidence.' Kearney's laptop lay open on top of the TV set, also switched on, though it displayed only wallpaper. Into it, Anna had plugged the pocket drive they got from Tate. Of all these gestures, Kearney thought, this was probably the most dangerous. When he said so, she shrugged. 'What I hate most of all is that you don't even need to kill me any more,' she said.

'Is that what you want? Me to kill you?'

'No!'

'Then what?'

'I don't know,' she said. 'Just please fuck me properly.'

It was awkward for both of them. Anna, instantly wet, presented herself determinedly; Kearney was less certain how to proceed. When he finally managed to penetrate her, he couldn't believe the heat of it. They began with what they knew, but she soon made him face her, urging him, 'Like this. Like this. I want to see you, I want to see your face.' Then: 'Is this better? Am I better than them?' For a second, he heard his cousins' laughter; Gorselands opened itself to him, then tilted and flickered away forever. He laughed. 'Yes,' he said. 'Yes!' It didn't last long, but she sighed and embraced him and gave further warm little sighs and smiles in a way she had never done before. They lay in front of the fire together for a while, then she encouraged him to try again.

'God,' he said experimentally. 'You're so wet.'

'I know. I know.'

The TV chirped almost silently to itself in the gloom above them. Ads passed across its screen, to be replaced by the logo of some science channel, and after that an image of great roseate streamers of gas and dust, studded with actinic stars, pocked and wrapped with velvety blackness, full of the beautiful false clarity of a Hubble telescope image. 'The Kefahuchi Tract,' announced the voice-over, 'named after its discoverer, may upset all our—' There was a sense of the screen filling suddenly, overflowing. Silent sparks of light began to pour out of it into the room, bouncing and foaming across the bare boards to the fireside, where they encountered Anna Kearney, biting her lower lip and moving her head back and forth in a dreamy, inturned manner. Into her hair they flowed, down her flushed cheeks, across her breastbone. Taking them to be a part of what she was feeling, she moaned a little, rubbing them in handfuls into her face and neck.

'Sparks,' she whispered. 'Sparks in everything.'

Kearney, hearing this, opened his eyes and got off her in terror. He grabbed up the chef's knife, then stood with it for a moment, naked and uncertain. 'Anna!' he said. 'Anna!' Fractal light poured from the TV screen like the fanned-out tail of a peacock. He ran aimlessly about the room for a moment until he found the Shrander's dice in their soft leather scrotum. Then he looked at Anna, looked at the knife. He thought he heard her try to warn him, 'It's coming, it's coming.' Then: 'Yes, kill me. Quickly.' Disgusted with himself forever, he threw down the knife and sprinted out of the cottage. That was it: something huge roared down towards him in the night, like a shadow out of the sky. Behind him he heard Anna laughing, and then murmuring again:

'Sparks. Sparks in everything . . .'

When Anna Kearney woke up, at five thirty the next morning, she found herself alone. The fire had gone out, the beach house was cold. The TV, still tuned to CNN, buzzed to itself and displayed images of current events: war in the Middle East, deprivation in the Far East, in Africa and Albania. War and deprivation everywhere. She rubbed her hands over her face, then, naked and shivering, stood up and collected her scattered underwear with amusement. I made him do it at last, she thought: but remembered the night only vaguely. 'Michael?' she called. The beach house had one external door, and he had left that open, allowing a little bright white sand to blow in across the threshold. 'Michael?' She pulled on her jeans and sweater.

Out on the beach the air was already bright, agitated. Kittiwakes swooped and fought over something in a clump of tidewrack. Up on the dunes Anna found flattened marram, the residue of some chemical smell, a long, shallow depression, as though something vast had settled there in the night. She looked down at Monster Beach: no marks.

'Michael!' she called.

Only the cries of the gulls.

She hugged herself against the cold breeze off the ocean, then walked back to the cottage, where she cooked eggs and sausages and ate them hungrily. 'I haven't felt so hungry,' she said to her own face in the bathroom mirror, 'since . . .' But she couldn't think what to add, it had been so long ago.

She waited for him for three days. She walked on the dunes, drove into Boston, cleaned the cottage from top to bottom. She ate. Much of the time she just sat in a chair with her legs curled up, listening to the afternoon rain on the window and remembering everything she could about him. Every so often she switched the TV on, but mostly she left it off and, staring at it thoughtfully, tried to picture the things they had done the night he went.

On the morning of the third day she stood at the door listening to the gulls fighting up and down above the beach. 'You won't come back now,' she said, and went inside to pack her things. 'I'll miss you,' she said. 'I really will.' She disconnected the outboard drive from Kearney's laptop and hid it under a layer of clothes. Then, unsure how it would be affected by the airport fluoroscope, slipped it in her purse instead. She would ask them at the desk. She had nothing to hide, and she was sure they would let it through. When she got back she would find Brian Tate, and hope – whatever had happened to him – he could carry on Michael's work. If not, she would have to phone someone at Sony.

She locked the beach house door and put the bags in the BMW. One last look along the dunes. Up there, with the wind taking her breath away, she had a clear memory of him at Cambridge, twenty years old, telling her with a kind of urgent wonder, 'Information might be a *substance*. Can you imagine that?'

She laughed out loud.

'Oh, Michael,' she said.

TWENTY-NINE

Surgery

The shadow operators flew to Seria Mau from all parts of the ship. They left the dark upper corners of the human quarters where, mourning the loss of Billy Anker and his girl, they had clung in loose temporary skeins like cobwebs in the folds of an old curtain. They abandoned the portholes, next to which they had been biting their thin, bony knuckles. They emerged from the software bridges and fakebook archives, the racked hardware on the smart-plastic surfaces of which they had lain undistinguishable from two weeks' dust in her father's house. They had undergone a sea change. Gossip rustled between them, bursts of data flickering like silver and random colours –

They said: 'Has she –?'

They said: 'Dare we –?'

They said: 'Is she really going out with him?'

Seria Mau watched them for a moment, feeling as remote as space. Then she ordered:

'Cut me the cultivar you have always wanted me to have.'

The shadow operators could scarcely believe their ears. They grew the cultivar in a tank much like her own, in an off-the-shelf proteome called Tailors' Soup, customised with inorganic substrates, code neither human nor machine, pinches of alien DNA and live math. They dried it out and eyed it critically. 'You'll look very nice, dear,' they told it, 'if you just wipe the sleep from your blue eyes now. Very nice indeed.' They brought it to the room in which she kept the Dr Haends package.

'*Here* she is,' they said. 'Isn't she lovely? Isn't she charming?'

'I could have done without the dress,' said Seria Mau.

'Oh but dear: she had to wear *something*.'

It was herself, twelve years old. They had decorated her pale hands with spirals of tiny seed pearls, and turned her out in a floor-length frock of icy white satin sprigged with muslin bows and draped in cream lace. Her train was supported at each corner by hovering, perfect, baby boys. She stared shyly up at the cameras in the corners, whispering:

'What was relinquished returns.'

'I can do without that, too,' said Seria Mau.

'But you must have a voice, dear –'

She didn't have time to argue. Suddenly she wanted it all over with. 'Bridge me in,' she said.

They bridged her in. Under the impact of this, the cultivar lost psychomotor control and fell back against a bulkhead. 'Oh,' it whispered. It slid down on to the deck, staring puzzledly at its own hands. 'Am I me?' it asked. 'Don't you want me to be me?' It kept glancing up and then down again, wiping compulsively at its face. 'I'm not sure where I am,' it said, before it shivered once and got to its feet as Seria Mau Genlicher. 'Aah,' whispered the shadow operators. 'It's all too beautiful.' Deco uplighters introduced to the room a gradual pearly illumination, wavering yet triumphant; while rediscovered choral works by Janáček and Philip Glass filled the air itself. Seria Mau stared around. She felt no more 'alive' than she had in the tank. What had she been so frightened of? Bodies were not new to her, and besides, this one had never been her self.

'The air smells like nothing in here,' she said. 'It smells like nothing.'

The Dr Haends package lay on the floor in front of her, locked up in Uncle Zip's red and green beribboned box – which, she saw now, was a kind of metaphor for the actual mechanisms of confinement the gene-tailor had used. She studied the box for a moment, as if it might look different viewed from real human eyes, then knelt down and threw back its lid. Instantly, a creamy white foam began to spill out into the room. *The Photographer* (revisioned from five surviving notes on a corrupted optical storage disc by the 22nd-century composer Onotodo-Ra) faded to the muzak it so resembled. Over it, a gentle chime rang, and a woman's voice called:

'Dr Haends. Dr Haends to surgery, please.'

Meanwhile, though dead by his own definitions since the collision with Uncle Zip's K-ship, the commander of the Nastic vessel *Touching the Void* flickered in and out of view in one of the darkened corners of the room. He looked like a cage made of leaky insect legs, but while his ship remained, so did the burden of his responsibilities. Among these he included Seria Mau Genlicher. She had impressed him as capable of behaviour even more meaningless than most human beings. He had watched her kill her own people with a ferocity that betrayed real grief. But she was someone, he had decided early, who struggled harder with life than she needed to: this he respected, even admired. It was a Nastic quality. Because of it, he had been surprised to discover, he felt he owed her a duty of care; and he had been trying to discharge it since he died. He had done what he could to protect her from the *Krishna Moire*. More importantly, he had been trying to tell her what he knew.

He wasn't sure he could remember all of it. He had no clear idea, for instance, why he had been co-operating with Uncle Zip in the first place: though he guessed perhaps that Uncle Zip had promised to share Billy Anker's discovery with him. An entire planet of unmined K-tech! On the eve of another war with human beings, this certainly would have seemed an attractive offer. It must, however, have begun to seem less attractive after the attempt to retailor the Dr Haends package. Uncle Zip had met with little success. All he had done was wake up something which already lived inside it. What that was, neither he nor the Nastic tailors had any idea. It was something much more intelligent than any of its predecessors. It was self-aware in a way that might take years to comprehend. If it had once been what Uncle Zip claimed it to be – a package of measures powerful enough to undo safely the bridge between the operator and the code: a kind of reverse signing-up – it was no longer anything like that.

It was alive, and it was looking for other K-code to talk to.

'If it's faulty,' Seria Mau said, 'there's one way to find out.'

Still kneeling, she leaned forward and extended her arms, palms up. The shadow operators lifted the red and green box until it lay across her arms, then streamed away from her like fish in an aquarium, flickering agitatedly this way and that.

'Don't ask me if I know what I'm doing,' she warned them. 'Because I don't.'

She got to her feet, and with her train spilling out behind her, walked slowly towards the nearest wall.

Foam poured from the box.

'Dr Haends –' it said.

'Take us up,' said Seria Mau to the wall.

The wall opened. White light spilled out to meet her, and Seria Mau Genlicher carried the package up into navigational space, where she intended to do what she should have done all along, and introduce it to the ship's mathematics. The shadow operators, rendered suddenly thoughtful by this decision, went up after her as demure as lace. The wall closed behind them all.

The Nastic commander watched from his corner. He made one more attempt to attract her attention.

'Seria Mau Genlicher,' he whispered, 'you really must listen—'

But – rapt, dissociated, pixilated in the way only a human being can be with the vertigo of commitment – she gave no sign of having noticed him, and all that happened was that the shadow operators chivvied him away. They were worried he would become involved with the train of her dress. That would have spoiled everything.

I hate to feel so weak and useless, he thought.

Shortly after that, events on his own bridge intervened. Uncle Zip, puzzled by what was going on and suddenly growing suspicious, had him shot. A realtime vacuum commando unit, which had been hacking its way grimly through the Nastic ship since the collision, finally broke into the command-and-control section and hosed it out with hand-held gamma ray lasers. The walls melted and dripped. The computers went down. The commander felt himself fade. It was a feeling of intolerable weariness, sudden cold. For a nanosecond he hung in the balance, beguiled by a shard of memory, the tiniest part of a dream. The papery structures of his home, a drowsy buzzing sound, some complex gesture he had once loved, gone too quickly to be pinned down. Curiously enough, his last thought was not for that but for Seria Mau Genlicher, chained to her horrible ship yet still fighting to be human. He was amused to find himself thinking this.

After all, he reminded himself. She was the enemy.

Two hours later and a thousand kilometres away, shrouded in blue light from the signature displays in the human quarters of *El Rayo X*, Uncle Zip the tailor sat on the three-legged wooden stool he had brought with him from Motel Splendido and tried to understand what was happening.

Touching the Void was under his control. He had nothing more to worry about in that direction. Nothing was alive down there in that rotten apple but his entradistas. Like the good team of lawyers they were they had begun to chop him out of his inadvertent contract with the Nastic vessel. It was a civil engineering project down there, with all the dull concussions and sudden flares you had to expect from that. Guys were getting a line open and saying,

'Hey Unc, could you give that a little more?' 'Could you give that a little less, Unc?' They were competing for his attention. And all the time now, his ship was gently trying to withdraw itself from the embrace of the cruiser. Uncle Zip thought of that embrace as a soft wet rottenness he would be glad to be out of. Trickles of particles flickered through the hull of *El Rayo X*, spun off from the destruction of the Nastic bridge. It was still hot down there. You had to give the guys their due, they were working in a heavily compromised environment. They had been dying for two hours now.

Touching the Void was his. But what was going on over there on the *White Cat*? It was total radio silence over there. K-ships had nothing you could call internal coms traffic: despite that you could usually tell if anyone was alive inside. Not in this case. Thirteen nanoseconds after the death of the Nastic commander, everything in the *White Cat* had switched itself off. The fusion engines were down. The dynaflow drivers were down. That ship wasn't even talking to itself, let alone Uncle Zip. 'I don't have time for this,' he complained. 'I got business elsewhere.' But he continued to watch. For another hour, nothing happened. Then, very slowly, a pale, wavering glow surrounded the *White Cat*. It was like a magnetic field, sketched slightly out from the ship's hull; or a faint diagram of some kind of fluid supercavitation effect. It was violet in colour.

'What's this?' Uncle Zip asked himself.

'Ionising radiation,' said his pilot in a bored voice. 'Oh, and I'm getting internal traffic.'

'Hey, who asked you?' said Uncle Zip. 'What kind of traffic?'

'Come to think of it, I got no idea.'

'Jesus.'

'It's stopped now anyway. Something was producing dark matter in there. Like the whole hull was full of it for a second.'

'That long?'

The pilot consulted his displays.

'Photinos, mostly,' he said.

After that, the ionising radiation died away and nothing happened for a further two hours. Then the *White Cat* jumped from blacked-out to torched-up without any intervening state. 'Jesus Christ!' screamed Uncle Zip. 'Get us out of here!' He thought she had exploded. His pilot went on ship-time and – ignoring the faint cries of the work teams still trapped inside – ripped the last few metres of the *El Rayo X* from the ruins of the Nastic vessel. He was good. He got them free and facing the right direction just in time to see the *White Cat* accelerate from a standstill to ninety-eight per cent the speed of light in less than fourteen seconds.

'Stay with them,' Uncle Zip told him quietly.

'France chance, honey,' the pilot said. 'That's no fusion engine.' Fierce annular shockwaves *in no detectable medium* were spilling back along the *White Cat*'s course. They were the colour of mercury. A moment or two later she reached the point where Einstein's universe would no longer put up with her, and vanished. 'They were building themselves a new drive,' the pilot said. 'New navigation systems. Maybe a whole new theory of everything. I can't deal with that. My guess: we're stuffed.'

Uncle Zip sat on his stool for thirty long seconds, staring at the empty displays. Eventually he rubbed his face.

'They'll go to Sigma End,' he decided. 'Make the best time you can.'

'I'm on it,' the pilot said.

Sigma End, Billy Anker's old stamping ground, was a cluster of ancient research stations and lashed-up entradista satellites sited in and around the Radio RX-1 accretion disc. Everything there was abandoned, or had the air of it. Anything new attracted the attention like a campfire seen in the distance for one night on an empty coast. This was deep Radio Bay. In places like this, Earth ran out of reach. Logistics went down. Supply lines dried up. Everything was for grabs, and the mad energy of the accretion disc lay over all of it. The black hole churned and churned, ripping material out of its companion star, V404 Stueck-Manibel, a blue supergiant at the end of its life. Those two had been locked together for a few billion years or so. This was the last of it: the wreckage of a fine old relationship. It looked like everything was going down the tubes for them.

'Which probably it is,' Uncle Zip's pilot told him. 'You know?'

'I didn't ask you here for your religious opinions,' said Uncle Zip. He stared out across the disc, and a faint smile crossed his fat white face. 'What we are looking at here is the most efficient energy transfer system in the universe.'

That disc was a roaring Einsteinian shoal. Gravitational warping from RX-1 meant you could see all of it, even the underneath, whatever angle you approached it from. Every ten minutes, transition states quaked across it, causing it to spike in the soft X-ray band, huge flares echoing backwards and forwards to illuminate the scattered experimental structures of Sigma End. Go close enough and this mad light enabled you to see clusters of barely pressurised vessels like leaky bathtubs, each hosting a failing hydroponic farm and two or three earthmen with lost eyes, bad stubble, radiation ulcers. You could see planets with ancient mass-drivers let into them, holding positions in the last stable orbit before the Schwarzchild radius. You could stumble over a group of eight perfectly spherical nickel-iron objects each the size of Motel Splendido, set into an orbital relationship which in itself seemed to be some sort of engine. But the outright prize, Uncle Zip said, went to the following effort: twenty million years before mankind arrived, some *fucker* had tapped off a millionth of one per cent of the output of the RX-1 system and punched a wormhole straight out of there to some destination no one knew. They had left behind no archeology whatsoever. No clue of how you would do it. Just the hole itself.

'Deep guys,' he said. 'Some really deep guys.'

'Hey,' the pilot interrupted him. 'I got them.' Then he said: 'Shit.'

'What?'

'They're going *down* it. There. Look.'

It was hard to lift the wormhole out of the overall signature of the accretion disc. But *El Rayo X* came with the equipment to do that, and on the displays Uncle Zip could just make it out, there in the boiling gravitational rapids just outside the last stable orbit: a fragile vulva of light into which the *White Cat* could be seen propelling herself like a tiny sliver of ice, those curious annular shockwaves still slipping regularly back along her brilliant raw trail of fusion product.

THIRTY

Radio RX-1

In the days that followed *The Perfect Low* wove her way across the halo. She was all bustle, her hull crowded to capacity, a warm, smelly node of humanity flying in the teeth of the vast Newtonian grin of empty space. A sense of purpose prevailed. Status-conscious and competitive at close quarters, the carnies were always dissatisfied with their accommodation, always, moving children and livestock from one part of the ship to another. Ed pushed his way up and down the packed companionways for a couple of days; then took up with an exotic dancer called Alice.

'I'm not looking for complications,' he warned her.

'Who is?' she said with a yawn.

Alice had good legs and bright expressionless eyes. She lay with her elbows on his bunk, staring out the porthole while he fucked her.

'Hello?' he said.

'Look at this,' she said. 'What do you make of this?'

Out in the vacuum, eighty metres from the porthole, hung an object Ed recognised: a mortsafe maybe fifty feet in length, brass-coloured, and decorated with finials, groins and gargoyles, its blunt bow shaped like a head melted and streamlined by time. It was one of Sandra Shen's aliens. They were never loaded aboard *The Perfect Low*. Instead, the day the circus left New Venusport they took off too, each firing some weird engine of its own – something that produced a mist of blue light, or curious slick pulses of energy that presented as a sound, a smell, a taste in the mouth – and giving new meaning to the words 'containment vessel'. Since then, they had followed the ship with a kind of relentless ease, flying lazy, complex patterns around its direction of travel, circling it when it lay at rest like aboriginals in the night in ancient movies.

'What do they want?' Alice asked herself. 'You know? I wonder how they think.' And when Ed only shrugged: 'Because they aren't like us. Any more than *she* is.'

She turned her attention to the world they now orbited, which could be seen – if you craned your neck a little and pressed your face up to the porthole – as a long bulge limned by its own atmosphere.

'And look at this dump,' she said. 'Planet of the Damned.'

She was right. *The Perfect Low*'s course was, in circus terms, as unrewarding as it was unpredictable. From the start they had avoided the halo moneypots – Polo Sport, Anais Anais, Motel Splendido – in favour of nightside landings on agricultural planets like Weber II and Perkins' Rent. Few performances were given. After a while, Ed noticed the ship's complement getting smaller. He never got the hang of what was going on. Sandra Shen was no help. He would glimpse her off in the distance, mediating an argument between carnies: by the time he had pushed his way towards her, she had gone. He knocked on the control-room door. No answer. 'If I'm not doing shows,' he said, 'I don't know why you made me train so hard.' Ed went back to his bunk and sweaty engagements with Alice while the dark matter trailed its weakened fingers down the hull outside. 'Another lot went last night,' she would say morosely after they had finished. The ship got emptier and emptier. The next time they landed, Alice went, too.

'We're not getting the work,' she said. 'We're not getting the shows.' There was no sense in staying under those circumstances. 'I can get a connection from here down to the Core,' she said.

'Take care,' Ed said.

He looked around him the next day and the circus was gone: Alice had been the last of it. Had she stayed for him? More out of nerves, he thought. It was a long way to the Core.

Madam Shen's exhibits still filled one hold. Everything else was gone. Ed stood in front of 'Michael Kearney & Brian Tate Looking Into A Monitor, 1999'. There was something feral and frightened in their expressions, as if they had used up all their effort to get the genie out of the bottle and were beginning to wonder if they would ever persuade it to go back in again. Ed shivered. In the other holds he found: a spangled Lycra bodysuit; a child's sock. The companionways still smelled of food, sweat, Black Heart rum. Ed's footsteps seemed to fill the hull, then echo out past it and into empty space.

Like any ship, *The Perfect Low* had her shadow operators.

They hung in corners like dusty spiderwebs: seemed less disused than cowed and anxious. Once or twice, as Ed roamed the empty ship, they detached themselves and flew about in shoals as if something was pursuing them. They clustered round the portholes, whispering and touching one another, then looking back at Ed as if he was going to betray them. They fled before him as he entered the control room, and flattened themselves against the walls.

'Hello?' called Ed.

The equipment dialled itself up at the sound of his voice.

Three hologram windows opened on to the dynaflow, featureless and grey. Recognising a pilot, direct connections offered themselves, to the drivers, the external coms, the Tate-Kearney mathematics.

Ed said: 'No.'

He sat in the pilot seat and watched thin ribbons of photinos stream past. There was no sign of a destination. There was no sign of Sandra Shen. Down by the side of the seat he found her fishtank, familiar but uncomforting, faint with the residues of memory, prophecy, applause. He was careful not to touch it: nevertheless, it knew he was there. Something seemed to shift inside it. At the same time, he felt changes in the dynaflow medium. A course correction had been made. He got out of the seat as if it had bitten him.

He called: 'Madam Shen? Hello?'

Nothing. Then alarm bells went off all over the ship and she popped out of the dynaflow very suddenly and the Kefahuchi Tract filled all three screens like a bad eye. It was very close.

'Shit,' said Ed.

He got back in the pilot seat. 'Direct connect,' he ordered. 'And give me the fakebooks.' He stared up at the screens. Light poured out of them. 'I've been here,' he said, 'but I can't— There! Rotate that. Again. Jesus, it's Radio Bay!'

It was worse than that. He was in his old stamping ground – the gravitation alley at Radio RX-1. The accretion disc roared up at him, quaking with soft X-ray pulses. He was coming in at a steep angle with his fusion torch full on. His coms were getting nothing but the identification beacons of the derelict research hulks – Easyville, Moscar 2, The Scoop: then, very faintly, Billy Anker's legendary Transubstantiation Station – communications as old as rust, Ed's past rushing back at him, partial, decoherent, twinked out. Any moment, he would be caught up in the Swartzchild surf, doomed to do the Black Hole Boogie in a fat tub. 'Get us out of here,' he told the direct connect. Nothing happened. 'Am I giving orders or not?' he asked the shadow operators. 'Can you see my lips move?' They looked away from him and covered their faces. Then he caught sight of a twist of frail light on the inner edge of the accretion disc.

He began to laugh. 'Oh fuck,' he said.

It was Billy Anker's wormhole.

'Come on, Billy,' Ed said, as if Billy was sitting next to him, rather than dead from this exact same adventure more than a decade ago: 'What do I do next?'

Something had entered the ship's mathematics. It was inside the Tate-Kearney transformations themselves, fractally folded between the algorithms. It was huge. When Ed tried to talk to it, everything shut down. The screens went dark, the shadow operators, who had sensed it there days before, streaked about in panic, brushing Ed's face like very old muslin rags. 'We didn't want this,' they told him. 'We didn't want you in here!' Ed battered at them with his hands. Then the screens fired up again, and the wormhole leapt suddenly into view, very clear and close, a spindle of nothing against the exposed grimace of RX-1.

The whole of the local space of *The Perfect Low* had, meanwhile, turned into a kind of agitated purple cloud, through which the alien mortsafes could be seen weaving their chaotic orbits, faster and faster like the shuttles of a loom. You could feel the ship shake to her frame with the approach of some catastrophic event, the phase change, the leap to the next stable state.

'Fucking hell,' Ed said. 'What's going on out there?'

There was a soft laugh. A woman's voice said: 'They're the engine, Ed. What did you think they were?'

In the calm that followed this announcement, Ed hallucinated a white cat at his feet: tricked thus into looking down, saw instead a spill of light emerging like bright foam from Sandra Shen's fishtank and licking out towards him.

'Hey!' he shouted.

He jumped out the pilot seat. The shadow operators spread their arms and streamed away from him into the dark and empty ship, rustling in terror. Light continued to pour out of the fishtank, a million points of light which shoaled round Ed's feet in a cold fractal dance, scaling into a shape he almost recognised. Each point, he knew (and every point which comprised it, and every point which comprised the point before that), would also make the same shape.

'Always more,' he heard someone say. 'Always more after that.'

He threw up suddenly. The entity calling itself Sandra Shen had begun to assemble itself in front of him.

Whatever she was, she had energy. First she presented as Tig Vesicle, with his shock of red hair, eating a Muranese fish curry off the end of a throwaway plastic fork. 'Hi, Ed,' he said. 'The fuck we are! You know?' But that didn't satisfy her, so she got rid of it and presented as Tig's wife, half-naked in the gloom of the warren. Ed was so surprised he said, 'Neena, I—' Neena got whipped away immediately and was replaced by the Cray sisters. 'Dipshit,' they said. They laughed. Between each version of herself, Sandra Shen filled up the control room with sparkling motes of light, like one of her own tableaux, 'Detergent Foam in a Plastic Bowl, 1958'. Finally she firmed up as the Sandra Ed first met, walking briskly along Yulgrave towards him in the blowing snow – a small, plump, oriental-looking woman, her gold leaf cheongsam slit to the thigh, her perfect oval face shifting constantly as she exchanged youth and yellow old age, her eyes sexy and fathomless with the charisma of something never human.

'Hello, Ed,' she said.

Ed stared at her. 'You were all of them,' he said. 'None of that was real. You were everyone in that part of my life.'

''Fraid so, Ed.'

'You're not just a shadow operator,' he guessed.

'No, Ed, I'm not.'

'There was no Tig.'

'No Tig.'

'There were no Cray sisters.'

'Theatre, Ed, every moment of it.'

'There was no Neena . . .'

'Hey, Neena was fun. Wasn't Neena fun?'

Ed couldn't think of anything to say. He felt more used and manipulated – more self-disgusted – than at any point in his life before. He shook his head and turned away.

'Painful, isn't it?' said Sandra Shen.

Ed told her: 'Fuck off.'

'That's a disappointing attitude, Ed, even for a twink. Don't you want to know the rest of it? Don't you want to know *why*?'

'No,' Ed said. 'I don't.'

'It got your head in the fishtank, Ed.'

'Another thing,' he said. 'What was all that about? What was happening to me in there? What was that stuff I had to put my head in? Because, you know, it's disgusting to do that, day after day.'

'Ah,' said Sandra Shen. 'That was me. I was always in there with you, Ed. You weren't alone. I was the medium. You know? Like the proteome in the twink-tank? You swam to the future through me.' She smoked her cigarette meditatively. 'That's not quite true,' she admitted. 'I misled you there. I was training you, but not so much to *see* the future as *be* it. How'd you like that idea, Ed? Be the future? Change it all. Change everything.' She shook her head, as if this was a bad day for explaining herself. 'Put it another way,' she tried. 'When you applied for this job, you said you flew every kind of ship but one. What's the only kind of ship you never flew?'

'Who are you?' Ed whispered. 'And where are you taking me?'

'You'll know soon, Ed. Look!'

A filmy twist of light, a faint vertical smile seven hundred kilometres high, hung above them. *The Perfect Low* shuddered and rang as the forces that kept the wormhole open engaged with elements of Sandra Shen's ad hoc engine. 'There are more kinds of physics in play here,' she informed Ed, 'than you people dream of in your philosophy.' Outside the hull, the aliens redoubled their efforts, shuttling faster and in more complex patterns. Suddenly Madam Shen's eyes were full of excitement. 'Not many people have done this achievement, Ed,' she reminded him. 'You're out in front here, you've got to admit that.'

Ed grinned despite himself.

'Just look at it,' he marvelled. 'How d'you think they *made* it?'

Then he shook his head. 'As to achievements,' he said, 'Billy Anker picked this peach. I watched him pick it ten, twelve years ago. If I remember anything, I remember that.' He shrugged. 'Of course, Billy never came back. You don't get the tick unless you come back.'

Something about this mindless philosophy made Sandra Shen

smile to herself. She stared up at the image on the screens for a moment or two. Then she said softly: 'Hey, Ed.'

'What?'

'I wasn't Annie. Annie was real.'

'I'm glad,' Ed said.

The wormhole opened to receive him.

During the transit, he fell asleep. He didn't understand why, though even in his sleep he suspected that Madam Shen had organised it. He slumped in the pilot seat with his head on one side, couch-potatoed and breathing heavily through his mouth. Behind closed lids, his eyes flickered in REM manoeuvres, a simple but urgent code.

What he dreamed was this:

He was back in the family house. It was autumn – heavy, felted airs and rain. His sister came down from the father's study carrying the lunch tray. Ed skulked about in the shadows on the landing, then jumped out on her. 'Haraaar!' he said. 'Oops.' Too late. The lunch tray slipped out of her hands in the wet light from the window. A hard-boiled egg rolled about in dipping, eccentric arcs, then bounced away down the stairs. Ed ran after it, going, 'Yoiy yoiy yoiy!' His sister was upset. After that she didn't speak to him. He knew it was because of what he had seen before he jumped out. She was already holding the lunch tray in one hand. With the other, she was pulling her clothes about as if they didn't fit properly. Her hands were already relaxing, soft and strengthless. She was already crying.

'I don't want to be the mother,' she was telling herself.

That was the point everything went wrong in Ed's life. Nothing after that was as bad, even when his father stood on the black kitten; and anyone who claimed it had gone wrong before that, they didn't know anything.

A voice said: 'Time to forgive yourself these things.'

Ed half-woke, felt the soft inside of the wormhole touch the ship, contract. He smiled loosely, wiped his lips with the back of his hand, slept once more, this time without dreams. Protected by the violent glow of alien engines, cocooned and cosseted by the ironic smile and unknowable motives of the entity at that time calling itself Sandra Shen, he was borne with grace and without incident down a birth canal a million years old. Or more. At the end of which, deep light would explode in upon him, in ways none of us can imagine.

THIRTY-ONE

I've Been Here

After he ran out of the cottage, Michael Kearney was thrown back for a last time into his own memory, where he saw himself, twenty years old, returning from his last innocent train journey to find a short, badly dressed woman walking up and down the taxi rank outside Charing Cross station, where the action of the Tarot cards had stranded him. She was holding up a letter in her right hand and shouting:

'You bloody piece of paper, you bloody piece of paper!'

Greying hair straggled down around a broad face reddened with effort. A maroon woollen coat, thick as carpet, compressed her fat breasts. 'You *bloody* piece of paper!' she cried. As if trying for some final, indisputable delivery, she varied the emphasis on this accusation until it had illuminated briefly every word. She had a duty of expression, you felt, to the forces inside her. It was work for her, work of the hardest sort, hawked up from somewhere deep. Kearney couldn't repress a shudder. But no one else seemed bothered: instead, they regarded her with a cautious, even affectionate, amusement, especially when her back was to them.

When Kearney's turn came at the head of the queue, she stopped in front of him and caught his eye. She was short, stout. The smell that clung to her reminded him of empty houses, old clothes, mice. Her sense of drama, the intractable rawness of her emotion, left him unnerved.

'Piece of paper!' she shouted at him. He saw that the letter was old, shiny with use, falling apart at the folds. 'You bloody piece!' She held it out to him. Kearney stared mutely away, aching with embarrassment. He tapped his foot.

'You bloody *written thing*!' she said.

He shook his head. He thought perhaps she wanted money.

'No,' he said, 'I—'

A taxi roared into the Charing Cross forecourt and pulled up next to him with a squeal of brakes. Dazzled briefly by the sunlight dancing in the raindrops on its bonnet, he seemed to lose sight of her. In a trice, she had reached in close and tucked the paper deftly into one of his jacket pockets. When he looked up, she was gone. On the paper he found not a letter but an address in Cambridge, written in blue ink as old as himself. He brought it close to his face. Reading it seemed to exhaust him. When the folds gave way, and it fell into lace in his hands, he redirected the taxi, caught another train and went home. There, depressed, worn out, unable to convince himself of the need to unpack his bag, he realised that he had memorised the address without wanting to. He tried to work. He sat dealing cards until it got dark, then – perhaps in a bid to remind himself of the triviality of all this – prowled from bar to bar, drinking restlessly, hoping to meet Inge Neumann and have her tell him with a laugh:

'It's just a bit of fun.'

Next afternoon he stood in the rain where the paper had led him, across the street from a substantial old suburban house, detached, three or four storeys high, in gardens half-hidden behind a wall of attractively spalled red brick.

He had no idea why he had come.

He stood there until his clothes were soaked, but made no move to leave. Children ran up and down the street. At half past four there was a brief increase in traffic. As the rain cleared and the afternoon light shifted west, the brickwork took on a warm orange colour, and the garden wall seemed to recede a little, as if the street had widened; at the same time it seemed to stretch, becoming taller and longer. A little later, the woman in the wool coat waddled into view, breathing heavily and wiping her face. She crossed the road and, walking straight through the wall, disappeared.

'Wait!' gasped Kearney, and flung himself after her.

He had the sense of penetrating something membranous which clung elastically to his face. Then he heard a voice say: 'It was amazing to them to discover they had always been in the garden without understanding it', and knew for certain that the inside and the outside of everything are always a single, continuous medium. In that moment he believed he could go anywhere. With a shout of elation he attempted to fall forward in all possible directions at once; only to find to his dismay that in the very exercise of this privilege he had selected one of them.

Odd items of furniture remained in the house, as if some tenant hadn't quite abandoned it. It was cold in there. Kearney went from room to room, stopping to examine an old-fashioned brass fender, a wooden ironing board folded up like an insect in a corner. He thought he heard people whispering in the rooms above; a laugh cut off by a sudden intake of breath.

The Shrander was waiting for him in the master bedroom. He could see her clearly through the open door, standing at the bay window. Light poured round her thickened, monolithic silhouette, transfiguring the bare floor of the room, then spilled out on to the landing at Kearney's feet, illuminating the rolls of dust beneath the cream-painted skirting board. Arranged on an inlaid table just inside the door he could see: books of matches; condoms in squares of foil; fans of Polaroid snapshots; a pair of oversized dice with symbols he didn't recognise.

'You can come in,' the Shrander said. 'You can step right in.'

'Why have you brought me here?'

At this a white bird flew past the three panes of the bay window, and the Shrander turned to face him.

Her head was no longer human. (Why had he ever thought it was? Why had anyone in the taxi queue thought it was?) It was the skull of a horse. Not a horse's head, but a horse's *skull*, an enormous curved bone beak whose two halves meet only at the tip, and which looks nothing like a horse at all. A wicked, intelligent, purposeless thing which cannot speak. It was the colour of tobacco. There was no neck. A few shreds of coloured rag – perhaps they had once been ribbons, red, white and blue, studded with coins and medallions – hung where the neck might have been, forming a kind of mantle. This object tilted itself intelligently, looking up and sideways at Michael Kearney like a bird. Breath could be heard inside it. The body beneath, wrapped in its maroon woollen coat, stained and smelly with food, raised its pudgy arms in a proprietary yet generous gesture.

'Look,' ordered the Shrander, in her clear, childish, counter-tenor voice: 'Look out here!'

When he did, everything lurched and there was nothing but blackness and a sense of enormous speed, a few dim points of light. After a moment, a chaotic attractor generated itself, churning and boiling in the cheap iridescent colours of 1980s computer art. Christ's blood, Kearney thought, streaming in the firmament. He staggered, nauseated and vertiginous, and put out a hand to save himself: but he was already falling. Where was he? He had no idea.

'Real things are happening here,' the Shrander said. 'Do you believe me?' In the absence of a reply she added:

'You could have all this.'

She shrugged, as if the offer was less attractive than she might have wished. 'All of it, if you wanted. You people.' She thought for a moment. 'The trick, of course, is to find your way around. I wonder,' she said, 'if you know how close you are to that?'

Kearney stared wildly out of the window.

'What?' he said. He hadn't heard a word.

The fractals churned. He ran out of the room. On the way, he stumbled into the little inlaid table and, grasping hold of it to keep his balance, found he had picked up the Shrander's dice. At that, his own panic filled the room, a liquid so thick he was forced to turn and swim his way through the door. His arms worked in a sort of breaststroke while his legs ran beneath him in useless slow motion. He stumbled across the landing outside and straight down the stairs – full of terror and ecstasy, the dice in his hand –

They were in his hand again now as he struggled through the marram grass, high on the dunes of Monster Beach. If he looked back, he could see the cottage, a milky illumination coming and going at its windows. The sky was black, and full of bright stars; while the ocean, clasped in the arms of the bay, appeared silver, and fell upon the beach with a faint shushing noise. Kearney, who was not a natural athlete, made perhaps a mile before the Shrander caught him. This time it was much larger than him, though its voice still had the counter-tenor quality that made it sound like a boy or a nun.

'Didn't you know me?' it whispered, looming above him so that the stars were obscured. It smelled of stale bread and wet wool. 'I spoke to you often enough in your dreams. Now you can be the child you were.'

Kearney fell to his knees and pushed his face into the beach, where he perceived with clarity and suddenness not just the individual grains of wet sand but the shapes between them. They looked so distinct and detailed that he did, briefly, feel like a child again. He wept for the sheer loss of this: the loss of himself. I've had no life, he thought. And what did I give it up for? This. He had killed dozens of people. He had joined with a madman to do terrible things. He had never had children. *He had never understood Anna.* Groaning as much with self-pity as with the effort of not facing his nemesis, his face thrust firmly into the sand, his left arm held rigidly out behind him, he offered it the bag containing the stolen dice.

'Why me? Why me?'

The Shrander seemed puzzled.

'There was something I liked about you,' it explained, 'from the very beginning.'

'You ruined my life,' Kearney whispered.

'You ruined your own life,' said the Shrander, almost proudly.

Then it said: 'As a matter of interest, why did you murder all those women?'

'To keep you away from me.'

The Shrander seemed surprised at this.

'Oh dear. Didn't you realise it wasn't working?' Then it said: 'It *hasn't* been much of a life, has it? Why did you run so hard? All I wanted to do was show you something.'

'Take the dice,' Kearney begged, 'and leave me alone.'

Instead, the Shrander touched his shoulder. He felt himself lifted and moved until he hung above the breaking surf. He felt his limbs straightened firmly but gently as if by some expert masseur. He felt himself turn in the air, hunting like a compass needle. 'This way?' said the Shrander. 'No. *This* way.' And: 'You can forgive yourself now.' A curious sensation – freezing yet warm, like the first touch of an aerosol anaesthetic – propagated itself across his skin, then, penetrating him through every pore, raced about inside, unblocking every cul-de-sac he had driven himself into in his forty years, relaxing the sore, knotted lump of pain and frustration and disgust – as clenched and useless as a fist, as impossible to modify or evict – his conscious self had become, until he could see and hear and feel nothing but a soft velvety darkness. In this he seemed to drift, thinking of nothing. After some time a few dim points of light appeared. Soon there were more of them, and more after that. Sparks, he thought, remembering Anna's sexual ecstasy. Sparks in everything! They brightened, congregated, pinwheeled up over him, then settled into the furious churning patterns of the strange attractor. Kearney felt himself fall into it, and come apart slowly, and begin to lose himself. He was nothing. He was everything. He flailed with his arms and legs, like a suicide passing the thirteenth floor.

'Hush,' the Shrander said. 'No more fear.' It touched him and said, 'You can open your eyes now.'

Kearney shivered.

'Open your eyes.'

Kearney opened his eyes. 'Too bright,' he said. Everything was too bright to see. The light roared in on him unconfined: he felt it on his skin, he heard it as a sound. It was light unburdened, light like a substance: real light. Great walls and arcs and petals of it hung and flickered, they hardened, they endured a moment, they tumbled and fell towards him, they somehow passed through him and were gone in a second, only to be replaced. He had no idea where he was. He felt the most extraordinary sense of surprise and wonder and delight.

He laughed.

'Where am I?' he said. 'Am I dead?'

The vacuum around him smelled of lemons. It looked like roses. He felt it tearing at him, inside and out. There was a horizon, but it seemed too curved, too close.

'Where is this? Are these stars? Is there anywhere really like this?'

Now the Shrander laughed too.

'Everywhere is like this,' it said. 'Isn't that something?' Kearney looked down and found it standing at his shoulder, a small fat thing the shape of a woman, perhaps five foot six in height, its maroon wool winter coat buttoned tightly, its great bone beak tilted up to face the roaring, toppling sky. He had the feeling it would have blinked, had there been any eyes in its sockets. 'That's the one thing *we* never seemed to get,' it said: 'How unpackable everything is.' Coloured ribbons fluttered and streamed from its shoulders in a completely invisible wind; while the hem of its coat trailed in the dust of some ancient rocky surface.

'Everywhere you look it unpacks to infinity. What you look for, you find. And you people can have it. All of it.'

The comfortable generosity of this offer puzzled Kearney, so he decided to ignore it. It seemed meaningless anyway. Then, staring up at the collapsing, constantly replaced towers of light, he changed his mind and began to wonder what he could offer in return. Everything he thought of was inappropriate. Suddenly he remembered the dice. He still had them. He extracted them carefully from their leather bag and offered them to the Shrander.

'I don't know why I took these,' he said.

'I wondered too.'

'Well anyway. Here they are.'

'They're only dice,' the Shrander said. 'People play some kind of game with them,' it added vaguely. 'But look, I did have a use for them. Why don't you just put them down?'

Kearney looked around. The surface they were standing on curved away, salted with dust, too bright to look at for long.

'On the ground?'

'Yes, why not? Just put them on the ground.'

'Here?'

'Oh, anywhere,' said the Shrander, making an offhand, liberal gesture. 'Anywhere they can be seen.'

'I'm dreaming, aren't I?' said Kearney. 'Dreaming or dead.'

He placed the dice carefully on the dusty rock. After a moment, smiling at the fears of his vanished self, he arranged them so that the emblem he knew as 'the High Dragon' faced upwards. Then he walked a little way away from them and stood on his own and turned up his face to the sky, where he imagined he could see among the clouds of stars and incandescent gas, the shapes of everything that had been in his life. He knew those things weren't there: but it wasn't wrong to imagine them. He saw pebbles on a beach. (He was three years old. 'Run here!' his mother called. 'Run here!' There was water in a bucket, cloudy with moving sand.) He saw a pool in winter, brown reeds emerging from the cat-ice at its margins. 'Your cousins are coming!' (He saw them run laughing towards him across the lawn of an ordinary house.) He even saw Valentine Sprake, looking almost human, in a railway carriage. In all of that he never saw Gorselands once: but over it all he thought he saw Anna Kearney's strong, determined face, guiding him to self-knowledge through the shoals of both their lives.

'You understand?' said the Shrander, which, having remained courteously silent through this process, now came to his side again and stared up in a companionable way. 'There will always be more in the universe. There will always be more after that.'

Then it admitted: 'I can't keep you alive for much longer, you know. Not here.'

Kearney smiled.

'I guessed,' he said. 'You mustn't worry. Oh look! Look!'

He saw the raging glory of the light. He felt himself slipping away into it, here in this fabulous place. He was so amazed. He wanted the Shrander to know. He wanted it to be certain he had understood.

'I've been here and seen this,' he said. 'I've *seen* it.'

He felt the vacuum empty him out.

Oh Anna, I've seen it.

THIRTY-TWO

Everywhere and No Place

What had happened inside the *White Cat* was this:

Seria Mau had gone up into the mathematical space, where the K-code ran without substrate in a region of its own. Everything else in the universe seemed to recede to a great distance. Things speeded up and slowed down at the same time. An actinic white light – sourceless yet directional – sprayed round the edges of every moving body. It was a space as lucid and intense and meaningless as one of Seria Mau's dreams.

'Why are you dressed like that?' the mathematics asked her in a puzzled voice.

'I want to know about this box.'

'It's so very dangerous to us all,' the mathematics said, 'for you to be here like this.'

'. . . so very dangerous,' echoed the shadow operators.

'I don't care,' said Seria Mau. 'Look.'

She raised her arms and offered up the box.

'It's very dangerous dear,' the shadow operators said. They picked nervously at their fingernails and handkerchiefs.

The code rushed out of Uncle Zip's box and merged with the code from the *White Cat*. Everything – box, giftwrap, and all – dissolved into pixels, streamers, dark lights like non-baryonic matter, and blew past Seria Mau's upturned face at near-relativistic speeds. In the same instant, she felt the wedding dress catch fire. Her train melted. Her loving cherubs flashed to powder. The shadow operators covered their eyes with their hands and flung themselves about like dried leaves on a cold wind, their voices stretched and garbled by unknown space-time dilation effects. Suddenly everything was out of the box: every idea anyone had ever had about the universe was available, operating and present. The wires were crossed. The descriptive systems had collapsed into some regime prior to them all. The information supersubstance had broken loose. It was a moment of reinvention. It was the moment of maximum vertigo. Mathematics itself was loose, like a magician in a funny hat, and nothing could be the same again.

Soft chimes rang.

'Dr Haends, please,' said a woman's gentle, capable voice.

Out he came, emerging from the universal substrate with his white gloves and gold-topped ebony cane. His tailcoat had a velvet collar and five-button cuffs, and down the outside leg of his narrow black pants ran a black satin stripe. His hat was on his head. His shoes, which Seria Mau had never seen, were chisel-toe patent leather dancing pumps. Hat, shoes, suit, gloves and cane, she saw now, were made of numbers, crawling so thick and fast across one another they looked like a solid surface. Was the whole world like that? Or was it only Dr Haends?

'Seria Mau!' he cried. He held out his hand. 'Will you dance?'

Seria Mau flinched away. She thought of the mother, leaving her to face things without a word of help. She thought of the father and the sex things he had wanted her to do. She thought of her brother, refusing to wave to her even though he knew he would never see her again.

'I never learned to dance,' she said.

'Whose fault was that?' Dr Haends laughed. 'If you won't play the game, how can you win the prize?'

He gestured around. Seria Mau saw that they were standing in the magic-shop window, a little-girl cultivar in a wedding dress and a tall thin man with a thin moustache and lively blue eyes. All around them were stacked the things she had seen in her dreams – retro things, conjuror's things, children's things. Ruby-coloured plastic lips. Feathers dyed bright orange and green. Bundles of silk scarves that would go into the top hat and hop out as live white pigeons. There were hanks of fake liquorice. There was a valentine's heart which lit itself up by means of loving diodes within. There were 'X-Ray Specs' and elevator shoes, trick eternity rings and handcuffs you couldn't take off. They were all the things you wanted when you were a child, when it seemed there would always be more in the world and always more after that.

'Choose anything you want,' invited Dr Haends.

'All these things are fake,' said Seria Mau stubbornly.

Dr Haends laughed.

'They're all real too,' he said. 'That's the amazing thing.'

He let go of her hand and danced elegantly about, shouting, 'Yoiy yoiy yoiy!' Then he said:

'You could have anything you wanted.'

Seria Mau knew it was true. Full of panic, she fell away from this idea in all possible directions, as if from the highest ledge in the universe. *'Leave me alone!'* she screamed. The ship's mathematics – which had been Dr Haends all along, or half of him at least – sent her to sleep. It had a quick look at some of the other parts of its project (this involved some travel in ten spatial and, especially, four temporal dimensions). Then, having reorganised the *White Cat* a little more to its satisfaction, it took the shortest possible route to Sigma End and threw itself down the wormhole. There was a lot left to do.

Sigma End.

Uncle Zip watched, his eyes narrowed.

'Get after them,' he said.

'Too late, Unc. They're already in.'

Uncle Zip was silent.

'They're dead,' the pilot said. 'We're dead too if we go in there.'

Uncle Zip shrugged. He waited.

'This isn't a place for human beings,' the pilot said.

'But don't you want to know?' said Uncle Zip softly. 'Isn't that really why you came?'

'Oh fuck it, yes.'

The *White Cat* cartwheeled silently out of the other end of the wormhole like a ghost ship. Her engines were off. Her coms were silent. Nothing was moving inside her hull; outside, a single blue riding light, normally used only in the parking orbit, winked, redundant and steady into nowhere. The hull itself – scarred and scraped, ablated through contact with some indescribable medium, as if wormhole travel meant a thousand years in a coffee-grinder, motion as Newtonian as a ride on a runaway train – cooled quickly down through red to plum-coloured to its normal thuggish grey. A lot of the exterior work was missing. The wormhole exit, a filmy twist of whitish light, fell behind. For two or three hours, the ship toppled out of control through empty space. Then her fusion torch flared briefly, and in obedience to some unspoken command, she shook herself and fell into orbit around the nearest large object.

Seria Mau Genlicher woke up shortly afterwards.

She was back in her tank. Everything was dark. She was cold. She was puzzled.

'Displays,' she ordered.

Nothing happened.

'Am I on my own here?' she said. 'Or what?'

Silence. She moved uneasily in the dark. The tank proteome felt lifeless and stagnant.

'Displays!' she said.

This time a coms feed came up, two or three visual images, garbled, intermittent, imbricated, speckled with interference.

A large white object could be seen sprawled across the floor in the human quarters of a K-ship, resolving, as the cameras moved carefully around it, into a partly dismembered human being. Its clothes, torn off by gravitational forces, were compacted into the corners of the room like wet washing, along with one of its arms. The walls above it were daubed and reddened. The second image was of Uncle Zip, playing the accordion as his ship tumbled endlessly down the wormhole. Over the music, his pilot could be heard shouting, 'Shit. Oh Jesus shit.' In the third, Uncle Zip's mouth was seen in close-up, repeating the words: 'We can get out of this if we keep our heads.'

'Why are you showing me this?' said Seria Mau.

The ship remained silent around her. Then it said suddenly:

'All these things are happening at once. This is a realtime feed. Whatever happened to him in there is still happening. It will always be happening.'

Uncle Zip stared out of the display at Seria Mau.

'Help,' he said.

He threw up.

'Actually, this is quite interesting,' the mathematics said.

Seria Mau watched one moment more. Then she said: 'Get me out of here.'

'Where do you want to go?'

She moved helplessly in her tank. 'No, I want to get out of *here*,' she said. And then, when no answer was forthcoming: 'It didn't work, did it? Whatever happened back there before you put me to sleep? I thought I saw the conjuror, but it was another dream. I thought—' She was like a thirteen-year-old girl, trying to shrug. In response, the fluid in the tank swirled sluggishly about. She imagined it washing what was left of her body like warm spit. Like fifteen years of despair. 'Oh well, what does it matter what I thought? I'm really tired now. I don't care what I do. I've had enough. I want to go home and this never to have happened. I want my life back.'

'Shall I tell you something?' the mathematics said.

'What?'

'Display up,' said the mathematics, and the Kefahuchi Tract exploded into her head.

'This is the way things really look,' said the mathematics. 'If you think ship-time is the way things look, you're wrong. If you think ship-time is something, you're wrong: it's nothing. You see this? This isn't just some "exotic state". It's light years of blue and rose fire, roaring up out of nowhere, toppling away again in real, human time. *That's* the way it is. That's what it's like inside you.'

Seria Mau laughed bitterly.

'Very poetic,' she said.

'Look into the fire,' the mathematics ordered.

She looked. The Tract roared and sighed above her.

'I can't give you your body back,' the mathematics said. 'You had this rage to live, but you were afraid of it. What you had them do to you was irreversible. Do you understand that?'

'Yes,' she whispered.

'Good. There's more.'

After a moment, the Tract seemed to frame itself in three tall arched windows, set into a wall covered in ruched grey satin. She was in the magic-shop window. At the same time she was in the tank-room aboard the *White Cat*.

Those locations, she saw now, had always been one and the same place. She could see her tank, EMC's corporate idea of what a thirteen-year-old girl would want: a coffin decorated with gold mouldings of elves, unicorns and dragons, all making heroic self-sacrifices over and over again, as if death wasn't a permanent state and heartbreak could always be risen above. It had a thick hinged lid – impossible to open from inside, as if they had been frightened all along she might get out – and sheaves of inlet pipes. She was above it, inside it, and behind it too: she was in the tiny shipboard surveillance cameras which fell like dust through every ray of light. As she watched, the upper body of Dr Haends bent itself slowly into the central window. His white shirt was freshly starched; his jet-black hair shone with brilliantine. After he had bent as much of his body into her field of vision as he could, Dr Haends winked at her. This time, instead of bowing himself out, he threw one long, elegant leg across the window sill and clambered into the room.

'No,' said Seria Mau.

'Yes,' he said.

In two strides he had reached her tank and thrown open the lid.

'*No!*' she said.

She thrashed and raged, what was left of her, so that the fluid in which she was suspended – thick and inert as mucous to absorb the Newtonian forces to which even a K-ship was sometimes prone – slopped over the side and on to his patent leather shoes. Dr Haends didn't notice. He reached down into that stuff and pulled her out. In the microcameras she saw herself for the first time in fifteen years. She was this small, broken, yellowish thing, its limbs all at odd angles, curling and uncurling itself feebly against the pain of the open air. What she heard as a scream of horror and despair was only a faint rough groan. The skin stretched over her like the tanned or preserved skin of a bog-burial. There was no flesh between that and the bones beneath. The withered lips drew back over small, even teeth. The eyes glared out of tarry sockets. When she saw the thick cables trailing from the core-points in the scholiosed spine, she felt numb and disgusted. She felt the most awful pity for that thing. She felt the most awful *shame.* To begin with, that was why she fought him: she simply didn't want him to see her. Then, when she saw what he was doing, she fought him for that, too.

He had landed the ship. The cargo ramp was down. He was taking her outside. Terror fell across her like the light from the Kefahuchi Tract. What could she do, if she was no longer the *White Cat?* What could she be?

'No! *No!*'

The Tract pulsed above her.

'There's no air,' she said pitiably. 'There's no air.'

The sky was on fire with radiation.

'We can't live! We can't live in this!'

But Dr Haends didn't seem to care. Out there on the surface, among the strange low mounds and buried artefacts, he prepared for surgery. On went his white gloves. Up went his sleeves. While out of his eyes and mouth poured the white foam of the K-code, to assemble from the dust itself the necessary instruments. Dr Haends looked up. He held out one hand, palm up, like someone testing for rain. 'No need for extra light!' he decided.

Seria Mau wept.

'I'm dying! How can you give me a new body here?'

'Forget your body.'

They had to shout to hear themselves across the silent roar of the Tract. Particle winds blew back the tails of his coat. He laughed. 'Isn't it amazing, just to be alive?' Behind him, the shadow operators poured out of the ship like shoals of excited fish, flickering and dancing.

'She'll be well again,' they called to one another. 'She'll be well.'

Dr Haends raised his instruments.

'Forget yourself,' he commanded. 'Now you can be what you are.'

'Will you hurt me?'

'Yes. Do you trust me?'

'Yes.'

A long while later – it might have been minutes, it might have been years – Dr Haends wiped the numbers from his forehead like sweat and stepped back from the thing he had made. His evening suit was less than spruce. He was bloody to the cuffs of his linen shirt. His instruments, which to start with had been state of the art, now seemed to him dull and not entirely the right ones for the job. He shook his head. It had been an effort, he now admitted, even for him. Thermodynamically, it had been the most expensive thing he'd ever done. It had been a risk. But what do you gain without that?

'Now you can be what you are,' he repeated.

The thing he had made raised itself and flapped its wings uncertainly. 'This is hard,' it said. 'Am I meant to be this big?' It tried to look back at itself. 'I can't really see what I am,' it said. It flapped again. Collateral electromagnetic events lifted dust from the surface. The dust hung there, but nothing else happened.

'I think if you keep practising—' encouraged Dr Haends.

'I feel terrified,' it said. 'I feel such a fool.'

It laughed.

'What do I look like?' it said. 'Am I still her?'

'You are and you aren't,' Dr Haends admitted. 'Turn round, let me see you. There. You look beautiful. Just practise a bit more.'

Seria Mau turned and turned. She felt the light catch her wings.

'Are these *feathers*?' she said.

'Not entirely.'

She said: 'I don't know how it works!'

'It will maintain any shape you want,' Dr Haends promised. 'You can be this, or you can be something else. You can be a white cat again, and pounce among the stars. Or why not try something new? I'm quite pleased with it now,' he said. 'Yes! Look! You see? That's it!'

She rose up and circled about awkwardly above his head. 'I don't know how to do this!' she called down to him.

'Some turns! Do some more turns! You see?'

She did some more turns. 'I'm quite good at it,' she said. 'I think I could be quite good at it.' The shadow operators flew up to her. They flocked to her whispering delightedly and clasping their bony work-worn hands. 'You took care of me *so well*,' she congratulated them. Then she made herself look down at the *White Cat*.

'All those years!' she marvelled. 'Was I *that*?'

She shed something that might have been tears, if an organism so bizarre – so huge and yet so frail, so perpetually emergent from its own desires – could be said to weep. 'Oh dear,' she said. 'I don't know how I feel.' Suddenly she laughed. Her laughter filled the vacuum. It was the laughter of particles. She was laughing in every regime. She tried out the different things she could be: there were always more; there were always more after that. 'Do you like this?' she called down. 'I think I preferred the last one.' Her wings lost

309

their look of feathers, and the Kefahuchi-light ran along them from tip to tip like wild fire. Seria Mau Genlicher laughed and laughed and laughed.

'Goodbye,' she called down.

She rose suddenly, faster than even Dr Haends's eyes could follow. Her shadow passed over him briefly and vanished.

After she had gone, he stood there for a time, between the empty K-ship and the remains of the physicist Michael Kearney. He was exhausted, but he couldn't seem to settle. He bent down and picked up the dice Michael Kearney had brought to that place. He turned them over thoughtfully; put them down again. 'That was tiring,' he said to himself. 'They can be more tiring than you think.' After a while, he allowed himself to slip back into a shape he was more comfortable with, and stood there for a long time looking up at the Kefahuchi Tract, a small pudgy thing with a huge curved bone beak and a maroon wool coat with food stains down the front, which shrugged and said to itself:

'Well, the rest is yet to do.'

THIRTY-THREE

Ed Chianese's Last Throw

The Perfect Low emerged from her journey down the wormhole. Her engine wound itself down then broke up into its component parts. She seemed to consider her options for a minute or two, then made off busily through local space, to arrive a little later above an asteroid in full view of the Kefahuchi Tract.

Ed Chianese sprawled in the pilot seat with his mouth open, breathing heavily. Except that one hand rested on his genitals, he resembled *The Death of Chatterton*; and if he was dreaming it didn't show. Looking down at him with an expression in her eyes both maternal and ironic, stood a small oriental woman in a gold cheongsam split to the thigh. She lit a cigarette, smoked it between shakes of the head. Her eyes never left him. You would have said, if she had been a real woman, that she was trying to work him out.

'Well, Ed. Time to get on,' she said eventually.

A few whitish motes seemed to drift out of her eyes. 'You know, we should have music for this,' she said. 'Something measured.' She raised her hand. Ed was lifted gently out of his seat by the gesture and propelled at a walking pace to *The Perfect Low*'s nearest hatch;

which, when opened, evacuated the atmosphere from the entire ship. Ed, too. He seemed unaware of this event, which was perhaps to the good. A little later he lay in the air – perfectly horizontal, legs together, hands folded on his chest as if for burial – two or three feet off the surface of the asteroid.

'Nice,' said Sandra Shen. 'You look nice, Ed.'

She tilted her face to the glare of the Tract, against which could dimly be seen the shape of *The Perfect Low*.

'I shan't need you any more,' she told it.

The ship manoeuvred for a second or two, the aliens in their mortsafes visible briefly in intermittent bursts of torchlight. Then they fired up the Purple Cloud again and were gone.

Sandra Shen stared after them. For a moment or two she seemed regretful, and reluctant to make decisions. 'Do I want another cigarette?' she asked Ed. 'No, I don't think I do.' She was restless, edgy: not quite herself. Her shadow became briefly restless too. Her hands were busy about her clothes. Or were they? Perhaps it was more than that. For a moment, sparks seemed to pour out of everything. She sighed exasperatedly, then seemed to relax.

'Do wake up, Ed,' she said.

Ed woke standing, on the curve of a small world under the desperate illumination of the Kefahuchi Tract.

Pillars of fire rose and fell above him – colours in suites, colours which had no business together, stained-glass colours. A little way off to one side, illuminated in a way he couldn't describe, lay a K-ship, its drive in park, its hull shimmering with the effort of repressing its weaponry; also, he noticed, the complete skeleton of a human being, brownish in colour, with bits of cloth and tarry cartilage still adhering to the bones. At his shoulder – odd and uncertain-looking in that raging, intransigent light, yet somehow less threatening than it first appeared – stood the entity sometimes known as 'Sandra Shen', sometimes 'Dr Haends', but most often down the years, and to most of its brief associates, 'the Shrander'. Ed eyed her sidelong. He took in the tubby figure, the maroon wool coat with its missing buttons; the head like a horse's skull, the eyes like pomegranate halves.

'Whoa!' he said. 'Are you real?'

He felt at himself with his hands. First things first.

'Am *I* real?' he said. Then: 'I've met you before.' Receiving no answer, he massaged his face. 'I know I've met you before.' He made a vague gesture. 'All this . . .' he said.

'Amazing, isn't it?' said the Shrander. 'And it's like this all over.'

Ed didn't mean that. He meant he had come further than he wanted to.

'I'm not sure where I am.'

'Do you know,' the Shrander said, with an air of delight, 'I'm not, either! There's so *much* of it, isn't there?'

'Hey,' Ed said. 'You're Sandra Shen.'

'Her too. Yes.'

Ed gave up. For a moment, he thought, it would be enough just to be kind to himself. Take it in. But the Shrander seemed companionable and considerate, and he soon felt more secure than he had when he woke up. That in its turn made him feel as if he ought to make some further effort: so after a little thought he said, 'You're from the K-culture, aren't you? You didn't die, you guys. That's what this has been all about.'

He looked at her in a kind of sidelong awe.

'What kind of thing are you?'

'Ah,' said the Shrander. 'I'm not sure you'd understand the answer to that. Whatever kind, I'm the last of them: that's for sure.' She sighed. 'All good things must come to an end, Ed.'

Ed was unsure how to respond to this.

'How are you with that?' he said eventually. 'I mean, in yourself?'

'Oh fine. I'm fine with it.'

'You don't feel alone? Let down?'

'Oh, of course. Alone. A bit sidelined. Anyone would. But you know, we had our day, Ed, and it was a good one!' She looked up at him animatedly. 'I wish you could have seen us. We looked just like

313

this, only if anything we had more ribbons.' She laughed. 'I won't show you what's under the coat.'

'Hey,' Ed said, 'I bet you look fine.'

'I'm not exactly Neena Vesicle down there.' She thought about this, perhaps for longer than she had intended. 'What was I saying?' she asked Ed.

'That you had your day,' Ed reminded her.

'Oh we did, Ed, we did! Life went as well for us as it does for you, maybe even better. One moment as dignified as a tea-dance in paradise; the next, fast, hallucinatory, last-chance, realtime. Oh, you know: absolute hell. We ate a few lunches. And you should have seen the achievements we did, Ed! We moved stuff about with the best of them. We had the code licked. We got all the answers you people want—'

She stopped. Indicated the sky.

'Then we came up against *this*. To tell you the absolute truth Ed, it stopped us as dead as the rest. It was old when we got here. The people who had been here before us, well they were old when we were nothing. We stole their ideas as fast as we could, the way you're doing now. We had our try at that thing –' the Shrander seemed to shrug '– and it failed. Wow, Ed,' she said, 'but you should have seen us. By then we had some control of things. It was an exciting time. But it all comes to nothing, all the pushing and the shoving.' She tilted back her head a moment and pointed her great bone beak at the Tract. Then she looked back down at her own feet in the dust. 'Oh,' she said, 'I'm not complaining. Even that was fine. I mean, it was an adventure, it was our adventure. It was part of being what we were.

'And that's the thing, Ed. Being here. Being up to your neck in what you are.'

'You feel you lost that,' Ed said.

The Shrander sighed. 'I do,' she said.

She said: 'We got off-base with ourselves. That's what happens with this thing. You fall back from it. You break yourself on it. You lose heart. It beat us: it beat our intelligence, our capacity to understand. In the end, we didn't have the juice.' There was a pause in which they both contemplated the idea of limits, which was a comfortable one for Ed, since he had spent his life pushing them. When he felt it had gone on long enough, he said:

'So. What happened then?'

'You pick yourself up, Ed. You try to carry on. We were missing something, we had to admit. But that in itself gave us our big idea. *We* couldn't know the Tract; but we decided to build something that could. I'm the last of my kind, Ed, you're right. They left me here to make the project work.'

The Shrander fell silent.

After a while she said tiredly, 'I'm a long way out of date, Ed.'

Ed felt the weight of that. He felt the loneliness of it. What do you do for an alien entity? Do you put your arm around it? What do you say: 'I'm sorry you're old'? The Shrander must have gathered some of this, because she reassured him, 'Hey, Ed. Don't sweat it'; then, after a moment, gathered up her resources and gestured in a way that took in the low ruins, the inexplicable artefacts in the dust, the K-ship squatting there like an evil demon of engineering, its systems cooking with radiation, its armaments extruding senselessly as it detected possibly threatening events a hundred lights up and down the Beach.

'I lived in these ruins, these objects and others, all across the halo. There was a part of me in all of them, and every part of me was all of me. After EMC discovered K-tech, I lived in the navigational space of this ship. I stole it. From inside its maths, and across the bridge into its wetware, I had the run of fourteen dimensions, including four temporal. I was halo-wide, I was backwards and forwards in time like a yo-yo. I could intervene.'

'Why?'

'Because we built you, Ed. We built you from the amino acids up. We made a guess at what we didn't have, and we built your ancestors to evolve into what we couldn't be. It was a long-term project, as long-term as anything here on the Beach. OK, maybe not so visible as some of this solar engineering stuff. But, you know, did any of that actually *work*? Look around you; I'd say it didn't. We thought our investment had a chance, Ed. It was low-end and elegant both at the same time; even more interesting, we gave the universe a hand in it and left some things to chance. All this time I was watching over it.'

The Kefahuchi Tract.

A singularity without an event horizon. A place where all the broken rules of the universe spill out, like cheap conjuror's stuff, magic that might work or it might not, undependable stuff in a retro-shop window. You couldn't make anything of an idea like that, but you couldn't stop trying. You couldn't stop trying to engage it.

Ed's visual cortex, as excited as an ion-pair in a Tate-Kearney device, hallucinated dice emblems in that vast flicker of sky. He saw the Twins, a horse-head, a clipper ship in a tower of cloud like smoke. Beneath these emblems of chance/not-chance, the surface of the asteroid – if that was what it was – stretched away from him, mostly even, covered in a fine white dust. Here and there could be seen the remains of low rectangular structures, their foundations worn to a three-centimetre nub by unknown ablative forces originating in the Tract. Scattered around them in this entradista paradise were the shapes of smaller artefacts, their outlines burred by layers of dust, each one worth a small fortune in the chopshop laboratories of Motel Splendido.

He tried to think of himself as an artefact.

He bent down and put his ear to the surface. He could hear the K-code not far beneath, singing to itself like a choir.

'You're still down there,' he whispered.

'Down there and everywhere else. So what do you want to do, Ed?'

Ed got back to his feet.

'Do?'

The Shrander laughed. 'I didn't bring you here just to look at it,' she told him. 'If you knew what it was costing in thermodynamic terms just to keep you alive in this –' she paused as if lost for words '– in this fabulous place, you'd blench. Honestly. No, Ed, I'd have been delighted just to bring you here, but it wouldn't have been cost-effective just for that.'

'So,' Ed said. 'What?'

'Don't be naïve, Steady Eddy. You can't stay still in this life. You go on or you go down. What'll it be?'

Ed grinned. He had the measure of her now. 'You were in the twink-tank, too,' he said. He chuckled. 'Rita Robinson!' he remembered. 'I bet you were Rita Robinson too.' He wandered over to where the skeleton lay, knelt down in the dust and touched its brownish bones. He pulled off a strip of light-bleached rag that had adhered to its ribcage, let it fall, watched the slow gravity take it down.

'So, look,' he said. 'What's the story here?'

'Ah,' said the Shrander. 'Kearney.'

'Kearney?' Ed said. 'Jesus. Not *the* Kearney?'

'Now there was someone who fell back from himself,' the Shrander said, 'exactly what I'm talking about. He was so promising early on, and yet so frightened of it all. I watched him fire up from nothing, Ed, then go out suddenly, just like a light. Oh, I know what you're going to say. He and Brian Tate got you people out here. Without him you wouldn't have quantum machines. You wouldn't have massive parallel processing. And without that you'd never have found your way around. But in the end he was a disappointment, Ed, believe me: he was just too frightened of the things he knew. I shouldn't have brought him here, but I felt I owed him.'

She laughed. 'Even though he stole something of mine and ran away every time I tried to ask for it back.' She bent down and sought about in the dust with her little pudgy hands.

'Look.'

'Hey,' Ed said. 'The Ship Game.'

'These are the originals, Ed. Look at that workmanship. We

never knew how old they were.' She stared at the dice on the palm of her stubby little hand. 'They were old when we found them.'

'So what do they do?'

'We never found that out either.' The Shrander sighed. 'I kept them for their sentimental value,' she said. 'Here. You have them.'

'It's just a game to me,' Ed said.

He took the dice and turned them so they caught the light from the Kefahuchi Tract. This was the way they were meant to be viewed, he thought. They were another device for trying to understand the place where the rules ran out. The familiar images flickered and yearned, as if they wanted to jump off the faces of the dice and cook in the light. He felt he owed her something for that understanding, so he said:

'What do I do?'

'Here's the deal: you take the K-ship. You go deep. It's the Kefahuchi Boogie, Ed: it's point and press. You go all the way.'

'Why me?'

'You're the first of them. You're what we hoped to make.'

'Kearney was the brains,' Ed pointed out. 'Not me.'

'I don't want you to understand it, Ed. I want you to *surf* it.'

Ed threw the dice thoughtfully.

He threw them again.

He said: 'I always wanted to fly one of those things. What will happen if I take it in there?'

'To you?'

Ed threw the dice.

'To it all,' he said, making a gesture which seemed to include the universe.

The alien shrugged.

'Who knows? Things will change forever.'

Ed threw the dice once more. The Kefahuchi Tract raged silently above him. War was breaking out in sympathy, up and down the Beach. He looked at the dice, lying in the irradiated dirt. Something he saw there – something about the way they had fallen – seemed to amuse him.

'Well, fuck all that,' he said, and came up grinning. 'Will it be fun?'

'Ed, it will.'

'Where do I sign up?'

A little later, paraplegic, catheterised and stuffed to the limits of his nervous system with brand new drugs, Ed Chianese, twink, felt the Einstein Cross light up his brain, and took control of his K-ship. Sandra Shen had trained him well. Navigation is an act of prophecy, a couple of guesses with your head in a tank of prophylactic jelly. You can leave the massive parallel processing to the algorithms: you can leave it to the quantumware. After signing him on, the mathematics had gone up into its own space, where Ed found it waiting for him.

'Hey,' Ed said.

'What's that?'

'One thing I wish. I had a sister, you know, and I did something stupid and walked away from her. I wish I'd see her again. Just once more. Sort that out.'

'That won't be possible, Ed.'

'Then I want to rename the ship. Can I do that?'

'Of course you can.'

Ed thought hard about his fucked-up life. 'We're the *Black Cat*,' he said. 'We're the *Black Cat* from now on.'

'Ed, it's a fine name.'

'So ramp me up.'

The mathematics was delighted to do that. Ed went on ship-time. Ten spatial dimensions spread themselves like legs for him; four of time. Dark matter boiled and flared. Out in the last place in the ordinary world, the *Black Cat* rose from the surface of the asteroid. She hunted like a compass needle, then turned herself slowly until she stood on her tail. For thirty nanoseconds, which is a million years down there where things are small, nothing happened. Then fusion product burst out of her stern. She leapt forward on a line of bright white light and shortly made a hole in nowhere.

'Well the engine's on. Let's just point the fucker.'

'Let's just do that, Ed.'

'Which of these switches is the music?'

The asteroid now stood empty, but for the bone dice and the dead physicist. The dice lay as they had fallen for Ed Chianese, and the dust sifted over them. Michael Kearney's bones browned a little further. Seria Mau Genlicher returned a number of times, sometimes happy, sometimes like a living winter, and looked down, and went away again. Years passed. Centuries passed. Then the sky began to change colour, subtly and slowly at first, then faster and wilder than anyone could dream.

THE BEGINNING